The
LAST PRINCE
of the
MEXICAN EMPIRE

warmest wishes

C. M. Mayo

C.M. MAYO

UNBRIDLED BOOKS

The

LAST
PRINCE

of the

MEXICAN
EMPIRE

 A NOVEL BASED ON THE TRUE STORY

This is a work of fiction. The names, characters, places and incidents are either the product of the author's imagination or are used fictitiously, and any resemblance to actual persons living or dead, business establishments, events, or locales is entirely coincidental.

Unbridled Books
Denver, Colorado

Library of Congress Cataloging-in-Publication Data

Mayo, C. M.
The last prince of the Mexican empire : a novel based on the true story /
by C.M. Mayo.
p.   cm.
ISBN 978-1-932961-64-5
1. Maximilian, Emperor of Mexico, 1832–1867—Fiction.   2. Mexico—
History—European intervention, 1861–1867—Fiction.   I. Title.
PS3563.A96389L37 2009
813'.54—dc22
2008053522

1   3   5   7   9   10   8   6   4   2

Book Design by CV • SH • NL

First Printing

For Agustín Carstens, como siempre

And for my godchildren, American, Mexican, and Mexican American:

Fernando Carstens
Sasha Miranda
Roberto O'Dogherty
Clementine Sainty
Mariela Solís Cámara
Gordon Sweeney
Katherine Pearl Zalan

In my dreams as a mother, I never thought that my
son should be a prince who would aspire to a crown

DOÑA ALICIA (ALICE) GREEN DE ITURBIDE,
to Maximilian, Emperor of Mexico

All that we see or seem
Is but a dream within a dream

EDGAR ALLAN POE

When that I was and a little tiny boy,
With hey, ho, the wind and the rain

WILLIAM SHAKESPEARE,
Twelfth Night or, What You Will

CONTENTS

BOOK ONE

BOOK TWO

BOOK THREE

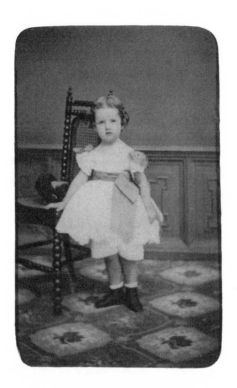

Agustín de Iturbide y Green

circa 1865

BOOK ONE

Contigo la milpa es rancho y el atole champurrado

*With you the corn patch is a ranch and the plain
corn-flour drink, hot chocolate*

—MEXICAN SAYING

THE DARLING OF ROSEDALE

*O*nce upon a time there was a little girl named Alice Green who lived on what people who don't know any better would call a farm, but which her family called their country estate. Rosedale's main house was not especially fine, a clapboard box with a center hall and, upstairs, a warren of bedrooms (Alice shared one of the smallest with two sisters). However, it had fireplaces in every room, a gleaming piano in the parlor, and Hepplewhite-style chairs in the dining room. It was said that Pierre L'Enfant, who laid out the plan of the city of Washington, had advised with the landscaping. There were avenues of dogwood and ornamental hedges; peach, pear, cherry, fig, and apple orchards, grape arbors, strawberry bushes, vegetable patches, including sensationally prolific asparagus beds. ("O Moses," Alice's mother, Mrs. Green, would lament each spring with scarcely disguised pride. "What am I to do with all this asparagus?") One might also mention their chickens, ducks, geese, prize hogs, and feeding on the hilly pastures that here and there dropped down to the wooded canyon of Rock Creek, a herd of scrupulously tended milk cows. As was common in those days, the family owned slaves; these had their dowdy little cabins out back behind the stables so as not to ruin the pleasing view from the main driveway. Rosedale crowned the heights above Georgetown, the nearly century-old tobacco port town that had been drawn into the western corner of the District of Columbia. From the dormer window of her bedroom, Alice could see hills undulating down for the few miles yonder to the one they called Rome, where the national capitol sat, then no more than a tooth of a building. To the south, below, lay the Potomac, with its jerry-built wharves and, shooting out from the foot of the Francis Scott Key house, the rickety-looking Aqueduct Bridge. On the opposite shore, in the blue distance: the chip that was Arlington House, with its back to the fields and forests of Virginia. Alas, oftentimes this vista was sullied by smoke from one of Georgetown's paper mills or bone factories.

Rosedale had been founded by Alice's maternal grandfather, General Uriah Forrest, who served with General Washington and, famously, lost a leg in the Battle of Brandywine. Her maternal grandmother was a Plater who grew up at Sotterley, one of the grandest of the Maryland Tidewater tobacco plantations. But so much had been lost by the time Alice was born: decades earlier, General Forrest had been bankrupted. As for Sotterley, the story went, it had slipped from a great-uncle's fingers in a game of dice.

Alice's father worked in an office in the city of Washington, but when he was a young man he had seen action in Tripoli with Commodore Decatur. Her father's uniform was in his seaman's trunk, a wooden box with handles made of rope, but impossible to lift. Alice and her brothers and sisters were allowed to take turns trying on the hat, which had an enormous plume, and posing in front of the mirror. They could take out the rusty musket, and the saber too (but they had to keep that in its sheath). There were a pair of high boots with cracked soles, yellowed breeches that had once been snow white, and a coat that smelled strongly of camphor but nonetheless was riddled with moth holes.

When she was seven years old, Alice knew: she loved uniforms. She wanted, with all her heart, to go to Tripoli.

"Girls don't wear uniforms," her older brother George said.

"Silly," an older sister said, rolling her eyes.

"Saphead," said another brother, Oseola, and he stuck out his tongue.

Thus was Alice persuaded to abandon her first ambition—but never the yearning for her destiny, which she felt as a blind girl might, laying a hand upon an elephant's side: this huge, warm, breathing thing. She had no notion of what it might be, no word to describe it, only the dim but solid knowledge that it was altogether different and inconceivably grander than the others'.

She, being the youngest of eight, had always felt small, but very special, and so this did not disconcert her. She took it as a given, as the color of the parlor's sofa was a given, that while whites went in that parlor Negroes, except to dust and polish and serve tea, did not. What was to ponder in the fact that winter was bitter, and the summer steamy and buggy? Whether it were clear or cloudy, the sun rose every day, and this included Sunday, which was the day Mr. and Mrs. Green and all the little Greens crammed themselves into the big carriage and drove down toward the Potomac and, to save their mortal souls, sat through mass (no talking, no pinching) at Georgetown's Holy Trinity.

And then came finishing school. At the Georgetown Female Seminary, in addition to French, music, and drawing, the history of Rome and such, Alice studied geography. She was diligent and she had a knife-sharp memory. Shown the Sandwich Islands once, she could pick them out of the Pacific, cold. In the parlor her father had a gold-edged *Atlas of the World*. She would sometimes lie on her stomach on the carpet and, propped on her elbows, study, say, Australia. Chile. Iceland. North Africa. She loved to trace her finger along the ragged curve of the Barbary Coast until it landed on Tripoli.

Tripoli. Alice whispered the names of the Arab cities: *Tangiers. Algiers. Tunis. Cairo.* She would close her eyes and imagine the musky scents of their bazaars, the tables piled with bangles and silks, oranges sweet as the sun. Her father had explored ancient temples, ridden a real camel, and held in his own hands a two-thousand-year-old kylix painted with the figure of the Minotaur. He had seen Malta, Mallorca, Gibraltar. On the map Alice would touch each of these magical places and then slide her pinky over the aqua blue swath of paper that was the Atlantic. And then her finger would arrive at Chesapeake Bay, sliding up the sinuous Potomac to . . .

Oh, Dullsvania. Blahsberg! Boringopolis!!

She knew there was another life waiting for her, a life as romantic as anything out of *The Thousand and One Nights*. Here, in the country, it sometimes seemed that she had nothing to do but sit at the window, her chin in her hands, and watch crows alight on the fence-rails. (Her mammy said that in the night the crows flew to Mexico, to feed on dead soldiers. In the day, they digested the flesh. But Alice knew better than to pay heed to Negro talk.) Sometimes, early in the mornings before school, her mother made her help feed the chickens and inspect the dairy. Was that not the rudest thing in the world? One day, she would wing across an ocean. She would be adored; like Commodore Decatur, she would be remembered for a hundred years.

No: more than a hundred years.

After her fourteenth birthday, when she began to read her older sisters's stash of novels, her daydreams became ever more baroque. Armor-clad knights on snow white steeds, damsels locked into sunless towers, Franken-stein, all class of ghoulish specters, and pirates, rakish lords and ruined ladies, and the personal memoirs of the white slaves, victims of shipwrecks on the wild Mogador coast, sold into brutal servitude to Mohammedans, then res-cued by the most dashing of British officers, titled gentlemen of the most polished minds and cultured sensibilities. Such were the stories that en-chanted her for hours at a stretch.

She was the youngest and the prettiest of all her sisters. On the cusp of the bloom of her life, she seemed the bud of a most glorious rose. Her father, she believed, was rich—and he was until he was thrown from his horse. He seemed to be all right at first, just a bump on the back of the head, but by morning he had sunk into a stupor. He slept, he ate, he slept. He spoke very little. This went on for some weeks. And then, one morning in 1850, he did not wake.

The subsequent decline in the family's income meant that Alice's dowry could not be so generous as some of her sisters' had been. However, the fa-therless girl grew up—it seemed to have happened overnight, her mother said—into a ravishing belle. She wore her fair hair in ringlets, and by biting them when she thought no one was looking she kept her lips plump and brightest pomegranate-red. Her teeth were a row of pearls; her laugh, a pretty brook. She had sylph-like arms and such dewy skin that, though some other girls may have been blessed with more in the material sphere, she was sure of it, they were all jealous.

For Alice's first winter, as the social season was called, her mother had four of her sisters' gowns refitted for her by the colored mantua-maker: emer-ald green silk with a satin bodice and lilac ribbons on the cuffs; buttercup yel-low silk with tulle and coral pink silk trim with three flounces of tulle; ashes of roses moiré with a whale-boned bodice; and, her favorite because it made her feel like a heroine out of *Ivanhoe*, Napoleon blue velvet with cap-sleeves and a scalloped train. She also had three wrappers; a fan trimmed with Alen-çon lace and another with swan's feathers; a coral bracelet and a pearl rope-necklace (her grandmother's); two adorable beaded bags (one jet, one white), and four pairs of dancing slippers (these not hand-me-downs but her very own), each dyed to match one of the gowns. In addition, four visiting toi-lettes: a suit of sky blue poult-de-soie embroidered in lavender; one dove gray with slate gray braid; another of the same but with beaver fur-trimmed collar and cuffs; and one in jet, but the dramatic effect, which would have, as the mantua-maker pointed out, made her face pallid, was lightened by ruches in rhubarb-sherbet pink, and ecru lace ruffles on the bodice.

A winter in Washington! As soon as they were old enough to put aside their dolls, this was what all the girls dreamed of: balls, receptions, concerts, opera, choice little dinner parties, skating parties, jaunts to the capitol, gath-erings . . . Come May, they liked to say, a belle just might find herself with an engagement ring on her finger.

Her mammy clapped her hands at the sight of her. "Miz Alice! Fo' de Lawd' sake!"

Alice, too, admired herself in the full-length mirror. Her eyes gleamed like wet hyacinths. One of her ringlets, soft as silk, rested on her collarbone. With two fingers she lifted it and tossed it behind her shoulder. She bit her lips, hard, to bring out their color. She brought her hands to her waist, pinched by the corset into the narrowest of "v"s. The corset, she was delighted to note, made her bust quite the opposite of an ironing board. She rose up on her toes, and then down, to see how her hoopskirt would bounce as she danced. Thanks to insisting on shoes a size too small, she had the daintiest feet. The daintiest of all of her sisters'. Indeed, the daintiest of all her class-mates' at the Georgetown Female Seminary.

"What do you think?" she asked her mammy. "In my hair, shall I wear the japonica or the silk rosette?" It was a pomegranate-red rosette, more suitable for the décolletage of a dowager actress.

The stout mammy, whose woolly hair was covered with a calico bandana, pointed to the japonica.

Alice plucked up the silk rosette. "*This* one."

A sister laughed condescendingly. "Alice, you are *de trop*."

• • •

With the greatest of ease Miss Alice Green navigated the social whirl. From her very first formal ball, she was enchanted by the pressing crowds— among them cabinet ministers! Sam Houston with a serape thrown over the shoulder of his dinner jacket! Senators and their attachés, army colonels, generals, corporals, their chests flashing with decorations for valor in the Mexican conflict. And above all, her heart would flutter at the sight of the men of the diplomatic corps—or, as a belle from the Georgetown Female Seminary properly referred to them, *le corps diplomatique.* They had the most beguiling uniforms—gold lace, gold buttons on crimson coats, or tunics as black as onyx, all with elaborate embroidery and froggings, hats trimmed with feathers, chests bespangled with exotic decorations. There was the inestimable Baron de Bodisco, ambassador of the czar, and his lovely, still youthful wife, née Harriet Beall Williams, of Georgetown. It was not uncommon for a belle, through this avenue, to marry into aristocracy. There were well-known examples such as Miss Gabriela Chapman of Virginia who had married the Marquis de Potestad Fornari of the Spanish legation.

"Eet iza mya pleazure," said the minister from Sardinia, as he kissed the belle's hand.

There were Prussians, Austrian counts, Spaniards, Italian chevaliers, Frenchmen with mustaches waxed into daggers, Danes, English lords, Swedes, and even Turks. The Turkish admiral! A gentleman to behold: he wore a turban with a diamond and jeweled crescent, the most luscious robes, a dagger studded with precious stones, a scimitar on his belt, and slippers with toes that curled up into points. He looked all the part (the belle had to agree with the army corporal she was waltzing with) of a genie out of Ali Baba's cave.

There was much hand kissing, wafts of perfume, blasts and trills of music, and always, the Negroes weaving their way among the guests with trays of flutes of champagne, or rum punches, platters of the recherché tidbits concocted by the most fashionable restaurateurs. The decorations: pink candle shades, spun-sugar swans, banks of hothouse lilies, poinsettias, heliotropes, red, white, and blue bunting, potted palms and profusions of ferns, and on one occasion, at a recital of *La Traviata,* no less than four dozen lemon trees (whose fruits turned out to be—on the sly, Alice squeezed one—papier mâché).

Her dance card was invariably filled. She had been taught that a young lady should be demure; nonetheless, in the mirrors, she boldly watched the others watching her—one of the French attachés in particular, an adder-eyed count with slicked-back hair and a mole on the side of his nose. He never asked her for a dance, but she had to be careful not to look at him because then their eyes would lock. Always, she felt her mother's watchful gaze from the sofa, the inevitable sofa in the back of the room where, crowded like sparrows onto a telegraph wire, the mothers sat together, her own mother in black widow's crêpe and the drabbest paisley shawl.

After dancing, breathless and flushed, fanning herself (and hoping the elegance of her Alençon lace fan would be noticed; it was *comme il faut*), Alice would make her way to the supper-buffet. At the end of her fifth ball, an Annapolis middy she had danced with twice before came up behind her.

"Miss Green?"

His Adam's apple seemed to have a life of its own. He simply stood there, breathing. His face, which could not be said to be that of a Romeo, was beaded with sweat. His name had quite gone out of her head.

"Miss Green, would you do me the honor of dancing this waltz?"

She had blisters on both heels. As it was, it would be a supreme effort not to be seen limping on her way back to the table where her sisters and their beaux were waiting for her. Already, she had turned down three would-be gallants. She decided to be freezingly polite: "No thank you, I'm quite tired." She turned back to the cavalcade of cakes and petit fours and puddings.

"Miss Green?" This specimen was a barnacle of tenacity.

She finished serving herself a slice of the apricot sponge gâteau. Someone jostled her from the left. She let out a peeved sigh.

"Miss Green," he insisted, "may I call on you at Rosedale?"

She almost blurted, yes, but—isn't it better just to be honest?—she said, "No."

The poor boy looked as if he had taken a cannonball in the gut. She was sorry. But not really.

Oh, the clod-footed boys. The ones with pimples on their necks and sweaty gloves. Annapolis middies, low-down-the-totem-pole army types, law clerks, a dry goods merchant's son . . . Why were *these* the ones who asked to put their names on her dance card? As Alice danced the mazurkas and quadrilles and waltzes, the air would grow uncomfortably warm, the whalebones in her corset would rub under her arms, the pins in her hair come loose, and her too-small slippers would rub her heels raw—for *this*?

And it provoked her to tears that other girls lived right in the thick of the social scene: in Lafayette Square, or on Pennsylvania Avenue, or Georgetown, whilst she and her sisters had to make the miles-long slog back up the dark road to Rosedale. In inclement weather, this was a cruelty to the horses, her mother would sigh.

The following winter, the night before the opening of the season, it snowed. Under a bright sun, the snow melted. By midday, came the report, the road from Rosedale into the city and all of Pennsylvania Avenue had become a rutted mess of mud. Which is why Alice almost decided not to go to the White House *levée*.

"What a bother," she said sourly, from the hall doorway.

Mrs. Green adjusted the pins in one of Alice's older sisters' coiffure. "Are you certain you don't want to go?"

"Per-fect-ly," Alice said. She was in her riding outfit, though she had stayed inside to eat cookies and play the piano.

"Oh, come on, Alice, it will be gay," her sister said, applying more powder to a shiny forehead.

Alice, slouching into the door frame, put a hand on her hip and rolled her eyes.

"Oh, Alice," her mother said. "If you don't go, we will all be talking about it, and you will just have to sit there staring at your oatmeal, Miss Glum."

Alice wrinkled her face.

"Go on," her mother said, shooing her out with the hairbrush, "Get dressed."

• • •

So Alice did go to that White House *levée,* and in her emerald green, her grandmother's rope of pearls around her swan-like neck, and a camellia in her hair. With her sisters and mother, she joined the throng that snaked from the foyer into the reception room. They greeted President and Mrs. Pierce, and then moved into the East Room. Anyone and everyone but outright vagabonds and Negroes, it seemed, had crowded in: there by the window, tête-à-tête, were Senators Jefferson and Slidell; an elfin gentleman in a plug-hat and his frumpy wife, admiring the chandelier; His Excellency the Baron de Bodisco, Mrs. Tayloe and Mrs. Riggs and Mrs. Lee, and her daughter in the fleeciest of gowns and a wreath of white rosebuds. There was the usual slew of middies and army boys, and also, gawkers of which the most rustic were those congressmen from the West (one could spot them from a country mile, and their wives in such gauche and badly made clothes).

Leaving their mother with Mrs. Tayloe, Alice and her sisters pushed through the crowd. They moved slowly, yet somehow, she became separated from the others. For a time she wandered, shyly fanning herself. In the Green Room, the air greeted her with a freshness that hinted of long-off spring, for it was filled with a veritable forest of palm trees and ferns and staggering bouquets of hothouse blossoms that camouflaged there, a pair of *très distingué* gentlemen, and there, what she supposed were junior Senate clerks, and chittering away on a green and gold sofa, their wives. No one paid her the least attention, not even the waiter who bumped her and caused her to drop her fan. No gentleman stepped forward to pick it up; she had to retrieve it herself, no small feat whilst encased in crinolines. As she waded through the crowds from room to room, she was beginning to feel angry—yes, that was it. Why should *she* play the ghost before all these nobodies, not worth a glance from Miss Alice Green of Rosedale? She swiped a glass of punch off the next tray that came floating by; she sipped it, found it too sour, and poured the rest into a potted fern.

She had just about fixed her mind on going back outside to wait out this annoying party in the carriage, when, nearing the door, she was stopped in her tracks by an excrescence of attar of roses. Its source was known to her: an acquaintance, a new member of their parish, Madame Almonte, wife of the as-yet-to-be-seen Mexican ambassador. It seemed the poor lady had found no one to talk to either (had she just been looking out the window?). Her tired old face, at the sight of Alice, dropped its mask of anxious decorum.

"Meez Green!" she said in her atrociously accented English, which nonetheless came out with the authority of a headmistress. "I introduce you." Gripping Alice firmly by the arm, Madame Almonte steered her into the crowd, around the punch bowl, and with a push at the small of her back, right in between two gentlemen. Madame Almonte tugged the older man, who had the top-heavy aspect of a pestle, on the sleeve.

"I introduce you! Meez Green." Then, to Alice, she said, "His Excellency General Juan Almonte."

From beneath heavy dark brows, two obsidian eyes now fixed themselves upon Miss Green, in nonchalant appraisal. A shade swarthier than his wife, this hawk-nosed gentleman had unmistakably Indian features, though these were compensated by side-burns well along in the process of turning a distinguished silver. He wore full court dress with gold braid (the buttons straining somewhat down his middle). He bowed deeply (the fringe on his epaulettes swinging) and, with expert grace, kissed her hand.

General Almonte: Alice had heard (she forgot where) that Mexico's ambassador had been in the Alamo with Santa Anna. He had a powerful charisma and what seemed to Alice a most peculiar sense of humor: for no reason she could fathom, he gave her a lopsided smile and then winked at his wife.

Still gripping Alice's arm, Madame Almonte turned to the younger gentleman who had been conversing with the general. "Meez Green, you know our legation's secretary?"

There before her, also in full court dress, stood Mr. Iturbide. They recognized each other from church, but it happened that they had not yet been formally introduced.

Alice, demurely, offered her hand and curtsied. *"Enchantée,"* she said, as Mr. Iturbide's mustache brushed the back of her glove.

Mr. Iturbide wore the most attractive and unusual fragrance; it had (was that it?) a hint of vanilla and lime. As all Georgetown knew, Mr. Iturbide was one of the sons of Mexico's George Washington, as it were. Unlike General Washington, however, General Iturbide had set himself up as emperor. His brief reign ended with his abdication, exile to Europe, and when he, soon after, very improvidently returned to Mexico, his execution before a firing squad. It was under the protection of the Holy Roman Church that his widow and her children had come to Washington, to live on Georgetown's Holy Hill, near the Jesuit College and Visitation Convent. Though the Iturbides could have, they did not use their royal titles. Having arrived here as a small boy, Mr. Iturbide spoke English just like a Yankee, and he looked, with his pallor, his sad eyes, raven-black hair, and broad and thoughtful forehead, the very twin of Edgar Allan Poe. Though, unlike the famous writer, the debonair Mr. Iturbide gave no indication of being anything other than an exemplar of rectitude.

It was, as the French say, a *coup de foudre.*

"*He is too old* for you," her mother warned.

Alice's youngest brother scrunched his nose. "A greaser!"

"I remember his mother," a sister said. "Before Madame de Iturbide decamped for Philadelphia, she rented that nasty little house on N Street. Her entire purpose in life, it seemed, was to stir up intrigues at Visitation Convent."

Her brother George snorted. "Madame de Iturbide has the disposition of a goat."

They were sitting around the dinner table. Aunt Sally, the cook, set down a steaming bowl of chowder. "'T ain't no she-goat nuther."

With that, the table went silent until Aunt Sally disappeared into the kitchen. Then everyone but Alice broke out laughing.

"Oh," said another sister, rolling her eyes, "her mustache!"

"Talk about *his*," said George.

Mrs. Green, who had been about to serve the first bowl of chowder, set down both the bowl and the ladle. "That mustache," she said, "is the sort worn by Kentucky hog drivers."

Alice, her eyes glittering with indignation, stood up. From the doorway, she cried, "You're all just jealous!" She flew up the stairs.

Miss Alice Green would not be budged: Mr. Iturbide was the beau for her. He was so handsome, sensitive as a poet, well read, he had been to New York, London, Paris, Italy, Havana, and Texas, too. And his handwriting, so frank, so elegant, however did he learn such penmanship?

"The priests always said, ask yourself, 'Can the pope read it?'"

That sent her into peals of laughter.

By springtime, several times a week, Mr. Iturbide came all the way up the hill to Rosedale to call on her. With a wary Mrs. Green chaperoning, they went to hear the Marine Band play, and one time, they took a buggy out to see Great Falls.

Angel, properly pronounced *Ahn-hel*, was his Christian name, but his family and friends called him Angelo, which was Italian.

Angelo stirred his coffee with a stick of cinnamon, wasn't that fascinating? Angelo drank Madeira wine, he smoked Cuban cigars, he had a piping of silver on his ruffled shirtsleeve cuffs. Such panache! And he was very brave.

They were picnicking at Mount Vernon, tossing leftover breadcrumbs to the gulls, when Alice made the little question that had been tugging at the corner of her mind. Not so long ago, her country and his had been at war. As she had been too young to be reading newspapers at that time she had not understood, nor cared since, to learn the whys and wherefores of it. (Her older sister had caught a glimpse of the war's hero, General Winfield Scott, at a White House *levée;* she had thought him "very wrinkly.") Now, anyone who had eyes to see colored pictures knew that Santa Anna, the "Napoleon of the West," had the smarter uniform, not that boring old navy blue. Santa Anna may have lost the war, but the Mexicans' leader did not just have epaulettes and a couple of rows of brass buttons, he had a crimson coat ablaze with the most arabesque gold embroidery!

Alice tossed her last handful of breadcrumbs at the gulls. "Why," she finally asked, "did you not go and fight in the Mexican conflict?"

"Santa Anna was my father's enemy."

"So?"

"If I'd shown myself in Mexico, he would have gone straight for me."

The meaning of this washed like a great wave into Alice's mind; as it receded, she was left with a sparkling new appreciation of her beau. She nodded sagely. "You stayed here to avoid assassination."

Angelo was lying on his side, propped on one elbow. He looked at her strangely and then gave her a wry smile. "I suppose one could see it that way."

For a time they were silent. Mrs. Green was napping in the buggy, parked in the cooling shade of an oak tree. There were others picnicking on this same lawn, but none close enough to overhear. A flock of geese was feeding near the water's edge. The breeze pulled at the strings of Alice's bonnet.

And then Angelo told her how it had been for him, that he had been heartsick with grief and shame, not so much that his country had been invaded but that the Mexican army had been so incompetent in its defense. "They were a gang of barbarians. Santa Anna is a creature out of a cesspit."

"And General Almonte?" Alice asked, because she remembered, hadn't the ambassador been at the Alamo with Santa Anna?

"Oh." Angelo twisted his mouth. "He's alright."

Angelo's family had been granted generous pensions by the Mexican government, he went on, but during the war years and for some time afterward, these pensions were not paid. It was bitterly hard for his mother. To save his pennies, he himself had had to go live in the country. For news of the war, every day that the Senate was in session, Angelo would cross the bridge over Rock Creek and walk the several miles up the gravel of Pennsylvania Avenue to the Hill, to sit in the gallery. When Mr. Thomas Corwin of Ohio spoke, one wanted to be sure to hear every word! Angelo did not say where he was going, but his landlady had suspected he was up to something. "Your shoes are wearing out," she'd said. "And you've got the appetite of a hippopotamus."

Alice laughed. She plucked a grape.

Angelo went on, "I would receive messages in Spanish that said, *Watch your back. Be careful.* I did not know what it meant, or who was sending them."

"You were in mortal danger!"

"Maybe . . ." He was watching a schooner glide by. Ducks bobbed in its wake. "I only wanted to know what was going on, but I could not show any concern about the war, because then people would think I knew something."

"Now that Santa Anna has gone into exile, will you return to your country?"

His gaze met hers. He looked all of a sudden very pale. He came up from his elbow, and he reached over and took her hand. "Miss Green—" he began.

"Yes," she interrupted. "I *will* go with you."

Mrs. Green was less than overjoyed. She had not yet fixed upon any particular beau for Alice, but of the four or five candidates she would have considered desirable additions to the family, all were at least ten years younger than Mr. Iturbide, and from old Virginia or Maryland families. His mother, Mrs. Green well knew from her acquaintance with Madame de Iturbide at church, would be a chafing rock around any daughter-in-law's neck.

Soon after Mr. Iturbide's proposal, an ominous cloud descended. One of his older sisters, a self-important spinster, came down from Philadelphia to meet Alice. After that, silence. A most disquieting signal was that Madame de Iturbide neither invited Mrs. Green and her daughter to visit her in Philadelphia nor volunteered to visit them at Rosedale. Indeed, neither lady initiated a correspondence. Most distressing to Mrs. Green was that, as a Mexican diplomat, Mr. Iturbide's income was precarious, and he would sooner or later take his bride to Mexico, a completely unsuitable country. Nonetheless, when she realized her warnings were falling on deaf ears, as she did not want the responsibility of having broken her daughter's heart Mrs. Green reluctantly gave her consent to the union. She was not one to flog a dead horse. Her final words on the subject were these: "Be careful what you wish, my bright and beautiful meteor; for you are likely to get it."

The wedding mass was held in the front parlor at Rosedale. Eyebrow-raising as it may have been, protocol dictated that the very swarthy His Excellency General Almonte be the guest of honor. Members of the Iturbide family did not attend.

Angelo let his wife and her family believe that his mother had been suddenly indisposed. But that night, he confessed the brutal fact of the matter: his mother had forbidden even the mention of Alice's existence in her presence. In Madame de Iturbide's way of thinking, her sons were destined to marry into Mexican or even Spanish aristocracy. At the very least, a handsome dowry should have been provided for the sons of Mexico's emperor. And, after all, her father, Don Isidro Huarte y Arrivillaga, a Spanish nobleman from Pamplona, was one of the richest men of New Spain. As for the Iturbides, they were descended from the Basque nobility.

"Does she not know of my family?" Alice meant, above all, her maternal grandfather, General Uriah Forrest, and her great-grandfather George Plater III, the Tidewater tobacco planter and sixth governor of Maryland.

Angelo had heard about these so-called Tidewater aristocrats. His mother would have called it "Bilgewater." With strong arms, he pulled his wife close. "Darling, it is her misfortune, not yours."

Ever after, Alice pretended she did not care. But the fact was, she was mortified to the quick.

Having taken leave of his mother in Philadelphia, a gloomy errand, Angelo then took his wife to his country, where she could not speak the language and did not comprehend the customs; and the poverty and filth, just as his mother had predicted, shocked her to tears; and the food, as much as the bullfights, upset her digestion; and the high altitude left her breathless. Why, just going up stairs made her dizzy. She frequently complained that it seemed to her these Mexicans were barking at her! She pined for her own people, who, as she said, would tell you exactly what they thought about things, who would not dally with the truth, twist it and stretch it like so much taffy, and certainly not embellish simple anecdotes with outré inventions. "Why, I could serve roast polecat and your amigos would tell me to my face it was delicious!" What especially exasperated her was when Mariqueta, their maid, deliberately used slang she could not understand. And the Indian bands in the street! Horns, drums, pot lids, rattles, fiddles fit for firewood! "How can a body get a wink with that unholy din, and right outside the window!" Those rascals would pull the bell and ask for money, their object being to induce one to bribe them to take their racket elsewhere!

Angelo listened with a pained and stoic expression. But, for each complaint he had a solution.

For lies: "Darling, if *you* were to serve roasted polecat, it might well be so toothsome, the others would want to steal your recipe."

"Oh," she said, batting her eyelashes.

For the disrespectful Mariqueta: "I shall have her sent back to her village next morning."

For the noise-mongers in the street: Angelo paid his landlady's *mozo*, or manservant, to keep them well away, and that night, he arranged for a band, a very good one, to play whilst he serenaded her. But—he insisted upon this—from the vestibule, not the street, as that was safer.

Things began to improve, and in fact, much sooner and more definitively than anyone had either hoped or expected. Being absolutely devoted to her husband, Alicia (as Alice began to call herself) studied the language diligently. It came easily to her, for was it not *le cousin du français*? She became friends with many of the wives of Angelo's friends. This was as easy as a hand sliding into a glove for, not only was Alicia ready with a smile and a generous gesture (breads, jams, and other little gifts, including the Maryland version, that is, Mrs. Green's recipe, of pumpkin pie), but the name of her husband's family was famous and, among those of their kind, revered. The most beautiful theater in the city was the Teatro de Iturbide; the finest hotel, the Hotel Iturbide; and in the National Palace, the grandest salon was the Salon Iturbide—just to give a few of innumerable examples. Whenever she was introduced to anyone new, the moment they heard her name, she could feel the frisson of alertness, the way the air in the room would, literally, change.

Good houses were scarce in the neighborhood of the *gente decente*, the better class of people, for the constant strife of the wars, revolutions, and the U.S. invasion had left so many in ruin and decay. Angelo was fortunate to have secured the top floor of a mansion on the Calle de Coliseo Principal. Its owner was the widow of General Don Manuel Gómez Pedraza, a renowned statesman and loyal friend to his father. In the tumultuous years after the fall of the empire, Don Manuel had been elected president, fair and square, though a disgruntled general got up a revolution against him before he could assume office. Three years later Don Manuel did hold the presidency but briefly—for by then, his lungs ravaged by disease, he had come to an understanding with that unstoppable force of nature, Santa Anna. Don Manuel's career had been an odyssey, the convoluted episodes of which only the most persistently interested in Mexican affairs could comprehend. His widow, Doña Juliana, was terribly kind; even in the early days, before Angelo's little wife could converse in the language, Doña Juliana would invite her to come down the stairs to her antique-filled drawing room for *café de olla* (spiced coffee) and *un poco de pastel* (a little bit of cake), by which she meant a fat slice of her pine nut-studded chocolate cake.

As Doña Juliana's English was almost nonexistent, in the beginning their conversation was of little consequence. But Doña Juliana would pat the little wife's pretty hand, and pat her golden hair, and kiss her on the cheek, and say, *"Ay, sí, qué chula, qué linda."* Later, when they could converse, Doña Juliana would ask about Alicia's family; after her mother, "Señora Green"; after Alice's brothers and sisters, each by name; and, for her part, Doña Juliana delighted to reminisce about the Emperor Iturbide. "Our Liberator," said Doña Juliana with a solemn shake of her head, many a time, "was betrayed, as was Our Lord." He was so brave, and an expert horseman . . . A paragon of discretion, she said little about him other than this. About the empress, Madame de Iturbide, she said nothing, though once she allowed, "Oh yes, Don Agustín and Doña Ana, they dined with us many a time."

Secretly Alicia pretended that Doña Juliana was her true mother-in-law. To protect his wife's dignity, Angelo had not spoken a word of his mother's thunderous rejection to anyone, except to the widow de Gómez Pedraza, who could be trusted to guard it with strictest silence. Indeed, not even Alicia was aware that Doña Juliana knew. Nor did she ever guess it.

After they had been living in Mexico City for a few years, in 1861 a letter came from Angelo's eldest sister, Sabina, that their beloved mamá, to whom God had granted seventy-nine years, was in peace, her mortal remains interred in Philadelphia's church of Saint John the Evangelist. Alicia sent her condolences to her sisters-in-law, and to her brother-in-law, the head of their family now, Don Agustín Gerónimo, who was also a diplomat, then with the Mexican legation in London (under, it so happened, General Almonte, who had abandoned Washington for the Court of Saint James's). With her husband, Alicia attended the several masses said for Madame de Iturbide's soul, all the while relishing the idea that this soul, a lump of charcoal, had thunked onto a smoking garbage pile on the bottom rung of Purgatory. But she went and confessed that.

Three months later, for the first time, she conceived.

And so it seemed to Alicia that all her troubles were a bridge that had been crossed. But alas, a bridge was not the most apt analogy; rather, her troubles were akin to a great mountain, such as Popocatépetl or Iztaccíhuatl, whose snowy crests made such a majestic background for the rootftops of Mexico City. Our Alicia was still—having conquered a few hillocks, as it were—in the neighborhood of the first foothills.

Her husband had another living sister, younger than the nun, Sabina, but two years older than himself, whose Christian name was Josefa, but she was known as Pepa to her intimates. Pepa had been very close to her mother, endlessly attentive to her care. In Madame de Iturbide's last year, when she had been confined to a wheelchair, it was Pepa who, even in inclement weather, pushed this conveyance and its obstreperous, shawl-and-blanket-swaddled occupant the five blocks to Saint John the Evangelist. Yes, Madame de Iturbide and her daughter attended mass every day. Although never in the realm of the darlings, in her bloom Pepa had been a handsome señorita. God had given her a dainty figure, pretty hands, and waist-length tresses, which she had diligently brushed each night with one hundred strokes. She never forgot anyone's birthday. Over the years Pepa's hair turned gray; what was left of it was pulled into a severe chignon and, when the occasion called for it (and rare were the occasions), augmented with hairpieces. Her corset, though tightly laced, could no longer disguise her predilection for potatoes, bread, and pies. But there was—let this be clear—nothing coarse about this señorita. She wore tasteful diamond earrings and, where a wedding band might have been, her great-grandmother's filigreed silver ring, set with a lustrous black pearl. (As a belle in Washington, she had been teased that her ring resembled a swollen tick. Mexican society, however, had the sophistication to appreciate this rare treasure, which had its provenance in the waters of the Sea of Cortez.) Her hands, dry and freckled with age, she kept meticulously manicured, and she used them with regal elegance, gesturing as she spoke, or flicking her fan, fingering a rosary, raising a teacup, one pinky out.

Upon her mother's death, Pepa maintained a composure that surprised everyone. Although militantly pious, she did not join her elder sister, Sabina, as a postulant in the convent in Philadelphia, because it was her conviction that now her God-chosen mission was to be of service to her little brother's family. With that Yankee wife and a new babe, no doubt, they would be in sore need of it.

Pepa had not approved of Angelo's taking an interest in such a young, foreign, and altogether frivolous girl. However, Pepa loved her little brother very much, and so, when he had first written to her that he had proposed to this person, this Miss (ugh, what a common surname!) *Green*, it was with a true feeling of Christian charity in her heart that she made a gesture of welcome. Actions speak louder than words, as their father used to say: she sent her little brother's fiancée the antique cream white mantilla that had been lying all these many years carefully folded in muslin in her own trousseau. Imagine her horror, upon her arrival in Washington, to have seen Miss Green with the precious family heirloom slung around her neck like some sort of scarf and pinned to her bodice with a brooch. A Scottish-style brooch of barbaric proportions! It left a ragged hole in the lace big enough to put a fist through!!

Pepa went straight back to Philadelphia and reported to her mamá, "He is not thinking with his head, I can tell you that."

Their mother had tried to talk sense to him, but Romeo had found his Juliet. After the wedding, when Angelo came to Philadelphia, without his wife, to take his leave before going back to Mexico, he did not have to tell them, they could see in his stiff demeanor and cold tone that he had been offended. Their mamá, never one to back down, was even more offended, and when

Sabina spoke kindly to Angelo and asked about Alice, Madame de Iturbide got up, and put her fingers to her temples. In an unnaturally low voice she said, she had seen ingratitude in her life, but never such as this. She went into her room and, from the inside, locked the door. From this date, her health began its final and precipitous decline.

The two sisters, Pepa and Sabina, shared many a discussion about their brother's unfortunate marriage, both between themselves and with their confessors. The convent's abbess was also consulted. The conclusion the sisters reached was that, like it or not, Angelo and this woman had exchanged their vows before a priest. If the Church of Rome recognized the marriage, then so should they. The sisters owed their grief-stricken mamá respect, but they also owed it to their brother and his future children to acknowledge his wife, for she would be those children's legitimate mother.

And so, over the four years since her little brother's marriage to this flibbertigibbet, Pepa had written her numerous brief but warmly polite letters containing a great deal of information about the weather. And more: whenever the little wife sent one in Spanish, Pepa would correct it, and return it with her own.

Now that Pepa had arrived in Mexico City and could examine her little brother's household with her own eyes, she found it—in no way to her surprise—wanting. She took the reins, which Alicia happily relinquished because, now that she was enceinte, she was feeling lethargic and, in the mornings, oftentimes so nauseous that she could barely lift her head to nibble a cracker. And, Alicia said with an extravagant sigh, she'd never had a head for managing staff. At Rosedale, naturally, her mother, Mrs. Green, had assumed all responsibilities. In any event, Negroes were one thing, Mexican servants quite another kettle of fish!

"Right you are about that!" Pepa said.

Under Pepa's firm hand, the rooms sparkled, the meals were served on attractive platters, the linens washed, ironed, and changed daily. The little wife had a husband who was now properly taken care of. Pepa treated Alicia as she might a feckless child. She criticized her piano playing (did Alicia not know how to use a metronome?), her pie recipes (too much cinnamon, scrimpy on the lard), her wallpaper (a bit "loud" and puckered at the corners). Another woman might have resented such overbearing interference, but Alicia was thrilled to be not only acknowledged but so actively supported by her husband's older sister. In front of other people, Pepa did not criticize; to the contrary, she praised her sister-in-law to the skies: *How well Alicia speaks Spanish, with very little accent (much less pronounced than Mrs. Yorke's, for instance). Alicia attended the Georgetown Female Seminary, you know, one of the best, well, in Washington. Alicia's fruit pies are divine. She grew up on a country estate, where they had peach and apple orchards, and fields of strawberries just baking in that humid sun.* Then, turning to Alicia, *I never thought I would say it, but your strawberry pie makes me miss Washington.* Best of all, with Pepa "minding the fort," Alicia was free to go out, without a worry in the world, on her rounds of visits, evenings at the opera, at the theater, to bullfights, and lots of parties.

Soon, however, Alicia's social life began to slow. She felt increasingly uncomfortable. The baby was growing very big, and then very, very big. For the first time in her life, Alicia was afraid.

"I have been praying for you," Pepa said, taking a seat next to her on the sofa.

Alicia rested her hands on her now taut watermelon of a belly. She slid her palm over it, and as she did, the baby gave her a kick that made her gasp.

"Alicia, what is it?"

Alicia burst into tears. "I want my mother!"

Pepa was about to say, *I miss my mother, too,* but just in time, she bit her tongue. Instead, she said, in her most soothing tone, "I am here with you." She gave Alicia her own handkerchief. "God is good. He has sent us Our Mother, Mary. Let us say the rosary . . ."

From that day on, Alicia and Pepa were inseparable, and the more so after the miraculous day, April 2, 1863—the day of San Francisco de Paolo—throughout which Pepa held her sister-in-law's hand, whether limp with half-unconscious exhaustion or gripping tight in screaming agony.

It was a healthy boy. They christened him Agustín, after his illustrious grandfather, the Liberator and emperor of Mexico. Agustín was a name revered in this family, both the eldest son of the Liberator and the youngest—born in New Orleans, shortly after his father's execution—were named Agustín.

The former, Agustín Gerónimo, a bachelor of fifty-six years, was a diplomat recently retired and returned from London to Mexico City, for his health had rapidly deteriorated, the result of a near lifetime of untempered drinking, pipe-smoking, and who-knows-what. The latter, Agustín Cosme, now forty-one years, had always been frail, obsequious, dreamy, and for near a decade now, tortured by a ringing in his ears of such volume it approached that of a trumpeting elephant. This he medicated with strong wines and tequila. As the youngest of so many, and lonely for the ones who were now in peace, from the moment he first met his lovely sister-in-law, Agustín Cosme had felt a great sympathy for her. But being of a livelier character, she found little about him to interest her. Mostly, like everyone else, she ignored Agustín Cosme.

The elder uncle, Agustín Gerónimo, was invited to be the baby's godfather, and Pepa, the godmother.

Baby Agustín was not a day in this world before his godmother pinned to his wee shirt a gold medal of Our Lady of Guadalupe. Pepa had already knit him five sweaters; needles clacking at a furious pace, she knit him five more and also stitched lace trim onto his caps and embroidered his sheets with his monogram. As his mother was confined to bed for the two weeks following the birth, Pepa took it upon herself to carry her godson downstairs to visit the widow de Gómez Pedraza. Touching her fingers to the crown of his shaved head, the delighted Doña Juliana would croon, *"Agustín, chiquitín."*

Pepa had decreed that the baby's head be kept shaved for his first year, as this would induce his hair to grow deeper roots. Well in advance of his birth, Pepa had hired the *chichimama* (wet nurse), and also a nanny. Pepa had happened to ask tiny Lupe, the *galopina* (kitchen maid), a redundant relic of Doña Juliana's household, "What do you know about babies?"

"All that God wants me to," Lupe answered in her quavering voice—and so the crucial matter was settled.

"You have given this family such happiness," Pepa said to Alicia, as she took the baby to show him to his godfather. (But before allowing him to touch the babe, Pepa instructed him with a click of her fingers and a gesture, to leave his pipe in the ashtray outside in the hall.)

Agustín Gerónimo stared at the little one who fell right to sleep in the crook of his arm. He said, in English, "My God, I have never seen anything so beautiful in my life."

Agustín Cosme, haunting the doorway, looked on with mute but beatific joy.

Pepa leaned down over the bed and kissed her sister-in-law's golden hair. "I do love you, Alicia." She patted her shoulder. "You are a true sister now."

Alicia felt her heart shine with a hundred suns of pride. She was, at last, not only accepted but adored by her husband's family: Mexico's most illustrious family. After so much disappointment, so much heartache, she had, she thought, achieved the pinnacle, the very Olympus, of happiness.

But there was more. Something wonderful, something that could have been lifted straight out of a novel: the French Imperial Army arrived to occupy Mexico City, which Alicia, with her two-month-old babe in her arms, had the privilege of watching from the flat-roof of the U.S. legation. She and her husband were the personal guests of the U.S. minister, Mr. Thomas Corwin. Alicia looked fetching in her new Parisian-style chapeau trimmed in pink grogram, and the baby, plump and rosy-cheeked, was so handsome in the blue knit jacket his doting auntie had made for him; everyone, including Mr. Corwin, admired him with cootchy-coos. Below, in the Calle de San Francisco, flowed the river of men. Bugles, flutes, drums, and the hobnails went *chum, chum*, on the cobbles: the noise was deafening, and it came with waves of cheers, thrown down with flowers from every flat-roof, balcony, window, doorstep:

"*¡Viva los franceses!*"

"Death to Juárez!"

"Long live the pope!"

These were the veterans of the stupendous battle for the city of Puebla: bronzed, a dozen abreast: Zouaves in their white gaiters and baggy red trousers, Hussars, *chasseurs d'Afrique*, infantry regiments, battalions, fusiliers, grenadiers—

Over the past year, the war had not come to Mexico City, except in the high prices and scarcities of corn, lard, coal, and cloth. From the Gulf Coast at Veracruz, the French had advanced easily, until the city of Puebla, that last stronghold before the capital. There, the year before, on the fifth of May, to everyone's astonishment the French Imperial Army was defeated! They'd had to retreat to Orizaba, that much closer to the coast, to wait for reenforcements. There was no taking Mexico City without first taking Puebla, and the battle for Puebla turned into a grinding year-long siege. The delay was a humiliation for Louis Napoleon; nonetheless, his was an army that retained deep reserves of power. The Republicans might put up a courageous fight, but few expected an outcome other than France's conquest of Mexico.

At news that Puebla had finally fallen, the Mexican Republic's president, Benito Juárez, and his cabinet ministers, packed up and fled north. The ragamuffin Republican Army marched out with them. It would not be long, Angelo supposed, until that army melted away, and Juárez himself would seek asylum, probably, in New Orleans. In the past several days, while waiting for the French troops to arrive, order in Mexico City, or rather, a semblance of it, had been kept by citizen volunteers and guardsmen lent by the foreign legations, including that of the United States.

The U.S. minister, Mr. Thomas Corwin, however, was disdainful of what he called "Louis Napoleon's Mexican adventure." Mr. Corwin was popular in Mexico with both Republicans and conservatives, for it was well-known that back in 1847, when he was the senator from Ohio, he had loudly and steadfastly opposed the U.S. invasion of Mexico, calling it "unjust and dishonorable." The land grabs, of California, Texas, and more, Mr. Corwin had called "hypocritical avarice." Now, arms crossed over his broad chest, Mr. Corwin, whose visage might have been carved in stone, gazed down upon the spectacle of the French Army with undisguised contempt.

Lined up along the ledge of the flat-roof, his fifty-odd guests were mostly men, Yankee traders, mining engineers, railroad people, and a Dane with a sunburnt nose. Mr. Wells, a journalist for *Harper's* and *The Overland Monthly*, wore an ill-fitting hounds-tooth suit and a derby. Leaning out over his elbows, he said, out of the corner of his mouth, which held a fuming cigar, "A fine candle to our Army of the Potomac."

Across the street, from a balcony, a woman upturned a basket of roses; from another balcony, a pink dot of a nosegay made an arc before disappearing beneath the river of men. Angelo and the Dane were discussing how the police had driven around the city this morning, delivering sacks of flowers. The baby began to mewl and turn his head toward his mother.

"He's hungry," Mr. Wells observed.

With the clamor from the parade, they could barely hear one another; Alicia could pretend she'd not heard that impertinence.

"Why's his head shaved?" Mr. Wells edged closer. "Got lice or somethin'?"

Alicia turned away. Shifting the baby from the crook of her elbow to her shoulder, she now rubbed his little back. Yes, she stayed right where she was, for she was enchanted by those uniforms: gold braid on the shakos, now kepis with sun-curtains, now a fluttering battle flag of yet a different regiment. *Tirailleurs algériens* in their white turbans. Cavalry. Artillery: siege, mountain, field . . . each a special world . . . The sun was precisely overhead, so that the walls of the buildings on the both sides were luminous. Everything shimmered and flashed. And the officers! So smart, their glittering chests, gold braid shining all up their arms, saluting with white gloves.

"Viva Forey! Viva Bazaine!" Someone was calling down the names of the generals.

More roses, confetti, and a lusty "Long live the Holy Church!"

Angelo wore an inscrutable expression. He pulled his cigar from his mouth. "What do you reckon, Mr. Corwin, fifteen thousand men?"

"No, sir. Substantially higher."

All the while, Alicia could not help but keep glancing down at the babe in her arms, into his sea blue eyes closing, then opening to search her face, or scowl at the sun. O, how his lips made an "O," how he curled and uncurled his tiny, perfect fingers. And what was wonderful to her was that his own grandfather, too, had come into Mexico City at the head of an army. Don Agustín de Iturbide, the Liberator, had received these same cheers from his grateful countrymen, and a rain of roses—Pepa, then a young girl, had heard the bouquets thudding onto the roof of the family's carriage. The Liberator had united Mexico under a tricolor of green for independence, red for the memory of Spain, and white, medallioned with the Aztec symbol of an eagle perched on a cactus and devouring a snake, for the purity of the True Faith. Alicia looked into her baby's eyes and in silent words from her heart told him this story, which ended this way: *And you are not only the Liberator's grandson; you are his* tocayo, *the one, the very special one, who has the same name.*

"*Tocayito,*" she whispered, kissing the top of his shiny head. And then (as Pepa and Doña Juliana were always urging her to do), she pulled the blanket over him.

Speaking now to Mr. Corwin, Mr. Wells said, "I wager the French'll bleed this country, then—" he made a slicing gesture across his throat. "Skedaddle."

Mr. Corwin squinted but offered no reply. The latest news to reach Mexico City was that a month ago, at Chancellorsville, General Robert E. Lee had routed Union forces twice the size of his own. All told, over thirty thousand men had perished. But for the Confederacy, Chancellorsville was an astounding triumph. It was the North that would oppose an empire in Mexico, and very possibly the North was whipped. As for what Washington wanted or did not want, that was moot. No one, it seemed, could stop the juggernaut of Louis Napoleon's Army. There, below in the Calle de San Francisco, was the proof for their eyes: artillery caissons, wagons, mules, more men, and then—when Alicia felt her arms becoming weak with fatigue from holding the baby—bringing up the rear, the ambulances. There were so many ambulances she gave up and went inside for limeade and pie. It was strawberry pie: her favorite.

Angelo and his brothers were not cheering the French Occupation, but neither were they so incautious as to oppose openly what could well be the permanent new order. Juárez had attacked the church. His government, crippled by bankruptcy, was incapable of maintaining order, and so perhaps General Almonte had reason to say, "Better this Devil than the other one."

After many years abroad, in Washington, London, and the Continent, General Almonte had returned to Mexico City, where, with French cannon behind him, he had assumed the office of Lieutenant General of the Realm, President of the Council of Regents. His was a breathtaking pole vault into power. Even his detractors had to shake their heads at the audacity of it. But unlike his onetime mentor, Santa Anna, General Almonte was not a flamboyant personality. He could throw out his chest and flash his medals, and he was jealous of the perks of his position, as all men of power wisely are, but he was, at bottom, a suzerain of simple tastes. Although he had dined at the tables of royalty, he was most at home with his mug of pulque, his plate of beans, and his wife's own tamales *de tinga*. He was, moreover, a very Scotsman of fiscal prudence, a tireless, shoulder-to-the-shovel worker, who worked most effectively behind the scenes.

Now, to be General and Madame Almonte's friend could be most convenient. To be their enemies, in a word, unhealthy.

The Iturbides were neither. In the weeks that followed the occupation of Mexico City, as the French Imperial Army now thrust tentacles into the countryside, taking over cities, highways, mines, and ports, for news the Iturbides had to content themselves with reading the heavily censored newspapers and third-hand drawing-room gossip, like other mere spectators. As was abundantly obvious to Alicia now, the Almontes were of a provenance distant from the exalted one of Mexico's distinguished creole families. In Washington, Alicia knew almost nothing about General Almonte. She had supposed the ambassador was a typical specimen of Mexican gentleman. Once in Mexico, however, from Doña Juliana and others, she heard earfuls about that *pata rajada* (barefoot Indian). What, did she not know?! General Almonte was the bastard of Father Morelos! Yes, Father José María Morelos, so-called Slave of the Nation, hero of the early wars for Mexican Independence? Oh, no, no, no, nothing—absolutely—to do with Don Agustín de Iturbide. Why, Iturbide, a colonel then, had fought *against* Morelos. Morelos was a mule-driver-turned-parish-priest who led armies of campesinos in bloody insurrections, until he was captured and, as God wanted, convicted by the Inquisition. Not until five years after his execution did Spain itself descend into liberalism; only then did good men, decent men such as Agustín de Iturbide, take up the cause of independence.

There were a multitude of stories about how Morelos's bastard received the name Almonte. The one toward which Doña Juliana inclined was that the peasant mother, when presenting Father Morelos with the baby, was told to "take it *al monte*, to the mountain."

As for Madame Almonte, nobody who was anybody knew anything about her family. She had directed some sort of technical school in Mexico City and, at her instigation, her husband had put his name as author onto the *Guía de forasteros*, an overpriced guidebook that featured her amateurish drawings of Mexico City's principal buildings. A decade out of date, the *Guía de forasteros* was, nonetheless and all of a sudden, prominently displayed in all the bookshop windows.

Ostensibly, General Almonte was working with the French to install a Catholic monarchy. The idea, as formulated by a select group of Mexican exiles in Europe, was that this form of government, this time with the unassailable prestige of a European prince, would provide Mexico with the stability finally to realize its potential, with the unquestioned reign of the True Faith and with protection, desperately needed, against an encroaching neighbor to the north. Of course, said monarch would ally himself with the interests of France. A Mexican imperial government would grant France generous trade concessions and make payments on debts—above all, it would satisfy, as the republic had not, the holders of the so-called Jecker Bonds. The expectation was that, with the gold and silver from Mexico's until now chronically underexploited mines, and the soon-to-be-abundant tax receipts on revived trade, the expedition would, voilà! pay for itself.

But not just any European prince would do. He had to be of impeccable royal blood. He had to be Catholic. Not too young, not too old. Ambitious but malleable. The candidate Louis Napoleon had drawn a bead on was the Archduke of Austria Maximilian von Habsburg, for he was all of these things, and (delectable icing on the cake) also a direct descendant of Carlos V, Holy Roman Emperor and (as Carlos I) king of Spain at the time of the conquest of Mexico.

Should the Archduke Maximilian refuse the crown, well, there General Almonte would be: difficult to dislodge. Perhaps, Agustin Gerónimo wondered, Santa Anna, from his Caribbean exile on the island of Saint Thomas, might have had something to do with this scheme, after all.

"Perhaps," Angelo said.

"Perhaps," Agustín Cosme echoed faintly.

• • •

Pepa de Iturbide, for her part, welcomed the French. She had no pity for Republicans. In confiscating church property, Juárez and his ilk had stolen the patrimony of the poor and they deserved to burn in Hell until they were *chicharrón,* that is, fried pork rinds. Alicia did not worry her pretty head with politics or religion (topics her nicely bred family rarely discussed at the dinner table anyway). However, she wholeheartedly agreed with her sister-in-law that the arrival of the French was an excellent thing, for the streets were now cleaner, the beggars more orderly, the officers so gallant and dashing. Best of all, there was a raft of new shops—one opened its door every day, it seemed.

For the past year, the Compagnie Transatlantique had been plying its steamships between Saint Nazaire and Veracruz; now, with the stagecoach highway opened from Veracruz to Mexico City, one could find imported corsets with genuine whalebone, Parisian silk stockings, quality trimmings and laces for bonnets. The newspapers were soon advertising shipments of pianos, umbrellas, sewing machines, champagne and cognac, billiard tables, gas lamps that were ever so much more efficient and smoke-free. Mexico City now had a proper patisserie; bookshops carried the most recent issues of *Revue des Deux Mondes, Le Moniteur,* Victor Hugo novels, and what-have-you. There were French language schools, French music schools; and a French tailor, Monsieur Bouffartigues, right there on the Calle de Refugio No. 19; not to mention the touring French theater troupes, French opera, and the Chirini Circus, direct from Paris with, as the newspaper announced, "trapeze artists and a battle of Moors and Christians on horseback." Alicia and Pepa were among the few Mexico City señoras who spoke French—or even were in-the-know that "ch" was pronounced "sh" and not to pronounce the "z" at the end of words such as "chez." As had been *très chic* in English-speaking Washington, they now sprinkled their Spanish conversations with bons mots—so much so that when (at Angelo's insistence), Alicia went to call upon Madame Almonte, this lady, in the crush, mistook her for a Frenchwoman!

"Ma cher Madame . . ." When Alicia answered her in English, "How do you do?" Madame Almonte blinked. She stared hard, pinching her brows to-

gether, and then let out a tiny scream of pleasure. She gripped Alicia by both shoulders, pulled her close, giving her the heartiest Mexican *abrazo*, finished with a clap on the back and a smooch on the cheek. Madame Almonte did say, "Remember me to Don Angel," but she neglected to ask anything about Alicia, her family, her new baby. Nothing. Madame Almonte just went on, retailing some story about her and her husband's tour to some dowdy mining town, to her rapt audience of the obscure. Some of these women were smoking! Fanning herself, Alicia nearly had a congestion, and not because of the smoke. The sofa was understuffed and the cake tasted dry. "You leave already?" Madame Almonte said in her awkward English. "Please to come again."

"O Moses," Alicia later told Pepa, "why bother?"

Meanwhile, baby Agustín was growing plumper by the day. He was a stubborn little fellow and a champion chewer. At four months, he had the habit of chewing on his toes; at six months, he gnawed off the corner of his mother's *Harper's Monthly*. One morning, Alicia found him teething on a button. "Lupe," she scolded the Mexican nanny in her now flawless Spanish, "you must watch what he puts in his mouth."

"*Sí, niña.*"

Alicia herself spoilt the baby with spoons of *nieve de limón* (lime sorbet) off her plate. When he was especially squirmy, she set him on the floor and let him crawl. At mealtimes she pretended not to notice when he went exploring under the table, where he would go tugging at shoes and trousers and skirt hems. The one who enjoyed this most was Salvador, the baby's thirteen-year-old cousin. An orphan, Salvador was the only child of Angelo's younger brother, also named Salvador, who had died in Mexico just two days before Angelo's wedding—though the news of that fierce blow had not come to them until many weeks later. A shy, thin, but big-shouldered boy, Salvador was living with an uncle in Toluca; now and again he came to Mexico City to visit. With an embarrassed smile, Salvador would lift the tablecloth and then dip his head under the table. "Ay, who's pulling at my shoe?"

Alicia, coquettishly, would say, "Father? Might we have a little mouse nibbling under there?"

Pepa would press her lips in consternation. This was not her idea of any way to raise a child.

Letters, very slowly, made their way between Mexico City and Washington. News might be three weeks or three months old when it was read; its reply would then be read another month or more after that. Some letters were lost. The War Between the States went on, and it was vicious. The baby was already taking his first unsteady steps when, one spring day of 1864, his grandmother Green, outside for the first time without her paisley shawl, held his photograph in her hand for the first time. Her heart leapt for joy—and stung with longing for this grandchild, for her dear, darling Alice was so far away. She had not seen Alice in seven years.

It seemed the photograph was taken when he was first able to sit up on his own. Posed upon an ornately carved chair, he was looking off at something or someone (Alice?) to the side. His frock was so large it covered his shoes and spilled over the sides of the chair. In the letter, Alice explained that Pepa and Doña Juliana, their landlady, had recommended shaving his head—a harmless concession to Mexican custom, it seemed to Alice, and what if there were something to it? After all, Alice's father's hairline had begun to recede when he was still in the navy.

The baby's face appeared blurred, but his expression, it seemed to Mrs. Green, was remarkably frank. He had intelligence. He had the same ears as his great-grandfather, her father, General Uriah Forrest. She wiped a tear from her eye.

Pride goeth before destruction, but Lord forgive her, she was proud of her Alice, her youngest, who had been the one Mrs. Green most feared for. It seemed like only yesterday that Alice, elbows on the carpet, her little chin in her hands, was poring over that old atlas. She had been such a headstrong child, prone to daydreaming, and as a belle so frivolous. Mrs. Green had tried to convince her, marrying a Mexican would be a trial beyond the strength of a mere Job. But now, Mrs. Green recognized, Alice had shown herself to be both brave and steadfast. No meteor that would streak to earth, her Alice was a true star.

Mrs. Green left the porch to go into the house for her spectacles. When she came out again, drums were on the wind; the soldiers were drilling at Fort Reno. Three years into the war, Mrs. Green had not yet become accustomed to the sound; it set her nerves on edge. She sat down on her rocking chair and put on her spectacles. In the photograph, the baby's face was still blurred.

Alice's letter began thus: *The baby is the greatest thing that could have happened for this family—a perfect Godsend.*

There was no one to see her; Mrs. Green burst into tears.

THE ARCHDUKE MAXIMILIAN
VON HABSBURG, OR A E I O U

*O*ur story turns now to an ivory castle, perched by an uneasy sea within sight of the city of Trieste. In the northeastern corner of Italy, then part of the Austrian Empire, Il Castello di Miramare, or Miramar, was the residence of the archduke who was second in line to the throne. Whereas Vienna's ancient gray Hofburg Palace huddled around shadowy courtyards, Miramar stood new, crisp, unafraid of the Italian sun. Even today, in the early morning, just before the sun rises from behind the hills, and all the birds are singing, its tower seems to glow from within. Yes, sometimes a story's beginning fools the eye, the way a fata morgana projects a landscape that may in fact lie hundreds of miles beyond the horizon. But sometimes, too, persons who do not appear to share even a footprint's worth of common ground turn out to have destinies bound together in painful knots.

Indeed, it was in the midst of the Iturbides' domestic idyll that, beyond the other side of the Atlantic Ocean, in his still-under-construction Miramar Castle, the Archduke Maximilian von Habsburg very reluctantly accepted the Mexican throne—that same throne that had belonged to the ill-starred Don Agustín de Iturbide. The archduke's reluctance was an ugly embarrassment for all concerned. However, the details of the episode were not generally known until years afterward, when most of the participants had already gone to their reward, for, in Austria and in Mexico during the French occupation, sharp-eyed censors inspected letters, magazines, newspapers, and telegrams, with not the least hesitation in confiscating matter their superiors might deem offensive. Which is not to suggest that no one in Mexico knew of the troubles surrounding the archduke's acceptance of the Mexican throne, merely that the Iturbides, as most members of Mexico City society, were not privy to the whole of it. This turned out to have exceedingly unfortunate consequences.

The troubles surrounding the archduke's acceptance were many, but the stickiest was the so-called Family Pact, a document the archduke referred to as "that accursed piece of paper." His version of events was that his older brother, Kaiser Franz Joseph, sprang it upon him without warning and then strong-armed him—literally forced him—to sign it. However, ample time beforehand, when the archduke visited Vienna in January 1864, the foreign minister, Count Rechberg, had mentioned that, of course, before accepting the Mexican throne, Maximilian would have to resign from the House of Habsburg, thus renouncing his rights as an archduke of Austria. Maximilian had coolly answered, "That I will never do."

How could one resign from the House of Habsburg? It was his blood, his fingernails, the very skin he wore. It was recorded in the *Almanach de Gotha* and would be, until the end of time: He, Maximilian von Habsburg, was the descendant of the kings of the Holy Roman Empire, rulers by Divine Right. It was as a member of the House of Habsburg, knight-errant for its glory, that he had given his word to Louis Napoleon that he would accept the throne of Mexico. The idea of giving up his rights was not only inconceivable, it was absurd!

Maximilian assumed that Count Rechberg had not spoken with the authority of the Kaiser. And indeed, subsequently, Maximilian met with his brother several times, and nothing was said about it. Not until the eve of Maximilian's departure for Brussels—very late in the game—did Count Rechberg press upon him the court historian's report on the matter of succession, again arguing that, before formally accepting the Mexican throne, Maximilian would have to sign the Family Pact. This report had the Kaiser's signature, but it was, Maximilian told Count Rechberg, so much intellectual flatulence. Maximilian heard nothing more about it—until after Maximilian and his consort, Charlotte, had been feted as emperor- and empress-elect in both Brussels and Paris, after they had floated the loan for the Mexican Empire in the Paris bourse, after they had crossed the Channel to pay their respects to Queen Victoria, that is, after everything, lock, stock, and barrel, had been recognized in the most public way. On their way back to Trieste, where the coronation was to take place in Miramar Castle in a matter of days, Maximilian and Charlotte visited Vienna where they were received at the Hofburg, not as archduke and archduchess but as heads of state. The day after the state banquet, lo! Count Rechberg presented that piece of paper. Either sign the Family Pact, or Younger Brother would not be permitted to wear a crown.

Bitter rage welled in Maximilian's throat. It was just like the fiasco of his governorship of Lombardy-Venetia when, notwithstanding his demonstrated competence, leadership, and popularity (really remarkable popularity given the restiveness of the Italian nationalists), Franz Joseph had dismissed him with no warning, no justification, and so made him appear ridiculous. Franz Joseph had never supported him. And now, their mother, Archduchess Sophie, stepped in. *You should not deprive Max of his rights. You are not being a good brother.* Franz Joseph argued right back, Felipe V, nephew of Louis XIV, renounced his rights to the French throne when he went to reign in Spain, as did their Aunt Marie-Louise forfeit hers to the Austrian throne when she married Napoleon Bonaparte.

Yet there was an undercurrent to Maximilian's raging feelings: relief. To begin with, though Charlotte insisted he was overreacting, it did seem to him, as to many of the older generation, rather unseemly for a Habsburg to accept a throne from a mere Bonaparte. And to put one's fate in the hands of a Bonaparte . . . Maximilian remembered, from the time he was a child, hearing them called "those dregs of the Corsican banditti." His aunt the Archduchess Marie-Louise was the one who had been made to marry Bonaparte, once the barren and infinitely less distinguished Empress Josephine had been divorced. Bonaparte, that rapacious parvenu, he was horrible: Krampus, the Devil, was what they'd called him in Vienna in those days.

And to erect an empire in Mexico was, perhaps, a Quixotic quest—alike to a march into Russia? The finances were somewhat convoluted and, well frankly, mystifying. By the Treaty of Miramar, which Maximilian was to sign once he was crowned emperor, Louis Napoleon would keep troops in Mexico as long as needed, but at Mexico's expense—the costs of the transports, the supplies, all arms, and the payrolls and interest, and indemnities, and—well, would that, ultimately, be feasible? In the beginning, although Louis Napoleon had assured Maximilian that they would, neither England nor Spain had offered their support for the Mexican expedition. The U.S. consul in Trieste came out to Miramar Castle to warn Maximilian not to swallow the honeyed words of the Mexican delegation. Who were these men, after all? Don José Hidalgo, a no-account expatriate Parisian society hanger-on; Don José María Gutiérrez de Estrada, another longtime expatriate, denizen of Rome, an ultramontane schemer; and General Almonte, a crony of Santa Anna's and, as it happened, bastard of the guerrilla-hero of Mexican Independence, the priest Morelos. At that time, General Almonte had already returned to Mexico City and was serving as Lieutenant General of the Realm, which is to say, regent under the French occupation. More than any of them, General Almonte's true purposes remained inscrutable. (Was Almonte secretly loyal to the exiled dictator, Santa Anna? Just another Albanian-style strongman? Or a visionary and true patriot? as was his father, Father Morelos, the glorified hero of the wars for Mexican Independence?) The U.S. minister in Vienna, according to the reports of the police spies, was dripping with disdain for the entire enterprise—he seemed to think Maximilian might as well have offered himself up to a rope and gibbet.

And the U.S. minister was not the only one of this persuasion. Queen Victoria had received Maximilian and Charlotte not as heads of state but as her cousins; at the dinner at Windsor Castle, at every mention of Mexico, she took on the expression of having bitten into gristle and changed the subject (to puppy-dogs and the unseasonable weather in Scotland!). On their return from London, Maximilian and Charlotte had stopped at Claremont to visit Charlotte's Grand-maman, Marie-Amélie, the ex-queen of France. That was a nasty scene. Grand-maman had gripped Charlotte's hands, crying, "Don't go, my darlings, you mustn't go!" She nearly shouted at Maximilian, "They will assassinate you!" The ravings of an old woman, perhaps, but there were many other warnings. One, in particular, blazed bright in Maximilian's mind, for it came from Don Pedro Montezuma XV, the sole legitimate descendant of the Aztec emperor.

French cannon have cowed some into submission; once tranquility reigns,
however, there will rise up all of a sudden a terrible counter-revolution . . .
Your Highness has been too precipitous in accepting the Mexican throne . . .
Those who today form the regency are of the most impious stripe . . . de-
praved evildoers, usurpers, they rob the Treasury, they rob even the Holy
Church . . . they will supplant Your Highness perhaps after a tragic end.

Indeed, when the Mexican throne was first offered, Charlotte herself had forebodings. Her uncle Prince Joinville had visited Mexico some years earlier. It was a barbarous country, he said, rife with yellow fever, malaria, the revolting spectacles of bullfights, and if that weren't enough, armed bands roaming the countryside. "And if Brazil was unsuitable for you, a white woman, to visit, Mexico is even less so. You, the empress of Mexico?" Joinville had laughed. *Une idée affreuse!* A dreadful idea!

However, when Maximilian began to give the invitation serious consideration, Charlotte not only warmed to the idea, she became its most energetic proponent. Neither had Maximilian, sunny by nature, been swayed by all this "doom and gloom." As Charlotte pointed out, the enemies of France and the enemies of the True Church painted the picture with their own tints. Maximilian and Charlotte both interviewed diplomats, bankers, mining engineers, and scientists. They read stacks of letters, reports, and between them a library's worth of books, including, of course, Baron Alexander von Humboldt's extensive and meticulously documented report, *Reise in die Äquinoktial-Gegenden des Neuen Kontinents,* all volumes, from cover to cover. Mexico, astride the world's two greatest oceans, rich with precious metals and fertile lands, had stupendous potential, and the catalyst, they both became convinced, would be himself.

As Charlotte said, quoting one of the gentlemen of the Mexican delegation, a Habsburg prince on that throne would be as the sun to the planets. Yes, to lend their personal prestige—the prestige of the House of Habsburg and, on her side, Saxe-Coburg and Gotha—would be an enormous help to Louis Napoleon, and they could count, as a cathedral upon its foundation, on his deepest, most reverent gratitude. And: the equally, nay, perhaps even more profound gratitude of His Holiness the Pope. Yes, Maximilian's ambition had been whetted. And was it not a sign of Divine approbation, that he, descendant of the Habsburg king of Spain who had commanded the conquistadores, should be the one to sit upon this throne?

Oh, and what a shining pleasure finally to have the chance to govern, to bring justice, peace, and prosperity to a people, without Vienna's boot on one's back! He revered his elder brother, but how trying, how absolutely exasperating at times, to be the Heir Presumptive, and after the birth of Prince Rudolph, second in line—inconvenient shadow or little chess piece, as it were, of those who were schemed to keep themselves close to the Kaiser, those ham-fisted reactionaries. Oh, right they were to fear Maximilian! Had he been All-Highest, he would not rule by instilling dread in the hearts of his subjects; he would earn their love with understanding and vision. Italian students should not be mowed down with guns, pulled off the streets to be beaten and tortured. *Bravo tutti!* The good ruler celebrates his people, he is of them, and so is lodged in their hearts. They had loved him in Lombardy-Venetia; many of his subjects had told him he was the best governor they had ever had. It would have worked out, he knew, he had tried to convince the Kaiser to just give him a chance—

Maximilian could almost feel the weight of the crown of Mexico upon his head; the cool metal of the scepter in his hand. He could see, in his mind's eye, his own imperial seal—the crowned Aztec eagle, the MIM for the Latin *Maximiliano Imperator de Mexico*, and his motto "Justice with Equity"—he had sketched it in his notebook, refining the design, many times.

But to separate himself from the House of Habsburg? Maximilian saw no way he could sign such a document. Therefore, he could not leave Austria. In his view, he had been bullied and betrayed by his brother. But his brother was the Kaiser; the All-Highest's word was an order. There was nothing to do but buck up.

He and Charlotte left Vienna for Trieste, and there, where the early spring winds tossed the Adriatic and the trees in the park were just beginning to bud, he told his wife, with a *sprezzatura*, a genuine lightness he had not felt in months: "We have much to do here." Miramar was still in part a shell; only the ground and first floors had been finished. The walls wanted paintings and draperies. The parterre needed work, the driveway more gravel, and the aviary could be expanded. It could be finished by June. This summer they could spend cruising, perhaps, as an appoggiatura, Corfu, Patmos, and then a few blessed weeks on Lacroma, the island that Charlotte, so thoughtfully, had given him as a present. Lacroma was silence itself: pines and myrtle, and Richard the Lionheart's ruin, an abandoned eleventh-century monastery, its walls laden with roses. Lacroma was so romantic, a place where he could botanize, read philosophy, and write poetry, whilst Charlotte painted or played the lute.

And so it was that, but three days before his coronation was to take place, with a mix of wounded pride, weltschmerz, and a heart secretly glad, Maximilian informed Don José Hidalgo, acting head of the Mexican delegation, that he was unable to accept. A telegram was sent to Paris. As for the pope, before cruising to Lacroma Maximilian would go to Rome to explain his decision in person. Thus ended the bittersweet might-have-been of the cactus throne, curious footnote within a footnote in history, so Maximilian imagined.

Louis Napoleon's answer thundered back:

Your Imperial Highness has entered into engagements that you are no longer free to break. What would you really think of me if, when Your Imperial Highness had already reached Mexico, I were suddenly to say that I can no longer fulfill the conditions to which I have set my signature?

And then Louis Napoleon lunged with the saber: *The honor of the House of Habsburg is in question.*

What to do, what to do, what to do? Maximilian was in a teeth-gritting dither. No, it was more than that. He felt himself in the sucking grip of a kind of quicksand.

The Mexican delegation had not yet departed Trieste. The Mexicans, shocked, were imploring him to change his mind. In Miramar Castle, from the window of his study, Maximilian could see, anchored out in the bay, the *Novara* and the French frigate the *Themis,* which was to be its escort for the voyage to America. The ships' captains, too, were waiting, expecting him to change his mind.

Charlotte pointed out that now, if he refused the throne, how could they possibly hold their heads up? "Louis Napoleon and Eugénie will ridicule you. In all the courts of Europe, you will be despised."

"You exaggerate."

"They would brand you a coward!"

He had never seen her so agitated. "No . . ."

"Yes!!!"

She had raised her voice at him. He lifted his eyes, but before they met hers, they slid over to the window. Slowly, a horrible expression came over his face; his breath went shallow. "Really? You really think . . . that . . . they . . . ?"

"Max," she cut him off. "It is too late."

They were in the library; above the double doors hung the portrait by Winterhalter of Charlotte as a small child. Maximilian was looking at it with the most heartbreakingly forlorn expression she had ever seen. Suddenly, he cast his gaze to the carpet. He whispered, "Oh . . . my . . . God."

"Max . . ." she touched his hand, but he pushed it away.

He bolted out to the terrace, leaned over the side, and threw up.

He took to his bed. Charlotte, a hive of anxiety, did not wait; she barged past Dr. Jilek, right into Maximilian's sickroom, and hovered there, urging him: *What else was there for him? The Kaiser was jealous of his talents and popularity. The men Franz Joseph surrounded himself with, rigid-minded officers, distrusted Maximilian; they would continue to intrigue against him, and now, his refusal of the Mexican throne would be ammunition for them!*

Maximilian was propped up on pillows, his face deathly pale. Under the covers, he clutched at his stomach. He protested weakly, "I *cannot* give up my rights."

Yes, Charlotte agreed, the Family Pact was a horrific injustice. "But consider, is it meet that you, a man born to govern, born to make a people happy, have been left at the age of thirty-one with nothing to do but build castles and sail around collecting bugs?"

She herself was on the verge with boredom in Trieste—this stuffy, fifth-rate, provincial town. They had been exiled, put out to pasture, and was *this* to be the rest of their lives? Wasted! She wanted so very much to be useful, to serve, which she knew in her heart had always been God's purpose for them both. She knew how terribly wounded he had been to have lost the governorship of Lombardy-Venetia—but now, God had delivered to him a throne. Not any throne, not a Poland or a Greece, no! This was a throne backed by the might of the French Imperial Army! A once-in-a-lifetime opportunity!

"You *must* sign the Family Pact."

Maximilian raised his hand, as if to make some gesture; it fell limp at his side. "I—" He closed his eyes. His voice had dwindled to a thread: "I . . . can . . . not . . ."

Now Charlotte reminded Maximilian that without a monarch, notwithstanding the fine work of the French Army (which had, by this time, pacified most of Mexico), the country would slide right back into the abyss of bloodshed and anarchy. Had not the Mexican delegation made it clear that Maximilian was their savior? Had not His Holiness expressed great gratitude? Thousands of men had fallen in the battles to liberate Mexico from godless terrorists; would their deaths be in vain? They had lost arms, legs, they had died like dogs of disease! Would so many wives be left widows and children orphans for nothing? For Maximilian's scruples about a piece of paper! He would let the Holy Church in an entire nation be sacked! Between Salvation and the fires of Hell, souls were tottering on the precipice! Millions—nine million Mexicans—were depending on him! She fell to her knees at his bedside. Tenderly, as if it were a child's, she held his hand in both of hers. She spoke softly, her voice on the edge of breaking:

"In the name of God, you *must* accept."

The awful wheezing sound brought Dr. Jilek into the room.

The patient was hyperventilating, he said. Indignantly, but with perfect formality, he ushered Charlotte out into the hallway and firmly closed the door behind him. Maximilian, he said, could not, absolutely not, be disturbed.

In Dr. Jilek's professional and personal opinion, and he gave it freely when asked, the archduke's going to Mexico would be tantamount to suicide. No, he himself would not go as part of the retinue, for he had no intention of leaving God's earth by way of the yellow fever or being shot by some Mexican. Let younger, rasher men than himself tempt Fate. Might it please God, he hoped to continue to serve the archduke right here.

Wisdom and its companion compassion are bought, as the saying goes, with years and tears. Had Charlotte been a few years wiser, she might have perceived the dangers and, it must also be recognized, the strengths, though in a very different line of endeavors, of such an acutely sensitive personality as her husband's. She might have realized that the esteem she so craved from him was not going to come from pushing him. She might also have realized that things are not always as they appear to be, for there are those who actively seek to deceive us, knowing that we look out at the world, and politics in particular, through the filters of our own fears and longings. We can be our own enemies, blindly injuring ourselves, but we must, if we are to go on with any hope of happiness, learn to forgive ourselves. At the hard, unripe age of twenty-three, however, Charlotte had the single-mindedness of an amazon. Mexico was Maximilian's destiny and duty, his rightful prize, and she, by God, was going to win it for him! Girded for battle, as it were, she took the train to Vienna to take on the Kaiser.

Franz Joseph, though so consternated he kept rubbing his eye and crossing and uncrossing his leg, was impeccably polite to his sister-in-law. He had thought his own wife, Sissi, was stubborn, but *Lieber Gott*, she had competition! In the three hours behind closed doors, there were two occasions of such high color that he got up and went to the window, but Charlotte went on arguing at his back! Insisting and insisting, swinging and lunging with her arguments, what-ifs and exotic interpretations, coming at it from this direction and that, until finally, the Kaiser put his hand up. He conceded a fig leaf's worth of money and a few thousand volunteers. On the Family Pact, however, he remained as immovable as a post sunk ten meters into the ground. Before accepting a throne, Maximilian was going to have to sign the pact.

Behind his back, the Kaiser heard the rain sleeting against the window, and through the closed door the growing hum of the crowd that had been kept waiting in the reception area. It was impolitic to keep people waiting.

Among them were the governor of Croatia and the chief of the Geheim Polizei, the secret police. To signal the end of this meeting, which had already (and only to mollify his mother's feelings) gone on far past the point of decency, he stood up. But Charlotte—this was a pungent breach of protocol—remained seated. The Kaiser stared at her. It seemed to him she was grinding her teeth. She pushed her palms into the edges of her chair's armrests. A strand of her coiffure hung at a peculiar angle over her ear. She noticed that he had noticed. She brushed it back.

A look of despair flashed across her eyes, immediately replaced with a face of steel. "Surely," she said, standing up at last, "you do not expect Max to have come *here* to sign the Family Pact."

"He can sign it at Miramar."

Charlotte thrust her jaw at him. Her earrings bobbled. "The least you can do is give him the dignity of your presence, as Kaiser and as head of the House of Habsburg."

He almost laughed. "You want me to come to Miramar?"

"Yes," she said.

"I do not think Max would want that."

"You are wrong."

Soon after Charlotte's return to Miramar, the letters came: Charlotte's father, King Leopold of the Belgians, advised Maximilian to sign the Family Pact. Maximilian's mother, Archduchess Sophie, also advised him to sign it. As she had told Charlotte back in the Hofburg: *It breaks my mother's heart, but it is too late. And there is nothing for him here; you know that better than anyone.*

Dr. Jilek, with a face like a victim of the Gorgon, permitted Charlotte to enter; at Maximilian's bedside, in tears, Charlotte knelt and said, "My love, I did my best."

Through the open drapes there was nothing to be seen of the Bay of Grignano. A foghorn sounded, low and mournful. "You are my angel," Maximilian said, and he kissed her hands.

He got out of bed and had his valet dress him.

AEIOU, *Alles Erdreich Ist Österreich Untertan,* the whole world is subject to Austria, the mystical motto of his ancestor, the Emperor Frederick, had been his creed, the creed of the House of Habsburg. He was an officer. He was a gentleman. He had given his word to the pope, to Louis Napoleon, to the financiers of Paris, and—this also counted for something—the Mexican people. His own mother thought he should accept the throne. And Charlotte so dearly, so valiantly, wanted it. He could not quite admit to himself that he had, for many months already, succumbed to the siren song of power. What he told himself was that to remain in Europe would be not only to forfeit his honor but to crush Charlotte's spirit. For her sake, he would accept. But a part of him yet hesitated, squeezed his eyes shut, and hoped that somehow— some way—perhaps—it might be possible to avoid having to sign that damned Family Pact.

On April 9, 1864, the Kaiser arrived at Miramar Castle with Count Rechberg, seven archdukes, three chancellors, the governors of Venetia and Istria, and a crowd of officers. With due pomp Maximilian and Charlotte received them, and then, alone, the two brothers met in the study on the ground floor. It was a cozy room looking out on the sea. The walls were covered in elaborate hardwood paneling, and the parquet floor shone with the oval reflection from the skylight. The room was not so bright as it might have been, however, for the ceilings fell unusually low in emulation of the officer's mess room in the *Novara.* Outside the window, in the bay, could be seen the stern of that frigate, the same frigate that had taken him once to Brazil. Coal and provisions and almost all hands on board, it was waiting to carry him and his retinue to a destiny on the far side of the ocean. He did not want to go. He did not want to stay.

The brothers faced one another across the table. Both slender as whippets, they had the same shape of face, the same large ears—though Franz Joseph's protruded slightly. The Kaiser was then thirty-four years old, and his blond hair, always thin, had begun receding. His eyes were warm but resolute. Maximilian was the taller, his whiskers redder, and extravagant by comparison. The All-Highest wore his general's uniform: white with a gold lace collar and red trousers. Maximilian wore his admiral's uniform, a midnight blue with gold epaulettes and gold braid on the cuffs.

Having kissed his brother's hand, Maximilian stepped back and stood to attention. (One did not sit in the presence of an emperor without an express invitation to do so.) The Kaiser, meanwhile, put his hands behind his back and with occasional deep breaths taken in by the nostrils, moved clockwise about the room, ostensibly inspecting the artworks in which, they both knew, he had no interest whatsoever. He was moving toward the spot, the exact spot where, as he could stand in shadow, Younger Brother would be blinded by light. This went on for what felt to Maximilian a Dante-esque eternity. It seemed that, having paused before the bronze of Marcus Aurelius, Franz Joseph was going to make some comment. But, with a sniff, he swung around and, taking the larger chair:

"Please," he said, indicating, for Maximilian, the smaller chair.

Maximilian sank into it and crossed his arms over his chest. "I cannot fathom the point in this."

Franz Joseph first helped himself to the dish of salted almonds. He chewed thoroughly. Then he answered with the exact words he had used before, that, though, as a brother it sincerely pained him, as a sovereign he was obliged by an oath before God to put the interests of the empire first. In the event of his death, in which case his son, Prince Rudolph, would assume the throne, it would be impossible to have the next in line on the other side of the sea, having taken a solemn oath of loyalty to an alien people, and with financial and military entanglements with France.

"But these are my birthrights!"

"But this is the situation."

"I *never* would have gotten into this if I had known these were your terms!"

They went round and round with the same arguments, until Maximilian burst out: "You want to be rid of me!"

"Max . . ."

Since they were children, it had always gone this way. "You humiliate me!" Maximilian banged his fist on the table.

"You forget yourself."

Maximilian stood up and began breathing hard. The veins on his forehead throbbed. He steadied himself on the back of the chair; then, without a word to his brother, he threw open the doors and stalked out onto the terrace. He could be seen out here by the men on the *Novara* and the *Themis,* by the gardeners—he didn't care. Up and down he walked, gulping the sea air, wringing his hands, shaking his head. He talked to himself: *I won't be bullied, this is an outrage, I won't go, no, no, I shall tell them, I want to stay here, but I shall be, I can't, I must, oh, God!* After a while, when he had calmed somewhat, he stood with his hands on the balustrade. A pair of gulls circled high above; below, a pelican trailed its shadow over the whitecaps. The water slapped violently against the seawall and the rocks. There was pattern in the surf; he watched the foam as it slithered, sparkling, over the rocks. The wavering shreds of seaweed. The breeze on his cheeks. The scissor-like screams of the gulls. If time could stop, he could stay here, right here, as if inside a bell jar. The unholy thing he was about to do—he was about to be forced to do—had not yet been done.

"Sir!"

Maximilian put his fingertips to his temples. Slowly, he turned around. It was the Kaiser's aide-de-camp.

"Sir, the Kaiser says that it would be good of you to come back inside."

Stiffly, Maximilian came back inside. The Kaiser had left the study; he was standing at the foot of the staircase. "Let's get it over with," he said, and without waiting for Maximilian's answer he started up the stairs. Maximilian followed. In the stateroom, there must have been thirty people assembled there. They had been waiting all this time, and Maximilian wondered now, with a tightening knot in his stomach, had they seen him down on the terrace stalking about like a lunatic? Before the Kaiser, the crowd parted. The air was ripe with cologne and hair lotions and bootblack. There on the table, upon a stretch of green and gold morocco leather, lay the document and the quill, a white feather.

Maximilian's heart sank to his shoes. *Lieber Gott in Himmel,* a small voice within him cried. *Dear God in Heaven, help me.*

With a trembling hand, he set down the quill. There it was: his signature. And with it he had sacrificed what was most dear to him in the world. Rage welled again in his throat. The child in him wanted to rip the paper to shreds and toss them in the air, let them fall over the carpet like snow. He put his hand on the edge of the desk. It took him a moment to find his breath.

There was a banquet afterward. With each course, as always, the instant the All-Highest set down his cutlery, all plates were whisked off the table. (Maximilian only poked at his food, but he noticed Charlotte, at the Kaiser's right, had had the chance for but a single spoonful of her *Topfenknödel* with chocolate gelato.) By one o'clock the Kaiser was at the train station to return to Vienna. In front of everyone, the Kaiser broke all protocol. "Max!" he cried, and he held out his arms. With all the feeling of a stone, Maximilian stepped up and allowed himself to be embraced.

His coronation took place in that same stateroom the following day. Maximilian wore his Austrian admiral's uniform. His skin felt clammy. His stomach lurched. Charlotte, serene and stately, was in rose pink satin and her diamond crown. The Mexicans spoke. Maximilian read a prepared statement. Then, the Bishop of Trieste received his oath, and Charlotte's oath. The document was placed upon a small but most apt table: a wedding gift from His Holiness, its round black scagliola top covered with oval mosaics, Saint Peter's, the Parthenon, the Colosseum, the ruins of the Forum, Temple of Vesta, Arches of Septimus, Severus and Titus.

Bugles, drums. The Mexican imperial flag, a tricolor with the medallion of the crowned Aztec eagle perched on a cactus and devouring a snake, was run up the pole on the tower.

For Maximilian, the next three hours dissolved in a smear. He woke slumped over his desk, the back of Charlotte's hand, so cool, on his forehead.

"You are burning up," she said.

Dr. Jilek prescribed strictest bed rest. No visitors. And, Maximilian told Charlotte, please, not one word about Mexico. And so it was that the empress of Mexico presided over the coronation banquet with the Mexican delegation, alone.

It took three days for Maximilian to "find his sea legs," as it were, but he did.

On April 14, with his empress on his arm, Maximilian descended the steps to the jetty. They moved slowly through the vast crowd that lined the seawall and the road all the way from Trieste. People were touching their clothes, kissing their hands, calling out, God keep you! *Arrivederci!* Goodbye! Flowers pelted his shoulders and sailed over his head: roses, daisies. The band struck up the thumping drone of the brand-new Mexican Imperial Anthem, so peculiar after always, for all one's life, reverently singing along to *Gott Erhalte Unsern Kaiser,* God Save Our King. At the end of the jetty crouched the little stone Sphinx, a souvenir of his cruise to Egypt; people crowded around it; a small boy was perched, legs swinging, on its head. Maximilian had planned, as was his custom, to touch its nose for luck, but it was impossible to do anything but help Charlotte into the launch, and then, somewhat shakily, step in himself. He waved to Dr. Jilek, Radonetz, all the faithful retainers and friends.

This dazzling day had a sky the color of a robin's egg. Beyond the jetty, the Bay of Grignano was filled with tugs and frigates and steamers and fishing boats. From the smokestacks of the *Novara* and the *Themis* sooty coils worked their way into the sky. Salvos of cannon erupted from the warships, from the forts, from the city itself. It was in this clamor, being carried over the water, as if not by the sailors' rowing but by the fading cheers of the Triestini, that Maximilian looked back upon his castle, its ivory towers luminous against the sky, the strange flag flapping in the breeze, and the hills rising lush and green behind it with ilexes, oaks, and ash trees, and he began to cry.

Once onboard the Novara, he went below deck, and giving strict orders that unless the ship were in danger of sinking he was not to be disturbed, shut himself into his cabin. The dim and the rumbling of the engines soothed him. It seemed to him that he had been murdered and, like a Hindu, sent back into a kind of womb to be reborn. *Yo soy mexicano,* I am Mexican: he practiced saying it, though it seemed ridiculous. He stood before his shaving mirror. *Yo soy el emperador de México.* He stayed there in anguished communion with himself until after breakfast the next day.

Then he joined the others up on the deck. There was Count Karl "Charlie" Bombelles, whose father had been their tutor, and old Professor Bilimek, the botanist, and Schertzenlechner, and Monsieur Eloin—a whole party of blue bloods and expert advisors. The thrill of the adventure of a lifetime coursed in their veins, lightening their eyes, and bringing bursts of laughter to every exchange.

They steamed down the coast of Apulia: Trani, Bari, Brindisi—ancient Brundisium, from which Octavian set out to conquer Mark Anthony and Cleopatra. By the time they rounded the coast of Calabria, his spirits were buoyant. They passed through the Straits of Messina without incident. On the other side, they caught sight of the two-thousand-foot-high smoking island of Stromboli. By late afternoon, they were cruising close enough to make out the goats grazing on its steep flank. When the sun sank behind it, the cone turned the most exquisite shade of dusky lavender, and the sea to blood. It was one of the most awe-inspiring sunsets that he, a connoisseur of sunsets, had ever seen. That night, a waxing moon polished the waves, and Stromboli's sparks danced, red sprites, in midair. The stars made a canopy of diamonds. God's blessing was upon their enterprise, Charlotte said, and again, he kissed her hands.

The following day, when they were enveloped in fog and could not see Mount Vesuvius, he was overcome by a pique of melancholy, but neither did this last. In Rome, where his reception by His Holiness was more than any sovereign could hope for, he felt young again, with more than enough energy to climb the Palatine Hill, and then hike through the Forum, leaving their cicerone, a German painter, behind with the ladies, and go leaping over fallen columns and rubble (Charlie was the only one who could keep up; Schertzenlechner and Eloin fell behind, those two fatties sweating like a pair of draft horses). Because of the Roman fever, it was imprudent to be outside at dusk— but one felt simply bulletproof! They toured the Colosseum under moonlight, and their cicerone gave such vivid descriptions that, as the Mistress of the Imperial Household Frau von Kuhacsevich said with a shiver, she could verily hear the roars of the lions and the screams of the Christian martyrs.

They visited the Baths of Titus, and the Pantheon, that sublime work of genius commissioned by the Emperor Hadrian, where they had the unearthly privilege of watching a light mist falling from the oculus. They admired the late baroque Trevi Fountain; they strolled through the gardens of the Villa Borghese with its superb statues and its trees and bushes dripping with the most delicious-smelling blossoms. One kept in mind Goethe's admonition: "Only in Rome can one educate oneself for Rome." This city of Michelangelo, Maderno, of Borromini and Bernini, and all the specters of emperors past: the Eternal City, Cradle of Civilization, of art and architecture of unparalleled majesty, how it made his spirit soar—and then plunge. Because after Rome, Mexico City? Having seen Brazil's Rio de Janeiro, he could well imagine what he would find: a child-like people whose sense of taste is all in the mouth.

On the month-long crossing to America, his moods came in waves: anger, galloping enthusiasm, bitterness, gratitude. Charlotte was often green with seasickness. They spent most of their days shut in their respective cabins, working. They both understood the iron rule of orderly government, the fortress, as it were, that defended a people's peace and prosperity against bloody anarchy: that the sovereign's prestige be preserved and maintained by means of an elaborate and rigidly respected protocol. There was much to do: rules of etiquette detailed, the court organized, categories of rank defined, privileges assigned, medals of honor created. Each afternoon, they met to take tea and compare notes. He found intelligence in a woman tiresome—he bristled whenever Charlotte contradicted something he had written—but he was grateful for her assistance. They were creating a monarchy from the ground up: a titanic task. As the daughter of King Leopold of the Belgians, first cousin of Queen Victoria of England, and granddaughter of King Louis-Philippe of France, Charlotte was an expert on protocol. Nonetheless, Maximilian considered her young, and more than a bit enamored of pomp. She claimed she was not, but it was obvious: she gloried in it. In Milan, when he was viceroy, Charlotte, so thrilled to be vicereine, could not wait to go out onto the balcony of her palace and receive the cheers of her subjects. With the Mexican delegation it was the same—and in the Hofburg! How she relished her elevation, being the equal in rank to her sister-in-law Empress Sissi.

Charlotte was like a little terrier after a chicken bone. It was a defect in her character; he had pointed it out to her many times.

But Charlotte looked out for him, she stood up for him. She always put his interests first, as a good wife should. She was not his first love, but he would trust his life to her. One balmy morning just south of the thirtieth parallel, there was a rare moment when they happened to be alone on the rear deck. Turquoise water churned by; two dolphins were porpoising in the foamy wake, which unrolled from beneath the ship into the endless plain that appeared to melt into sky. To the east, perhaps twenty leagues distant, there was the broom-like smudge of a rain shower.

"Aren't they beautiful creatures?" Charlotte said.

Perhaps it was the sweetness in her face as she watched those dolphins from beneath the shade of her parasol or, perhaps that over her hair she wore a blue silk scarf just a shade darker than the sea, and this reminded him of a certain Madonna by Botticelli: he opened his heart. He confessed that, though he was, as the English say, *taking it coolly,* to have had to sign that Family Pact . . .

"I know," she said.

Tears sprang to his eyes. He had tried to bury it, but his rage rose again bitter in his throat.

"It was so," he said shakily, "unjust."

She set the pole of her parasol on her shoulder and turned to face him. Her nostrils flared. "The grossest injustice."

The next day, he was both surprised and deeply touched when she came to his cabin with a draft of a—he blinked twice to read her crisply molded handwriting—"Repudiation of the Family Pact." It had not occurred to him to protest. But she, who had been up most of the night consulting the various law books in the ship's library, argued that, first, the Family Pact was unconstitutional; modification of the order of succession to the throne could not be effected with a document such as this; second, Maximilian had known nothing about it until the last minute when he was forced to sign it; and third, he had not even read the whole of it. Therefore, she concluded, the Family Pact could not be considered legally binding.

"Bull's-eye!" Maximilian said. "But . . ." He pulled at his beard. "I don't know . . . it might not be wise to send it."

"Well, isn't that what we have our advisors for?" They had with them onboard two chancellors, good old Schertzenlechner and also Monsieur Eloin, a Belgian mining engineer Charlotte's father, King Leopold, had commended to them. (Suffice to say, neither of these advisors spoke Spanish—not a pertinent skill in this particular instance, but very telling.)

After both Schertzenlechner and Monsieur Eloin had read the draft, Maximilian said, "Gentlemen: I am inclined to sign it, but be so good as to give me your unbiased opinions."

Monsieur Eloin first looked at Charlotte. She nodded, almost imperceptibly. Monsieur Eloin turned to Maximilian. "I would advise Your Majesty to sign it."

Maximilian addressed Schertzenlechner. Not long ago a mere valet, Schertzenlechner was not the usual sort of advisor for an archduke, to say nothing of that of an emperor, but Maximilian appreciated both his skill at billiards and his earthiness, what he thought of as a peasant-like honesty. "And you?"

Schertzenlechner, miffed at not being asked first, puffed out his cheeks. "Well." He waited a beat, to gather all attention securely upon himself. "Well," Schertzenlechner said again. "Better now than later."

"What do you mean?"

"They ought to know it right now. They can't kick Your Majesty around."

"That's right!"

But to be absolutely sure, Maximilian summoned Count Karl Bombelles. Charlie, as he called him, had come along to head the Palatine Guard. Charlie had a sure compass for the precise point at which Maximilian's needs coincided with his own. He had a smooth, chocolatey way about him, a gravelly voice, a long nose and long fingers, ferret-like eyes, a bristling beard that made his jaw appear to jut out, and a mustache that covered his mouth. He had been down in the billiards room and he smelled of beer.

"You are a Habsburg," Charlie said. "Document or no document. That is God's truth, sir."

At once Maximilian signed the repudiation, and with such heavy pressure he nearly tore the paper. His signature was bigger than it was before, and the sweep of underlining more elaborate. The envelope was sealed by a dot of scarlet-red wax into which was impressed his imperial monogram: MIM, for the Latin *Maximiliano Imperator de Mexico*. At the next port of call, Fort-de-France on the island of Martinique, this document was put onboard a French packet boat and telegrams to that effect dispatched to all the courts of Europe.

Maximilian might as well have sent back bags of putrid fish. In a letter that arrived in Mexico City more than two months later, Charlotte's father, King Leopold of the Belgians, scolded them both and said that he had had to work double-time to avoid a rift in Austrian-Mexican relations. No other government deigned to comment. And unfortunately, because the telegrams had been relayed via New Orleans, Juárez's agents picked up on the news sooner than anyone. *You see,* the Republicans jeered, *Maximilian has come to Mexico in bad faith.*

Despite the French censors, by the spring of 1865, Angelo de Iturbide was aware of the rumors about Maximilian's protest of the Family Pact, but as he remarked to his elder brother, Agustín Gerónimo, it was difficult to know what to believe. After all, in the north of Mexico, and in pockets, the war was still going on between the French and the guerrillas; lies were raining down on all sides.

Agustín Gerónimo replied with a *refrán,* one of their mamá's rhyming sayings: *"No firmes carta que no leas, ni bebas agua que no veas,"* Don't sign a letter you haven't read, nor drink water you haven't seen. Whatever the truth or untruth in this story about the so-called Family Pact, certainly, Mexico's second emperor had taken on his realm sight unseen.

It had occurred to the Iturbide brothers that Maximilian must have been given pause by what happened to their father, though, perhaps, he had not heard the most gruesome details. In her bitter moments, and these were many, Madame de Iturbide had often said, Mexicans are a people who do not deserve their heroes.

Maximilian's ship was due in at Veracruz any day. That morning, General and Madame Almonte and a party of the most enthusiastic conservatives had departed under heavy guard for the coast.

Seldom did the Iturbide brothers reveal their political views. But in Angelo's parlor, the shutters closed and drapes drawn, the women having retired, a bottle of cognac down to its dregs and a game of dominoes arrayed before them, the youngest brother, Agustín Cosme, spoke.

"If beards gave wisdom, goats would be prophets."

Angelo said, "You take Maximilian for a fool?"

"Eh, ship of fools," the eldest, Agustín Gerónimo, said, waving his pipe to signal he had no interest in the subject, or perhaps he meant his comment to encompass the whole of creation.

A BREEZE RIFFLING THROUGH
AN AUTUMN FOREST

*J*t was June of 1864, well into the rainy season, when Maximilian and Charlotte arrived in Mexico City; nonetheless, as if the Almighty Himself intended to show His pleasure, the day's sky was as clear as newly washed glass. Thousands thronged the main street of the capital, the Calle de San Francisco; hundreds more waited out in the sun on open flat-roofs and balconies. A series of wood-and-plaster triumphal arches had been erected, each spanning the street, and as tall as five-storey buildings: The Arch of Peace, the Arch of Flowers, and so on, with allegorical figures and cornucopias and elaborate inscriptions, *O Carlota, Mexico's flower-gardens salute you with palms, roses, and laurels*... For days this street had been the scene of frantic hammering and tinkering, potholes filled in with sand, curbs swept, balconies draped with banners, and bowers, and the green-white-and-red Mexican imperial flags. Once again, the police had gone around early in the morning, dropping off sacks of flowers for people to toss. The best balconies were being rented at between eighty and a hundred pesos a head. Rumor had it that a newspaperman had offered a certain Mrs. Yorke five hundred pesos for hers!

Angelo and Alicia de Iturbide, however, did not enjoy their privileged perch of the previous year when the French Imperial Army marched in down this same street for, in protest at French ambitions in what it regarded as its own hemisphere, the United States had recalled its minister, Mr. Thomas Corwin, to Washington. The building that had served as the U.S. legation, vacant for the length of time it would take to whistle a ditty, was being used to billet French officers. From the Iturbides' third-floor dining-room balcony, to the extreme right, if one leaned out over the railing, one could see a tight slice of the main street. Angelo and his brothers could not be enticed to the window. They remained at the table, smoking and playing dominoes. The baby was left in his bedroom with his nanny; they could all hear him wailing and her trying to shush him with a lullaby. Alicia and Pepa had been waiting for some time out on the balcony. The sun was intense. In the small space, their parasols kept bumping.

For Pepa, the thought of seeing these foreigners fêted as her own papá and mamá had been was bringing back heart-wrenching memories. And she was already in a testy mood because a promiscuous number of Mexican society had been invited to watch the fireworks from the flat-roof of the Imperial Palace this evening, however, not a one of her family had been included. The guest list must have been concocted by General and Madame Almonte and their ilk—that lowest class of parvenus and flimflam artists.

They could hear the drums, but the parade did not seem to be coming any closer. Alicia said, closing her parasol with a snap, "What a bother! Oh, let's go inside."

"Yes, let's," Pepa said, and she went in first.

Within the week, the shops were inundated with cartes de visite, collectable photographs of the imperial couple. Doña Juliana de Gómez Pedraza, the Iturbides' elderly landlady, peered at the most recent photograph through her tortoiseshell lorgnette. This was Doña Juliana's at-home day, a Tuesday. Handing the carte de visite back to its owner, Mrs. Yorke, Doña Juliana observed drily, "In life, Maximilian's beard is redder than one would guess."

"It hides a weak chin," said Pepa, taking the carte de visite and with scarcely a glance passing it to Alicia, who was sitting next to her on the sofa, close enough that their elbows touched. Alicia put the magnifying glass on it.

From the opposite sofa, Doña Juliana's sixteen-year-old niece, Pepita de la Peña, said, "I don't think it's half so bad, but his teeth—"

"Did you say, 'his teeth'?" Pepa had to cup her hand to her ear. She looked at Pepita de la Peña incredulously. "Child, you can see *that* without a glass?"

Mrs. Yorke, a longtime resident whose Spanish was excellent, said, "*Pues,* it is a very good photograph."

Pepa gave Mrs. Yorke a withering look. "I have seen much better."

With the magnifying glass, however, Alicia was examining the other end of things: Maximilian's shoes. They were different. The toes came to more of a point. She pushed the photograph back into its slot in Mrs. Yorke's album. There were two cartes de visite to a page, each with a gilded edge. The album itself, of handsomely tooled leather with a brass clasp that might have been inspired by the door of a medieval monastery, was the size and heft of a brick. Alicia turned the page. The cut and quality of their clothing was stunning. Alicia studied the empress's gown, the pattern of its pleats, the scalloped lace on the cuffs, and the sweep and precise volume of her coiffure. Carlota, the Mexicans were calling her. Just as she, Alice, had so easily, abracadabra, become Alicia.

"*Ay, como!* Oh, now! I would not go so far as to call Carlota homely," Doña Juliana was arguing with Mrs. Yorke.

The women nitpicked over another photograph, comparing it to what they had glimpsed when the imperial landau had happened to pass by. Nearly every day the emperor swept down the Calle de San Francisco, nodding and raising his stovepipe hat to enthusiastic cheers. Carlota's carriage, too, was frequently seen hurtling to and fro; as the new newspaper, the peach-colored *La Sociedad,* detailed, Her Majesty maintained a heavy schedule of visits to schools and hospitals and orphanages—though, not the orphanage of which Doña Juliana, widow of President Manuel Gómez Pedraza, had long been a patroness. Lesser members of Mexican society had been attended to; but, other than Mrs. Yorke, none of these ladies had yet been invited to one of the *tertulias* at the Imperial Palace. Resentment and hope, like vinegar and orange juice, make an unappetizing mix. Status hierarchies in Mexico City society, to put it bluntly, were being crudely rearranged by witless foreigners, by General and Madame Almonte, and their cronies. There were all sorts of complete nobodies, who happened, in these first golden weeks, to have the emperor's ear. But, welcome or unwelcome, adored or disdained, Maximilian and Carlota were a topic of endless fascination. No European royalty had ever before set foot in Mexico. Or Washington—except for the visit of the Prince of Wales, which to Alicia's inconsolable disappointment had taken place in 1860. She'd had to hear about that in letters that took forever and a century to arrive.

"Wales?" Pepita de la Peña asked. "Where is that?"

Alicia covered her mouth to hide her smile. Pepa said, with arch-backed dignity, "Never mind about Wales, Pepita dear. The Prince of Wales does not live there, it is simply the title of England's Crown Prince."

Pepa was a fount of information on royal genealogy. Consanguinity was the rule, she declared. In other words, royalty are all related. Carlota, for example, was Queen Victoria's first cousin as Carlota's father, King Leopold of the Belgians, was Victoria's mother's brother. And his first wife was the Princess of Wales, but she died in childbirth. After that, the Belgians took him on, on condition that he marry the daughter of King Louis-Philippe of the French, who—

"Now there's an eggplant patch!" Doña Juliana interjected. She found Pepa's patronizing her niece annoying; however, after that warning shot, Doña Juliana said nothing more; she sat back and fingered her black lace mantilla.

"Didn't that king get his head chopped off?" Pepita said.

"No, no," Pepa corrected Doña Juliana's little niece. "You confuse the Bourbons with the Orléans. Charlotte's grandfather, King Louis-Philippe, abdicated in 1848 and subsequently died in exile."

Pepita said, "Where?"

Pepa said, "In England."

"So he knew the Prince of Wales."

"You can be sure."

Pepita de la Peña, unblemished and long-lashed, had the face of an archangel, at once child-like and womanly, and with a touch (perhaps it was the dimple on her chin) of the masculine. She was exceptionally beautiful, even in consternation. "But . . . What about his queen then, that one who got her head chopped off?"

"No, I tell you, that was a different king—King Louis the Sixteenth, the

Revolution, 1789, all that. Carlota's grandfather, Louis-Philippe, assumed the throne much later, in 1830."

"Um, is Louis Napoleon Carlota's uncle then?"

This time, Alicia had to bend forward and cough to hide her laugh.

On many an occasion, Alicia and Pepa had commented to one another about the appalling level of what passed for "education" in Mexico, especially for women. A one like Pepita de la Peña would not know Rome from Ragusa, or the *Iliad* from *Ivanhoe*. Her French, though respectable in terms of vocabulary and grammar, came out with the most atrocious accent. Her English? Nonexistent. The same could be said of her dowry. What hope was there for her?

Afterward, when they were back upstairs, and the nanny had handed the baby to his godmother, Alicia said, "Sister, you are so right about the importance of education. I really want—"

Pepa finished the thought: "—the best for our Agustín."

"Yes." His mother came around behind his auntie, so that she could kiss his curls. He looked nothing like his auntie, but he did resemble his mother, and, so everyone said, he was strikingly like his paternal grandfather, Agustín I.

As his doting auntie carried him back down the stairs, he said in English, "Goo' bye."

"Tootle-oo," his mother said, wiggling her fingers.

With his toy bunny, Mimo, in his hand, the baby waved back.

The winter of 1865 saw the first formal ball in the Imperial Palace, and at last, the Iturbides were invited, or as Alicia's oldest brother-in-law, Agustín Gerónimo, wryly put it, commanded to appear.

On the appointed evening at the appointed time (for they had been advised that latecomers would be locked out), their buggy moved slowly through the throngs of Indians and gawkers. At the main doors of the palace, French Zouaves armed with rifles and batons pushed the crowd back, away from the descending guests. Above the palace roof, illuminated with alternating red and green lanterns, the Milky Way sparkled in a chilly sky. Beneath their *mantones,* as they called their embroidered Chinese silk shawls, Alicia and Pepa wore gowns of satin and tulle, not new, alas, but re-fashioned by the best mantua-maker in Mexico City, after the latest patterns imported from Paris. Pepa's décolletage glittered with one of her mamá's antique necklaces; Alicia wore her grandmother's rope of pearls, and earrings, a gift from her husband on the birth of their son, which were also of pearls. They had been advised that the protocol of an imperial ball was both strict and elaborate. Gentlemen had to bow, women to curtsey, one could not speak to a Highness unless spoken to. Alicia had only read about such things. By comparison, a White House *levée,* with its bumpkin of a president, was a rustic pileup. Oh, that Potomac backwater with its third-rate consular bureaucrats, those were as reed birds to real eagles! As donkeys to a Pasha's elephant!

If those belles from Lafayette Square and Georgetown could see her now! To think that anyone had looked down upon her marrying a Mexican and going to live in Mexico. Things were going to be radically different with a Habsburg here: that was clear to Alicia from the moment she caught sight of the Palatine Guards, Vikings in snow white coats and silver helmets shining in the dazzle of fantastic torches, and inside, the gargantuan Venetian teardrop chandeliers, dripping light over the rustling mass of perfumed guests, officers and diplomats in dress uniform, civilians in tails and white tie, the women alight with jewels. Hundreds of people, indeed perhaps a thousand, were all craning their necks. Who had been invited? Whom did one recognize? *Don Roberto, ¡qué gusto! Ceci, ¡qué tal!* Alicia recognized a Mexican countess, the Hungarian cavalry captain who lodged down the street, the Belgian ambassador, and, in a huge velvet cummerbund and a diamond the size of a garbanzo bean in his cravat, Don Eusebio, the richest man in Mexico.

A buzzing roar filled the air of the stairwell. Kisses for friends, handshakes for acquaintances, and up the crimson-carpeted stairs they swarmed, past tapestries, Sèvres vases, wondrous peacock-like bouquets. Once in the main hallway, still clinging to her husband's arm, Alicia happened to look up: the cedar beams had been gilded! It was hard to believe this was the same lice-infested wreck that Doña Juliana de Gómez Pedraza refused to inhabit, back in the 1830s, when her husband briefly had been president. Neither had Alicia's father-in-law lived here. (The Emperor Iturbide's palace, so-called, was now the stagecoach hotel on the Calle de San Francisco.)

What's more, Their Majesties were only using this palace for formal entertainments; though they had apartments here, they had established their Imperial Residence in Chapultepec Castle, which had lately housed the Military College. (This Alicia completely understood, for, as she had remarked to Mrs. Yorke and others, her family's country estate, Rosedale, was at the same easy-commuting range from the city of Washington.)

If the inside of Chapultepec Castle were half as sumptuous as this, it would be something out of a fairy tale, Alicia thought, pressing her hand to her fast-pounding heart, sincerely hoping that one day she might be invited there, also.

The Imperial Palace extended the entire length of the east side of Mexico City's Plaza Mayor. The rooms given over to the ball were one extravagant stretch of brightly lit parquet after another, all drapes and mirrors and chandeliers, until they ended with the closed doors of the throne room.

At nine o'clock the doors to the street were bolted, and now the Master of Ceremonies, with the aid of a silver baton and two assistants, divided the crowd; the ladies to line up along one wall, gentlemen the other. The buzz faded to whispers and then a sudden hush. Alicia went up on tiptoes: yes, the doors to the throne room had swung open.

Soon she could see Maximilian in his Mexican general's uniform greeting the men, and the empress, trailed by her ladies of honor, working her way down the line of women.

Carlota's dark hair was arranged cushion-like over her ears. She was not wearing a diadem, but, *à l'espagnole*, a single blood-red rose. Her necklace and bracelets were of diamonds; these sparkled in the candlelight. Her gown was of mint green and scarlet brocade with a train of gossamer lace. She moved smoothly, with hauteur relieved now and then by the slightest of smiles. Next to Alicia, two rotund little señoras, nervously fanning themselves, began whispering and giggling. "Shsh!" Pepa scolded. It was an effort to stay back near the wall; everyone wanted a better view of the approaching imperial couple (always, one of the assistants to the Master of Ceremonies nudged them back). Alicia could now hear the conversations, Carlota's murmurs of

"Enchantée," and some question about the work on the telegraph or, in Spanish, a bland, *"Buenas noches."* Carlota spoke the language of each lady she addressed, a word of Spanish here, Flemish there, German, or French, or English. This daughter of the king of the Belgians spoke no less than seven languages! Alicia could feel butterflies in her stomach. She batted her eyelashes and her hand flew to her pearls: Her turn had come! She tipped her head forward and sank into the reverent curtsey she had been practicing all week.

Once she straightened, Alicia was startled to realize that she and the empress were exactly the same height.

"Buenas noches, señora," Carlota said, and said the same again with a slight nod, her diamonds flashing, as Pepa bowed her head (but, as her hip was troubling her, she did not curtsey). The empress was about to move on when Madame Almonte, chief lady of honor, rushed up and whispered into the empress's ear.

Carlota turned to Alicia and said in an unnaturally slow, deliberate, perfectly pronounced Spanish, "Señora de Iturbide, we are pleased to have you here."

"Ma'am, oh, delighted!" Alicia's voice came out strangely high.

Carlota said, switching to English, "Oh, you speak English?"

"I do? I did? Oh, oh, did I—"

Pepa interrupted: "She is from Washington."

"A very beautiful city, I hear, with the boulevards of Monsieur L'Enfant." And before Alicia could recover, Carlota had moved on down the row and was greeting the wife of the Mexican foreign minister.

The orchestra erupted into music; Their Highnesses took their seats upon their thrones beneath the canopy of crimson velvet. The platform for the thrones was covered in the same rich crimson carpeting that ran the entire length of the hallway and all down the stairs. Sitting very erect, Maximilian rested his slender arms on those of the chair and crossed his ankles. Carlota clasped her hands together; the bracelets in her lap threw sparkles, like freckles, onto her throat and face. Maximilian and Carlota now stood; he took her hand and led her down to the dance floor. They opened the ball with the quadrille and then retired to their thrones.

The imperial couple sat watching silently and, it seemed to Alicia, tenderly, as in a rustling swirl of tulles and satins, the ladies and their cavaliers came back together and, with the aid of the Master of Ceremonies and his assistants, took their places on the dance floor. It was a sight Alicia would never forget as long as she lived: in one of the mirrors, she saw herself, her golden hair crowned with a wreath of miniature yellow tea-roses, her dainty gloved hand in her husband's, and to the left, and to the right, and behind them, the rows of the other dancers, so many splendid uniforms, gowns all the colors of the most breathtaking bouquet. Then, she danced as she had never danced before, with a lightness and such precision it seemed the music—*ba-bum, tra-la*—was her own heart, galloping, singing. Oh! surely, her slippers, like Mercury's ankles, had sprouted wings!

When the orchestra took its break, in the crush Alicia was separated from her husband. She wandered, fanning herself, tucking stray hairs behind her ear (the dancing did mischief to her coiffeur). One of the several balcony doors was open, and by happenstance, as she approached, three French officers who had been enjoying the cool evening air brushed past her. Rudely, they looked her up and down. *"Bonsoir, mademoiselle,"* said the last one, a captain, in an oily tone. She answered sharply, *"Madame."*

So it was that she had the balcony to herself. Below, in the vast Plaza Mayor, was an astonishing sight: hundreds of faces turned up in silent wonder. Moonlight cast their shadows before them over the pavement. Some of these people began pointing at her. Behind her the music began again, trilling and soaring; for the first time she realized that they too, the humble people, wrapped in their blankets, had been out here, listening. They had never heard such music; they had never seen such finery, and the whole palace, so long decrepit, now pulsing with light . . . Of its own accord, her hand moved up— she almost waved but, instead, put her gloved fingers to her lips. *This was what it would feel like to be royalty,* she thought. A heady feeling, headier still, knowing that her own husband had once, long ago, been a real prince. Had history played out differently, it would have been her bachelor brother-in-law, Agustín Gerónimo, sitting on that throne. *Imagine that!* she thought, then, *her own husband would have been Heir Presumptive!* She would be known to all as—she silently whispered—*Princess Alicia.*

Her bare arms were turning to gooseflesh, but Alicia could not bring herself to leave this magical perch. Her husband would have scolded her severely, for Mexicans believed that to become chilled by night air could cause earaches, or paralyze one's face. Simpler sorts believed the night belonged to ghosts, bogeymen, and all class of *nagualli.* Such was the magnetic power of royalty that it could pull all these people out into the open night. She thought, the pavement must be awfully cold. She wondered if some of them were hungry. She bit her lips. Shivering slightly—oh, she could not help herself: she raised her right hand. But only one person waved back. It was the mounted policeman.

After the midnight supper, Angelo wanted to sit down, but Alicia insisted that they go on dancing: the waltz, the schottische and redowa, the habanera; her feet were blistering, but on she whirled, light-headed with one too many glasses of pink champagne. She was sure (it was so odd, but she *could* feel it) that from their thrones, Maximilian and Carlota were watching them. Her fanciful musing had turned into a persistently glittering conception: that she would have been, as she whispered again, *Princess Alicia.*

"What, darling?" her husband said.

She giggled and squeezed his arm, and at that moment he stumbled. Wax from the chandeliers had begun to drip onto the parquet; one had to be careful, Angelo said. He'd had enough. Mopping his brow with his handkerchief, he steered her to the side. She pouted. There was nothing else to do but go sit with her sister-in-law on one of the brocade-upholstered benches.

"Too much pudding," Pepa said sourly. Her face was flushed and because she had lost her fan, she was fanning herself with the musical program. Alicia waved at Madame Almonte, but she sailed on, an imperturbable ship in another sea.

To make conversation, Alicia said, "And our brother, Agustín Gerónimo?"

"Who knows."

"Did you dance?" Alicia asked.

"Not at my age."

Most of the ladies were sitting down now; the men had gathered in clusters, smoking. Only a widely scattered few of the younger couples were still dancing. The parquet, like a stretch of sand revealed by the receding ocean, was strewn with detritus: a fan, flowers, an earring, a crumpled dance card.

Pepa glared across the room at Maximilian and Carlota. "I do wish they would get up." That, they had been informed by the Master of Ceremonies, would be the signal for the end of the ball. No one would be permitted to leave the premises any earlier. No sooner had Pepa said this, however, than the conductor, a bald-headed German in spectacles, sliced down his baton, the music crashed to a stop, and as if by Pepa's personal command, the imperial pair rose from their thrones. This action was answered by a rustling that would have brought to mind a breeze riffling through an autumn forest, had it not been accompanied by so much coughing and scraping of furniture. Alicia looked around: as if bewitched, every single person in the ballroom had stood up also.

BOOK TWO

Take what you want, God said. And pay for it.

—ARAB SAYING

THE PRINCE IS IN THE CASTLE

*A*tín had batted his blue ball with his hand but not hard, what makes it roll-a-roll away so fast, a piffle of breeze? This strange big sky-house feels breezy, wind chuffs in beneath the cracks of the doors, wind whips the flag on its pole outside, Atín hears it—*thwik, thwik*—as he has all this morning since he has been left here to play. Atín toddles after his ball, but over the edge of the yawning sweep of bone white it drops: *benk, b-benk—*

Gulping with astonishment and grief, he plops down, his bottom on the cold hard floor, and he begins to cry.

Prince Agustín de Iturbide y Green is his too-big-a-mouthful of a name, and he is tall for his age, which is two, but smaller than anything around him in this place: assorted plum- and jet-fringed sofas, a mottled green urn on a stand, a moon white statue of a woman in a sheet, twisting one arm toward the massive blown-glass chandelier. Behind him a tapestry shrouds the wall; with the breeze coming up the stairwell the tips of its fringe lift slightly.

He does not see his Auntie Pepa, coming up to him from behind the urn, her hands pressed together, and her hard, nearly lashless eyes melting into gluey tenderness.

"Shsh, Agustinito," Pepa says as she strokes his hair. "Shsh." Brusquely she wipes his tears with her handkerchief, and then—Atín does not expect this—she hefts him to her hip.

"Ball," Atín says in English, aiming a finger behind her, toward the stairs. He shouts to make Pepa understand, because sometimes she does not hear. He tries to wriggle down, but she squeezes him around the waist in the stout vise of her arm.

"Stop fussing. That's enough—" Pepa is breathless already—"Aren't you a big boy? Big boys do not fuss."

Atín does not like it, being jounced, he does not like that her stiff gray hair smells of perfume. Her dress makes too much rustle, and her heels stamp heavy like Papa's. Down a long tunnel of a hallway his auntie carries Atín, and around, back, and down a stairwell with walls that stink of paint.

Checkerboard floors now. And then two soldiers in green with swords on their belts swing open the doors into a high-ceilinged room so brilliant that Atín scrunches his face. Through the glass, which for a moment he does not realize is there, he sees that flag snapping on its pole, a colorful, strange kite. Pepa keeps him on her hip as she threads through the crowd. His aunt is bigger than his mamma, and her big-hipped dress makes her huge. Pepa takes up room, she makes people (that man with the gold fringies on his shoulders) have to step back, out of her way! Her steely gaze says: I know where I'm going.

"*Es el chiquillo.* It's the little one," murmurs that wheezy grandpa whose eyebrows droop like pasted-on caterpillars. His eyeglass, plugged into his saggy skin, mirrors the window. A lady who looks like she's swallowed an egg whispers, waggling her fingers at him, "Agustinito, *hola* Agustinito!"

In front of a man in a chair, Pepa sets Atín down and gives a yank to the back of his frock. Atín whirls his gaze around the blur of colors, faces—

Where is his mamma? His papa?

Pepa bends halfway over from the waist—but there's nothing to pick up from the floor.

"*Ven, niño.* Come here, child," says the man on the chair. He leans forward, his pale hands reaching for Atín from the ends of his dark sleeves. On his left hand he wears a fat gold ring.

Atín wrinkles his forehead; he stays put with his Auntie Pepa. The lady on the other chair next to him, her eyes wary, coughs behind her fan. Atín can hear his own breath as he pushes it out of his nostrils.

The man on the chair claps. "*Niño! Digo, ven para acá.* Child! I say, come here."

That lady on the chair next to him glares down at Atín as if he were something on the bottom of her shoe.

"*Ve cuando te llamen.* Go when you're called," Pepa commands, waving her hand toward the man in the chair. Her bracelet scatters pinpricks of light against the wall. "*Debes ser mi niño bien portado.* You must be my good boy."

What for is Pepa speaking to him in the nanny language? Atín pushes out his lip. He likes to shout, in English, *No!* And he's about to, but the man on the chair grasps him round the waist and lifts him up onto his lap.

The man's breath smells of tea. And his whiskers are so firelight golden, and combed smooth and lion-wide away from his chin and all up to his ears. The ends of the beard curl the way Atín's hair does when his nanny, Lupe, wraps it around her finger. It looks soft as lamb's wool. Might Atín touch the lion beard? He clenches his hands into fists because . . . because he is not sure.

No one speaks as the lion man looks Atín up and down. His eyes, fringed with sparse apricot-red lashes, are the same watery blue as the stones in Pepa's bracelet. They are at once weak and kind and cold.

The lion man says, "*Que rojos cachetes tiene.* What rosy cheeks he has," and claps Atín between the shoulder blades, too hard (he feels that ring). The man begins to talk to the grown-ups, his lips quivering as if he has trouble moving them over his teeth, but his voice swims through the room strong and clear; he is telling everybody all about everything and what to do. That lady next to him snaps open her fan and begins to whisk it furiously, its shadow flits over her nose, black, quick. Pepa stands before Atín and the lion man, her cheeks flushed and eyes glistening as if something exciting is happening, but it isn't.

"Ball!" Atín tells the lion man. Again, he tries to tell Pepa. "My ball, down!"

"*Tu pelota.*" The lion man interrupts.

Atín sighs, because *pelota* is a word that's all elbows in his mouth. Now, as if on tiptoes, all the grown-ups are staring at Atín. That grandpa with the eyeglass leers over Pepa's shoulder at Atín, showing his snaggly-peg teeth.

"Ball dow'." Atín points at the doors where those soldiers stand, stiff as tin toys and their hands by their sides in fists. Oh, where are those stairs that his blue ball bounced down? This house is too big, and Atín is all turned around. And why does he have to sit on this strange man's lap?

"*Se le fue su pelotita.* He's lost his little ball," the lion man throws back his head and roars out of his golden beard—and an echo of titters ripples from the crowd. "*Pues que te encuentren tu pelota.* Well, someone will find your ball, and if not, how's this? You—" He taps a finger on Atín's nose—"shall have a new one!"

"No!" Atín wants back *his* blue ball.

Against the arm of her chair, that lady smacks her fan closed. Outside the window, that flag whips in the breeze. A bird plunges: black flash. The lion man is talking to the grown-ups again, he doesn't care about Atín's ball. His beard moves back and forth with his head, brushing the back of Atín's shoulder. His skinny knees jut sharp (not like Papa's). The lion man, still talking, sets him down, and as if slingshotted, Atin dashes back to his Auntie Pepa. But, however softly upholstered, the iron gray satin of her skirt resists his groping arms like a slippery wall. He pulls at her hand. Pepa's hand isn't like his mamma's; it closes around his own, cool and dry as an old leaf. Slowly, Atín and his auntie move through the silent, smiling crowd, a parting sea of fabrics.

A tremendously long time goes by. It's time to eat, something cheesy, and the cheese pulls away from the tortilla in gooey, greasy strings.

"Stop fussing." Pepa has a harsh voice.

"*Callate niño,*" that nanny hisses at him, but low enough so that Pepa can't hear her. "*Ya.* Enough."

This nanny's blue-black hair, pulled tight behind her ears, has the shine of crow feathers. The parted V of it points at her nose, which makes Atín think of a beak. And there is a gap between her front teeth, and when she leans in close, her hair smells of lamp-wick oil. Her lips pinch as if she wants to peck him! Olivia is her name, but he won't say it. He *won't*. She is *not* his nanny Lupe. She doesn't like Atín, she should take care of pigs.

• • •

Not until after the pudding does Salvo try to find Atín's blue ball for him. Salvo is Atín's cousin; he has a friendly, dumpling-chinned face and his fingers smell of cigars. He has a few hairs for the beginnings of a mustache; mostly his dough-pale skin shows through. Salvo is strong! Salvo hoists Atín to his shoulders—"ya set in the saddle?"—and clasps Atín's ankles with damp, meaty hands. Salvo lets Atín pull his ear, slap at his jaw—"Grrrr!" Salvo growls, because he's Grizzly Bear, and Atín lets out a peal of giggles. Around a corner, Salvo carries Atín, and down the cold of a corridor where the crystal sconces—Atin holds his hand out—klinkle as they pass.

And then, through doors nearly as tall as the ceiling, they burst into a room where rectangles of sun yawn across the floor. Dust dizzies itself in midair. There is a long black piano; a fly buzzes lazily over its vase of roses. Everything else is pushed against the walls, sofas and hard-looking apple-green chairs, the feathery palms, screens, and tables clumped with masses of more roses. Their fragrance is syrupy, and tinged with a grassy bitterness; pink petals, their rims brown, litter the floor. The ceiling (with his hands on Salvo's ears, Atín cricks back his neck to look) is carved all over with cheese white leaves.

Salvo sets Atín down. "Your blue ball, ya say?"

Splat like a monkey Salvo is on his knees. He spies beneath an ottoman. Atín trails behind his cousin, his thumb in his mouth.

"Nothing here," Salvo says, springing up again, and not bothering to brush the dust from his knees. He scrapes a table away from the wall. "No ball here, little man." Salvo hops around a screen: "Uh uh." Now Salvo peers under a sofa. How silly Salvo looks, with his behind in the air. He has a hole in his shoe.

Salvo lifts the lid of the piano and props it open with a stick that was inside. He peers in. "Hmmm . . ." Salvo scratches at his mustache.

Now Salvo comes around the front of it, diddling his fingers along its teeth, *bink, bink, dooong.* As Salvo parts the tails of his coat and aims his bottom at the bench, Atín's stomach twists with the knowing: Salvo is not going to look anymore.

"How's about 'Hail Columbia'?"

"*No!*"

But Salvo doesn't care what Atín wants, he starts to play, loudly mashing the chords. Atín's mamma, she plays chiming, twinkly songs, and she sings to him, where is she? Atín wants to go home now. Almost the *whole day* has gone by! And he's lost his blue ball. Atín hangs his head and begins to whimper. Salvo pounds and bellows on:

> *Ever grateful! foooor the! prize!*
> *Let its altar! reeeeeach the! skies!*

Atín wails, but Salvo is trying to drown him out! In a rage, Atín throws himself beneath the piano's thundering black body and screams.

The lid bangs down. "Do you mean to wake the dead!" Pepa says. "What kind of example—" she sputters. "Your behavior is an abomination! Upstairs, this instant!"

The piano is still vibrating.

"Are you deaf? I said: upstairs!"

From under the piano Atín can see Salvo massaging his fingers. "You might've broke one!"

"*What* did you have the cheek to say to me?"

"You might've broke my finger!"

"Must you always answer with insolence! Are you blind to your station? The importance of your example!"

Salvo gives the piano leg a kick with his shoe, and he stalks out.

"And you!" Pepa hauls Atín up by the back of his collar. "Carrying on," she huffs, "like a weeny baby!" She whacks him on the bottom. Atín howls louder. Her hand clamps tight around his, and he stumbles after her, all the way hiccupping with sobs.

After his nap, Atín plays with his blocks. His mamma sent along his other toys all in a wicker hamper, his velvet kitty, his bunny, Mimo, with button eyes, but Atín does not like these, not even Mimo, not anything so very much as his blue ball. He clacks the blocks together, and *"Ayyy, Beee, Seee,"* he sings the alphabet song to himself, the rest of it as best he can (he hum-a-hums), and then, *"an' Teee, an' Veee."* It's their special song (his nanny Lupe doesn't know their language). Pepa, she sings it fast, as if she just wants to get it over with. But Atín's mamma sings it tilting her head and with her finger tracing each letter in the air, A, which is up, then down, then slash across the middle, the lace on her sleeve flouncing. After she comes to the end, the zig and zag of Z, his mamma claps her hands together and very slowly, the words dropping like down the stairs, she sings, *tell me what you think of me . . .*

Atín sings softly, *"Meeeeeee."* He clacks the red block on the green block.

He does not like that the rug rubs scratchy and air seeps in through the crack beneath the door, brushing cold on his legs. Outside the window there is nothing but sky. This is a bad windy place with too many people. Do they all have to live here, or is it time for them to go home, too? Now. Atín is ready now. Now he wants to go home.

In the greenish light of dusk, that bad nanny, Olivia, feeds him his supper. His mamma and papa have not come for him. Why? And why can't his nanny Lupe be here?

"Ay, niño," Olivia says every time she roughly wipes his chin. She wants Atín to open his mouth again, but she can't make him. His nanny Lupe, *she's* the one who should give Atín his supper! Lupe knows that Atín does not like the red sauce, but only the mild green sauce with the little seeds, and that Atín eats his melted cheese always with the tiny bacons. Olivia aims another lump of that gritty red mush at Atín, he swats it, and the spoon clatters to the floor.

Pepa gives Atín his atole. She helps him hold the cup of the thick, sweet corn drink. He slurps it loudly.

"Goo' bye," Atín says what his mamma said.

"What did you say?" Pepa stands over him. "Speak clearly."

"Goo' bye!"

"No, you are not a good boy until you drink up all of your atole." Pepa tips the cup for him, and with his hands flat on his high-chair tray, he bends his head back for the last drop to slide down the inside of the cup. He does not want to, but he swallows.

Pepa pats his shoulder.

The wind has died when Pepa wraps him in a strange blanket and then lowers him into a strange crib. The blanket's trim touches cold and slidy beneath his chin, but he is too sleepy to cry about that. As Pepa leans down to kiss him, her earrings tickle cold on his cheek.

"*Que Dios te bendiga.* May God bless you," Pepa says a little too loudly, in the nanny language, "and may all the saints and the angels look over you." She makes the sign of a cross over his forehead.

You are safe, Atín understands this to say, and you are cared for. In the morning, then, Pepa will get his blue ball back. In the morning, they will go home.

He is a special child; he dimly senses this already, though he has no idea how beautiful he is with his cupid's bow of a mouth, slightly parted. From beneath his nightcap, his silk-soft curls spill palest gold over the pillow.

The stars are just beginning to wink; with two firm tugs, Pepa pulls the curtains closed.

Nunc et in hora mortis nostrae. Amen.

Just as the mantel clock chimes half-past eight, Pepa has finished saying the rosary. She rises painfully from arthritic knees, steadying herself with a grip on the bedpost. Shivering slightly, she draws her diaphanous lace-trimmed chemise *de nuit* around her shoulders. Foolish, she chides herself: why didn't she think? Of course it would be colder up here in Chapultepec Castle; without the sheltering of trees, the wind carries any warmth away. However, having spent such a fabulous sum on her new wardrobe, a wardrobe not in any way extravagant, merely necessary for the dignity of her rank, she really ought to wait another month before buying the flannel for a warmer nightgown. She drops the rosary beads in a dish. Her bedroom jitters with shadows from the candlelight. She is not happy with the way the footman has trimmed the lamps, however, she is gratified to note that this bedroom is as spacious as her little brother's parlor, and her sitting room twice again as large. Flowers adorn almost every surface, at the foot of the bed is a divan upholstered in brocade, and the porcelain wash jug—she had turned it over and put on her spectacles to examine the mark—is Sèvres.

Pepa sits, (the frame creaks), on the edge of her bed. In her lap, her palm. That vulgar woman Alicia invited to dinner was mistaken. The line—she traces her finger along the curve of the fleshy base of her thumb—is broken, *¿y qué?* It is glorious fortune! Which not everyone can recognize, can they? "*Mi querida prima*, my dear cousin," Maximilian von Habsburg condescends to call her now—every time she thinks of it, she feels a swell of pride. No, *not* pride, Pepa swiftly corrects herself. This splendid feeling is gratitude, *heartfelt* gratitude, to be able, at last, to serve her country. It has been forty-two years since her own father, may his soul rest in deserved peace, was crowned Emperor and Protector of the True Faith. In exile, there was no dowry for the murdered Liberator's daughters. A cloistered life was a destiny she resisted; she had, so stingingly, wanted children. How she prayed to San Antonio the matchmaker! The young men with promise, they flocked to the belles with names their mothers recognized. Not a one wanted to court the exotic and nearly penniless Señorita Iturbide. Of course, few of them were Roman Catholics. In any event, Mamá had a visceral prejudice against the idea of her children marrying foreigners. A Chilean diplomat? *Impossible.* That Peruvian gentleman from church? *I will have no such son-in-law.* Yankees, Mamá often said, had no culture. By nature, they were greedy and lowborn. Tidewater "aristocrats"? Mere merchants, tobacco traders. It took supreme effort for Mamá to acknowledge the neighbors. In Georgetown, there was one who introduced herself from the back alley, whilst taking out her pail of potato peelings!

And so, as the years slid by, Pepa had been left with the increasingly grinding realization that her voice had gone unheard in Heaven. This was what God wanted. God, after all, had an all-seeing wisdom. For who else was left to care for Mamá? As Pepa told herself, it would be very selfish for her to go on hoping for something so unsuitable and inconvenient for everyone else.

Although disappointed by San Antonio, Pepa has never wavered in her faith—the True Faith. She has worn it like armor, and is it not so? To serve here, now, is the Divine's reward. The Almighty, she reminds herself, gave Maximilian the inspiration to accept the throne of Mexico, as He gave Maximilian the inspiration to make her nephew and godson his Heir Presumptive.

Domine Salvum Fac Imperatorum, God save the Emperor—this same chant she heard when her own father was standing there at the top of the crimson steps in his imperial robes, and Mamá beside him, with the stars on her swan white gown and pearls braided through her hair. Yesterday, how magnificently the archbishop's voice had filled the cathedral! To think of her father being so honored in God's own house, Pepa feels as if a flock of doves might fly out from her breast. Yesterday, Mexico's Day of Independence, in the ceremony, she had to bite her lip to keep from sobbing. When it was over, from the balcony of the Imperial Palace, Maximilian shouted out, *"Long live Our Lady of Guadalupe! Viva México! Viva Iturbide!"* From the Plaza Mayor, up came the roar of the crowd; how the cheers washed over her with their silken caress. Later, with Carlota and Madame Almonte, Pepa—now Her Highness Princess Doña Josefa de Iturbide—came out on the balcony again, to see the night mortared with whistling Chinese rockets, chrysanthemums of diamonds and rubies.

On her bedside table, next to a dish with the coil of rosary beads, is the *Reglamento y ceremonial de la Corte* (Ceremonies and regulations of the court), big as a Bible. It is being reprinted with an all-new Chapter One, "On the Iturbide Princes," specifying their rank, which is above all others, with the exception of imperial princes (of which there are none); cardinals; those rare few, such as General Almonte, upon whom the emperor has bestowed the medal of the Order of the Mexican Eagle; and Their Majesties. Princess Iturbide may make visits in society and leave her card; however, she need not return visits except to cardinals, Mexican Eagles, ambassadors, ministers of state, and their wives. When Their Majesties are on their thrones, she must place herself at their feet, on the first step, to the left of the empress. In church, her place is in the first row, and the bench covered in velvet. But she shall not be presented with the holy water. There is so much to study, too much to remember. But God will help.

"Please," said the Master of Ceremonies when he brought her this book, together with the loose manuscript pages of Chapter One. "I am at your service."

"I am obliged to you," Pepa answered, but with the firm intention of making questions unnecessary.

The Master of Ceremonies, rather than put the book in her hands, took a slight step backward. Holding this tome as a waiter does his tray, he lifted the cover and then slid his glove over the small square of a certificate that had been pasted on the inside. "Please," he said, "you will see here that this book is for your personal use. However, it remains, now and always, the property of His Majesty."

Pepa put on her spectacles. The Master of Ceremonies could have, but did not, turn the book around for her to be able to read the certificate.

"Each book," he went on, "has a registration number."

"I see."

His tongue pushed against the inside of his cheek. It seemed the Master of Ceremonies was going to say something more; but no. With an air of infinite reserve, he closed the lid of the book and, dipping his head slightly, presented it to her.

It was so heavy she had to carry it with both hands.

Now, on the edge of her bed in Chapultepec Castle, Pepa kisses her thumb again, for luck. She presses her hand to her heart and smiles with grateful satisfaction, remembering how this morning, before the whole court, Prince Agustín had run to *her*.

She has her child now.

She thrusts her legs in between the chill sheets. She reaches her hand down to the candle and, with a pinch, cuts it.

Down the hall, in a cold bedroom unadorned but for a crucifix, the emperor snores—and this rare for him, for he is a shallow sleeper (and often his valet is kept awake by the lamplight from beneath the door that connects their rooms). Maximilian's is the sound sleep of the self-satisfied, for he has, as brilliantly as Metternich, bagged not two, not three, but five birds with one arabesque toss of a stone. To celebrate Mexico's independence, raise the status of the Iturbides to princes, and bring the two grandsons, Agustín and Salvador, under his tutelage, he has, first, demonstrated he is no puppet of the French; second, signaled favor to General Almonte, son of the other hero of Mexican Independence, the insurgent Father Morelos; third, co-opted a possibly dangerous element of conservative society; fourth, provided an Heir Presumptive; and fifth, given a powerful inducement to the Kaiser to rescind the Family Pact. Oh, what a flock of pretty birds. And now, one's brothers will see that a Habsburg empire in the Americas is viable, and all to be handed over to the grandson of a creole parvenu? They will be too jealous of a throne to allow *that* to happen, surely. Avid one's brothers will be to enjoy the fruit of this magnificent work of the House of Habsburg! *Etiam sapientibus cupido gloriae novissima exuitur,* the desire for glory is the last infirmity cast off even by the wise, as Tacitus well knew. Yes, the moment one's quill touched that contract with the Iturbide family, one had felt—it was an almost physical sensation—the ropes uncoiling, and then, as if . . . the anchor had bit! Charlotte, good soldier, has already offered to sail to Europe and bring back one's nephew, his nursemaid, and a doctor. The bait, the news of the little "Prince" Agustín de Iturbide being brought into this court, has been telegraphed to Veracruz; within the week it will be steaming across the Atlantic. Letters will follow, and soon, in Vienna, everyone will be talking—and soon everything, the whole storm-tossed, listing ship of this Mexican enterprise, will be set aright!

His face mashed into his pillow, Maximilian sails on through blue dreaming . . . and then gaily, he is in Brazil again, chasing monstrous fluttering *Saturniidae,* moths as big as starlings. There are palm trees, and high in the jungle canopy, parrots the colors of candy scream. He watches the parrots, how they swoop down, fast as bullets, and then fly out—

—to where? One has lost oneself over a lavender horizon.

In a nearby, more spacious bedroom, the empress has fallen into the bilious dreams of one who has allowed herself, dazed within a labyrinth of sugar-encrusted rationalizations, to collude in her own—there is no other word for it—humiliation. She feels the way water feels when it is just about to run over the lip of its cup. Among the snowy linens and down-stuffed pillows, Carlota has curled into herself, her knees touching her chin. The oil in her bedside lamp allows only a weak bluish bud. The book she was reading, *Imitación de Cristo,* has dropped to the carpet. She will be sorry, tomorrow, to find that its loose-leaf color plate of the five wounds of the Savior has been creased. She will not be sorry, however, because no one will tell her, that her orders for the little "Prince" Agustín de Iturbide (that he be given a daily cold-water bath and a spoonful of cod liver oil) go blithely ignored. The *susto* of cold water, Mexicans believe, can cause sickness, and that fish oil—the nursemaid, Olivia, will pinch her nose and fling it out the window onto a bush. "I wouldn't feed that to a pig," Olivia will tell Pepa—and Pepa, despite herself, will chuckle.

In between Carlota's bergère and a gilt mirror a slim door leads to another bedroom, this one no bigger than a closet, where her wardrobe maid, Mathilde Doblinger, raises herself on an elbow to see, beneath that door, the wand of grayish yellow light.

Ja, the empress must still be awake . . . Don't poor Charlotte's eyes ever tire of all that reading? A person could go blind. Mathilde sinks down again into her pillow. This day was too strange for her German blood. It is like the trick of a magic lantern to have those Iturbides here, under the roof of a Habsburg and a Saxe-Coburg! About that tin-horn "Emperor" Iturbide, she's heard all about that affair, so uncannily similar to the story of Murat, that upstart son of an innkeeper that Bonaparte made the king of Naples. Like Murat, Iturbide was an incompetent scoundrel and his subjects threw him out. Like Murat, Iturbide was too ambitious to stomach his exile; like Murat, Iturbide was fool enough to return, and he had hardly stepped off the boat when he got himself hauled in front of a firing squad. And after that, the Mexicans, those apes, they dug up the cadaver to steal the boots off its feet! And the son of Iturbide, for a pension, sells his child like a box of *spécaloos,* the mother must be mad as the moon. The baby's aunt, that witch, anyone can see it, she's gobbled him up, delicious little lozenge. A nice arrangement for a no-account spinster to live here, and as an Imperial Highness! That costume she wore for the audience, Mathilde saw it afterward hanging in the wardrobe—a rag! Cheap moiré, the color of three-day-old fish scales.

Mathilde tugs her nightcap over her ears. How will poor Charlotte cope with this perversion of nature? A duckling put into a peacock's nest!

By now Charlotte, a vigorous twenty-five years old, in the perfection of health, after eight years of marriage, might have had five, six children of her own. Why, her cousin, Queen Victoria of England, she pops them out, buns from the oven. But Maximilian does not visit his wife. In Miramar Castle, Maximilian spent his nights in a cramped mop-closet of a room directly off the main entrance hall. Mathilde would not have believed it had she not overheard Charlotte tell a visitor that the little bedroom was a copy of Maximilian's quarters on his yacht! As was the study next to it, which was why the ceiling fell so low.

It is true: Mathilde hates Maximilian a little, though she would never, on her mortal soul, let slip from her lips one word of disapproval. Serving Charlotte is Mathilde's life. What will happen, or should happen, or should not have happened, is not for a wardrobe maid to know or question. Whatever comes to pass is God's will. All Mathilde allows herself is to pray, with her fingers laced tightly together, her knuckles pressing into her forehead, *Santa María, ora pro nobis . . .*

The words float out into the chilly night.

The air dead-still, sky solid black, it is about to rain. From Chapultepec Castle, an immense stretch of mud-dark fields bring the road into the edge of the city at Buenavista, a gem of a baroque palace. In this "city of palaces," Buenavista is one of the most dignified, but peculiar, for it is not made of the customary reddish *tezontle* but of gray stone, and its chief feature is an enormous elliptical central courtyard. Its curving rooms open onto this courtyard, and on the one side onto the street, and in the back, onto gardens. It is a palace, its occupant often grouses, with a few too many windows.

The scrape of boots: a sentry on the roof. They cannot be seen from the back balcony, but in the garden, there are two more: one stationed beyond the line of apple trees, another at the gate.

This, for now, is the residence of General François-Achille Bazaine, supreme commander of the French Imperial Forces. In his robe and babouches,

General Bazaine has gone out onto this balcony to smoke the last of a superb cigar. He considers the lights in the distance: the scattering of pin-stabs that is Mexico City, and yonder to the west, lit up in midair like a house afire, Chapultepec Castle. He pushes his cigar to his lips.

So—Bazaine begins to puff—yesterday, the anniversary of Mexico's Independence, Maximilian makes a fiesta for Iturbide, the martyred hero, a way of throwing some flowers at the *mochas* and the priests—and kicking dirt in the faces of the French! Disdaining the services rendered to him, Maximilian had not consulted Bazaine, nor the French ambassador. General Almonte must have put him up to it or, God knows.

And to make the little Iturbide his heir presumptive, and fork over to that family such pensions, such a pile of lucre—when the Mexican treasury cannot even equip or properly feed that piss-ant excuse for a Mexican Imperial Army!

And to ship the child's parents off to Paris with this so-called Status of the Murat Princes? It about made Bazaine fall off his horse!

As his aide-de-camp pointed out, such an arrangement prompted serious concern. Was it even within the Mexican constitution for Maximilian to name his heir? His aide-de-camp had studied the Treaty of Miramar, but it was mute on the matter.

The guerrillas are putting up hot resistance in the north, kidnappings are rife, along with regular attacks on the stagecoach highways . . . No, this throne is not yet firmly rooted. Should the experiment fail, well then, France cannot be expected to defend a dynasty it has had no say in shaping!

As his aide-de-camp, red in the face, sputtered, "The high-handed ingratitude of this Austrian is chilling."

Bazaine, however, had merely raised his eyebrows and rubbed his mouth.

Bazaine is a soldier, which means he follows orders, and his orders until further notice are to support Maximilian. Moreover, Bazaine does not easily anger. He has gotten as far as he has because, when everyone else goes off on their high horse, he maintains a low center of gravity.

Coolly, he draws on his cigar, and Bazaine turns over in his mind what might be Maximilian's motivations . . .

So. The Iturbide question, if there was one, has been stomped.

Hsss, Bazaine exhales.

Perhaps yes, Maximilian was concerned that conservative society (which is becoming disenchanted with him) could rally around a member of the Liberator's family. Why, at dinner the other day, once again, the archbishop had compared Iturbide to Our Lord Himself. The archbishop, having impaled a spear of asparagus, fixed Bazaine with such a vicious expression it might have unnerved anyone else. But Bazaine, with the sangfroid of a stone, noticed that the prelate's hand was trembling. A droplet of butter sauce landed on the lace tablecloth. The archbishop's voice came out thin and nasal, "Our Liberator was betrayed by Freemasons, as the Hebrews betrayed Our Lord." Bazaine had gone on slicing his veal. This took some doing. The cutlet was cooked tough as mule hide.

"That, sir, was the beginning of the disgrace of this country."

Bazaine, one elbow on the table, put a piece of meat in his mouth.

This was the same pig-headed ultramontane who, before Maximilian set his pretty foot on Mexican soil, had threatened to excommunicate anyone Bazaine appointed to office. That cork was an easy one to pop—just took positioning a few artillery pieces in front of the cathedral's doors.

De toute façon . . . Iturbide, Freemasons, that could—Bazaine now muses, puffing his cigar—have been true. *N'importe.* It was before his time.

Et bien, what's to be done when what the empress has got is a chinless candy-ass? Chases butterflies, looks for every chance to show his mercy, to the guerrillas his—Bazaine's—men have died like dogs trying to capture. Last week, the guerrillas got three of his officers, castrated them, strung them from a tree by their ankles, and left them like that to die, covered with blood and flies, of thirst. There is much worse. *Oui.* When he is out with his men in the campo, riding over the burned fields, past ruined huts and rubble-strewn courtyards, the starving dogs, gangs of begging children, Achille Bazaine knows it in his bones: this is a godless country. And he and his men have been sent to plough the sea. Until they are recalled to France—or shipped back to Sidi-bel-Abbès, or, Devil knows, Cochin China.

Bazaine raises his fist to his mouth and belches. Too much roast. That gravy had onions. He tosses his cigar butt over the side, and with a small yawn, then a lusty, lips-peeled-back yawn, he turns to go in.

• • •

The French general is quick-witted as a fox, and durable as a camel, in both body and character. His father, an engineer, abandoned the family in Versailles. François-Achille was sent to a good school, but not good enough; he failed the entrance examination to the Ecole Polytechnique. What did that matter? From the time he was a bantam-sized boy, François-Achille had known what he wanted: action. Was not his middle name that of the invincible warrior? In the French Foreign Legion, Bazaine fought in the mountains of Spain, the sands of Algeria, the Crimea, Solferino—countless times he has had bullets sing by his ears. Men all around him have been shot, bayonetted, hacked, pummeled, trampled, decapitated. He has had seven horses shot out from under him, been knocked flat by three explosions, and several times had mortars land right where he'd just been standing. His stars, he knows, have been lucky ones, too lucky not to displease the jealous gods. Bazaine was one of the senior officers on the troopship to Mexico, when out in the middle of the ocean, he first sensed a change, something he did not quite have the words for, something gritty and bitter in the back of his throat. He is beginning to understand that this is dread.

Bazaine's years chasing after Abd-el-Kader and his ruthless horsemen—laying siege to oasis towns, and then, bayonet fixed, entering their stinking labyrinths—have impressed upon him a deep-seated suspicion of anything that appears too easy to walk up to, and yet, he has preserved an almost child-like openness, the flexibility to bend toward the ripe, fragrant fig of opportunity.

Mexico: *pourquoi pas?* Its latest "president," some little Indian lawyer named Benito Juárez, attacked the church and refused to honor Mexico's debts with France. The United States invaded Mexico back in 1847, but as the Union and the Confederacy became embroiled in their civil war, France had no obstacle to pressing its claims, and in the process, bringing to these unfortunate people law, order—in short, civilization. Bazaine was not the only officer who had bragged that what they were about to gear up for was a mere victory parade. They could expect to suffer casualties in the port city of Veracruz, mainly from typhoid and yellow fever, but to drums and fifes, chanting songs while lovely señoritas tossed them flowers (and *bien sûr,* other favors, if you liked your women as you did your coffee), the main body of the French Imperial Army would march over the hot lands, and the sierras, easily liberating Orizaba, Puebla, and finally—touché—Mexico City. They had not yet left the docks in France when General Lorencez had gone around saying, "We are so superior in organization, discipline, and morality, we are already the masters of Mexico!"

The Arabs have a saying: he who despises the little lamb will weep for the herd. Vanity dulls the senses, and for battle they need be razor-sharp. Lesson one, basic training. And you must think like the enemy, anticipate his every step.

Oof, what happened? On the fifth of May, 1862, the French Imperial Army slammed into the city of Puebla and broke like a goddamned pencil. In that one day, they pissed away half their ammunition, shells lobbed onto dirt, 462 men slaughtered by Mexican artillery and Mexican calvary . . . Like whipped dogs, the French Imperial Army had to retreat to Orizaba and wait for reinforcements. Before French prestige could be avenged, it took twenty thousand more men, Lorencez's replacement with General Forey, another year, and a ferocious siege of Puebla that stretched for sixty-two days and ended with street-by-street, house-by-house fighting. After the triumphant entrance into that shell of a city, and then into Mexico City, Forey was promoted and called home, and François-Achille Bazaine was made supreme commander in Mexico—a promotion he had dreamed of, schemed after, grasped at. And strangely, now he had it, it left him cold.

At first, he would regard himself in the mirror and tell himself: *I am the Master of Mexico.* Then he would see a sprinkle of dandruff on his collar. In the year before Maximilian arrived, Bazaine sometimes thought of himself as one of those dogs that chases after carriages. Now that he'd got the carriage, and a bloody whopping big one, a goddamn municipal garbage wagon, what the hell did he want with it? Sleeping on a featherbed, nothing to do but sit half the day on his derrière in thumb-twiddling meetings with pinheaded bureaucrats, opportunists, schemers, sticky-palmed contractors, journalists, and greedy-minded little clerics (with those ones, it was Father, Son, and Holy

Peso). Then, after Maximilian arrived, more lunches, dinners, teas, balls with groaning buffets and pink champagne; of course, Bazaine has been packing it on. He feels it in his ankles and his knees when he jumps from his horse. He's had new uniforms made, and still his trousers are tight and his jacket cuts around the arms. Life has so much deliciousness to offer, not only those beef tamales *bien picantitos* and refried beans: in the last days of spring he married a pretty mexicana, Pepita de la Peña, who is young enough to be his grand-child—and *pourquoi pas?* He himself is young, at least at heart!

"*Mi corazón* . . . my heart," his Pepita calls him.

Pepita de la Peña, Madame Bazaine, has the grace, the sparkle, and the fierce sweetness of an angel.

Doña Juliana de Gómez Pedraza, her elderly aunt said, smiling at him from behind her lorgnette, "Dare I say, General, you are a lucky man."

His Pepita lives for him, he now lives for her, and the children they will have—for he has longed to have children. Until now he had been sad to think that he would march into the sunset of his life without them. He'd had a wife, Marie, whom he'd had to leave behind in Paris. He and his brother officers had thought they could call for their wives, or be recalled to France, within a matter of months. But things dragged on too long. After the fall of Puebla, soon after he sent for Marie, the news came that . . .

But he has promised himself not to dwell on Marie.

After Mexico, in the end, which will come quickly, *la belle France,* his white-gloved honor, his chestful of ribbons and medals won for the glory of Louis Napoleon's empire: they will matter to François-Achille Bazaine's true heart no more than that cigar butt he just tossed over the balcony.

It lies on the paving stones below, abandoned, still glowing.

Meanwhile, in their apartment on the Calle Coliseo Principal, Angelo and Alicia throw things into trunks! Boxes! Baskets! An old iron parrot cage! They are rushed, they've been ordered to quit Mexico, not at their leisure but before dawn. In less than one hour, palace guards will escort them to the Ho-tel Iturbide where, just before the cock's crow, they are to board the stagecoach to Veracruz. From there, they are to take the next steamer to New York, and from there, without delay, to Paris. The Iturbides shall be received in the court of Louis Napoléon as Highnesses of the Mexican Empire. It is to be a life gilded with glamor and ease, and they should be grateful. Any other ideas they might entertain would be, as the Palatine Guard intimated, "not the best for your health."

Alicia races down the stairs with an armload of petticoats. Angelo scoots up to his desk and begins frantically sorting through his papers. In the next room his elder brother, Agustín Gerónimo, propped on a rolled blanket, is getting quietly squiffed on the last of the cognac. Agustín Cosme—where is he? And in the midst of this madness, the child's dismissed nanny, Lupe, a wizened little woman with a frightened and despairing expression, steals into the dining room. She looks right, looks left, then grabs a silver candelabra and wraps it into her shawl.

"Lupe!"

Lupe's heart skips a beat—but it is only Doña Alicia calling for her from the top of the stairs.

Lupe comes out into the hallway to answer, *"Sí, niña."*

"Lupe, bring me the market basket, I'm wanting it for the shoes. *¡Apúrate!* Hurry!"

But Lupe does not go into the kitchen to fetch the basket. In the dining room, she waits until she hears Doña Alicia's footsteps disappear into the bedroom; then Lupe picks out a silver teaspoon from the drawer and drops it in the little purse she wears under her blouse. She buttons the purse tight.

"Lupe! Do hurry!"

"Sí, niña." But what Lupe does is, she removes her huaraches so as to come silently down the stairs.

In the kitchen she stuffs a bag with tortillas, cheese, and several handfuls of raisins. Then she puts her huaraches back on and, leaving the back door open, slips into the alley, into the night.

Upstairs, Alicia dumps her apronful of shoes on the mattress. She huffs. *Oh, that lazybones Lupita, she's got* tzictli *on the bottoms of her huaraches!* As she comes to the landing, Alicia catches sight of her reflection in the barred window. But she won't worry about how she looks (her pale hair sweat-soaked and wild), she won't stop, she won't think about Lupe and the other servants and the thousand things, she must run, run past her baby's shut bedroom door, down the stairs for the basket for the shoes. There is a dam of numbness inside of her, and it is holding back a Niagara.

PAST MIDNIGHT

*P*ast midnight, as the sky tears itself open, pouring needles of silver over Mexico City and the whole vast Valley of Anahuac, uncounted thousands of souls lie awake for the noise and their worries of flooding, ruined roads, drowned crops and animals. General Bazaine, in his bed with a bear-like arm over his wife's waist, thinks guiltily of his men in their field tents. But the French are not the only soldiers suffering tonight. At the gates to Chapultepec Castle, an Austrian volunteer shivers in his slicker. His rifle is so cold, his fingers have gone numb. To keep from drifting off, he sing-hums through chattering teeth a beer-hall song, *Ein, zwei, drei und der Hündschen* . . . his words are soused in rain; twelve paces away, the other sentry cannot hear them. On the topmost floor of the castle, where the flat-roof thrums and, just outside the window, the drain spouts dribble and splash, the empress's wardrobe maid, Mathilde Doblinger, having prayed, and having then recited the rosary one hundred times, stitches lists in her mind, counting on her fingers the tasks for next morning, dress-hems washed of mud and mended, slipper soles scrubbed, a silk rosette stitched back onto a bodice . . .

But Carlota, though her bedside lamp glows, sleeps; down the hall, Maximilian sleeps; around the corner, Pepa, serene princess, sleeps; and, most sweetly of all, an angel on pillows of gossamer, the tiny Agustín sleeps with his thumb in his mouth, never dreaming that his home is being abandoned, his father's and mother's clothes, shoes, knickknacks, jewelry, books, and papers packed up. By three in the morning, all the beds and his crib have been stripped and the bedclothes wadded into a trunk. The bookcases, the piano, and the inlaid mahogany wardrobes will be picked up by an agent for auction (the proceeds to be forwarded to an account in Paris). His father's library, a last crate of Madeira wine, and the portrait of his grandfather, the one of Don Agustín in his uniform as Imperial Military Commander that had hung over the piano, have been entrusted to Doña Juliana de Gómez Pedraza for safe-keeping. And if the draperies have been left hanging on their rods, a China coffeepot forgotten in a debris-strewn corner of the dining room, and a silver candelabra and several teaspoons gone missing, along with the nanny, Lupe, no matter: under the watch of two Palatine Guards, Alicia, Angelo, and his brothers, Agustín Gerónimo and Agustín Cosme, and every last rain-spattered basket, box, and hand valise—and that iron parrot cage crammed with shoes—are loaded onto the stagecoach to Veracruz.

Angelo is the last passenger to climb aboard, and he has not yet sat down on the bench when the door slams shut. The guards, a pair of Hungarians, ride alongside the stagecoach, as they will, Angelo guesses, until it leaves the city. They are aristocrats of some minor sort, but they had stood watching as the coach was loaded with the grim, stupid expressions of workers in an abattoir.

In utter gloom Angelo rakes his hands back over his hair. Then he presses his fist to his mouth. He had suspected Maximilian would stoop to this. Yes, he had: the hammer of that thought pounds in his head louder than the rain. It makes his throat tight to think: *they have been made to travel in the rainy season!* When the yellow fever is at its peak. Agustín Gerónimo took it the way he takes everything—with another drink. The other brother also: Agustín Cosme reeks of cognac and he's snoring already, his chin lolling on his chest. Beside Angelo, Alicia is wedged in next to a colossal Belgian grocer, with a hatbox crowding her lap. There are eleven passengers, packed tighter than ja-lapeños in a jar. Before reaching the coast, how long will they be trapped in this wretched contraption, two weeks? Five? The roads, if they can be called that, are troughs of mud. Last week *La Sociedad* reported that, past Orizaba, an entire team, eighteen mules, had fallen into the muck and suffocated. The ravines will be flooded; at any point along the way, the wait to cross, in some roadside inn acrawl with vermin, could last for days. In the high sierra, nearing the pine forests around Río Frío, they could be attacked by bandits. Then, down in the hot lands, typhoid, cholera, malaria, yellow fever . . . Veracruz this time of year is a deathtrap. Angelo is livid: with Maximilian, yet more so with himself. Ah! the elegant lunch in Chapultepec Castle, the shiny medals of the Orders of San Carlos for Alicia and Pepa, and of Guadalupe for himself and his brother . . . So goes the fuchsia flip of the matador's cape!

Never would Angelo have signed such an agreement of his own volition. He would have withstood the pressure from Pepa alone, but they all, including Alicia, were rock sure that this would be the best for the family, the best for the baby, the best for Mexico. Alicia argued, "Our son *is* heir apparent to the throne, this only makes the fact official, and promises for him—"

"You are out of your mind." Angelo had cut her off and for days refused to listen to one word about it. But if his wife was nearly twenty years younger than himself, a belle who liked nothing better than to chatter about dress trimmings and flubdubs (how it charmed him when she would toss her head, *darling, for my chapeau, which do you think the more* recherché, *the jonquils or the ostrich feather?*), she was as strong-minded as a man. She kept at him, a pestle to a mortar. She pointed out, "You were the one who wanted to name him after your father. You were the one who insisted, it is his rightful heritage."

Yes, Angelo had insisted they name their son Agustín, but only after his elder brother had suggested it. Agustín Gerónimo: he was the one whose son should have carried on the name. But of course there was no such person, and with his health in ruins, there never would be.

"Eh, it's yours." Agustín Gerónimo had turned fifty-six that year, but with the web of veins reddening his nose and bags under his eyes, he could have passed for seventy. A decade earlier, he had announced he would never marry. Women, he said, they expected castles in the air, or else, as far as he could pull a bead on it, their manner of thinking was Chinese. Angelo guessed that Agustín Gerónimo's bluster was a cover for wounded pride.

Alicia's mother, Mrs. Green, wrote that she voted (as if this were a democracy!) for the name Uriah, after her father, General Uriah Forrest, who had served with General Washington and lost a leg in the Battle of Brandywine. *"Uriah?"* Pepa said, as if she smelled turpentine. Agustín Gerónimo's response was to slap his knee and guffaw.

So, their son's name was Agustín de Iturbide. *"¿Y qué?"* Angelo had said to his wife, meaning, he wanted nothing to do with Maximilian's scheme.

Alicia gasped. "How can you not care about his education? We cannot dream to give him the education Maximilian can!"

"But—" Angelo began.

Pepa cut him off. "A Habsburg—"

Alicia leapt in, "Think of it, knowing Europe, Paris, London, Vienna, all of Italy—and having chances to travel to Brazil, Egypt, and he will know Maximilian's nephews, and—"

Pepa cut in, "The princes of France, of Prussia—"

"And Russia," said Alicia.

"And England! He can be sent to the best school—"

"In London or Yorkshire and then Oxford—"

"Heidelberg," Pepa said.

Alicia reached over the arm of her chair to touch Pepa's arm. "San Michel in Brussels is first rate."

"Saint Cyr—"

"The Sorbonne!"

Turning from Pepa, Alicia now fixed Angelo with her most business-like look. "You yourself have had an education that would have been impossible in this country. It hardly seems fair to deny such an opportunity to your own son."

Angelo, aghast, turned to his older brother.

Agustín Gerónimo had been stroking his chin. He made a steeple with his fingers. He raised his eyes to the wall above the piano. There, in a gilt frame, hung the portrait of their father. The Liberator, with his glorious sweep of reddish hair, looked younger than all of them, except Alicia.

Agustín Gerónimo hiccupped. "Important, education." He hiccupped again. "A man needs. Exactly."

• • •

Pepa, she was the one who first wormed the idea into Alicia's head. Months ago, she'd said, "What Maximilian is offering us is our sacred duty to accept. Brother—" she gripped Angelo's arm. "Can you not see?" Her eyes were shining. "It is for the Holy Church. Our father and mamá, you know they would have wanted this."

"No," Angelo said, and he brushed off his sister's hand. He'd been up to the neck with these women.

But Angelo had no lack of respect for his father. To the contrary; Angelo may have kept a poker face with his wife and siblings, but a secret chamber in his heart had thrilled to think that after their desert of exile, and the thousand and ten insults to their name, their father was once again being shown respect and gratitude.

"Don Agustín de Iturbide was our envoy of Providence!" It was last Easter Sunday that the archbishop spoke those words before the assembled multitude. For Angelo, to hear the reverence and unassailable authority in that voice, he felt at once joy, and the knifepoint of fear. Did the archbishop want to provoke Maximilian? Earlier this year, when Maximilian would not reinstate the church properties that had been confiscated by the republic under Juárez, the papal emissary left for Rome in a white-hot fury. The archbishop had been chafing under the French. It was no secret that he detested General Bazaine, and lately, it was rumored that privately he had been calling Maximilian *"ese alemán,* that German."

To every one of the Iturbides it was an article of faith that their father had been both a genius and Mexico's greatest patriot, and if his rivals called him ambitious, this was only because they had jealous designs. Mamá always said, as his intimates knew and as his every action revealed, Don Agustín de Iturbide harbored no ambition but the pure and blameless desire to serve his country—which was Spain, until in its own upheavals, it abandoned its children in the Americas. In 1821, out of the ashes of two roiling decades of civil war, insurrections, and anarchy, the Liberator proclaimed the Plan of Iguala, thus erecting this nation—he decided to call it Mexico—as a constitutional monarchy under three guarantees: independence; the union of Mexicans and

Spaniards (as all men were held to be equal); and the Catholic religion as its one True Faith. The Liberator then offered the crown of Mexico to Fernando VII of Spain, and his brothers, and they refused it. Undaunted, the Liberator sent a delegation to Vienna for an Austrian archduke—but that court offered nothing but scorn. Mexico was an orphan and, without a king, slipping back into the morass of chaos. France had suffered its Reign of Terror; how long until Mexico would be soaked in that same blood? Every city from Acapulco to Zacatecas had ready thieves, pillagers, Jacobins, the Mexican people began to clamor for their Liberator, their *generalíssimo,* to be their king. As a Christian and as a patriot, what choice did he have? As he told the family, he was morally obligated to accept "these golden chains." The empress, the princes, the princesses, they all had to accept them. If they were made prisoners, and it already felt that way to Angel, surrounded every moment of his days and nights by bodyguards, the Iturbides had been—as his older sister Pepa, who was eight, explained it to him—chosen by God.

They could no longer call their father Papá. He had become "Your Majesty." He looked very beautiful with his rings. Whenever he entered a room, everyone stood up. Always, there were many people around him. Always, outside his office, there was a crowd waiting to see him. Before, as was the custom, children kissed their parents' hands, but now they were to kiss His Majesty's ring. His Majesty was like a Roman Caesar, so broad-shouldered and with his reddish hair. Priests, officers, all sorts of important men, so many people, even Indians in their colorful dress and bare feet, would come to kneel before him on one knee and kiss his ring. Angel believed that the throne, its limbs carved to resemble sheaves of wheat, was of solid gold, even after Pepa told him, "Don't tell, it's just painted."

Big brother Agustín Gerónimo was the Prince Imperial, gangly, big-footed, his face pocked with acne. He was annoyed to outrage by the little ones who wanted to put grubby fingers on his sword and pistols. For Angel, a bewildered six-year-old, it was all over almost as soon as it began. In their palace, glass shattered over the carpets, they could hear shouting down in the Calle de San Francisco, "Death to Iturbide!" Outside the city, the family had to sleep in their carriage and in the fields. The priest who came with them went into the farmhouses to beg for food. At the coast, they found the sea raging like something alive. They could all drown, their father said, but Mamá answered, with a hard edge in her voice, that it were better they all die than endure one moment more among people so ungrateful. At sea, in the rolling, pitching nights, Angel was tumbled out of his bunk. At meals, soup splashed, dishes slid and crashed. Soon everyone was plagued by head lice, and maggots infested the salt pork and hardtack. Someone tried to poison their father and Angel, and the captain refused to stop, he had strict orders to continue no matter what, he said, though for the retching (his father had given Angel an emetic), Angel nearly died. The ship was a pesthouse, but when they docked at Leghorn, they were made to stay onboard, under quarantine, for another thirty gruesome days. The Iturbides were not wanted in Italy, nor in Paris. They had no place, it seemed, anywhere. In London their father learned of a Spanish plot to invade Mexico. Out of patriotism, he was inspired to return to Mexico to deliver the news and offer his help.

For the little ones left behind in school in England, that summer dragged by, each day slower and soggier than the last. The games the English boys played were dull beyond words—marbles, jacks, and they would trot along guiding a hoop with a stick, like girls. In Mexico Angel had flicked knives at dogs. His bodyguards had taken him to bullfights. In England, his elbows on a ledge, Angelo—this was his name now—stared through a lead-glass window at cows chewing their cuds in the rain. One gray morning, he was brought into the rector's library. It had mildewy-smelling books from the carpet to the curlicued ceiling, and behind a desk, a leather globe on a stand. He spun the globe with his finger and it squealed. A priest appeared; Angelo saw his dark expression and he expected he would be struck, but instead, the father, who spoke Spanish, told him that his papá was *con Dios*, with God. God is here on earth, one of the teachers had said, so Angelo wanted to know, when is my papá coming back to get us?

For many years afterward, Angelo had the feeling that time had stopped, at that moment he touched his finger to the leather globe, evil magic. They were sent to the United States where they joined their mamá and the new baby, Agustín Cosme, in New Orleans. Then they went to Washington, to live on Georgetown's Holy Hill near the Jesuit College. They lived on there, but outside of time; in an English-speaking dream, if Mexico were real or, remembering this *sueño,* this dream sweetly dappled with harp music, if that is what their country was.

Angelo is forty-eight years old. Educated by the Sulpician Brothers in Baltimore, and later by the Jesuits at Georgetown, he is, if by nature a stylish man, meticulous and guarded. He was glad to serve his country as a diplomat in Washington, but he has never sought to be a public man. Many are dazzled by the glamor of it. But he has always known, public life is riddled with indignity. You lose your humanity and become a thing, a puppet to be loved, or bashed, slandered, decapitated. Your fate depends upon your fellow citizens who can be noble friends or, when you least expect it, murderous ingrates. Whether emperor or president, you and your family are the property of the nation, and the nation is a Janus-faced beast.

He had thought he had escaped the fate of a public man.

He has heard of ships plowing into icebergs in the dark. Having to leave Mexico again was like that: sudden, implacable. Horrific.

Of exile Mamá used to say, *es nuestra jaula,* it is our cage. In her blacker moods, when she did not know how she would scrape together the money to pay the rent, she would rage, her fists at her forehead, "*Válgame Dios!* This is being buried alive!" She had lost everything. She hated Washington—"*ese fangal,* this swamp," she called it, and she found living in Philadelphia unbearably cold. Madame de Iturbide, as she insisted she be addressed by all but her children, spent her days gossiping about Mexicans she had not seen in years and, in the convent, intriguing with the sisters over bureaucratic trivialities. With the exception of Pepa, for daughters, there was the convent. For her sons, her object was that they marry into the best families, that is, those whom she knew and who had both titles and land enough to provide substantial incomes—which was tantamount to expecting them to find a phoenix in a henhouse. In Washington, what Mexicans? Mamá had a low opinion of Chileans, Peruvians, "all those from down there." Spaniards were another matter, but in the United States, Spaniards of consequence could be counted on one hand, nay, two fingers, and certainly, they had superior alternatives for their daughters. It did not help that Agustín Gerónimo was notorious all over Georgetown for once waving around his pistol at a brandy-soaked tea party.

Angelo was nearing forty when, like a spring breeze, Miss Alice Green, she of the golden hair and laughing eyes, whose dainty, silk-slippered feet seemed to float over ballroom floors, alighted in his life. Nothing mattered but Miss Green. His every thought, every breath, every action was for Miss Green. He brought her flowers, he made her a valentine, and on her birthday, he brought her a corsage of orchids. In summer, they went to concerts on the White House lawn; in the autumn, the opera and to National Theater to see a play. In winter, after ice-skating, did she fancy roasted chestnuts? He bought her a newspaper cone of the hottest ones, fresh off the fire. He was not Miss Green's only suitor, and her mother, Mrs. Green, merely and barely tolerated him. Time was of the essence, for, to advance in his diplomatic career, he would need to return to Mexico City, which he could do now that so many of his father's enemies were dead and Santa Anna in exile. He proposed to Miss Green and, to his joy, was accepted. He had thought her mother would object, but to his surprise, she quickly, though without enthusiasm, gave her consent.

It was Mamá's reaction that stunned him. From Philadelphia, she wrote that she had taken to her bed, prostrate with grief. Angelo replied in a respectful and soothing manner, reminding her of what he had already told her, that, naturally, Miss Green was a Roman Catholic; surely she remembered Mrs. Green, a convert, from Holy Trinity. (Mrs. Green, he carefully added, was the lady who would sometimes sit next to Mrs. Decatur, widow of the commodore.) The Greens were a respected family in Washington society; Miss Green was the great-granddaughter of Maryland's Governor Plater, and of General Uriah Forrest, who had served with General Washington and lost a leg in the Battle of Brandywine. Angelo furthermore explained, underlining this twice, that he fully intended to take his bride to Mexico, to which she had agreed. *I am certain, dearest Mamá, that you will understand me, and you will find for your devoted son's beloved an honored place in your heart.* He enclosed with the letter a train ticket, that she and Pepa might come down from Philadelphia to attend the wedding. But he received no answer until the morning of his wedding day.

My beloved son:

It is clear to me that your head is not in its proper place. I pray to God that this letter comes into your hands in time for you to be able to refrain

*from taking such a step. But if, against <u>all my will</u>, you are resolved to dis-
obey me, then you must never mention this woman to me and if, sometime,
you come to visit me, for my peace of mind, I demand your word of honor
that you will never present her to me.*

Mamá had no conception of how cruel she could be. She had a heart, yes,
but it had become calloused. Her life had been played out on so big and broad
a stage; she had been one of the richest girls in all of New Spain, wife of the
nation's hero, crowned an empress, and then found herself in exile, a widow,
with the problem of educating her children, dependent on the charity of
priests. She had gone on craving drama as an addict craves opium. And it so
galled her to have to live in the United States, which would with such easy
contempt, such hypocritical arrogance, pluck off pieces of her country like so
much fruit ripe for the taking.

The wedding took place in the front parlor of Rosedale, the Greens' farmhouse, which overlooked the heights above Georgetown. Afterward, alone,
he took the train to Philadelphia. He did not mention his bride to Mamá,
but he did not hide the new ring on his finger. When he was taking his leave
the next day, she gripped his hand with both of hers. "Promise me, my grandchildren will be Mexicans." He kissed her hands. He promised her. "You will
stay in Mexico," she said. He promised her that, as well.

Angelo and his bride arrived in Mexico just in time for a bloody merry-go-
round of governments, laws, constitutions concocted by clowns and radicals.
Mexico seemed to be bound to a wheel, undergoing the same tragedies and
travesties over and over again. The United States had invaded his country in
1847, now it was the turn of the French. Not that it was so easy this time—
when the baby was born, the French were still battling for the city of Puebla.
Then Juárez decamped, the French occupied the capital, and in June 1864,
Maximilian and Carlota arrived. There was a whirl of balls, dinners, *tertulias*—
Alicia and Pepa were thrilled, they had all-new wardrobes made up with Parisian-style chapeaux trimmed with swan feathers, ostrich feathers, Belgian lace,
all quite the sight, as before Carlota's appearance on the scene señoras wore
mantillas, not hats. But it was all the same to Angelo; he could care a fig for

these Europeans! Pepa and Alicia could curtsey, but he and his brothers, sons of the Liberator, they were not going to bow and scrape. Nonetheless, they were careful with words. They had always had reason to be very careful.

Both at home and in public, the Iturbides spoke English to one another, and even still, they rarely discussed politics. Where they might be overheard, they used code words: General Bazaine was "Grandpa" and Maximilian, "Younger Brother." Privately, however, Angelo had expressed his reservations on the larger questions of diplomatic strategy. The French intervention in Mexico had been constructed, in part, upon the assumption that the Confederacy would achieve its independence, and so the Mexican Empire could count on a friendly neighbor and buffer between itself and the North. But Louis Napoleon had underestimated the Union. Angelo had been friendly with Lincoln's ambassador, Mr. Thomas Corwin, before he left Mexico, yes, but Angelo had himself seen the ports, the shipyards, the railways of Baltimore, Philadelphia, New York—not Boston, not personally, but the thing was—last year, he had said it to several gentlemen—"The North is a juggernaut and the Confederacy is going to be crushed."

"It is *rouge et noire*," General Bazaine responded, through his cloud of cigar smoke.

Atlanta had already been burnt to the ground. "Respectfully, sir," Angelo countered, "the South is buried. And the United States are going to be no friend to this empire."

By February 1865, the news had reached Mexico City that Charleston had fallen. In May they learned that, in April, General Lee had surrendered at Appomattox. Angelo had expected to see grim faces all around, but no; with the *mochas*, the Mexican conservatives, everything with Maximilian's empire was *de maravilla*. That same month, when they learned that Lincoln had been assassinated, some of the *mochas* celebrated with champagne toasts. *La Sociedad* declared that the new U.S. president would recognize His Majesty the Emperor Maximilian and soon trade would be bustling not only over the Texas border from Matamoros, that hole in the Union blockade, but now also from Campeche, Tampico, Veracruz. Mexico would become a magnet for colonists! Confederate refugees, the best people with education and capital—it went without saying.

"What is your view, Don Angel?" the Prussian ambassador, Baron Magnus, had asked Angelo. This was all very *sotto voce*, but Baron Magnus had seen a copy of Carlota's letter of condolence to Mrs. Lincoln. "Will they acknowledge it?"

Angelo said, "It is naive to think so."

Agustín Gerónimo muttered, "Bloody hell they will."

That was it; the Iturbide brothers had said nothing more. Angelo was proved correct on all counts: the Confederacy did fall, and the new U.S. president not only refused to recognize Maximilian but sent forty thousand troops straight down to the bottom of Texas, where they could, at any moment, open fire and pound Matamoros to dust.

Last June, at General Bazaine's wedding, the men gathered in a corner of the garden. The Spanish ambassador asked him directly, "In your judgment, Don Angel, will the United States troops cross the Rio Grande?"

"It's a bluff," Angelo said. "The states are weary of war."

An English journalist, elbowing in and making an obsequious little bow as he introduced himself, said, "Is it your opinion then, Mister Iturbide, that the Americans will now be handing over their arms and ammunition to Mister Juárez?"

"*¿Quién sabe?* Who knows?" Angelo sank his hands into his pockets. One could never be sure who was a paid agent for whom.

Soon afterward, Angelo and his brothers were followed whenever they went into the street.

Then Alicia made jest of the emperor's *charro* costume—but blazes, who hadn't? Pepa said Maximilian looked the part of a ranchero about to rope a calf. Even their elderly landlady, Doña Juliana, the widow of Don Manuel Gómez Pedraza, the aunt of Madame Bazaine, and a complete *mocha* from her velvet slippers to her black lace mantilla, when she caught sight of Maximilian cantering by in that tight little jacket and washtub of a sombrero, cried (if only loud enough for Alicia to hear), "God spare us this burlesque."

Three days later, a Palatine Guard left an envelope for him. Doña Juliana's maid took it for an invitation, brought it upstairs, and placed it on the mantel with others. That evening, with only a feeling of smugness, Angelo slit open the heavy ivory paper embossed in gold. But this was not an invitation to another ball. It was a clap of thunder out of a clear sky: an order, without explanation, that the Iturbides quit Mexico. Alicia burst into tears. To hear her, the baby began bawling.

Angelo felt he'd been horse-kicked in the gut. Why? Who was it? Who had slandered them? It happened all the time; people made things up, forged documents. His mind raced through the mirrored maze of possibilities.

Or, was someone fishing for a bribe?

He had no idea what this was, no idea what to do, but he spoke calmly. "Darling, do not upset yourself." He rested a calming hand on her shoulder. "I will go to Agustín Gerónimo. He will arrange things."

By protocol, his elder brother should have been the one to receive such a communication. The next morning, Angelo found him in his hotel. The darkened room smelled of unwashed clothing. On the bedside table a plate of cheese crusts had already attracted ants. There were two glasses and an empty champagne bottle. The cork lay on the floor by a pile of clothing. As was his custom, for his sick headache, Agustín Gerónimo had a lady's white leather opera glove packed fat with ice on his forehead. The thing reminded Angelo of an obscene, skinned trout.

"Brother! Brother," Angelo shook one of the bedposts.

Agustín Gerónimo groaned, "Eh. Balls." He flung the glove. Angelo stepped aside. It landed with a wet thump at the foot of the bed. Angelo picked the thing up in his fingertips and carried it to the washbasin. His brother, meanwhile, rolled over to face the wall. After that Angelo was unable to rouse him. He left the letter propped on the bedside table.

Not until late that day was the family able to gather in Angelo's parlor. They were stunned, Angelo most of all, when Agustín Gerónimo announced that he had already dashed off a reply, that His Majesty consider it had been more years than the French had been in this country since the family's pensions had been paid by any government. Should Maximilian reinstate their pensions, and perhaps also grant them a little extra, for a style of living commensurate with their station, then the Iturbides, all of them, would gladly go.

Pepa cried, "I would not be glad!"

"Enough of a pension and you would be," Agustín Gerónimo said.

Alicia looked crushed. "I don't want to live in Washington!"

"Who says ya hafta?" Agustín Gerónimo was about to say more, but he doubled over in a paroxysm of coughing. Angelo thought: it was ghastly the way his older brother had declined. Wherever they ended up—Philadelphia? London?—that was where Agustín Gerónimo was going to be buried.

They all waited for the head of the family to compose himself. They were arranged around him in a horseshoe, Alicia and Pepa to one side, together on the sofa; Angelo standing behind the straight-backed chair, upon which sat the youngest brother, Agustín Cosme.

Pepa could no longer contain herself. "You should have waited to hear what we had to say about it." She sniffed with indignation. "What are we supposed to do now, wait on tenterhooks for a reply?"

"Or a midnight knock at the door." Angelo uncovered his eyes. "My God," he muttered to the ceiling. "We could all be arrested."

"Eh!" Agustín Gerónimo said, stuffing his handkerchief back into his pocket. "Not with the landlady you have . . ."

Alicia cut in, "Yes, Doña Juliana would help us! She could go to General Bazaine! Why, he's practically her son-in-law."

That made Agustín Gerónimo guffaw.

Pepa gave Agustín Gerónimo a lacerating look. "I see nothing amusing about any of this." She turned now to Alicia. "Involving General Bazaine would not be the best idea."

One thing they all agreed upon: They could not risk appearing in public.

Angelo gave away his opera tickets and, claiming to be indisposed by the gout, declined all invitations to dine. Alicia and Pepa gave up their morning rounds of visits. To avoid their being seen in church, Doña Juliana arranged to have one Father Fischer, a German recently arrived from Durango by way of Texas, come and take their confessions and say mass in her drawing room. Doña Juliana had plenty of sofas, a pair of prie-dieux and an age-darkened altar once the pride of the chapel of a Dominican cattle hacienda. Before that altar stood a manila chest, upon which the curate spread his altar cloth and placed the chalice and the host. Afterward, they would all troop upstairs to Angelo and Alicia's dining room for coffee and apple pie. Father Fischer always took three heaping spoonfuls of whipped cream, saying with a satisfied sigh, *"Ach, mit Schlag."*

Father Fischer had the pudgy, friendly face of one who has invariably eaten well. But he had an oily way about him, a Roman nose, pelt-like red hair, and ferret-like eyes that darted about, as if secretly sizing up the furnishings, the better to estimate his tithes. Most unattractive was his habit, in the middle of hearing a confession, of examining his fingernails, and every now and then he'd give one a good chew. Alicia pouted that Father Fischer smelled of beer and pickled cabbage, and he mumbled the Lord's Prayer to gibberish—why, his Latin was atrocious. He certainly was not the elevated kind of German she had become acquainted with among the *corps diplomatique* in Washington. She'd heard it said that his father was a butcher in a village north of Stuttgart. Further, he'd gone to San Francisco during the gold rush and, in violation of his oaths as a priest, taken a lover and then abandoned her and their children. But, Pepa countered, idle gossip was best overlooked. The fact was, Father Fischer had made Maximilian's acquaintance in Rome. He had high-level connections within the Vatican— "*Va-ti-can,*" Pepa said, pronouncing it as if for a small child. "And Father Fischer is German."

"So?" Alicia rolled her eyes.

Pepa said, "Have a lick of common sense, for once."

Doña Juliana, meanwhile, had advised General Bazaine. He knew nothing of the letter to the Iturbides, and dismayed as he was by it, he judged it "outside his purview." With utmost discretion, Doña Juliana attempted to learn more, but Maximilian's court, being so largely composed of parvenus and foreigners, remained opaque.

Three weeks went by before the Iturbide brothers dared dip a toe in the water. Angelo, with Father Fischer as his companion, showed himself in the Restaurant Parisien. General Bazaine and Baron Magnus, the Prussian ambassador, stopped by their table and shook hands. As they exchanged pleasantries, Angelo searched their faces. So little of importance was ever said directly; one had to parse out what went unsaid. One watched for subtle changes in the shades of gray—was it a sharpening of the tone of voice? An inflection, was it of deference, or however infinitesimal, annoyance? Was a smile one of affection, or a mask for nervous embarrassment?

From the Imperial Palace there came a blast of silence.

Soon afterward they read in *La Sociedad* that His Majesty was touring in the provinces, beginning with some canoeing on Lake Texcoco, and then Teotihuacan to see the pyramids of the Sun and Moon, and on to Chapingo, Otumba, and Tulancingo. His Majesty visited a school, a hospital, and a glass factory. He admired the aqueduct of Zempoala and then traveled north to visit the silver mines in Pachuca. There was much to read about Pachuca, pages and pages. "It does seem," Pepa said, "that Maximilian might move his whole court to Pachuca!"

After Maximilian had been back in residence in Chapultepec Castle for another week, the Iturbides had still heard nothing. Agustín Gerónimo said, "Maybe he's kicked the ball downstairs to the treasury." He meant the question of their pensions. After another week, however, Angelo was coming to suspect that they might never be arrested, if they kept quiet. Very quiet.

In the meantime, Doña Juliana learned a piece of brilliant intelligence: Father Fischer had become friendly with Frau von Kuhacsevich, Mistress of the Imperial Household, and also with Mathilde Doblinger, the empress's Viennese wardrobe maid. These were some of Their Majesties' closest, most trusted people; they had come with them from Miramar Castle in Trieste.

Angelo put it to Father Fischer directly: Did he think the danger of their being arrested for not obeying the imperial order to leave Mexico was past?

Father Fischer's ferret-like eyes slid to the left. "It is not for me to say."

On the first Sunday of August, after the mass in Doña Juliana's drawing room, and after the apple pie and whipped cream, and after Doña Juliana, leaning heavily on the arm of her old cook, had gone back downstairs, Father Fischer made his proposition.

Angelo thought he must have misheard. "Maximilian wants to do *what?*"

Father Fischer smiled greasily as he repeated: "His Majesty desires to bring your son, Agustín, under his tutelage."

A mammoth might have crashed through the ceiling and flattened the piano to splinters. Angelo opened his mouth, but he could not form words. He found himself standing, but his knees felt suddenly uncertain; he put a hand on the edge of Alicia's chair. Alicia, however, lit up like a Christmas tree.

"Our Agustín would go to Chapultepec Castle? With Their Majesties?"

"With Their Majesties." Father Fischer and Pepa said it at the same time.

Angelo looked at Pepa and his jaw dropped. "Sister—you—?"

Father Fischer continued, "His Majesty would assume the responsibility of his education. He would also assume your nephew Salvador's education in France."

Pepa said, "We would *all* be made Highnesses, with the titles of Prince and Princess." Pointedly, looking first at Agustín Gerónimo and then at her two younger brothers, she repeated, "All."

Agustín Cosme, the one son of the Liberator who had never had the rank of an Imperial Highness, for he had been born shortly after his father's death, came quite alert now, though he said nothing. No one wanted his opinion anyway, and had he given it, its weight would have been that of a feather.

From his chair, Agustín Gerónimo cleared his throat loudly. "Eh! Got that title more than a few years ago. You got it, sister, when you were knee high to a puddle duck."

Father Fischer said, in his oily way, "Dear sir, you might consider it as the palace taking your esteemed family under its—" he looked to the ceiling as if there the words were a-fluttering—

"*Special* protection," Pepa said.

Agustín Gerónimo said, "Hot air, Father." He put a hand on his hip. "What about pensions. There is the nut of the matter. We cannot be leaving Mexico without means."

Father Fischer said, "All your pensions would be fully reinstated. And there would be other sums that would be more than generous."

Agustín Gerónimo tipped back his head. "How generous?"

"For each of you, one hundred fifty thousand dollars."

"*En écus bien comptés?*"

"Thirty thousand dollars in cash, and the balance in bills, payable on February 15, in Paris."

"Paris!" Agustín Gerónimo laughed. He raised his glass. "Cheers—well—" He remembered himself, and twisted around to Angelo. "He's your boy. What say you?"

"N—no!"

"Well, that's that." Agustín Gerónimo turned to Pepa. "Tough potatoes."

"*Tough potatoes?*" Pepa's expression was rabid.

"Keep your bonnet on, sister." Agustín Gerónimo flipped his hand. "What do you say, Father, can you go back and tell Maximilian, how 'bout he gives us our pensions, and Salvador the education, but not for my infant nephew, Agustín. He stays with his parents."

Father Fischer's eyes seemed to sink into his fleshy cheeks. "As you wish," was all he said.

Angelo had been flummoxed, not only at the unexpectedness—the audacity!—of this proposition, but that, then, in the days that followed Alicia entertained the idea. She implored him, pestered him, pushed him! *Do you care nothing for your family? Your son could have the finest education in Europe! Think of his future! Your country's future!*

Where, *how* had they lost the thread of reason in this fog of sparkles and genie dust?

One night, over a game of cards with his two brothers, Angelo said to Agustín Gerónimo, "I do not want to do it, but Alicia . . ."

Agustín Gerónimo counseled, "This is what the woman's got a fix on, she's the mother, you ought to agree." He covered his mouth with his cards and coughed. "I would."

"You *would*?" Angelo blinked.

Agustín Gerónimo pulled a card from his hand and placed it on the table. Jack of spades. "Go deaf, never hear the end of it."

"You would?"

Agustín Gerónimo palmed another card. When he'd arranged his hand, he looked out the window to the street. "That's what I said."

"It's so damned much money," Angelo said darkly.

The youngest, Agustín Cosme, said soothingly, "It's not just the money. But, yes . . . and Pepa says—"

"I know what Pepa says." Appalled, Angelo pushed himself to his feet so violently, his chair tipped over behind him. He walked out. He was not going to hand over his own flesh and blood to some other man. And the idea that little Agustín would be Heir Presumptive—or Apparent, or whatever—maybe so, but that anything would come of it, this was laughable! Maximilian and Carlota were still young; Carlota was only twenty-five years old!

Had he not given the clearest possible signal?

But the very next day, preceded by an arrangement of birds-of-paradise, orange blossoms, lilies and roses, and orchids and tuberoses, and ferns so extravagant that the thing could not fit through the door (the servants had to take the bouquet apart and then put it back together), the empress herself arrived at number 11, Calle de Coliseo Principal. Leaving her bodyguards in the street, she ascended the stairs to their third-floor apartment. In a rustle of silk and taffeta, Her Majesty alighted on their sofa and accepted a cup of coffee. The servant who brought it shook so badly she nearly dropped the tray. The rest of the servants pressed their ears to the door (Angelo could see beneath it the shadows of their feet). To Angelo, it was not thrilling but grimly disconcerting to have Carlota—daughter of King Leopold of the Belgians, granddaughter of King Louis-Philippe of the French, first cousin of Queen Victoria of England, sister-in-law of Kaiser Franz Joseph of Austria—here in this Mexican apartment. Everything was wrong with it, the torn thumb of wallpaper behind the sidetable, the cheap carpet, the frayed upholstery on the arms of the chair. The stale smell of fried bacon. On the sofa cushion, next to the sleeve of Her Majesty's lace-and-velvet pelisse, was a stain where, months ago, the baby had spit up. (To flip the cushion would have revealed a coffee splotch.)

After the baby had been handed back to his nanny, Carlota said: "We can assure you that you will have frequent news of Agustín."

Alicia, her face innocent as a child's, was on the edge of her chair. "Every day?"

"Constant communication," Carlota said.

Alicia had placed the bouquet, precariously, on the mantel. The sight of that thing, so ridiculously out of proportion, and its cloying stink, made Angelo ill.

That night he had a dream that he was at sword point, being backed up to a precipice, and then, with no one to help him, he fell. He woke with a start, covered in sweat. Within the week he had an attack of gout so excruciating he had to hobble with a cane. And then a nasty boil on the back of his neck.

They would have to flee Mexico, but how?

In the north, insurgents controlled the countryside. The French had finally taken Chihuahua, but they were still waging pitched battles against the guerrillas in the pueblos. On all the roads heading north, stagecoaches were regularly ambushed. There were snipers on the cliffs.

Instead, the family might take the stagecoach road southeast to Veracruz, on a route almost as treacherous, and from there a steamship north. But to arrive in Veracruz now, in the rainy season, the season of yellow fever, would be madness. And if they made it out of Mexico alive, without a post in the diplomatic corps, without land, without pensions, where could they live?

Angelo knew the answer, and it made his intestines grind: Washington, under the same roof with Mrs. Green. On her damned farm.

"You are being selfish," Alicia accused him. "We must consider our son's future!"

It was, Angelo had to admit, fabulous to consider that their son could be educated under the tutelage of a Habsburg.

Pepa, like a second in a duel, came in right behind her sister-in-law. "This is larger than you are, brother. Our sovereign is requesting our help and making a magnanimous offer. Is it not dear to you also that Mexico be a Catholic country? Would you have Juárez and his criminals destroy our country? Are you not godfearing? We are, all of us in this family, and you, brother, in a crucial position to be of service."

The maid saved the teaspoon that had touched Carlota's lips, tied a ribbon around its neck, and left it out on the mantel by those awful flowers. The cook put the teacup and saucer on a high shelf, apart. Angelo had never seen his sister so energetic, so smilingly solicitous of Alicia—whom, up until now, she had merely tolerated, as one would an inconvenient and silly child. The empress visited their apartment again, urging them with honeyed smiles to do this beautiful, noble thing, but underneath Her Majesty's polished-as-silver poise, which so awed the women and the servants, Angelo could detect the threat: *Or else! Nothing will come of it for any of you.*

Maximilian could, after all, take their child by force and then exile the rest of them without a peso. Or much worse. Maximilian relished the grandiose show of mercy (it was an open secret that General Bazaine was increasingly provoked), but His Majesty was, after all, the younger brother of Kaiser Franz Joseph, whose Geheim Polizei plucked scores of inconvenient people off the streets of Vienna, Trieste, Milan. Liberals, anarchists, hotheaded students, no matter, they were shot, strangled, tortured, gang-kicked to pulp. Such things had always happened in Mexico, and only a simpleton could expect it to be different now. Last week, for example, the milliner, whose shop was on their corner had been frog-marched out, with his head bleeding and his hands roped behind his back, in broad daylight. Why? Doña Juliana did not know, and neither did the servants. There was nothing about it in *La Sociedad*, of course. One's luck could change with the snap of His Majesty's fingers. Or with the snap of a flunky's. Without favor in the highest echelons, one was vulnerable, a bull without horns—or, more apt, a wrinkled little turtle crawling along without its carapace.

But with Maximilian's arrangement, Pepa said—Alicia nodded, yes, yes, yes—"we can not only count on His Majesty's protection, but brilliant prospects for our Agustín."

On the drive to the signing ceremony at Chapultepec Castle, Angelo had to stop the carriage twice so he could get out and throw up. In Chapultepec Castle, they were shepherded up the marble staircase and then down a hall hung with Venetian glass chandeliers, then past a gauntlet of footmen and guards, into a red-velvet-draped salon. The contract lay on a spindle-legged table shining with ormolu. Maximilian took up the pen and signed. How it stung Angelo, that sound. Like metal scratching on glass. Agustín Gerónimo was the first of the family to sign, then, because Angelo did not step forward, Agustín Cosme signed. Pepa signed, *scratch-scratch*. And then Alicia signed, *scratch*.

When again Angelo did not move to pick up the quill, Father Fischer pressed it into his hand.

"For Mexico," Father Fischer said. His little eyes darted about, but his voice was a bell, low and mellifluous. "For Mexico."

Don José Fernándo Ramírez, Mexico's foreign minister, put his fist to his mouth and coughed.

Angelo could feel their stares. Maximilian, ripe with hair lotion, waited with one hand's fingertips pressed to the table, as if posing for a photograph. It struck Angelo at that moment that the fabric of His Majesty's uniform was uncannily fine; the gold-fringed epaulettes—it was remarkable—fit him perfectly. Angelo's father's uniform never did hang so well. He had worn-at-the-heels boots and the old-fashioned starched collar that brushed his jaw. Where was his face? Why could he never, in all these years, conjure in his mind his own father's face? Angelo was groggy with nausea. His right toe, afflicted with the gout, was throbbing agony. His eyes filled with tears (he blinked them back) and, in such a jagged movement it seemed some outside force moved his feet to the table and his hand to the sheepskin, he signed. He lifted the quill from the paper, and he felt the blood drain from his face. It was as if, in that instant, a limb of his soul had been amputated. *Dear God,* a small voice within him cried. *Dear God.*

Now in the stagecoach, Angelo cannot get comfortable, not with his cane between his knees and his shoulder jammed against the window, his elbow to his wife's hatbox. Through the downpour, dim outlines of doorways file by. Now and again, the coach's lantern casts a veil of light over a length of telegraph wire, a dripping bank of bushes, a cross, askew in the mud. A moth, he notices for the first time, flutters, trapped inside the lantern just outside the window. The Belgian grocer snores. Agustín Gerónimo starts coughing, a dry, trembling hack.

Angelo has such a sick feeling. In Paris, if they make it that far, there is a slim chance that the Mexican legation might have something for him to do, translating, tasks of that nature, he cannot expect more, as the ambassador there will be jealous of his own responsibilities and relationships. It has occurred to him that, with the money from the pensions, he could set himself up with some kind of exporting company, sewing machines or pianos, but when he thinks of having to arrange permits, calculate customs duties, budget for bribes, it is as if he were watching someone else, some soulless marionette of a philistine, and from a great distance.

He might play scholar and write a history of his father, the revolutions for Mexican Independence, the First Empire, and its fall. Many people, including the archbishop, have suggested it. But for Angelo to dwell on those times would be to peel back his rage and expose such grief, he knows he is not equal to it.

God protect you, the widow de Gómez Pedraza had said. For the first time since Angelo was a child, Doña Juliana put her hand on the back of his head and kissed him on the forehead. She had stayed awake, so long past midnight, to send them off.

Angelo says, "Darling?" He leans toward his wife, and the hatbox on her lap jabs him in the rib.

"What."

He touches her hand, and it is so cold, the horrible idea penetrates his mind: they are dead. In a way, he realizes, they are, and this, this pitching, cramped box of misery, is their Purgatory. An image of a bullfighting ring comes to mind: the antique ceremony finished, the *mulillas,* the team of mules, dragging by ropes the carcass, and the *areneros,* behind, stirring, raking the sand.

"What?" she says again, raising her voice over the creaking and the thundering of the hooves. "What is it?"

He warms her hand in both of his. "Nothing."

"Your hands are ice," she complains, and she takes her hand back.

Half an hour ahead of the stagecoach, a covered wagon rocks along on wobbling wooden wheels. In its back, Lupe sits huddled among jiggling stacks of boxes. She is as old as Methuselah, but she fears, far more than this wet cold, it is the *sustos,* the frights she's suffered that will be the death of her. The first *susto* was when Doña Alicia told her the baby was going to live with the emperor. Then, last morning in the full of the sunshine, the empress came to the apartment, and she and Doña Pepa took the baby away. Then, Doña Alicia and Don Angel said they were leaving. They were going to cross the sea. Even now—it comes in nauseating rolls—Lupe feels as if the floor she's been standing on has given way.

For a time, in the back of this rattletrap wagon, she'd rubbed and clapped her arms to keep from shivering, but now she simply sits, her teeth chattering and her eyes squeezed in numb, exhausted sorrow. The jouncing and jolting is torture on her old bones; she's banged her shoulder twice and bruised her back; every joint from the crick of her neck to her toes aches. Rain roars onto the canvas, and rushing in through a tear in the cover, cold water has been puddling around her huaraches. They are tiny huaraches. Lupe is no bigger than a malnourished twelve-year-old.

She has no family. She does not know how old she is, only that she was still a very little girl in the orphanage the year the earthquake brought down the coal shed's roof. She might have been eleven or fifteen the year the nuns sent her off forever, as a *galopina*, a kitchen maid, for one of their patronesses. For some sixty years, the Gómez Pedrazas' was Lupe's home. The nuns had taught Lupe to make many things, which she, as a child, had imagined to be the worldliest, *quesadillas* and *gorditas* stuffed with the brilliant orange squash flowers, and *tostaditas* of beans and shredded chicken with cinnamon shavings. Lupe had been allowed to stir the stew of pigs' feet with onion, that, the nuns all agreed, tasted even better reheated. On special occasions, such as the day of Our Lady of Guadalupe, or when a priest or patron would come for a visit, Lupe helped to make the *mole*. She got down on her knees to grind the chiles, chocolate, and spices in the stone *metate*, and she tended the fire under the big pot, hour after hour, long into the night. Before dawn, Lupe helped prepare the jugs of watermelon water, mango water, *horchata*, and in the fall, after the rains, *agua de tuna*, cactus fruit water sweetened with *piloncillo*, molasses flavored with orange peel and spices.

But in Doña Juliana de Gómez Pedraza's house, it was another level! The cook there learnt her to grind almonds fine to powder, how to whip sweet cream to fluff. Doña Juliana had them make fancy things—oh, the fancies! Cream white trout on a bed of pickled lime-skins, sweetly mild *poblano* chiles stuffed with sautéed walnuts and minced beef and sprinkled with pomegranate seeds, and duck, and goose, and quail, pheasant in butter-nutmeg sauce with crisp diced peppers. Soon, by watching Chole, Lupe knew how to make the turtle soups with sherry, and the salads of lettuce, bananas, and peanuts broken fine (on top, very carefully, as Doña Juliana showed her, Lupe would arrange slices of strawberry into stars). Before the midday meal, for his digestion, Lupe served Don Manuel his shot glass of *tepache*, pineapple liquor. Lupe always added a squeeze of lime, for that was the way he liked it.

"*Gracias*, Lupita," Don Manuel would murmur, lifting the glass from the tray.

Lupe would cast her eyes down to her feet and murmur, *"Para servirle,* to serve you, señor."

Don Manuel towered over most other men, and the thick hair that he brushed up from his forehead made him appear even taller. Knife-like sideburns framed his pale, narrow, clean-shaven face. He had thin lips that seldom smiled. But there was nothing mean about him.

"I declare," Don Manuel said to his wife, "there must be angels in your kitchen."

Well, huh, Lupe could have become the cook, but that was about as likely as a mouse laying an egg, because Soledad—Doña Chole, those bootlicking vendors in the market called her—was the cook. Doña Chole, old garlic breath and flabby arms, who stood a head taller than Lupe, but she shrank as she got older until—the day did come—Chole and tiny Lupe stood eye-to-eye.

But old or young, Chole could have made wax melt, she was that ugly. She had hands that could wring the neck of a big male *guajolote* on the first twist. Jutting up her lantern of a chin, Doña Chole always had her way of looking down on one. For no reason but spite, Chole would give Lupe a clout on the head. If Lupe burnt a tortilla, Chole slapped her. "You're not worth a mustard seed," she would sneer, never mind that Chole herself had burnt enough tortillas to feed an army, and more than a few cakes, ay, once Chole burnt a whole suckling pig to a blackened brick! Didn't that cost the señora a pretty peso; she had to serve her guests leftovers, sliced up venison sausage from breakfast into the soup, and there was not enough of it. And how could anyone forget—it happened the year the cannonball crashed down the portico of Count Villavaso's house across the street—the time one rainy season, when instead of putting it up in the *zarzate,* hanging basket, Chole left a bag of rice on the floor. For weeks afterward, the kitchen was overrun with mice, and their droppings, and cockroaches. Once, when she was taking it down from the high shelf, Chole dropped the blue-glass bowl that had been one of Doña Juliana's own wedding gifts—smashed to bits! The señora came running into the kitchen, and in her camisole! It was a holy miracle Doña Juliana did not die of the grippe she got after that *susto.*

But did the señora say one blessed word about any of this? Ay, never. Chole's mamá had been Doña Juliana's own nanny, so from all whichways, upside down and inside out, Shrove Tuesday to Shrove Tuesday, Chole was the hands-down favorite servant in the Gómez Pedraza house. Chole walked on water, and her farts were perfume of lilies. Chole knew it, too. If they had a cake to decorate—and Lupe, having prepared the pine-nuts, candied ginger, orange peel and raisins, set them out each in their little bowls—Chole would pick out the biggest onion, and say, "You, chop this." Or, "You, throw the garbage in the alley." Or, "You, sweep out the ashes." Her Highness Doña Chole wouldn't rinse a teacup if she could order the *galopina* to do it.

Many a time Lupe climbed up to the flat-roof, to the bedroom she shared with Chole and the other maids, and threw herself on her blanket and cried. But if Chole or any of the other girls were in there, they would tease her, so Lupe stayed out on the flat-roof and hid herself among the sheets and clothes hanging there to dry. She hated being up there, alone, exposed like a rabbit under the open sky. The sight of snow on the volcanoes made her feel so cold. The dog that was tied up on the flat-roof next door would snarl and bark at her. She would scream at it, "Devil take you!" She kept a supply of pebbles to throw at it.

Chole was Lupe's cross to bear. At the orphanage, the nuns had taught her, *The Almighty has given each of us a station in life. It is His will that you obey your superiors. Faith in His wisdom is as necessary to your salvation as the air you breathe is to your earthly body.*

Sometimes Lupe would gaze up at the crucifix on the wall above the bed, or the crucifix over the big iron pot, or the crucifix in the hallway to the drawing room (certainly, crucifixes were not in short supply in the Gómez Pedraza house), and she would remind herself, whatever she was suffering, was it nails being driven through her hands and feet? She wore no crown of thorns; there was no blood running down her face. She was not being lashed and stoned by soldiers and Hebrews! This house had Chole in it, but the fact was, the Gómez Pedrazas' was a decent, God-fearing house. Don Manuel and Doña Juliana spoke to all with respect: one another, their relatives, their friends and guests, their servants. For the servants, there were always beans and tortillas, and even if just the calf's head, or the tripe, or the overcooked and gristly bits—the servants did eat meat every day but Friday, and on Fridays plenty of eggs, and cheese, too.

The meek shall inherit the earth. This was the promise of the Heavenly Father, and the idea never ceased to seem wonderful to Lupe, wonderful as the orphanage's chapel had been, *ay,* with its soaring, light-swollen dome and the altar covered all over with golden cockleshells, and the vanilla-pudding faces of saints and angels. And the Templo de la Profesa, the church that the Gómez Pedrazas and their servants went to, it was bigger, with ten golden chandeliers that cast their shadows on a shrimp pink marble wall and the long line, all up the nave, of pictures of the Stations of the Cross. There were many of suffering saints, and suffering prophets, too. When the priest and the altar boys swung the silver censers, out wafted plumes of the most fragrant smoke, the same, Lupe was sure of it, that Our Lady of Guadalupe was sniffing in Heaven along with bouquets of her beautiful roses.

Her tattered grease-stained shawl over her head, Lupe would come home and shuffle into the gloom of the kitchen.

"Boil the water for the señora's tea!" When it wasn't fast enough, Chole would pinch Lupe's eyebrows or smack her with the wooden spoon.

"Bitch," Chole might say, and not even for anything.

Twenty years went by. One day, the Demon made Lupe whisper, "Who talks?"

Chole, at the washtub shelling peas, whipped around and glared at her. "*What* did you say?"

Lupe's heart raced in her chest. She dropped her eyes. "Nothing."

Lupe should be meek, she scolded herself, again and again. The nuns had slapped it into her: *Obey. Obey your mistress, obey your betters, and above all, to obey your superiors is to obey God.* Or else, burn in the flames of Hell.

Pride stained the soul, and so maybe then it was Chole, *she* was the one who would burn. This idea pleased Lupe very much, and soon, whenever she might be, say, carving up a watermelon, she would imagine Chole not there at the washtub shelling peas, or pulling the meat off a boiled hen, but with her hands roped behind a stake. The pile of logs and twigs beneath her feet would begin to spiss and smoke; soon Chole would be screaming, writhing, sobbing, *Mercy! Have mercy on me!* But Lupe would watch the flames lick up her ankles, and then her calves. Chole's skirt and apron would bloom into fire, and then it would race up the sleeves of her blouse, and then, with the most beastly stink, her braids would shrivel, her flesh sizzle . . . a smell like bacon . . .

Hee hee hee! Lupe would rinse off the knife, wipe it dry on her apron, and begin arranging her work on a platter.

"What's so funny?" Chole would ask.

"Nothing."

At first Lupe confessed her unclean thoughts to the priest, and in penance, said her Hail Marys. Ten Hail Marys, one hundred Hail Marys, five hundred Hail Marys . . . But the Demon insisted. Over the years, the wicked scene played out in her daydreams ever more vividly. One time Lupe imagined herself standing there before the bonfire with a pail of water. Chole's voice squeaked through the black billows of smoke: *Mercy! Lupe, I beg you, pleeee-eee-ease!* Lupe dipped the wooden spoon—the spoon Chole smacked her with—into the pail of water. Lupe flicked just a teaspoonful. It landed on Chole's blistering red thigh, *zuzz!* and gave off the tiniest cloud of steam.

Such were Lupe's sweetly secret consolations, as years passed by, the one the same as the next it seemed, but when she thought back on it, *ay*, there had been many changes. In the Year of Our Lord 1822, Don Manuel was made Commander of Mexico City. What a splendid uniform! The house had a parade of people coming and going, dinners, entertainments, and sometimes in the dead of night important men would come to meet with Don Manuel. The servants knew they were important because, from the flat-roof overlooking the street, they could see the bodyguards, shadowy in the lamplight, smoking and throwing dice on the steps. There were always a lot of military officers at the dinner table. From the kitchen the maids could hear the rumble of their voices, the sudden bursts of loud laughing, first one, then all together, *To Don Manuel!* and the clinking of glasses, *Salud! Salud!*

In the year 1828, Don Manuel was elected president. What a beautiful celebration dinner the family had—aunts, cousins, first, second, third cousins, such a lot of relatives Lupe had never seen before in this house. First there was a consommé with sherry ladled over a boiled quail egg in each bowl.

There were four turkeys and two hams, and for dessert, a mousse of papaya (didn't that give Lupe a sore shoulder!), pineapple fritters and "buttons" of egg yolk, *nata*, and sugar. But right away, a cabal of generals got up a revolution. From the Plaza Mayor, just a few blocks yonder, they could hear the boom of cannon and from the next alley over, crackles of rifle fire—the servants covered their ears and lay down on the floor. Later, Doña Juliana came into the kitchen to tell them, just as cool as you please, not to worry, as soon as things settled down, Don Manuel would return. Which was exactly what happened.

And in the year 1832, once again, Don Manuel was made president. Because the palace had taken so many cannonballs and been used as a jail, Doña Juliana refused to set up house there; her household stayed right where it was and, anyway, Don Manuel was president for only a few months before Santa Anna came back. And the Yankees came, and then the Yankees left. Most of the servants, all Chole's relatives, went back to their village, San Filomeno de Cuaujimalpa. Lupe was the only one in this house who had never set foot in San Filomeno de Cuaujimalpa, and she never would.

With only Chole to share it with, the bedroom on the flat-roof seemed much colder. They would have to pluck and cook only one chicken, not four or five. One day after dinner, while he was reading the newspaper in his wing chair by the window, Don Manuel asked Lupe to bring him his shot glass of *tepache*. When she returned with the tray, she found her master slumped over to one side. His lips had turned blue! His pale eyes stayed wide-open with their pupils staring blackly. His spectacles lay on the carpet. Lupe did not dare touch the señor's shoulder; she ran for the feather duster, and held it before his lips. This was how she knew: General Don Manuel Gómez Pedraza, whom the Lord had granted sixty-three years on this earth, was in peace.

For a long time the house was as quiet as a tomb.

It was only a few years later, however, that Doña Juliana let out the top floor of her house to Don Angel de Iturbide, the son of that emperor. Don Angel and his brothers had come back from the north, everyone was a-twitter, the shoeshine boys and the watchman, and the boys who sold the newspapers and pamphlets, the broom-maker, the water-seller, the rag-picker, and the knife-sharpener, all sorts would linger near Doña Juliana's front door for a glimpse of the prince. Don Angel de Iturbide had a barrel-chested military kind of bearing, a wonderful mustache, and he wore ruffles on his shirt-cuffs and a stovepipe hat. From the front steps to his waiting buggy (his coachman would bring it around front), he walked with long, quick strides (unless he happened, as he sometimes was, to be afflicted with the gout). Later, their spinster sister, Doña Pepa, arrived. She was stout and had so much gray in her hair that many people mistook her for their mother, the empress, Doña Ana.

But Doña Ana had died in the north. Lupe got that straight from Doña Pepa, and Lupe made sure to inform the watchman, the shoeshine boys, the broom-maker, and whomever asked, as well as many people who didn't think to. *Ay*, a queen, just like her mother, Doña Pepa wore a ring with a black pearl. When she went outside, she wore butter-soft kid-leather gloves and, rain or shine, carried a coal black silk parasol.

As for Don Angel's wife, Doña Alicia, she was a Yankee, but a decently mannered one and pretty as a doll. She had a heart-shaped face, and hair the color of clover honey that she wore somewhat loose, and the daintiest, most precious shoes. They had rounded toes, not like the shoes with buckles that Doña Juliana wore. No, not a one of the señoras in Mexico City wore shoes like Doña Alicia's.

Don Angel and Doña Alicia wanted a cook, and so whom did Doña Juliana send upstairs?

The worm had turned!

Chole was wild with envy. And for Lupe—Doña Lupe as the vendors in the market began to call her—oh no, she wasn't just *marchantita* (customer) anymore—there was no nectar sweeter than to trounce into the kitchen, for it was the same kitchen, they shared it, and in a loud voice command Chole: "Move aside, Don Angel wants his breakfast."

Lupe was delighted to let Chole know that in the Iturbides' upstairs apartment, where their pantries were kept, only the wine cabinet had a lock. That's right, Lupe could eat whatever she wanted, bacon, sugared almonds, raisins, five boiled eggs for her breakfast, nobody counted.

Doña Alicia had showed Lupe how to make pies of apples, but you could make them, Doña Alicia said, with strawberries, apricots, sweet potatoes.

That was something to see, when Doña Alicia turned up her sleeves and rolled out that dough herself, and sprinkled so much flour on it they both sneezed! The secret to perfect dough, Doña Alicia explained, was to work it just to the point, no further, where a little piece of it, rubbed between your fingers, feels like your earlobe. Lupe, to demonstrate this principle to Chole, gave her own earlobe a tug. And Doña Alicia had a cookery book as fat as Doña Juliana's Bible. It had colored pictures of pies. Lupe giggled. "Yankees, that's all they eat. Pies."

Through all of this, Chole sat on her stool, quiet like a toad.

Chole had little to do other than make tortillas, rice pudding, and to fret boiled vegetables through a sieve. Doña Juliana's digestion could tolerate little else. The fancy dinners were years in the past. Other than Sundays, when there was a stew to cook for the relatives who came to visit, and Tuesdays, her at-home day when she wanted a cake and such for her visitors, Doña Juliana spent her days in the wing chair by the window, knitting baby sweaters for her grandnieces and grandnephews and the orphanage. Her house was dark, and the drawing room smelled of old leather and mildew.

But upstairs, on the top floor where the Iturbides lived, the furniture was all bright, the air fresh and sweet. Don Angel wanted chunks of raw coconut with lime and chili powder, *chilaquiles* smothered in a tomatillo sauce so fiery it could make your nose run, and raw pineapple spears and orange sections peeled and arranged in spirals and sprinkled with toasted walnuts. They had their walls repapered in mango stripes on sunflower yellow. And Lupe helped Doña Alicia hang the new drapes, made from cloth she had brought from her country. It was as soft as deerhide. The Iturbides had brought many things from her country: a piano, and a music box with a brass bee on its handle, and a grizzly bear hide, which they used as a rug in Don Angel's library, and, for the dining room, a wee fluted bell. Whenever it was time for Lupe to bring in the next course, or to clear the dishes, Doña Alicia would tinkle that bell.

Lupe often thought it must be sad for Doña Alicia to be so far from her country. When Doña Alicia arrived, her Spanish was no better than a child's. Doña Alicia did learn to speak Spanish, but at first, she was always having to ask, what was a word. In the market, Doña Alicia would point.

"*¿Cómo se dice?*"

Chícharos, Lupe would say for the peas, or *huitlacoche* for the baskets heaped with corn smut. Doña Alicia scrunched her nose at that, but Doña Lupe showed her: for the Iturbides' Sunday supper, she made Doña Juliana's recipe for *crepas de huitlacoche,* and Doña Pepa said it was the best dish she had tasted in many a year. *Crepas de huitlacoche* was, Don Agustín Gerónimo said, the most toothsome dish in Mexico.

Don Angel said, lifting his glass of wine, "*Exquisito,* Lupe."

And Doña Alicia said, "*Gracias,* Lupita."

Lupe bowed her head and bent her knees a little, too, for she felt sure, if she didn't keep her huaraches flat on the floor she would float to the ceiling! She murmured: *"Para servirle, niña."*

Niña: Child, that was how older servants called their mistresses, if they were fond of them.

Chole did not call Doña Alicia *"niña."* And Chole would have told Doña Alicia the wrong word, just to hear a Yankee use it, then she could laugh behind her back.

Ay, Chole was black as the inside of a goat and with a belly full of envy. Another person's envy, Lupe believed, could make a body wither up inside. Chole wore an amulet of she-goat hair around her neck, and for troubles with a certain cousin named Mariqueta, she paid a *bruja* for a *limpia,* a cleansing with a chicken egg. But the nuns had taught Lupe that these "superstitions," as they called them, were an invitation to the Demon. *Pray to Holy Mary, Mother of God, and on your knees, that is all you need to do.* They had taught her the magic words in the Divine Tongue of the Saints: *Santa María, ora pro nobis . . .*

Lupe did pray and with all her tiny might, and it seemed that, though it had been God's plan that she suffer, in her new life upstairs she was becoming ever more blessed. One day, Doña Pepa said to Lupe, "What do you know about babies?" Lupe, startled, answered, "All that God wants me to." Which is to say, nothing—but so it was settled: Lupe would be the nanny for Doña Alicia's baby. They named him after his grandfather, the Emperor Don Agustín de Iturbide.

Lupe could not remember when she had last held a baby. Always, even in the orphanage, her place had been in the kitchen. It surprised her: he was light as a rabbit. His squeezed red face looked like an old man's. She slipped her pinky beneath his fingers, so tiny, tiny. She had to share him with a *chichimama,* a wet nurse, but whenever her Agustinito needed his nappies changed, he came right back into Lupe's arms. How she could drink in his sweet milky smell. She would wrap him in a blanket like a little tamale in its husk, but she loved to lift the edge of it and press her nose to his down-soft, golden hair.

Whenever Doña Juliana saw him, her eyes turned tender as if she were gazing upon the Holy Child Jesus himself. "Good morning, Lupita," Doña Juliana would say warmly. She would lean over the perambulator. A wrinkled finger would emerge from the black lace mantilla to tickle his chin. "Who is this *pollito,* this little chick, is he Agustín, *chiquitín?* Is Lupita taking good care of my precious?"

"Yes, señora!" Lupe would chirp.

As he grew, Lupe's old arms became muscled. He soon learned to stand, shakily balancing himself by holding onto her skirt, and then, holding her hand, he could toddle. Soon Lupe had to chase after him. He had a blue ball, and he was forever sending it down the stairs. This child, Atín, he called himself, all she wanted to do was hug him, sweep him up, and kiss him. How his face became a sun! She loved this little boy with every last piece of her soul, more than she had ever imagined it was possible to love. If Atín wanted to have his cheese with the tiny bacons, that's what she made for him, and if he wanted to sing the piggy-toe song before bed, that's what they did, and when he became fussy and sleepy, in her arms she would carry him to his crib.

But now these arms must be hacked off—for Agustinito was being sent to Chapultepec Castle, and that was how the news felt to Lupe. She knew, without it being said, an old *galopina* such as herself could not expect to set her huaraches in that place. No, her heart was to be ripped out, thrown to the dogs! Lupe tried to keep herself from trembling, but this *susto!* Her soul had been shattered. She could feel the pieces beginning to scatter, float away.

Doña Alicia said, touching her shoulder, "There's no need to cry."

For her tears and sobbing, Lupe could not hear what Alice saying. *"Niña,"* Lupe said, pulling at her sleeve, "take me with you!"

"It's impossible." Doña Alicia had already spoken with Doña Juliana, she said. Lupe could stay right here, she had a place in the kitchen.

Under Chole? To scrub pots, to take slaps and beatings with a wooden spoon, after having been not only the cook to the Iturbide family but nanny of the grandson of Mexico's own king! Lupe's answer shot out of her mouth:

"I am going back to my village."

"I understand," Doña Alicia said. But no, Doña Alicia did not understand. Lupe had not seen San Miguel de Telapón in over sixty years. In truth, she was not sure it was a village; perhaps it had been only a *ranchería*, a few huts in a clearing. Aside from its name, Lupe remembered a stony pine-forested slope. She also remembered, dimly, watching chickens scratch among the shards of a bottle—from the post she was tied to by the ankle. A stooped old man would limp out back and chop wood, with a lot of noisy sighing and wheezing in between each swing of the axe. Always, she'd had a knot of hunger. At night, the howls of coyotes made her whimper. She did not know who this man was, if he was her father, or grandfather, or someone else. Even if she could find San Miguel de Telapón, perhaps not a soul would remember her. She'd heard that out in the country, the French (weren't these the Hebrews who killed Our Savior?) were burning villages, torching the cornfields, stealing animals, abusing women. They shot the men they captured. The countryside was a hive for bandits and guerrillas, and who knew which was which, or which was worse?

And at night, everyone knows, the open country is the territory of La Llorona, the weeping Ghost-Woman. The nuns warned the orphans, "Stay in your beds at night or else . . ." La Llorona's filthy, rancid shroud and long, tangled, wet hair drags behind her on the ground, though her ghost-feet do not touch it. She flies, eyes like black roses, wailing for her murdered children, searching for them, and with her long cold fingers La Llorona takes whomever she finds.

Now, hurtling through the rain-drenched night in the back of this jolting, fish-tailing wagon, Lupe's heart is beating like a hummingbird's, and her knees are jelly. She had been so proud. Is this why God is punishing her? Her one consolation—thanks to Holy Mary!—is that the driver of this wagon is a priest. Yes, a young, strong-looking priest with a bright gold tooth. She had asked him, "You know of San Miguel de Telapón?"

He'd given her a slow lopsided smile. "I know the whole country like the back of my hand, *abuelita*, little granny."

"Father, how many days' journey is it?"

"We will arrive when God wants us to. Go on, *abuelita*," he'd said, gesturing to the back of the wagon. "Get in."

She could not; she was too tiny. So the father lifted her by the waist and set her down among the boxes.

"What's in these?" she'd dared to ask before he closed the canvas.

He patted the side of one of the boxes. "Statues of saints."

He did not lie outright, but neither did he tell the whole truth. Alas, his saints, made of plaster, have no purpose but to be smashed, for they encase Yankee bullets, powder, and six dozen breech-loading carbines. This wagon driver is no priest—but El Mapache, the Raccoon, so called for the pair of black eyes, long since healed, that he been given in a brawl, right-hand man of El Tuerto (One Eye), the bandit chief who has lately joined forces with the Juáristas. Los Ciegos (the Blind Men), the bandits call themselves, because, as one of them had once joked, in the land of the blind, is not the one-eyed man king? Los Ciegos have dodged into the Sierra de Telapón, in the neighborhood of Río Frío. Word is, they're harassing an Austrian brigade, and since Sunday, they've looted the stagecoach twice.

El Mapache's mission is to drop the weapons cache at the Hacienda de los Loros, but, as he was informed by the Republican Army lieutenant back at the warehouse, after he'd loaded the last box onto the wagon, Hacienda de los Loros has been shelled and burned.

They were still standing behind the wagon. El Mapache had demanded, "When!"

"Two weeks ago."

"*Hijo de puta!* Son of a bitch." He put his fist through the side of a crate.

The lieutenant, moving his hand to the hilt of his sword, said, "You'll show some respect."

El Mapache rubbed his knuckles. He'd cut one of them open. "Yessir." It came out a hiss.

"And by the way," the lieutenant said, as with the tip of his saber he lifted the flap of the canvas off its hook, and let it fall, "the *contreguérilla* has hung seven of our men from the trees along the entrance road."

A grisly parade, and El Mapache might've rolled right up to see it, a fly to a smear of shit! Anger boiled up inside him. This lieutenant was thin in the face, and though a head taller, El Mapache could have beaten him in any fist-fight, any knife fight, except, maybe not with that saber. (El Mapache's speciality was the dagger, in the kidneys.) The tuft that hung from this officer's boyish chin was a sorry excuse for a goatee. But there was something about this officer, his ramrod bearing, his level-eyed gaze, that inspired El Mapache, grudgingly, and against all habit, to respect him.

The lieutenant slipped his saber back into its scabbard. "You'll keep your fists in your pocket."

"Yessir."

But now, the lieutenant explained they wanted him to haul the whole wagonload to a granary a league southeast of Orizaba—three fucking days past the city of Puebla! With the rains, the only way to get there is the stagecoach highway, patrolled by French Zouaves. A mission for a *cabrón*, was that what this lieutenant took him for? El Mapache answers to nobody but El Tuerto. He had decided, then and there, what he was going to do was haul the load to Río Frío, the first overnight stop for the stagecoach. There, in their camp deep in pine forest, he would meet with his chief. If El Tuerto gave it the thumbs-up, the boys could help themselves, and bury the rest. Answering to an officer who leaves his head up a donkey's butt, *carajo*, was that what being a Juárista amounted to?

"Listen," the lieutenant said, softening his tone. "It has to be done. If anyone can do it, you can."

The lieutenant was just buttering him up . . . but damn, it worked. And the Juáristas, El Mapache reminds himself, they're the ones getting money and Yankee arms. From San Francisco, boatloads of rifles and powder are coming into Acapulco, and then over the mountain trails through Guerrero and into the bowels of Mexico City, right under Maximilian's nose. The

French can torch every hut from here to the Pacific, they can shoot every man, woman, and child and pound all the cities to gravel, and the priests and the nuns and all their fancy *mocha* traitor-friends can help them do it—but the Juáristas, they're the ones who are going to win this game! And Los Ciegos are on the winning team.

"Down with imperialism!" El Mapache shouts into the rain. "Down with the white traitors!"

The old woman in the back of the wagon, shrieks, "What?!"

He shouts back at her. "Shut up!"

That shrimp of a granny: she said her village is in the sierra, two days up a trail behind Río Frío. San Miguel de Something-or-Other, it was Cuautit-lán to him, but he told her what she wanted to hear. She said she could cook for him, so he didn't think to ask her for anything, but she pulled out from her shawl a candelabra. Solid silver and more arms than an octopus. Who knows who she stole it from, but who gives a sow's tit, because silver buys bullets, and any one bullet might be the one to kill Maximilian.

The thought of that so-called emperor makes El Mapache clench his jaw and want to punch somebody. *That Austrian clown! Puppet of foreigners and papist lackeys!* He lashes the exhausted mules, yelling into the downpour, "You sacks of shit! Git!"

But for the rain and his own shouting, he does not hear the stagecoach powering up behind him. All of a sudden, the stagecoach's twenty mules and its great wheels thunder past, slapping out a confetti of sludge. His mules bolt right, and the wagon, careening, the boxes sliding, overturns into—he cannot see—

A ditch?

OLIVIA CANNOT UNDERSTAND

*T*he lion man promised Atín a new ball. Well, where is it?

But Atín wants his own one. His *blue* one.

The new nanny, Olivia, pulls his bunny, Mimo, from the hamper. She flaps the toy in his face.

"*Conejito.* Little bunny," she says. "You like your little bunny."

Atín gives the bunny a punt, and it skids beneath the chaise.

Olivia gets down on her knees, reaches under, and brings it out by its ear. "Here, your bunny!"

Atín's chin trembles. Where is his nanny Lupe? Mamma?

Later, he's been dressed in a frock and new shoes. They feel stiff on his feet.

Atín needs to blow his nose again; he breathes through his mouth. He does not like it when Pepa squeezes him. Her side is hard, that thing she wears has bones in it.

His nanny Lupe, she's the softest with her soft shoulders, her cotton white braids, and her nut-dark face. Her cheeks are like the skin of old apples. When she waggles his pinky, Lupe sings to Atín in her wavery voice, "*El bonito y el chiquito . . .* the little, pretty finger . . ." With her rough brown fingers, Lupe holds each of his in turn: "*El que lleva los anillos,* the one who wears the rings; *El tontito,* the silly one; *Ese que lame las cazuelas,* that one licks the cookpots." And when she comes to Atín's thumb, Lupe taps her thumbnail to his and she says in a man-like voice, "*El que mata los bichitos,* this one squashes the little bugs."

Where is Lupe? Why does he have to be all day with Olivia?
The stringy cheese again and without the tiny bacons: he screams.

Poor Olivia. And worse for her: it so happened, in her first moments inside the Imperial Residence, that she had witnessed the unlikely fate of Agustín's blue ball. She had been following the Mistress of the Imperial Household, who had hired her only the day before, after the most informal of interviews. Some German priest, a Father Fischer, had asked her family's parish priest to ask around, was there anyone with an unmarried daughter available to serve as nursemaid to Prince Iturbide? Olivia had applied as a lark; such a vague invitation was not the kind of leverage to hope for results, and anyway, her family knew no one who worked in the Imperial Residence, nor the Imperial Palace. When Olivia told her mother and sisters she had been hired, they could not believe their ears. *You?* Her mother said. *A position in Chapultepec Castle?! I'll have a stone for my breakfast!* They were sure she was teasing them.

And so, that golden morning, here she really was: her heart pounding and palms of her hands sweating so much she'd had to keep wiping them on her frock—her best jet-black bombazine. Tied around her waist she wore the purse embroidered with marigolds that her mamá had made for her, especially for this day, and she wore her granny's silver-and-jade earrings. Her granny had pressed this treasure into Olivia hands saying, *These were for you to wear on your wedding day, but how could I wait? We are so proud of you.* When Olivia went out the door, every member of her family had lined up to give her an embrace, including her little brother who, on other occasions, pulled her hair until she had to slap him.

For Olivia, to be here, inside Chapultepec Castle, was to have stepped into some fantastic dream. Never in all her seventeen years had she imagined that she, Olivia Pérez, daughter of an apothecary (her grandpa a mere herb-vendor in the market), could be the nursemaid of the grandson of the Liberator! Nor that Chapultepec Castle, which she had seen sitting atop its rock, every day of her life, could be so grand inside. *María Santísima,* this was waking up into a fairy tale, these urns as tall as a man, and masses of draperies, emerald green malachite dripping with gold, apple green velvet chairs from the emperor of the French, chandeliers of such staggering size! The chandeliers were Venetian, the Mistress of the Household said (whatever "venetian" was). It made Olivia feel faint to look up into them. The diamond-shaped droplets of glass tinkled slightly. And, *por dios santo,* what if they were to crash down in an earthquake?

Señora von Kuhacsevich was the name of the Mistress of the Household, and as it was a foreign name, Olivia did not dare attempt to pronounce it. Señora von Kuhacsevich had a mass of dyed curls beneath her lace cap, which squashed the coiffure like a pot lid on so much licorice. She minced along lugubriously; it appeared that Señora von Kuhacsevich's shoes pinched her as much as her corset. On a velvet cord around her belly (it could not be said she had a waist), she wore a bristling ring of keys; this swung alongside the pleats of her crinolines like a pendulum. She stopped often to catch her breath, or to right a lampshade that had been left askew, or with her toe, to nudge a small carpet back into place—all the while giving Olivia rapid-fire instructions in gutturally accented Spanish peppered with the strangest words.

"Here we have a carpet, of course," Señora von Kuhacsevich said, "but it has been sent out for *riparazione.*"

They were in the entrance hall, a black-and-white checkerboard marble expanse. Señora von Kuhacsevich had stopped at the foot of a staircase. It was the grandest staircase Olivia had ever seen in her life. The entrance hall was bathed in a chilly gloom, but this staircase, brightened by the skylight, almost hurt her eyes. Olivia, squinting, swallowed. Gooseflesh prickled her arms.

"Riparazione." Señora von Kuhacsevich said that word again. "Do you understand me?"

Olivia lied, "Yes."

Señora von Kuhacsevich shot her an irritated look. "Yes, what."

"Excuse me?" Olivia was afraid her teeth would start chattering; she hugged herself.

"You should say, 'Yes, *ma'am.*'"

"Ma'am. I mean, yes, ma'am."

Señora von Kuhacsevich pursed her lips. "And quit rubbing your arms. It is unbecoming."

Olivia would have liked to answer, *Unbecoming? And what do you know about it, you sausages-for-arms tub of lard?* Instead, Olivia fixed Señora von Kuhacsevich with an insolent mask of politeness, a barely-there smile. She'd had practice. As her grandfather, the herbalist in the market, often said, it did not pay the rent to allow rude customers to provoke you. Sometimes they were rude because they were in pain, or else God, in His Infinite wisdom, had made them soft-headed enough to not know how to treat other Christians, and the older they were, the less probable they would learn and better to pity such creatures and remember to praise God.

Olivia uncrossed her arms and murmured, "Yes, ma'am."

"Voilà!" said Señora von Kuhacsevich.

Olivia did not know that word either, but she followed the Señora's gaze to a little blue ball that was bouncing toward them, down the steps. *Benk, b-benk*—the ball gathered speed as it fell, bouncing high enough to skip two, three, six steps, until on the next to last, it shot slightly to the side, so that it hit Señora von Kuhacsevich on the exact middle of her bosom.

"Uf!" Señora von Kuhacsevich had caught it. She dropped it into her jacket pocket.

From above the landing, a child began to whimper.

Olivia's hand flew to her throat. "Is that Prince Iturbide?" *Of course you stupid girl,* Olivia scolded herself, but to her relief, Señora von Kuhacsevich had not heard her; she was mincing up the next hallway.

At the door to the Iturbides' apartments, Señora von Kuhacsevich, breathing heavily, set her plump hand on the doorknob and paused.

"Do you have a cigarette?"

"Yes, ma'am."

Olivia fished her silver cigarette case from the purse on her belt. To her surprise, Señora von Kuhacsevich took not a cigarette, but the case, snapped it shut, and handed it to a footman! With his white gloves, the footman turned it over, and over again; it seemed a mystery to him what he was supposed to do with it. "Ma'am?" he said to Señora von Kuhacsevich.

Señora von Kuhacsevich turned her back on him. To Olivia, she said: "Ladies do not smoke, and they would not dream of smoking in the presence of any member of this court."

The blood burned to Olivia's cheeks, but she managed to stammer, "Yes, ma'am."

"I see," said Señora von Kuhacsevich, "that we need to review some basics."

"Yes, ma'am."

"When addressed by a superior, you are to keep your eyes on the floor."

Olivia looked at the floor. "Yes, ma'am."

"You are not to speak to anyone, most especially to Their Highnesses, unless spoken to."

"Yes, ma'am."

"That includes Princess Iturbide."

"Yes, ma'am."

"No nosy questions."

"Yes, ma'am."

"No silly questions."

"Yes, ma'am, but what if—"

Señora von Kuhacsevich cut her off. "No questions!"

"Yes, ma'am." Olivia could feel Señora von Kuhacsevich's gaze boring into her skull.

"Unless for some reason you are summoned into their presence, you are to *evitare, evitare,*" Señora von Kuhacsevich said, sweeping her hands for emphasis, "encountering Their Majesties. If, despite your supreme efforts, you were to find yourself alone in the hallway when the emperor or the empress approaches, you must duck into the next corridor, and if that is not handy, then a closet—and indeed, any open door will do. If this were to happen in the garden, hide yourself behind a bush. You must be neat and you must be clean, and this means," she shook a finger at Olivia, "*every* morning, not just when it occurs to you, wash your teeth with a *spazzolino da dente,* and scrub behind your neck and below your jawline. Your hair must be without adornment, combed and pinned, up out of the way, no excuses. Jewelry must not be vulgar, no dangling earrings, such as you are wearing, do take them off."

"These?" Olivia brought a finger to her granny's silver-and-jade beads.

"*Ho fretta.* I do not have all day."

"Yes, ma'am." Olivia took them off quickly, for she feared they might be confiscated as was the cigarette case, and she tucked them in her purse.

And then, Olivia was presented to the Princess Iturbide—or was it acceptable for her, as did Señora von Kuhacsevich, to address the princess by her Christian name, "Doña Josefa"? Or, without exception, must it be "Your Imperial Highness"? Just, "Your Highness?" (Or was "Ma'am" alright?) And was Olivia supposed to curtsey to Princess Iturbide *every* time? This was worse than school lessons, too many names and rules to stuff into her rattled head! And nobody here wanted questions!

The prince, a red-faced brat, took one look at Olivia, and lay down on the floor and yelled louder than her pet parrot—what lungs! He needed his nose wiped, but he wouldn't let her get near him; he went on kicking his legs.

"Lupe," he screamed over and over, "I want Lupe!"

The day went by in a blur of frustrations. All through it, Olivia's stomach felt like it was going to somersault. She should have stayed at home, in her family's shop, helping measure out the powders and ointments, tinctures of laudinum and such. Her sisters were right, these were peculiar people, these aristocrats and nose-in-the-air foreigners. The likes of Olivia Pérez had no business being in Chapultepec Castle. But she was afraid to go home, for her family had been so proud of her. And they needed the money. On the other hand, she was afraid to stay, because she was certain—she could feel it coming, like cold water on the face—she was going to get fired. The question was, how soon?

An hour before vespers, Princess Iturbide said to Olivia, "Prince Agustín has lost his ball. It's gone down the stairs, I suppose. Tell one of the footmen to bring it up at once."

"Yes, Your Highness, ma'am," Olivia said. But she wondered, how in God's good heaven could a nursemaid, a servant on her first day, presume to ask the Mistress of the Imperial Household to give it back? (And the silver cigarette case!) Olivia badly wanted a cigarette, and in this country, ladies of even the highest rank had always smoked, if they fancied the taste. Olivia's mamá smoked! All of her sisters, and her granny enjoyed a cigarette after their meals. Madame Almonte and the general used to live just up the street from the shop—well, Madame Almonte smoked, too. *Era la costumbre.* It was the custom. And who was this foreigner, this Señora von Cucaracha, to tell her about that?

About the prince's blue ball, Olivia said nothing. Señora von Kuhacsevich never did bring it back. Why, Olivia wondered, would that lady want to keep his toy? He may have been a brat, but wasn't he just a little boy? It was a cruel thing to do.

What kind of people were these?

Olivia's eyes took on a hard shine; in her mind, resentment, fright, and confusion lashed as the wind that whipped the flag out on the terrace.

Señora von Kuhacsevich, or rather, as the Mistress of the Imperial Household thought of herself, Frau von Kuhacsevich, had a bundle of things on her mind. Her work, she frequently complained to her husband, was akin to being asked to push a wheelbarrow piled with sawdust in a high wind whilst juggling coconuts and a watermelon and fending off marauding monkeys! Once she had brought the nursemaid Olivia to Princess Iturbide's apartments, so as not to be late for yet another interview she'd hurried back down, all out of breath, to her office. Tucked in behind the pantry, it was a mean little room without much light, just big enough for her desk and a stool, a straight-back chair for visitors on business, and a shelf for the heavy leather-bound ledgers, a cuckoo clock, and the pie basket she used for the receipts. The wall behind her desk had a moth-shaped water stain that had, during this rainy season, spread into a very big moth indeed and begun to turn a greenish black at the edges. But she had covered this with a framed watercolor of orchids. It was an amateurish picture, but she treasured it because it had been given to her by the botanist, Professor Bilimek, one of Maximilian's favorites. Professor Bilimek was a Capuchin friar, and so shy that people laughed behind his back about how little he spoke, how he kept to himself, always busy, busy pinning butterflies, cataloging beetles. All the Germans who happened into her office remarked on this watercolor. They would say, "Professor Bilimek gave that to you, really?" And because she was a respected married woman, Frau von Kuhacsevich could answer with a smile and proudly.

Out the window, birds were being blown about in the sky, and in the distance, rain clouds draped like a filthy rag over the sierra. At the rate the clouds were moving, rain would arrive in a matter of minutes. This room smelled disagreeably sour. For a bit of air, she pulled the one small window in, just a crack. The receipts in their basket rustled.

She checked her schedule, which was pinned to a corkboard by the door. Interviews were marked with a red pencil. A candidate for the just-opened position of assistant pastry chef should have been here already. Well, with the rain, probably, he would arrive later, if at all. Heavily she sat down at her desk, and then, ignoring the calls of the cuckoo that popped put of the clock, dipped her pen in a pot of ink.

Meine Lieber Freundin!

She had just begun this letter to her dearest chum in Trieste, when a gust of wind pushed the window further in, knocking over her inkpot. *"Ach!"* she cried out in horror. Not only was a good quantity of scarce letter paper now ruined; ink had splashed her jacket. This was a costly turquoise blue chamois jacket, with toggles of carved horn that fastened with Chinese red froggings; she'd had it made the year she and her husband came from Vienna to look after Maximilian, a bachelor then, in Trieste. It had been meant to be worn over a bulky sweater; for this reason, it was one of the few articles of clothing she'd brought with her from Europe that still fit her.

For such a stain there was no remedy. *Ach,* and wasn't it just like everything in this waterlogged pesthole of an "Imperial Residence"? Frau von Kuhacsevich was sick to the teeth with this wind, the smell of mold in her rooms, mice droppings in every cupboard, her poor husband suffering with cramps and diarrhea, and the altitude—her lungs had not adjusted to it in a year and half. Having to trudge up and down, and up these stairs, oh, it was pure, wheezing torture! But worst of all was having to manage these lazy, thieving Mexicans. Did they think she didn't realize they were pilfering the candles and soap? It was going to cut short her days, and her husband's too. He was the Purser for the Imperial Household, a job for a Hercules! Whoever claimed Arabs were the best liars had not been to this country!

And bullfighting! Not only the footmen but the housemaids also went to that hideous Plaza de Toros to roar and cheer "Olé!" and toss around their sombreros, oh, they were as thrilled as Romans watching Christians being torn limb from limb by lions! As she'd already written to her chum in Trieste (and more than once)—for savagery, Mexicans outdid even Croats. And in today's letter, she had been about to write: *what's more, the new nursemaid to the little Iturbide came into the residence with a cigarette case! She has a hook-nose, a gap between her front teeth you could drive a team of horses through, and such a complexion she could pass for a gypsy—and this is the flower of the lot one has to choose from!*

Cork it, woman, her husband would say to her, the times she got going like this. *A bitter pill is better swallowed than chewed.*

With tears blinding her eyes, Frau von Kuhacsevich wrestled herself out of her ruined jacket and dashed the thing on the chair. Bitter pills, bitter pills, she was bone-tired of bitter pills. She swallowed them, by Jove, but she, who had no political responsibilities, should not have to lie about Mexico, that it was all sugar plums. She gritted her teeth. She yanked the bell for a servant.

In the Hofburg, a footman would appear before one could recite a *paternoster.* In Monza, when Maximilian had been viceroy of Lombardy-Venetia, it was the same as at Miramar Castle in Trieste, one never had to wait more than three minutes; more, and someone would have been dismissed. But here in Chapultepec Castle, it was just the same as everywhere, with everyone, about everything, in this pigsty: *¿Quién sabe?*

Rain had begun to spatter the little window. She couldn't help herself, she was weeping. She had no handkerchief! And why was that? Because the laundress had brought the handkerchiefs folded, but without having taken the trouble to iron them! Frau von Kuhacsevich, in a high dudgeon, had sent them back. She wiped her face with the back of her wrist, but that wouldn't do; she picked up a sleeve of the ruined jacket and pressed the chamois to her face, which only—oh!—it was so soft, such a turquoise blue!—made her sob.

She collected herself. Sniffing, she rang the bell again.

A year ago, she would have had the charity to pretend that no one had heard the bell because of the rain. Last week, when she wanted tea, she had ended up going down to the kitchen herself for it, and she nearly tripped over the assistant pastry chef, who had drunk so much cooking sherry he was conked out on the floor. Where was Tüdos, the Hungarian chef? Sick with diarrhea. And the rest? She got it out of that bleary-eyed Mexican: they were having a fiesta in a footman's room!

With these Mexicans it is *nada, nada,* and *nada. No hay,* there isn't any. *No sé,* I don't know. *Es la costumbre,* it's the custom. *Ahorita,* in a little moment—they hold up their fingers as if to show a pinch of salt—but Frau von Kuhacsevich had learned the correct translation of that: *Don't hold your breath.*

These people, they could not conceive the half of what she and her husband, not to mention Maximilian, had given up in order to bring civilization to their country. Gratitude? There was plenty of bootlicking around here, but not once did a Mexican express genuine, comprehending gratitude.

It would be good if . . . and she had been about to confess this in the letter to her chum . . . (she bit her lip at the catastrophic and lovely possibility) . . . that . . . Maximilian . . . might . . .

Abdicate.

God forgive her, how she longed to go home! To Trieste! Oh, to anywhere within the realm of the merest gloss of civilization! If staying with Maximilian meant being sent to live in Dubrovnik, or God help her, winters on Corfu—she *would* manage on Corfu—oh, yes, Corfu, broiling hot, full of Greeks and their oily food, but it was Greece! The very cradle of civilization! Land of Aristotle! Euripides! Socrates! What had these Aztecs come up with but barbarous piles of rocks carved with snakes and skulls? Altars to the Demon!

And it could happen . . . soon . . . Frau von Kuhacsevich had a cherrystone of a secret that she had been about to give herself the luxury of sharing, because she suspected that her chum in Trieste already knew. The gardens at Miramar Castle were open to the public on certain days, and so anyone in Trieste who took the trouble could go and see with their own eyes: Max was still constructing and decorating Miramar Castle.

For what possible purpose but his return?

It was her own husband, Jakob von Kuhacsevich, Purser of the Imperial Household, who was arranging the payments to the architects, decorators, and gardeners. Maximilian wanted eggshell white on the door trim and moldings, crimson damask on the walls and draperies with his imperial insignia, extra cages for the aviary, and four more loads of gravel for the drive.

What's more, Count Bombelles, head of the Palatine Guard, had let slip that Maximilian would be sending him to Vienna to renegotiate the Family

Pact. What a heartless thing for the Kaiser to have done, force his brother to sign such a document. In the Hofburg they were afraid of Maximilian, because Maximilian was so good, so capable, and dangerously popular, especially in Hungary. It was Franz Joseph's old fogey hardliners who had made a muddle of Lombardy-Venetia, *not* Maximilian—though they blamed him for it. The Prince Imperial, Rudolph, is a frail child, and the Empress Sissi such an eccentric sickly girl, she is unlikely to provide another son. And who is in line for the throne of the Austrian Empire, directly after Prince Rudolph? Maximilian! And if Prince Rudolph is made emperor, who would likely be the natural choice for regent? Maximilian! Ah, but not when they have cut him off with that "Family Pact." And after Mexico, if he were to return to Europe, could he have a future? Frau von Kuhacsevich had been bold enough to ask Bombelles. That little peacock puffed his chest out.

"I am going to Vienna to assure it," he said.

And now, to think of Trieste, and the good God-fearing people there, it made Frau von Kuhacsevich's heart break.

Oh, instead of these oceans of dusty cactus and corn stubble, what she would give to gaze upon the Adriatic again! The Hungarian chef, Tüdos, was doing his best, especially with the goulash, but oh, to be properly served an honest dinner of *Tafelspitz mit G'röste,* and cakes not with lard but with good German butter! A little spaghetti and a glass of Chianti. To sleep in a fresh sweet-smelling room, to find a mantua-maker who knows how to cut on the bias and stitch in a straight line, decent shoemakers, decent servants, priests who can say mass without making a mishmash out of the Latin, and to a congregation wearing shoes and sitting upright in pews, with proper respect for God. Here, half-naked Indians squat and loll in the aisles! When they fancy, they hack up a gob and spit on the floor! In Mexico City's cathedral, she has seen cats and dogs, too, running right by the chapel of San Felipe Mártir, oh, the Mexican curs are scabrous. Get a mile near them, and you are infested for life. Let that little Prince Iturbide have Mexico, yes, hand it over to him on a platter and with a solemn mass, tacos for the people, and with firecrackers, too! Let Princess Iturbide, she certainly appears capable, be named regent . . . And to run the charade, General Bazaine and Generals Almonte, Miramón, Mejía, Uraga—there are generals aplenty, like locusts in Egypt!

By the cuckoo clock, it was eight minutes before a housemaid answered: the same moonfaced girl Frau von Kuhacsevich had caught smooching the assistant pastry chef in a closet. Holding the jacket by her fingers as if it were a dirty rag, Frau von Kuhacsevich dropped it in the girl's arms. She had completely forgotten the little blue ball in its pocket.

"Do with this what you will," Frau von Kuhacsevich said coldly. "Do not let me see it again."

꧁꧂

ONE TAKES IT COOLLY

*O*ne takes it coolly, Maximilian reminds himself. But a woman cannot be told everything; how easily Charlotte works herself into a lather.

"When *he* was that age," Charlotte is saying, "the Child of France had a specially built-up seat for riding in the carriage, so that the people could *properly* view him. Letting the child *stand* on your knees, letting him *stumble* around like a ninepin, why, he could have been *injured*."

"He was not."

Charlotte stiffens. "The Child of France—"

"Enough!" Maximilian says, dropping his head in his hand. "One has heard quite *enough* about the Child of France."

They are alone in his study, facing the windowed doors to the terrace overlooking the Valley of Anahuac. The day's work is finished, and they sit, each in a chair, solemn as the deities of Memphis. It was years ago, on his first cruise to Africa, that Maximilian began to be religious about watching the sunset; here in Chapultepec Castle, it is like watching from aloft in a balloon: a luxury of sky. Miramar, "view of the sea" is the name he had given his castle in Trieste; Chapultepec, then, must be Miravalle. This stupendous valley with its lakes of molten silver, and the snowcapped volcanoes, Popocatépetl and Iztaccíhuatl, the one a cone, the other a sheered-off wedge: nothing in the Alps compares. For this alone, one would have come to Mexico.

Kein Genuss ist vorübergehend, No pleasure is transitory, as Goethe said. Each moment of life engraves itself upon Eternity.

"Bonbon?" He holds out the bowl of bonbons, *Brombeeren mit Mandeln*. It is a stunning bowl, orange red as a harvest sun, and curled around it, carved deep into the clay, a black caterpillar. The bowl is Totonac; possibly several hundred years old.

"Thank you," Charlotte whispers. She picks at the wrapper, but it has melted stuck.

"They are old," he says.

"Who?"

He looks at her as he would a dunderhead. He plucks up another bonbon. *"These."*

On the other side of the glass, the horizon, jagged with mountains, is paling, and the snowcaps of the volcanos tinged a fiery lavender, the exact shade, it occurs to Maximilian, of the inner lip of a *Phalaenopsis* orchid. For the past month, it has rained almost every afternoon, and sometimes all through the night, but this afternoon, the clouds, titanic puzzle pieces, have sailed apart to reveal a stretch of translucent ocean blue. To the east, a cloud bank soft as charcoal smudges the sierra; closer in, an island cloud shoots out swords of gold. The birds are coming in to their roosts around the lake in the park below. An eagle skims the tops of the ahuehuetes. In the distance, church bells begin to gong and chime.

A southern twilight: can there be anything in this world more sublime? Until coming up here to Chapultepec, "mount of the grasshoppers" in the Aztec language, one had believed that the *ne plus ultra* was the sunset over the Gulf of Naples, as seen from Capodimonte. The burning orb, the very eye of the Great Artist—Helios-Huitzilipochtli—how its setting sears one's thoughts with longing and the tender hope that one shall behold it again.

But to consider the next day, more meetings with the finance minister, and then that antediluvian, General Bazaine, one's stomach knots.

Bazaine won't say so, but he will consider this morning's carriage ride with Prince Agustín both a provocation and a serious miscalculation. One intended to content one's subjects, to impress upon them that the empire is securely anchored—to use General Almonte's words, that one's government is *not* a French puppet show! But, more likely, to Bazaine's crude way of thinking, the sight of the little Iturbide, who behaved no better than a jackanapes, served merely to remind one's subjects that, after eight years of matrimony, their sovereigns have not produced a child. The Juaristas have been spreading propaganda about syphilis, gynecological deformities, calumnies too vile to deign to think about.

But the worst was not that some rascal had the audacity to smack the imperial carriage with an egg. Nor that some lunatic was executed this morning for plotting to assassinate one (such things one must steel oneself for; it comes with the job). No, it was that the little Iturbide's American mother, having breezed through Río Frío and then spent several days in the city of Puebla, got the notion to turn around! And go straight to General Bazaine! That vain fathead, who is at this very moment, no doubt, mocking one to his officers.

The day before yesterday, one read Bazaine's letter, and that American Iturbide woman's, which Bazaine had enclosed (such pathetic whining! *Poor me*, and, *justice to my feelings*), and one quaked with anger. One threw down the both of them on the desk.

And then, that same afternoon, came another letter, from Agustín Gerónimo de Iturbide, the head of that family—a letter so audacious, so lacking in protocol, the penmanship so absurdly sloppy, one had to read it thrice, to believe it. Every word is pricked into one's brain.

Puebla, 23 Sept. 1865
To HM the Emperor, Mexico.

Sir

I don't know what's been YM's experience with these things, but mine are, it's better to take on 500 head of savages than an emotional and furious woman who wants her son back. My opinion is, YM should let my sister-in-law keep her son, for two or three years, rather than let her go all over the world with her accusations and complaints.

My recommendation for YM is, give her back the boy and keep her

nearby in an excellent establishment, one of those of which there are many in
this capital, and where I also would receive special relief.

    Sir, I am, with the most profound respect, YM's faithful servant,

A. de Iturbide

That insolent, indolent drunkard! And what, was he to have his brother, Angel, abandon his own wife? To think of it, one cannot help blinking. Where is *the sense?*

How dare that woman sneak back and show herself in this city. She wants two years with the boy, well, then she'll want three, and bloody likely she would change her mind again. Had not she, and all the Iturbides, signed a solemn contract? A contract signed of their own free will, signed by witnesses, stamped, sealed, a contract binding by law, because if that is not binding, by God, what is?

And, have they not each been awarded $30,000 cash and $120,000 in bills payable in Paris, plus generous pensions? $6,100 per annum! For life! Furthermore, have they not agreed, indeed expressed in written letters, their *sincere and immense gratitude,* that not only would Agustín be educated under one's personal tutelage but that the orphaned Salvador would be educated at Sainte Barbe des Champs? They have been honored in a public ceremony. And then, having signed that solemn contract, and twenty-four hours, in fact, *after* delivering the child to the Imperial Residence, that woman writes to Charlotte: *Having put my adored child under Your Majesties' special care, I am honored to offer to you, madame, my sincere gratitude and friendship.* And, the lot of them, one condescends to make Highnesses of one's empire, when what are they, after all, but the progeny of a trumped-up creole parvenu! No better than the Murat princes, indeed, descendants of an innkeeper. Revolutions extrude this sort of person.

What to do? This American woman's dishonorable scheming has made it perfectly plain that she does not have the moral character, nor the mental balance, to be a fit mother.

But, as ever, one *takes it coolly.*

One conferred with the child's aunt and governess, Doña Pepa, a well-educated and levelheaded lady; one is satisfied to condescend to address her as "cousin."

Doña Pepa, though deeply mortified, held herself with soldierly dignity.

Alicia, Doña Pepa stated flatly, *was like a child.*

"You would agree then, that she could be said to . . ." How to put it, one wondered, rubbing one's hands together . . . "Have a tendency to hysteria?"

Doña Pepa had not a feather of hesitation. "I would, sir."

Afterward, privately, one said to Charlotte, "My God, this is piteous."

Charlotte said, "The woman ought to be put in an asylum."

That was a repulsive suggestion. But what to do, what to do? Charlie Bombelles has gone to Vienna, to renegotiate the Family Pact. Father Fischer is away on a round of visits in the provinces. One's chancellor, Schertzenlechner, he advised arresting the woman like a common criminal. Schertzenlechner put his fist on the table. "Make her husband and his brothers come back for her, lock them up, too."

"And throw away the key?"

"Yes!" Schertzenlechner growled.

"And put them on bread and water?"

"Neither!"

One had a good laugh. Well, one is not bloody-minded. This morning, one had the Iturbide woman detained and returned to her husband and his brothers, who have been waiting, with all the bravery of a pack of hyenas, in the city of Puebla. One did not condescend to reply to those letters from the Iturbides; one had the Secretary of the Civil List convey the order that they are to depart the city of Puebla for Veracruz without delay; they are to board the steamship scheduled to leave on October 2. The secretary's letter concluded precisely as one dictated:

> *His Majesty the Emperor hopes that you will not put him in the unfortunate position of having to demonstrate to you that, if he is good-hearted, he also has the severity necessary for his role as Sovereign and his own dignity.*

La Sociedad will not print a whisper of this affair, but no doubt gossip is already festering. If only one's younger brother would accept to send a child to Mexico, and quickly—perhaps Franz Ferdinand, or the baby Otto . . . One feels confident one's family will accept one's magnificent invitation and, in so doing, rescind the Family Pact . . . but if not? It will look bad, very bad in Vienna.

Now, in the chair looking out over the valley, one puts one's hand to one's head and grits one's teeth. How contemptible it is to have one's mind thrashing around, a squirrel in a puddle.

"It is so beautiful," Charlotte says.

Mango has washed the sky. A pink streak deepens to the color of papaya. It's happened so quickly: her dress, gray with a sapphire blue trim, appears nearly black. With a slight drift of a smile, Maximilian twists the end of his mustache. "You do not like them."

"Who?"

"The *Brombeeren mit Mandeln.*"

Charlotte says, "I am sure I would have. I could not get the wrapper off."

She says something else, but Maximilian is not listening; he throws open the doors to the terrace. After the rain, the air smells so sweet—it reminds him of how, after the endless desert of sea, one sniffs that first, knee-weakening perfume of land. His hands rest on the damp stone of the balustrade. Below, a flock of starlings explodes from a tree as if commanded by a genie's wand. The air is staccatoed with birdsong. These Mexican sunsets, how they bring back Egypt, and the fiery sky from the Kasbah of Algiers. There is a peculiar quality in this southern evening air, a lightness, a quickness that excites the imagination. The Emperor Moctezuma, in his sandals of beaten gold and quetzal feather headdress, must have stood on this spot, surveying his realm. The Aztecs knew that Cortez was coming before anyone had seen a white man; their soothsayers had dreamed the future: the comet, then, the smoking ruin of Tenochtitlán. But the dreams confused time. They believed Cortez was not their destroyer but Quetzalcóatl, Toltec god and ruler, the feathered serpent, who had, at last, returned from the east. And so the Aztecs welcomed Cortez, as the Trojans their horse. The wonder of a sunset is that each is strange to the past, and will be forever unique to the future. The flock of starlings disappears into velvet scarlet; the beauty of it—one rests a hand on one's heart—is almost painful.

Charlotte has come out; one is slightly annoyed by the rustle of her skirts. But she also understands that these skies are a glimpse of God's glory. And how profoundly that glimpse provides one with the gentle passion of an ever-renewed sense of faith and peace.

But an hour later, on one's own narrow cot, one cannot sleep. One turns this way, arranges the pillow that way.

Does one appear ridiculous?

One should have followed Schertzenlechner's counsel and kept that Iturbide woman under arrest in Mexico, in the jail in the basement of the Imperial Palace. But what an appalling idea! One is a Christian; mercy, it is right to show mercy. Schertzenlechner is a pig.

Why, Charlotte is forever pestering one, does one suffer such low company as Schertzenlechner's? One answers her as the king of France once said, *"Je me repose."*

But ought one to have handed the child back to its mother? Bazaine did strongly suggest it. What a horrid, jelly-like tingling in the knees. But it was, the Iturbides signed it—every one of them signed a *solemn contract!* Never mind that, now they are going to take a steamship to *New York,* then to Washington, and then, arriving in Paris—they will make one's government ridiculous!

Tacitus knew it: *For he who would have an empire, there is no middle ground: it is the heights or the precipice.* One must maintain the steadiness of a tightrope walker. Rigidity, no; one wants balance, balance.

And this wavering, is this not precisely what tipped Lombardy-Venetia into revolution? Evil tongues say that the Kaiser dismissed one from that viceroyalty for softness, but it was not softness. Italian nationalist unrest was a dangerous matter, requiring perceptions far subtler than those ham-fisted old soldiers in Vienna could conceive—the Kaiser was blind as a mole to it, but one *had* set a wise and carefully calculated course for the viceregal government. What need was there to mow the opposition down! Brutality not only alienates students and workers, it frightens the businessmen, the money-men—those who most matter for a peaceful and prosperous realm. From Milan, one had tried to explain, telegrams, letters, but Franz Joseph had ears only for those sausage-for-brains generals. The pettifogging, slope-headed cretins! Hard-hides rigid as chain mail, with a sense of civil justice fitting for the eleventh century! It is one thing to be fond, as Franz Joseph is, of uniforms and military pageant (though what trite, ear-splitting little boy stuff that is)—but to take sole counsel of men for whom life is nothing but drills and sweaty soldiers in barracks—men who could not recognize Beauty, in any of its multitudinous forms, if the Madonna of Michelangelo's *Pietà* looked up, dumped the body of Christ on the tiles, walked across the nave, and slapped them across the cheek.

A good captain sets his course, and then he stays it. Batten the hatches, tacking as need be, but *stay the course!*

So . . . No, this morning's carriage ride was not a miscalculation; to the contrary, it was brilliant politics! As one's wise father-in-law, King Leopold of the Belgians, is fond of putting it, *We royalty have a job akin to a stage actor's. Put on the plumes, and every medal you can pin on your chest, stand tall, let the people see their sovereign. The more we give them spectacle, the more they love us.* Leopold goes so far as to have face powder and makeup put on him.

Ugh, pomp. It wears one to a shadow. One is content in mufti: a cotton blouse, peasant's boots, a straw hat, for walking where, with Professor Bilimek for one's sole companion, one is looked upon only by milk cows, or perhaps a solitary hawk.

The more one cannot sleep, the more keenly one desires it! The pillow this way. The pillow; hug the pillow.

The ballast of this ship—Charlotte said it herself—is the child. The Child of Mexico: like the Child of France, he should be sturdy, attractive, bright, and above all—and the time to begin is yesterday—superbly educated, both morally and intellectually. He must have Philosophy, History, Latin, Greek, and Sanskrit, as well as extensive study of Egyptian hieroglyphs (this will aid him in deciphering the Mayan), and Geography, and Mathematics, and Astronomy, Natural History, of course, Law, and Forestry. Lots of hiking in the fresh mountain air!

If one must make do with the little Iturbide for an Heir Presumptive, it is fortuitous then that, at this early age, he has been removed from such unsuitable parents. The clay, unbaked, is malleable. He will forget them, which is convenient.

It was quite right to show this child to one's subjects. If anything, in the course of these past days, one has been perhaps overly hesitant. After all, Franz Joseph made Crown Prince Rudolf a colonel in the army on the day he was born. That mewling little monkey with a diaper under his uniform! (Six years old and still a sickly and oversensitive child, one hears.)

The Child of France, now that is a beautiful boy. Before the last state dinner in the Tuileries, the little prince was brought out. He wore a moss green velvet suit and cream white satin collar and cuffs. But for the freckles, his face, dark eyes so somber, could have been painted by Caravaggio. Eugénie brushed his hair with her hand.

"Louis, tell Their Majesties about what you have been reading."

He looked up at his mother, lost.

Eugénie said, "Your picture book of Mexico, Louis."

He then recited a marvelously long list of fruits and vegetables. *Avocatl. Chicozapote. Garambullo. Maguey . . .* The prince bit his lip and searched the ceiling. One wanted to hold one's breath to watch him. *Mamey. Papas. Plátano . . .* He had such a serious, flute-like little boy's voice that it made one want to change every prejudice against the French into open-hearted laughter.

It is true: such a prince is worth more to an empire than a hundred chest-bespangled generals.

Louis Napoleon and Eugénie bring the Prince Imperial out to meet every ambassador, all the bankers, whatever military attaché. Crowds gather wherever his carriage passes, in the Bois, at the circus. He has his own escort of Cent Gardes. They wear helmets with white horsetails. Sharp. He has two pretty little spaniels, Finette and Finaud—oh! Why does one sink into such blistering nonsense.

Turn onto the other side. Elbow *not* under the ribs.

But the Yankees, what do they care, *they will not cross the Río Grande,* General Almonte says, and Bazaine, leaning on his elbows over his map, through his cloud of cigar smoke, says, *No, not if we continue to be careful to avoid any engagement.* But what are the Yankees up to, huddled there against one's back door? Waiting to swoop down on what they can, the pack of vultures. But if they were going to invade, Bazaine pointed it out, they would have crossed over from Texas last June. By July it was too hot. August! At that time of year the area around the Río Grande is hot enough—what did Bazaine say?

Bazaine said, *to fry the gizzards in a squawking chicken.*

What a ridiculous thing to say. Bazaine has a fat head, and such calculating, shifty Chinese eyes. Bah, he's a peasant. He has hair growing in his ears. How his little Mexican bride can stand him, there's a mystery. Bazaine with his vain blustering, as if, for having won a few battles, *he* were the sovereign. How it irks one, how it really oppresses one to have to treat with the likes of Bazaine, who has made his entire career in the Foreign Legion, that tattooed rabble of mercenaries, cutthroats, drunkards, and knuckle-draggers.

So now October has come around: cooler, but still the Yankees are camped, shoulder to the Mexican border, waiting to—

Reports have crossed one's desk that the Juaristas have been opening recruiting stations in New York, New Orleans, and San Francisco. Can it be true that Juárez has floated a loan to purchase armaments in New York? *(Can it?)*

There is no credit for Mexico, *rien,* one's French finance expert said, with his horse-jawed stare. He has a detestable habit of twiddling his pencil stub. Bean counters, how they make one groan.

Any credit in New York should be tied up with Reconstruction. And Americans are dog-tired of war. They've had enough bloodbaths: Gettysburg, Sherman's March to the Sea. They must be. *(Aren't they?)*

But don't forget, Charlotte pointed out, the Yankees, every chapter of their history has shown it, are rapacious for land. As the Mexicans say, they serve themselves with the big spoon.

Like that American Iturbide woman, yes, she wants to be a princess, she wants her pension, she wants her son honored, she wants her son to enjoy the education of a prince of the House of Habsburg, she wants the whole roast with gravy and champagne and a whipped-cream sweet, but then, *tra-la!* she trounces out of the place without paying. *So sorry, that was not quite the meal I wanted!*

One could strangle her with one's own hands.

One lies on one's stomach. One thrashes onto one's back. One kicks off the sheet.

What nuisances, those Iturbides . . . if they go to Paris . . . if they go to— God!—Vienna . . . ? Should one have Bazaine's Zouaves run out on the high- way and arrest the Iturbides before they reach Veracruz? Yes? No? One does not want to involve the French . . . General Almonte, he could . . . no . . . but maybe . . . before the Iturbides get as far as Orizaba . . . and then . . .

Despicable dithering! The decision has already been made: Let them go.

One tries lying on one's left side; knees bent.

With the Juaristas it is sliding into a war to the death. Every day the ani- mal savagery worse than the day before. Bazaine, like an old schoolmaster, lecturing one: *The guerrillas are criminals worse than animals, and Your Majes- ty's showing them mercy goads them on. They see you as weak. Your Majesty, if one has a saber, one must use it! Cut them down.*

One's own minister of war is pressing one to sign a barbaric Black Decree: *Anyone found with a weapon, shoot them like the vermin they are.* It is medieval what the minister of war is suggesting, the same game the French have been playing in Algeria—a crude conquest, nothing more. One saw it on one's visit there years ago, the way the sheiks bowed low to the French, but their eyes revealed the burning hatred born of humiliation. Here it must be different. One has been *invited* to Mexico to *serve*, and if one is to conquer anything, it is people's hearts, which one must achieve by Christian example and wisdom.

One must *stay* the course, stay the course, stay the course . . . God. Bol- locks. But the way it's going, one may end up having to abdicate. But unless that Family Pact can be renegotiated with the Kaiser, one cannot possibly go back to Europe. One shall certainly *not* go back to Europe with no pension, no position. One shall *not* be humiliated.

Rip the velvet glove off, your Majesty, and show the guerrillas your iron fist! Schertzenlechner agreed with the minister of war.

Father Fischer has been saying all along: *It is a Christian monarch's duty to crush the enemies of God.*

Other side. Fling that accursed pillow on the floor!

One has spoken with Professor Bilimek.

"Should one agree to let the *contreguérrilla*, in the name of law and order, shoot anyone found with a weapon?"

Professor Bilimek gripped the pole of his butterfly net in his hands and turned it around twice. Behind his spectacles, his small eyes grew round. "The Christian religion is one of love, not hate or vengeance. I beg you, in the name of all that is sacred on earth and in heaven, refuse such godless advice."

So . . . No.

Charlotte said, with the face of one who has been awakened from a dream, "It cannot have come to that."

No to butchery, because what has one brought this godforsaken country, if not Civilization?

One has not asked Professor Bilimek about the Iturbide situation. Why should one? It is a family matter and it is—*yes*—decided.

The Child of Mexico.

In the Tuileries, that last night before they left Paris, the Child of France said that he should like to visit Mexico.

Charlotte took his hand and patted it. She said, "We should be *very* happy to have you visit our country."

His beautiful face broke into an enormous smile, and he puffed his little chest. "I should like to climb its tallest mountain!"

Charlotte said, "The Pico de Orizaba is very tall, and you are very brave to think of it. One day I am sure you will."

Eugénie said, "Say good night, Louis."

"Good night," the little boy said, with all the seriousness of a Siamese ambassador.

Now . . . The Prince of Mexico is just as attractive a child—or more so, for he looks like a little Anglo-Saxon, golden haired and rosy-cheeked. (And he has healthy lungs, that's for bloody sure.)

Well, and has Bazaine not punched Juárez out of Chihuahua and right up to the U.S. border? One might as well claim that Juárez has abandoned Mexican territory—in which case Juárez could no more call himself "President of the Republic of Mexico" than President of—

One sits bolt upright. One shall proclaim it, let it be printed in *La Sociedad:* "JUÁREZ FLEES TO THE UNITED STATES." And, how about this morsel: "Juárez has set up his government in exile at . . ."

Oh, what, what, what . . . Santa Fe! Ha, that's better than a hundred warehouses packed to the rafters with gunpowder!

Those scoundrely Juaristas lob lies, well, one can smack that same ball right back! And on top of it all, yes, then it makes perfect sense: *Anyone found with a weapon shall be considered a bandit and may be shot.* One *shall* sign that decree.

But one is not bloody-minded. To kill or be killed?!

However . . . What if . . . this decree were to soften up Juárez, make him see that there is nothing in it for him but to come to terms with one's government? This brass-knuckled punch—or, an open-armed welcome for him and his sympathizers? To tame a beast, one must first feed it. One shall offer Juárez a nice, fat, polished apple. Why not—for, he is reputed to be a talented lawyer—the presidency of the Supreme Court?

Ah ha! As ever, one has the wings to soar above mundane paradigms. Charlotte has always said, *You are a man who was born to govern.*

And Charlotte, as ever, is right: one must tell Kuhacsevich, straightaway, to procure a child's seat for the carriage.

꠵

HER MAJESTY, EN ROUTE
TO YUCATAN

*A*t highway's edge a burro lifts its head from a feast of hay. Through a stand of eucalyptus, sunlight splinters the tile roof of a stable. A broken wall, a broad yellow meadow, and Mexico City, distant shining domes, disappears.

Like startled crows the days have flown off; already the year has plunged into an unusually chilly autumn. In a chocolate brown frock she has not worn since two winters ago in Vienna, her shoulders swaddled in a mink-trimmed cashmere shawl, coiffure snugly fitted with a black velvet cloche, and her face behind its veil, Her Majesty the Empress of Mexico—en route to Veracruz, from which port she shall depart for Yucatan—proceeds into the mountains over a highway that is badly rutted. It has not, evidently, been improved. These jolts could knock the teeth out of one's head, and this pace, *pour Dieu,* would try the patience of a Saint Marina!

Equally atrocious, communications have been flowing at the speed of cold treacle. Telegraph lines have been strung through these mountains and down over the hot lands all the way to the Gulf at Veracruz, but even when none has been cut, or a pole or two knocked down or bombed, messages can take hours longer to arrive than they should, because a number of the operators hold them up. On at least this one thing Her Majesty can agree with General Bazaine: a good number of them are Juaristas. They ought to be hauled out and shot. And then, the steamships from La Havana, New Orleans, New

York—and the one from Saint Nazaire? The mailbags might as well be set-ting out across, as Max so aptly puts it, a lake of oblivion.

Last night, the eve of her departure, she had received the Belgian consul's wire from Veracruz (sent more than *seven* hours previously!) that the *Man-hattan* had docked, and the *New York Herald* reports that King Leopold of the Belgians has fallen gravely ill. But of what? Is it his lungs? Kidney stones? The news is four weeks old. Perhaps by now, *à la grace de Dieu,* Papa has re-covered and is at this moment at his desk in Brussels, working through his dispatch boxes. But for worry, she could not sleep, and this morning, her eyes aching with exhaustion, when she should have been thrilled to be setting off, she feels like a watch on a fob, swung this way, then that: Is Papa well? Is Papa dying?

Has he been poisoned?

It was also yesterday—not until then!—that the mail that had come on the packet from Saint Nazaire *ten* days previously, finally arrived in Mexico City. Letters from Paris were dated mid-October; those from Vienna and Trieste as long ago as September 27—ancient history! And oh, would that among all that flurry of paper there had been one jot from Papa.

Her face behind her veil flushing with shame, she thinks how deeply, how horribly wrong she was to have complained in any way about Papa's letters. She had always found reading his handwriting a trial ("such scrawls, it might as well be Urdu," she'd snipped to Max). That last letter had taken Max the better part of an hour to decipher. Back in August, Max had queried Papa, what would he think of paying agents in Washington to spread word of how splendidly things are going? Because to Max, and his minister of foreign af-fairs, it had seemed a capital idea to counter the Juaristas' propaganda, which is prejudicing not a few members of the U.S. Congress against recognition of the empire, when that recognition would be so nourishing for the trade and investment that Mexico desperately needs. U.S. Secretary of State Seward, a New York lawyer with the nose and all the manners of a macaw, has been rattling his sabers with the "Monroe Doctrine," an absurd assertion that the United States should hold sway over the whole of the Americas! Papa had answered Max, *In America the only thing that counts is success.* But then, Papa's handwriting did look something like Urdu. After she had squinted at the letter a very long time, it seemed to her that Papa might have written, *Everything else is poetry and a waste of money.*

But in yesterday's mail, no word from Papa, and the only letters from family and friends were a nasty surprise. They were all in a twizzle about Max's October 3rd Black Decree, that anyone found with a weapon can no longer be considered an "enemy combatant" and may be shot. Well, what is Max supposed to do, coddle terrorists? His October 3rd Decree was *entirely* justified, as Juárez had abandoned Mexico (anyway, it is credible to claim so, it will happen any moment now) and therefore, these people have no business bearing arms. Bandits and murderers, vermin, they should be shot! Max's responsibility is to *save lives.* His October 3rd Decree was the only responsible course of action! This is the sad reality of necessity in Mexico. One has tried, one has truly tried to convey in one's private correspondence the nature of the evils of this terrorism, which is so pernicious, so similar, really, to the kinds of things France itself has had to confront in the past. Alas, one's talents are unworthy of the task. In his letter Uncle Joinville, who has a habit of reading liberal newspapers, wanted to know, what was this "atrocity," as he called it, 450 so-called "bandits" shot by firing squad in Zacatecas? One is fond of Uncle Joinville, but that was an impertinence.

And Grand-maman remains flustered about the honors Max conferred upon the Iturbide family back in September, and also, Grand-maman once again made a lot of hurtful criticism about, of all things, one's having appeared "dripping in diamonds" and wearing "a sumptuous scarlet and gold robe" for the ceremonies on Max's birthday. That was a *thousand* years ago, and had one not made it *abundantly* clear in one's previous letter, that these were the same diadem and same cloak, that old mended thing, that one wore when one was vicereine of Lombardy-Venetia? The trouble is, Grand-maman is a touch forgetful sometimes. And she has never supported the Mexican project. Grand-père's abdication and their having to flee for their lives gave her too thin a skin. When they first arrived in England, Victoria invited them, but Grand-maman never could bring herself to go out on shoots, she was that rattled by the cracks of the guns. When the bagpipes start up, Grand-maman cringes and makes up excuses to go inside. Her sensitivities seem to

have become more delicate over the years. Before sailing to Mexico, in Claremont, one had hoped, at the least, for encouraging words and glasses of
champagne—but Grand-maman offered only tea. Grimly, she pleaded,
"Don't go, you mustn't go." She had scolded and argued, and in the end, she'd
grabbed Maximilian's sleeve. "They will assassinate you!" After they took
their leave, as a cousin wrote, Grand-maman had had to be helped up the
stairs; she had collapsed on the chaise on the landing, sobbing. That was
really malicious of that cousin.

Marie-Antoinette, that Habsburg relative from the time of powdered
wigs, she may have shirked her responsibility to God, caring for nothing beyond card games and jewels, frivolous days away in her Petit Trianon. But
Charlotte—Carlota—granddaughter of King Louis-Philippe of France,
daughter of King Leopold of the Belgians, consort of the genius Maximilian,
she is a modern sovereign, fully in her realm. Mexico: raw as meat. Every day,
without fail, Carlota goes out among her subjects, touring orphanages, or a
school, a hospital, a house for prostitutes rescued from the street, cripples,
and yes, lepers. She has fanned away flies that would land on her gloves as
thick as fur. She has eaten fiery-hot *guisados* of God-knows-what glopped
onto tortillas. She is a nun to service! No peacock, no girl-child becharmed,
as she may once have been, by baubles, flattery from flunkies, and cheers of
"viva!" Without mercy, she has beaten down the snake heads of her vanity.
Why cannot one's intimates, and most of all Grand-maman, recognize that,
on whichever side of the ocean, for pity's sake, newspapers *profit* by *entertaining* their readers with *manufactured* novelty! It is to be *expected* that reporters
will describe one's robe, and each jewel, however many times they've seen
them, as if they were newborn wonders.

As for the honors Max conferred on the Iturbide family, she had *already*
explained to Grand-maman (in precisely the words Max had approved) that
it was nothing more than an act of *justice* to provide *protection* for the family
of a dethroned emperor, who are, in any event, not of royal blood. An infant,
Agustín, is being educated under Max's supervision; an older cousin, Salvador, has been sent to the college at Sainte Barbe des Champs near Paris; the
parents (who, after their many years in the United States, have, unfortunately,
degenerated into gamblers and drunkards) will also go to Paris. A daughter of

that emperor, a spinster, has agreed to serve as her little nephew's governess. Aunt and nephew have been provided with apartments in the Imperial Residence, but this is merely *temporary*, until something suitable can be arranged for them in Mexico City. *C'est tout dire*, that's all there is to say! But Grandmaman sends back questions, questions, a plague of questions. *Do you have any idea how this appears? What is this really about?*

It is about the one thing Charlotte will never tell, not to Grand-maman. Not to anyone.

She could be gotten rid of. This idea, which had been lapping, agitatedly, at the edge of her mind suddenly crystalized last spring, on the Hades-like day they visited the island of Martinique—first land after seventeen days crossing the Atlantic. She had expected things would be different now that she and Maximilian wore crowns. She had fought for his going to Mexico so valiantly because she was fighting for so much more than a crown. For these many years, Maximilian had avoided her. A monarchy required an heir, obviously. But on the crossing, Maximilian did not visit her cabin, not once. If she approached him, he turned to converse with someone else. When she touched his hand, he withdrew it. As soon as they were finished with work, he disappeared below to play billiards with his favorites, Bombelles and Schertzenlechner. If she found him later on the deck, he made an excuse to go to the library; if she followed him there, he needed to go to his cabin and lie down and rest. She had not been able to forestall the abomination of his having to sign that Family Pact—but she had drafted a well-founded and eloquent protest, had she not? She was loyal, oh, she loved him valiantly, why, *why* was he so rejecting?

Years ago, her older brother Leopold had warned her, *Maxie is an odd fish, a Narcissus, an Icarus.* But to Charlotte, not at all! When they first met, she thought Max the most romantic prince, so refined, so cultured and worldly, and—this made him stand far above the others—capable of the most profoundly noble sentiments. He was in mourning for his betrothed, their cousin Princess María Amelia de Braganza, daughter of Dom Pedro of Brazil. Delicate as a porcelain rose, she had died of consumption on the island of Madeira. Max wore a ring that encased a lock of her hair. He showed it to her: a curl as golden as an angel's—for María Amelia was an angel, he said, and when God had called her, it was to her only rightful home. Max had made a solemn pledge never to remove this ring.

"Not even when you bathe?"

"Not even when I bathe."

This was a man who deserved total commitment. If he was viceroy of Lombardy-Venetia, she would go there and serve him. If he wanted to go botanizing in Brazil, well, her heart sighing, she would be his Penelope. She had wanted to join him in Brazil, but, as she had suffered from seasickness, by the time they reached Madeira, Max had determined to forbid her to continue on. He gently kissed her on the forehead, "It would be too risky for the mother of my children."

"But I could help you with your botanizing!"

"Professor Bilimek will manage."

For Charlotte, those winter months on the island of Madeira were almost unbearably lonely. It often rained. In the mornings and evenings, fog drifted over the cliffs. Of course, she visited the grave of María Amelia. She went inside the house where María Amelia had died. She went into the bedroom. She sat on the edge of the bed. Every Sunday she went to mass where María Amelia had attended mass. And when she took the host upon her lips, Charlotte could not help thinking, this had also passed *her* lips. And so with Madeira's wine, with the garlicky fishballs, with every spoonful of muscovado sugar stirred into her tea. The air, always, smelled of cold ocean. Black moods poisoned Charlotte's days—but these, she chided herself, were the portion of a sinner whose felicity had been secured by the death of another.

When Max returned from Brazil, bronzed and muscled, she threw herself into his arms, her face wet with tears of happiness. That night, overcome, she said, "Please, for me, take off that ring." There was enough light in the bedroom to see that he had begun to twist and pull at it; finally, it came loose, revealing a white circle of skin. But then a peculiar look stole over his face. He pushed the ring back down.

"Never," he said, and he turned his back. He curled up small.

"Forgive me." When she touched him, he flinched as if stung. She lay in the dark as still as a corpse, listening to his ragged breathing.

She said again, "Forgive me." She touched his shoulder. "Max?"

He got up, sweeping his robe around him, and left the bedroom.

That was in 1860; since then, it seemed that a bed shared with her was to him as a bed of scorpions.

Because she had not made that voyage to Brazil, Charlotte's first experience of the tropics was Martinique, when they first disembarked at Fort-de-France, to take on coal and provisions for the rest of their journey to Mexico. She had smelled the tropics long before she could make out the buildings and wharves of the so-called petit Paris of the Windward Isles: a perfume of sugar and rotting vegetables, at once alluring and repellent. The town's central plaza was banked by thickets filled with so many chattering birds that guano carpeted the pavement. There was nothing to do but walk on it. In the middle of that plaza stood a marble statue of Martinique's most famous native, the Empress Josephine. A widow with two grown children, she had aided the little Corsican artillery officer in his meteoric rise, but soon after he made himself emperor, as Josephine was too old to provide sons for his dynasty, he divorced her.

The governor's wife, a mite of a woman in a muslin turban, prattled on about this statue, the only artwork of note on the entire island. Although an army of Negroes went on fanning the party with palm fronds, the air, a Turkish bath, was maddening: Charlotte could feel it cooking her brain. Heat shimmered up from the pavement. The statue, though pocked and splotched with tropical fungus, was almost too bright to look at. The men, scarcely interested, scowled at it and mopped their brows. Monsieur Eloin worked his handkerchief around the inside of his collar. Beneath his floppy yellow hat, Professor Bilimek's cheeks burned an alarming red. Frau von Kuhacsevich held her arms out, the better to take the breeze from the fans. The little plot of earth that surrounded its pedestal had been freshly planted with roses, but already the sun had burnt them. Several hung in clumps; brownish petals littered the dirt. As all the world knew, Josephine, née Rose Tascher of Martinique's Trois-Ilets Plantation, had been beautiful, the toast of Paris, despite her blackened teeth. But as an empress who could not bear her emperor sons, she had known what was coming. She had gone around telling everyone she was going to be poisoned.

The governor's wife said, "You wouldn't believe the slanderous things people say about Josephine, even today on this island."

Bombelles gave a wicked chuckle.

The marble face, whose blind eyes were impenetrable with shadow, faced the water. The sea drummed in. It insisted: *Divorce or poison. Divorce or poison.* Charlotte—Carlota—her sense of herself so uncertain—squeezed her eyes shut, trying to push those words out of her head. But they had found purchase.

In the distance, clouds cast shapes over the sierra. Agave, cornfields, a roadside chapel with its cross knocked askew. In the carriage Carlota adjusts her cashmere shawl and squeezes her eyes shut. It is *so* vexing, so very much more than one had imagined, to be unable to see one's family, to kiss dear Grand-maman's papery cheeks, to take her hands in one's own—and Papa? *Cher* Papa. Carlota's eyes brim with tears. Her two ladies-in-waiting, Señora Plowes de Pacheco and Señorita Varela, cannot see her face through the veil; Carlota therefore allows the tears to slide down her cheeks. Two, then three, splash hot on her wrist. The voice in her mind hisses: *For all that is at stake, your pissy personal problems are insignificant.* Why must one be a glutton for this putrid self-pity! *Putrid, putrid, you glutton, you stinking sinner.* She must stop: *Stop it.* Mortify the flesh. Sliding a hand into her sleeve, she probes for the softest part of her arm and pinches, hard. She swallows a sob, which she imagines is camouflaged by the violent rocking of the carriage.

"Ma'am?" Señora Plowes de Pacheco leans forward from the opposite bench.

Carlota swivels her head to the sound of the voice. She tries, when she feels unmoored, to pretend she is Eugénie. Serene, beloved, wise. She must be as impervious to pain as Joan of Arc. She must have the rectitude of Queen Victoria. The courage of Mary Queen of Scots. Cleopatra . . . done in by the venom of an asp! Marie-Louise de Bourbon, queen of Carlos II, last of the Spanish Habsburgs, ten years without child, all of a sudden lost her finger-nails. Cholera, they said it was, but her body did not decompose. *Tlapatl,* so much better than arsenic, it erases the appetite while it deranges the mind. *Mixitl* constricts the throat and causes the tongue to crack. *Nanacatl* in a spoon of honey promotes one to fly—off a cliff. There are myriad ways to get rid of a queen.

"Ma'am, are you not well?"

Through the blur in her eyes and her veil, Her Majesty regards her lady's face, its forehead creased with worry.

She studies the brooch at her lady's throat. It is Her Majesty's own por-trait, ringed with silver rosettes.

On the seat, cookie crumbs bounce.

"Ma'am?" Señora Plowes de Pacheco says again.

And does not the *Reglamento y ceremonial de la Corte* make it abundantly clear, that it is a gross breach of etiquette to initiate communication with a sovereign?

Her Majesty's voice is polished marble. "It feels stuffy in here. Be so good as to open a window."

In the last and meanest of the dozen passenger carriages of Her Majesty's convoy, her wardrobe maid, Mathilde Doblinger, worries, can Charlotte be warm enough in the mink-trimmed shawl? Every now and again, depend-ing on the curve the road takes, above the pines, there appears the hump of shining snow. Mathilde herself wears only a boiled wool jacket over her che-mise, but she's plenty warm, squeezed in with these seven of the Mexican chambermaids. Mathilde thinks sourly, Frau von Kuhacsevich said it, these people sound like parrots crazed on coffee, *Yakita-yakita-yakita.* Her chin on her knuckles, Mathilde looks out at the dust churned up by the other car-riages. To the rear follow some fifteen luggage wagons, all piled precariously high and covered with canvas. Mathilde had supervised the loading of Char-lotte's wardrobe trunks. It is but one of the snags in her daily work, having to treat with these brick-headed Mexicans who cannot understand, a wardrobe trunk must be loaded *upright*. The Triestini, Mathilde had given up for hopeless, but these hateful, tobacco-spitting, chili-chomping numskulls! She'd lost her Spanish along with her patience and shouted at the foreman, *Aufrecht! Aufrecht!* Upright! And this never-ending thundering of hooves: forty French Zouaves are escorting Her Majesty's party, but Mathilde could believe they were a hundred or more. Each carriage has a pair of soldiers sitting up on the box with the driver; at least a dozen ride in brisk file along either side of the imperial carriage, and uncounted numbers more ride two abreast along the edges of the highway—if these rutted tracks can properly be called that.

At a turn, the highway opens into a broad, marshy meadow skirted by pine forest, and the Zouaves up front, at a full gallop, fan out. Three, then five break off, their scarlet trousers billowing back over their horses' flanks, and their weapons, rifles, sabers, bandoliers, flash with sun—until they are swallowed into the trees. They are forever reconnoitering.

Mathilde has kept a sharp eye out for bandits, but all she has seen are goats, and a few Indians trudging along, bent double under the loads strapped to their foreheads. Up top, a luggage strap has broken loose; it begins slapping against the window, with each jolt, like a snake. *Slap, slap.* Dust coats the front of her apron, however often she brushes it away with the little clothes brush she keeps handy in her pocket. To protect her lungs, Mathilde presses the sleeve of her jacket to her mouth. Enough with this dust-filled window; already she has seen more of this country than the Devil could shake his tail at. Or have a notion to.

Mathilde Doblinger's people are Germans, and that is that. A big-boned woman with mouse brown hair, she has the forgettable features of a clerk one might find behind a counter in a provincial shop. Mathilde is not a friendly person, but she has become closer to the other Germans on the staff than she would have in Europe, where the differences in rank would have put an uncrossable gulf between them. In Vienna, the likes of a Mistress of the Imperial Household would never have deigned to sit at the same dining table with a wardrobe maid! Here they are lonely, they want to speak German and complain. The one thing Mathilde will not miss this month is Frau von Kuhacse-vich's nonstop blather about food.

"*Ach*, Matty . . ." Frau von Kuhacsevich's shoulders sagged the other day in the staff dining room when they were served *arroz con leche*, Mexican-style rice pudding. "At home, it is still the season for plum tarts . . . Do you re-member, Matty, in the Obersalzberg, the *Reisauflauf* with whipped cream and cherry syrup?"

Mathilde could feel Frau von Kuhacsevich's yearning eyes upon her as she tucked into the *arroz con leche* with her spoon. It was watery with raw egg white. As far as Mathilde was concerned, food was fuel, and if it did not make her sick, she was glad to have it.

"Tell me, Matty, what do you miss the most?"

Mathilde hated that Frau von Kuhacsevich called her that. She an-swered: "Beer."

"Yes, the beer . . . Oktoberfest . . ."

As Frau von Kuhacsevich would have it, in Austria, the veal was more tender; in Austria, the carrots sweeter; in Austria, the sauces milder yet more flavorful. Oh, the *Backhendle* and *Schnitten* and *Guglhupf!* Frau von Kuhacse-vich was always complaining about Mexican food, but this did not stop her from eating it. In a month's time, Mathilde thinks, Frau von Kuhacsevich will have to have yet another wardrobe made for herself. And with the seam-stresses here? Good luck!

With the carriage now running downhill, the springs make ear-splitting squeaks and squeals. A bottle rolls up the floor; one of the chambermaids kicks it, another kicks it back, and they giggle. Every one of these underbred girls wears the dangling earrings Frau von Kuhacsevich has expressly forbid-den. Brazen they are! Mathilde cannot follow the thread of their chatter. She could care a cruller why they laugh when they do. *Planchar*, iron; *botones*, but-tons; *tijeras*, scissors—Mathilde has learned the Spanish she needs, and not a word more. Her father was valet to an archduke of the House of Habsburg. What this *meant*, such as these could not begin to understand.

She feels as if she has endured ten lifetimes in Mexico but, in fact, it has been only a year and five months. She had arrived on the *Novara*, with the rest of the imperial retinue. From Veracruz, they had traveled to Mexico City on this same stagecoach highway, and so, she has already seen and suffered every inch of it. But she does not remember the pine forest being so black. It reminds her of the Vienna Woods. Scattered along the roadside are the little flowers that might be edelweiss, but their leaves are longer, tapering, like daggers. She should like to ask the names of these flowers, but the girls have begun singing and clapping. It's enough to make one stuff wool into one's ears. *La go-lon-drin-a!* (clap clap) *La go-lon-drin-a!* And then, the road slopes, the carriage tilts—another eruption of giggling—and that luggage strap starts slap-slapping at the window again.

It is strange to be headed so far as Yucatan, and on the way, be traveling back to the beginning, to Veracruz. With a shiver, Mathilde remembers those last days of May 1864, when they got their first sight of that fetid port. As they approached it from the Gulf, for some time they had seen the Pico de Orizaba—it floated, a chunk of soap upon the sea. Gradually, it rose into the sky until it appeared to be a snow cloud. The horizon was sand, and then, slowly emerging, buildings that appeared to be blackened along their rooflines. On shore, sand swirled into ghost-like clouds. Frau von Kuhacsevich's bonnet flew off and was lost in the wake. In a sudden gust, Charlotte's parasol flipped inside out. The mechanism had jammed; Mathilde hurried inside for another parasol, and when she came back onto the deck, they had all been set upon by biting flies. From the fortress, the guns had begun to boom; the *Novara* had been recognized. Smoke drifted over the water. Tüdos, the Hungarian chef, even as he slapped away flies, began sketching like mad. Soon, with the air still shuddering from the cannons, they were cruising near the fortress' ramparts, blackened blocks of coral, rising sheer out of the harbor, astreak with slime. From the battlements, soldiers shouted "Viva!" and threw down bouquets, most of which fell on the water. Metal gray harbor water swirled by, and ropes of kelp, an apothecary bottle, and a dead seal, its bloated belly glinting. Waves peeled back over shattered hulls, splintered boards. By this time in her service to Charlotte, Mathilde had seen many harbors—Trieste, Ancona, Civitavecchia, Funchal, Fort-de-France. Not a one was such a ship's graveyard as this horrid Veracruz. And what was that blackness atop the buildings? Another, louder church bell began to clang, and the blackness peeled up like a strip of felt. Rising into the sky, it became a flock of huge black birds. Their metallic-sounding cries chilled Mathilde to the bottom of her soul.

Charlotte asked, "What is the name of those birds?"

Professor Bilimek was about to answer, but he deferred to Maximilian, who said, lowering his field glasses, "*Zopilotes.*" He slapped a mosquito on the side of his neck. "Turkey buzzards."

Those filthy, gruesome birds, they took the starch out of her! And to see her expression, Maximilian laughed!

Now, November, past the height of the yellow fever, they say the hospitals in Veracruz are still filled. The boys die of it right off the troopships. And they are carried in from the fields shivering and delirious with malaria. They die of gut-worms, gangrene. No one in their right mind would set foot in that pesthole unless it be to board a ship and depart at full steam—which they will, for Yucatan. As for that province, Mathilde imagines a Hades-like jungle crawling with vipers, scorpions, leeches, and as Professor Bilimek told Frau von Kuhacsevich, a species of salamander that can grow to the size of a cat.

Why does Maximilian send Charlotte to these places when he did not allow her to accompany him to Brazil? It was no place for a white woman, he told his new bride, and left her alone for months on Madeira. But the rules have changed. Maximilian snaps his fingers!

Frau von Kuhacsevich says the reason Charlotte has to go to Yucatan is that Maximilian cannot risk leaving Mexico City, and if the expedition were to be canceled, Yucatan could break away from the empire. Do not believe it, said Tüdos, the Hungarian chef. No, Frau von Kuhacsevich said, it is *not* true, it is a *total* lie that Maximilian is planning to abdicate. "That's right, Matty," Frau von Kuhacsevich said, "the rumors that Bombelles is going to Vienna to renegotiate the Family Pact with the Kaiser, so that Maximilian will have a position when he returns? Mischievous slander! You don't believe that tripe, do you?"

"Didn't say I did."

Frau von Kuhacsevich had helped herself to a second piece of flan. She balanced the jiggling wedge upon her knife blade then let it fall, plop, to the plate. "You can be sure, Matty, such stories are concocted in the headquarters of General Bazaine." Now she eyed the bowl of whipped cream. "*Ach,* I shouldn't . . ." Frau von Kuhacsevich took a heaping spoonful. "But you know . . ." Frau von Kuhacsevich looked up and down the kitchen. They were alone. "You know . . ." She leaned forward and lowered her voice, "General Bazaine is a thief."

Mathilde sat on her hands and studied her own scraped plate. It would be unwise to say anything; but less wise to say nothing.

"Well, he's French."

"Right as rain you are," Frau von Kuhacsevich said, the French are jealous, and this and that and blah, blah, blah. *Did this woman ever give that tongue a rest?*

It is not a wardrobe maid's place to question, never mind getting into discussions of matters above her station—but this, too, worries her. What will happen in Mexico City where, for more than a month, Maximilian will be alone? With Charlotte away, Mathilde wonders, by protocol, won't Princess Iturbide be the highest-ranking female personage and so take Charlotte's place at the imperial dinner table? Princess Iturbide will have every opportunity to weave a dangerous swath of influence. Mathilde imagines, for a pucker-lipped moment, Princess Iturbide stuffed into her fish-scale moiré, standing by Maximilian's side, receiving ambassadors.

Maximilian's valet, Grill, heard it from his coachman, and he told Tüdos, who told Frau von Kuhacsevich, that the Iturbide brat's mother, a half-mad American, had changed her mind, she wanted her boy back, and so she went to General Bazaine to stir up an intrigue. Maximilian had no choice, Frau von Kuhacsevich explained; he'd had to have the woman detained. If that story is true, Mathilde thinks, then, it is strange Maximilian keeps the little boy—unless, Maximilian really does mean to make him his heir. But Tüdos said that, the way he heard it, making the child a prince and bringing him into the residence was not what it might look like, that it was "five birds and a stone."

"I do not understand," Mathilde had said.

Tüdos had shrugged. "I wouldn't try to make soup out of it."

A palace is a hive; a worker bee must do her work and take care not to fall into the delusion that she is in on the half of what is really going on. Nonetheless! Mathilde Doblinger does not have to eat the whole pig to know that it's pork. For Maximilian to bring that Iturbide infant into the Imperial Residence is an insult to Charlotte's womanhood.

It is strange that Maximilian keeps his distance from his wife, Mathilde has always thought so. Charlotte is so fetching, and he, clearly (anyone can see the way she looks at him from across a room), is the all in her life. There is some seam between those two that has not been properly stitched together. There is something off in the cut of the fabric of their matrimony; it does not hang right. Charlotte has not been eating. Last week, Mathilde began moving the buttons and hooks on her dresses, a lot of work, especially as she has no one to help her—that is, no Mexican she could expect to do the job to her standards.

But worse: Charlotte has been pinching herself again. The other morning, when Charlotte lifted her arms so that Mathilde could lace her corset, on the tenderest part of her inner arm, there were two livid bruises. She makes these where her clothing can disguise them. But when Charlotte realized Mathilde had seen the bruises; she tensed and pulled her elbows in. She lifted her chin, regarding herself in the mirror—no, not herself. It was something behind her. Mathilde turned around. There was nothing there but the closed door.

Mathilde has heard the news that arrived last night on the *Manhattan;* Frau von Kuhacsevich tattled about King Leopold's illness to everyone. Here, on the other side of the sea, Charlotte is so far from those who truly love her and might console her. And warn her: it is courting danger to so overwork herself, the charity works, the teas, *tertulias,* dinners, tours—and now, this expedition to Yucatan! It will be killing.

Maximilian expects too much of his young wife. He does not see the appalling strain he puts her under. No one will tell him the truth, except, perhaps, Father Fischer. Father Fischer is the one person on earth whom

Mathilde would confide in, but he has not yet returned from Rome. Early this morning, in the hallway, before leaving, Mathilde found herself alone in the vestibule with Frau von Kuhacsevich, and in her anguish for Charlotte, Mathilde very nearly said something. But she reminded herself, the von Kuhacseviches are not Charlotte's, but Maximilian's people. Mathilde Doblinger is no Judas. She keeps her eyes keen, her ears pricked, and her lips buttoned.

The road disappears beneath a swollen river, then it reemerges, dangerously soft with sand. The Zouaves lay down planks. The mules, dripping water, creep forward, straining under the whips.

In the afternoon, one of the empress's luggage wagons overturns, but is righted.

Later, nearing Río Frío, a stag leaps between two carriages. From his mount a Zouave takes a rifle shot; the bullet chips a cypress.

In the gentlemen's carriage, the Belgian ambassador observes, "*C'est maigre.* It's thin."

"*Ni valió la bala.* It wasn't worth the bullet," says the Marquis de la Rivera, the Spanish ambassador, and thus, like the expert horseman he is, reins the conversation back into Spanish.

The one member of their party who cannot converse in Spanish is Monsieur Eloin, the empress's Belgian advisor. Sandwiched between the two ambassadors, his silver cane across his paunch, massive head bent forward, Eloin goes on napping. Facing this trio, his back in the direction of their progress, is Mexico's foreign minister, Fernando Ramírez, who is glad indeed that Eloin has nodded off, for, though Ramírez speaks passable French, having to converse in it leaves him a wrung-out rag. And for General Uraga, seated to his right (wooden leg stowed beneath the bench) French is an even greater mountain to climb.

It is a relief to Ramírez to dispense with at least some of the diplomatic formalities en route—court dress, for example (how the collar of that uniform cuts into his neck, and he can never get his hat's ostrich plume to stay up). Eloin had made fun of him and the Belgian ambassador for showing up this morning in identical hounds-tooth and thick-soled boots. The marquis, who sports English riding boots, had brought a sack of oranges. The peels litter the floor and their scent sweetens the air made chokingly acrid with cigar smoke. They've launched into debating again.

"*El problema*," the marquis is saying, in such a low voice that he pulls all but the slumbering Eloin toward him, "is that Louis Napoleon is under increasing pressure to bring the troops home—"

"There's pressure," the Belgian ambassador interrupts, "but—"

"Louis Napoleon's back is against the wall," the marquis counters, "politically and financially. Honor and glory, bringing peace and prosperity, the civilizing mission, without support in the Legislative Chambers, it's a fart in a windstorm."

"But!" The Belgian ambassador leans out, around Eloin's bowed head, to wag a finger at the marquis. "By the Treaty of Miramar—"

"Hog slop." The marquis flashes his beautiful teeth.

Ramírez says nothing but removes his spectacles and, furiously, wipes at them with his handkerchief.

"That is a dim view," the Belgian ambassador says coolly, sitting back in his seat and crossing his arms. He pushes out his bottom lip. "But I grant you, militarily, Mexico has been a tougher nut to crack than anyone anticipated."

The marquis slides his eyes away to the window. "Unlike a certain *paternal figure*, I do not view the situation through a glass of pink champagne."

"Paternal what?" General Uraga barks.

"Champagne! I do hope someone brought some!" Ramírez slaps his knee with a hearty laugh. He's willing to make himself the Punchinello. *A certain paternal figure*—Ramírez understands perfectly: the marquis means King Leopold of the Belgians, Her Majesty's father, and the Mexican Empire's single steadfast ally in Europe, other than Louis Napoleon. All Belgium has done is ship over a few hundred volunteers (such greenhorns that, in their first major engagement, eight officers were killed and two hundred men were taken prisoner), but the goodwill of King Leopold, the very Nestor of Europe, is no minor thing. And neither should the dignity of its ambassador and of Mexico's sovereigns be besmirched.

The marquis looks like a harmless little peacock, with his short legs encased in boots, his manicured hands, and a comb-over that does not in the least disguise his freckled pate. But the Spanish ambassador is an intimate friend of the Countess of Montijo, mother of Eugénie. The marquis's words in French ears could be exceedingly damaging.

It strains him, but Ramírez goes on with his pretend-nonchalant bonhomie. "With all this shaking, why, any champagne on board might explode!"

Eloin jerks awake, his cane clattering to the floor. *"Quoi! De quoi parlez-vous?"*

And so, the conversation reverts to French. As the road winds through pine forests, General Uraga says nothing, and Ramírez little more than that, as Eloin, the Belgian ambassador, and the marquis ramble through the cost, positively criminal, of importing photographic equipment; whose wife owns the superior collection of cartes de visite, and is it better to collect circus performers, actresses, or opera singers; the quality of the Algerian stallions as compared with those of Andalusia; and, apropos of bizarre accidents, the marquis swears that once, out front of a café in Valletta, on Malta, he saw a midget, a dead ringer for the Crown Prince of Prussia, flattened by a flower cart that had careened down a hill out of nowhere.

But through it all, laughing, puffing his cigar with the others, Ramírez remains alert to the chilling fact that the Spanish ambassador has spoken, however briefly, so brutally. Although the marquis directed his comment to his Belgian counterpart, the barb was in fact aimed at himself, Mexico's minister of foreign affairs, as he is the senior official in Her Majesty's party. In Veracruz, the marquis's letters and reports will go into the mailbags for New York, Cadíz, Saint Nazaire. Spain is out of this game, but its ambassador's assessments of Mexican affairs will be widely read, including in the Tuileries.

Certainly the marquis will report that General Bazaine has been unable to defeat the guerrillas, whose attacks are escalating. Curfews and rhetoric have not done a damn. Almost every day an ammunition depot is blown up, train tracks pried loose, telegraph wires pulled down, mules stolen, caches of pistols, food, blankets, hospital supplies commandeered, patrols ambushed and slaughtered. There are so many murders, stagecoach holdups, bank robberies, kidnappings, it has become impossible to discern whether a given act was perpetrated by a criminal or a guerrilla, and the more so because now even little street thieves will proclaim for Juárez when it suits them. Maximilian's plans for foreign investment and colonists are fantasies if a man cannot expect to arrive in Mexico City with his life! A wasps' nest of bandits infests the sierra around Río Frío—the first overnight stagecoach stop on this highway to the coast—and in all this time the French have not managed to knock them out of there. What has been widely reported in the foreign newspapers is true: at Mexico City's Hotel Iturbide, the *mozos* run out to meet the stagecoach with blankets, because it frequently happens that the passengers arrive mother-naked.

In the diplomatic realm, one crucial step is proving stickier than Ramírez anticipated: recognition by the United States. Soon after the French took Mexico City, Mr. Corwin, the U.S. minister, was recalled. Then Mexico's minister to Washington, bringing Maximilian's personal letter to President Lincoln, was refused an audience. Carlota's letter of condolence to Mrs. Lincoln was returned unopened. This so-called Monroe Doctrine is a term now on everyone's lips. (Ramírez had to explain it to General Uraga, who at first could not believe it. Never in his life, the general said, could he have anticipated that even a Protestant people would lend their support to Juárez's so-called republic—a regime on their own border that stands for anarchy, institutionalized robbery, and the wanton destruction of the Mother Church.)

As for himself, like General Uraga, not long ago Ramírez had been leaning toward the liberal cause, for the idea of foreigners occupying Mexico was distasteful to him. As time went by, however, he had come to the conclusion that Mexico was not ready for democracy. Perhaps in another century. What Mexico needed was a firm hand. Mexicans squabbling among themselves were helpless before the United States—which would, sooner or later, attempt to expand its territory further, at Mexico's expense. About the French, one had to be realistic. As General Almonte put it: "Better this devil than the other one." General Uraga was more vivid: "If you cannot knife your enemy, bring him close, kiss his hands." And surely, once the French have set things to rights here, then the United States will recognize that a monarchy is the most natural form of government for Mexico, and a stable prosperous neighbor is in their best interest.

In recent weeks, however, Ramírez has had many an occasion to reconsider what he heard, last June, in the garden at Bazaine's wedding, when Angel de Iturbide insisted: *The United States are going to be no friend to this empire.*

The brothers, Agustín Gerónimo and Agustín Cosme, well, someone shot the dots off their dice. But Angel is an experienced diplomat who had resided many years in Washington. After the U.S.-Mexican war, he served as the secretary of the Mexican legation there, indeed served as its head, for it was some time before the ambassador, General Almonte, could be sent up from Mexico City. Scarce few men could have had their finger more on the pulse of things in Washington than Angel de Iturbide. Ramírez realizes now he should have given Angel's comment more credence. But at the time, it had seemed a prophecy so outlandish, so peevish, so—?

What *was* this arrangement the Iturbides made with Maximilian?

Ramírez himself witnessed the signing of the secret contract in Chapultepec Castle; his own signature is on that paper. But more than two months later, he remains befuddled. Honors and pensions are always welcome, but to hand over one's flesh and blood? How could Angel and the mother, a young American, have put their names to such a thing? And, to boot, agreed to go live abroad?

The single time that Maximilian mentioned the matter, it was to instruct that the Iturbides' status be "as that of the Murat princes to the Emperor of France." Ramírez had nodded sagely, though he hadn't a clue what Maximilian was talking about. *Murat? Murat princes?*

Fortunately, the Grand Chamberlain had an *Almanach de Gotha*, which, discreetly, and on another pretext, Ramírez could consult. Joachim Murat, he learned, was a French officer who, in the time of the revolutions, had married the sister of his comrade Napoleon Bonaparte. The coincidences were so extraordinary, they verged on the supernatural: Murat, as Iturbide, was a military hero. Murat, as Iturbide, was not of royal blood (Murat, son of an innkeeper; Iturbide, son of a wealthy provincial creole). Murat was crowned king of Naples; Iturbide, king of Mexico. Both abdicated and then, on an ill-advised return from exile, were captured on a beach and executed by firing squad.

And there was more: the portrait of Joaquim Murat sent a shiver down his spine. The man could have been Iturbide's own brother: the thick masculine sweep of hair, the high collar, the expression of active genius infused with hapless ambition, eyes forever fixed upon some star invisible to mere mortals.

Very, very peculiar . . .

The Murat princes, descended from Napoleon Bonaparte's sister, were therefore first cousins of Louis Napoleon, who was the son of Napoleon Bonaparte's brother Louis and Hortense (who was, by the way, the Empress Josephine's daughter by her first husband, the Viscount Beauharnais). Oh, these labyrinthine genealogies: just thinking about them makes Ramírez remove his spectacles and massage the bridge of his nose.

So, now, Ramírez's conception of the arrangement with the Iturbides is that it was Maximilian's way of forging a stronger alliance with Mexico's clerical party and distancing himself from the French, who are arrogant and increasingly unpopular. Ramírez categorically refuses to believe it, but Eloin, among other intimates of the imperial couple, has conjectured that Maximilian adopted the little Iturbide as a lure. The idea, supposedly, is that Maximilian's younger brother, Archduke Karl Ludwig, will become jealous and so agree to provide one of his sons to be Mexico's Heir Presumptive, and apparently, the Kaiser will approve, as it would keep the throne of Mexico for the House of Habsburg. It is a steadying thing for a monarchy to have an heir, but why the hullabaloo? Carlota is young and in blooming health. There are those who whisper that Maximilian suffers from a venereal disease, those who claim he is impotent, others, that Carlota—*tsk,* Juarista swill. Ramírez dislikes gossip. It makes him feel dirty and disloyal to his sovereign.

His Majesty is a visionary man. Well Ramírez remembers the morning, now many months past, when he was summoned to the Imperial Palace and led, not to His Majesty's office, but—the billiards room! Maximilian was not in his customary cut-away coat, but a general's uniform and gleaming boots. There on the game table's felt lay an enormous map. It had been painted on the back of a tablecloth.

"Behold the Americas," Maximilian said, and with the tip of his cue, he tapped the city of Washington, which was (Ramírez had to bend over the table to get a closer look at the letters) quite a bit further south from New York City than he had realized.

"You see, the United States, the North." Maximilian then swung the cue down to the other end of the table. "The Brazilian Empire, the South."

Ramírez had hurried to the opposite end of the table and bent down to see, yes: *Río de Janeiro*. Through his spectacles, he squinted at the letters beneath the point of the cue. *Petropolis*. This, he knew, was the hamlet that had grown up around the summer residence of Dom Pedro II, Emperor of the Divine Holy Spirit, the cousin of Maximilian and Carlota.

Maximilian said, raising the cue, "And the center?"

Ramírez considered the map. It was spectacular with color: the mountains cinnamon and russet-red, the valleys emerald and fern green, deserts tinted orange; the Pacific and Atlantic Oceans indicated with a wash of aquas. Above Canada the *glâce flotante* was represented by icebergs and spouting whales. At the bottom, below South America's curling tail at Tierra del Fuego—

Ramírez was distracted for a moment by the ingenious little crowd of orange-footed penguins.

The middle of it all? Of course! Ramírez pushed up his spectacles. "The Mexican Empire."

"No."

Across the expanse of the table they stared at one another. Maximilian's blue eyes were laughing. Then with the cue, in the air above the map, Maximilian drew an enormous circle encompassing Cuba, all of Sonora, Chihuahua, Lower California, the Revillagigedo Archipelago, and the isthmus of Panama.

"Behold, the new world power, the Central American Empire. A Habsburg empire in the heart of the New World." Without warning, Maximilian tossed him the cue.

"Uh," Ramírez said, as he caught it.

"And what will be the anchor, my minister of foreign affairs?"

"Why, Mexico City, sir."

"No."

Ramírez blinked. He felt his spectacles slipping down his nose.

"The anchor—" His Majesty leaned over the table and placed his fist on Mexico's fist-like peninsula—"is Yucatan."

"Yucatan?"

"The Egypt of the Americas."

Yes, the Yucatan peninsula was known to have some pyramids left by the Mayan Indians but . . . "The *Egypt?*"

It took time for Ramírez to comprehend His Majesty's vision, but it was brilliant, farseeing. Yucatan with its sisal hemp plantations could be richer than Georgia, Mississipi, and the Carolinas combined. It would be the anchor of the empire—or, another way of seeing it, Yucatan, as the hub of the Caribbean, could serve as a counterweight against the encroaching United States.

Yes, Yucatan is rich, but it is also a tricky customer, as His Majesty was ready to learn. Its Divine Caste, as its aristocratic families call themselves, is not invariably loyal to Mexico City—not long ago, they tried to break apart and join the Republic of Texas. The Maya have revolted in bloody rebellions. The Yucatecs could remain happily in the fold of the Mexican Empire, but it would take a personal visit from their shepherd. That is, both highly skilled diplomacy and His Majesty's personal prestige.

Working closely with His Majesty, Ramírez had planned the expedition down to the number of luggage wagons, the imperial gifts (two hundred monogrammed silver watches and four hundred monogrammed silver brooches), the seating arrangements at the state dinners, the speeches, the supplies for the fireworks—a thousand and eleven details. But over September and October, the military and political climate in Mexico deteriorated, and Ramírez was seized with dread. Medicines, meat, and charcoal every day became more dear, and in Mexico City itself Carlota had been hissed in the streets.

His Majesty's expedition to Yucatan could be fatal for the empire. With the emperor absent from the capital for an entire month, the Juáristas would claim he had gone back to Europe; there could be rioting, looting, murder in the streets. But what if Ramírez were mistaken?

It was not his place to question his sovereign—or, was it?

His heart told him, *Tell His Majesty the truth.* But was it the truth? His wife had chided, *You sound like a defeatist.* As Tacitus warned, *Impunitatis cupido . . . magnis semper conatibus adversa*—the desire for escape, that foe to all great enterprises. Was he being "defeatist"? There were numerous and very complex considerations. Nonetheless, expressing his concerns now could make him appear weak, even traitorous. To put it bluntly, to speak up could cost him his position in the cabinet. Then, without power, how could he help his country? Ramírez agonized, he prayed to God, what to do?

The day of departure approached. Maximilian was showing no sign of hesitation; on the contrary, at every meeting he enthused about the collecting he would do for Professor Bilimek's Museum of Natural History, the ruins he would explore, have surveyed and photographed. The pyramids of Uxmal interested him especially, and every time the subject came up, he recalled having climbed the Pyramid of Giza. In earlier stages of the planning, Maximilian had cannily weighed the various political and economic concessions to be granted to the Yucatecs, but now, he seemed lost in fanciful dreams.

Ramírez could no longer bite his tongue. He requested a private audience and was granted a quarter-hour, just before His Majesty's luncheon with the Austrian ambassador. He was ushered in; Maximilian, seated at his desk, did not look up. Ramírez tugged his waistcoat down. With his heart a stone in his throat, he waited for the signal that he might speak.

Maximilian was surrounded by a swirling halo of smoke. He had been reading a book. The desk was littered with bonbon wrappers. *Brombeeren mit Mandeln:* he had taken to keeping them in a Totonac bowl encircled with a sinuous, lobster-like caterpillar. It had become a gentle joke in the court that one knew one was in His Majesty's favor when he offered a bonbon. He did not offer one.

Maximilian took his cigar from his lips and held it in his fingers. "Yes?"

"Your Majesty, I urge you, sir, to postpone."

"Luncheon?"

"Sir, I mean, the expedition to Yuc—Yucatan."

"For what reason," Maximilian said, without expression.

Ramírez felt a knife of fear slice from his gut to his ankles. He stood at his usual respectful distance of about two and a half meters, but to stress the life-and-death urgency of this matter, he willed himself to take one step closer to the imperial desk.

"Sir." Ramírez cleared his throat. "With all due respect, sir, the situation, sir, I mean, politically and when the people see your, the imperial coach heading in the direction of Veracruz—um, sir, they may say, sir—"

"My good man, get it out!"

Ramírez whipped off his spectacles. "Our emperor has abandoned us! You see, he is going back to Europe!"

Maximilian puffed his cigar. The space between them had filled with smoke. A fly buzzed at the window. On the ledge, ninepins of pigeons. From the Plaza Mayor below, confused trills of music and shouting. This was it, Ramírez thought: he was going to get the axe.

"The empress will go to Yucatan in my stead."

Ramírez was so stunned by the wonderful simplicity of this solution, he did not know what to say.

"I entrust the empress, and the expedition, to your hands."

"Sir!"

"I am confident that you will do nothing less than superb work."

"Thank you, sir." Ramírez bent over in the deepest bow he had made yet; so low, that, after the style of General Almonte, he let his hands rest on his knees.

Maximilian brought his cigar to his lips, but instead of inhaling, he yawned. "That is all," he said, and he opened his book and, with a flick, began leafing through it.

Ramírez bowed once again and walked backward out of the imperial office.

Now, in the carriage nearing the first overnight stop at Río Frío, Ramírez has not quite adjusted himself to the idea that such a young consort might replace the august presence of the emperor. Carlota, as a matter of fact, is the same age as his youngest daughter-in-law. It is one thing to preside over palace balls and court ceremonies, to look and act the part, chatting prettily in seven different languages with the awestruck guests . . .

Nonetheless, Ramírez recognizes, Carlota has a man's stamina. He has seen her riding through Chapultepec Park (something no respectable Mexican señora would do), and he has seen her sit for hours with an iron-mask of politeness, listening to eye-crossingly boring speeches. Carlota is a worker, tireless and diligent worker, an excellent helpmate to His Majesty. The day will soon come that the Mexican Empire shall sit astride the saddle of the Americas, strong, prosperous, united, and peaceful.

Ramírez thinks of his grandchildren. They will live in a Mexico transformed; not the one he has despaired for, where he has had his friends and relatives murdered, kidnapped, knifed, and bludgeoned in the streets, where he has lived all his life in a house locked down and barred like a fortress, and that anyway, in the last revolution, had a cannonball bash through its roof and kill one of the maids. His Mexico is one where, year after year, one has trembled for one's life to go out at night, or onto the highway—only fools and renegades venture onto a highway unescorted. His has been a Mexico without honor, a Mexico where no property is safe, the mine shafts abandoned to fill with water, fields to lie fallow, and the patios of once splendid haciendas left charred and overgrown with weeds. A Mexico that would murder its Liberator. This Mexico of the vainglorious Santa Anna, who would attend a cockfight before troubling himself with the matters of the nation, who would stand by and allow Mexico to be violated, dismembered, sold to the highest bidder. Thank God for Maximilian! Thank God that Mexico, at last, has a Catholic, European prince to rule it! Ramírez's prayer is that he may live to one day tell these dear children how their own *abuelito* traveled to Yucatan with the Empress Carlota.

With his sleeve Ramírez rubs the fog of his breath from the window. In midair a falcon chases two tumbling sparrows. They are coming into the highest country now; the men have been drinking cognac from flasks to keep warm. The road cuts across a pasture dotted with white goats and then it winds down another mountainside in a series of hairpin turns, switchbacking beneath the telegraph wire. The outriders lean far back into their saddles. On the steepest parts, some walk alongside their mounts. Ramírez wonders whether, from deep in that darkening forest, bandits are watching their progress. Another turn in the road, and smoke from the inn's chimney rises from the pines like a finger into paling sky. Down its length, the valley of Río Frío is drowned in a weird blue light.

A CHILL IN THE AIR

After so many sleeps the world has turned, Pepa explains, rotating her hands as if she were holding a ball between them. The terrace shines with dew. Then she lifts Atín, so that he can see over the railing something important.

"Po-po-ca-te-pet-l. You can say it."

"Po," Atín tries. And he sees the other volcano too, its jagged crown blazed white as a cake's frosting.

"*Es nieve*. It's snow. If you climb way, way up there, you could touch it, and it would feel cold."

Atín knows that word. Once his mamma gave him a spoonful of green *nieve*. It tasted of limes as it melted on his tongue.

"*Corazoncito*, little heart," Pepa says, kissing his hair, "you are my clever boy."

A strand of her hair plays across his cheek. Far below beyond the treetops, down in the park, stretch the fields. Broad patches have faded to yellow. A man and his tandem-blade of a shadow move so slowly it almost seems they might be standing still. And then, in the haze-blue distance, there spreads the clot that is the city: unchanged, waiting. The thought of his mamma and papa presses heavy into Atín's chest.

And he misses Lupe. Sometimes, too, he thinks about Doña Juliana, who lived downstairs. He did not like her mantilla, it was black and it smelled of camphor. But he liked her. She would tickle his chin and say, *Who is this* pollito, *this little chick, is he Agustín? Is he my Agustín* chiquitín?

Pepa is explaining that it is a time called November, and in the north, very far, over that way, where she and her brothers and sisters and her mother, his granny, had to live before Atín was born, all the trees have turned red and gold as if they were on fire. They will drop their leaves. And then everything, the fields, the roads, the roofs of the houses, even the ponds and rivers, will be covered by a cold white blanket called snow. Here that will not happen, Atín does not have to worry. No, not all of the trees here will keep their leaves but most will. "And the only snow—the *only* snow, I promise you, *corazoncito*, will stay where it is, there, the caps on those mountains. But the air feels cooler, yes? That is why, even though he does not always want to—" Pepa taps his top button with her finger—"Prince Agustín must wear his sweater."

Atín pouts.

"Haven't you seen in the park how the ducks and the other little birds fluff themselves fat?"

Atín sighs into her shoulder.

"And I must wear my shawl. Isn't it a pretty shawl?" Pepa lifts the jet-fringed end of it, and flings it over Atín's head. "And so—" she bumps her nose into his and says, just the way Atín's mamma says, "we're snug as two bugs in a rug."

"Bugs, rugs." Atín giggles.

Some things are different now. Some of the footmen are not the ones that were here at first. And the lady who comes to fix the hairdos. Olivia, that bad nanny, she's gone.

Tere says, "Give me your little paw," and she laces her fingers with his. Tere's hands are smaller than Pepa's; like his nanny Lupe's, they are the dark of *piloncillo*, and Tere's feel so soft. Holding hands with both Tere and his auntie, that's how Atín likes to walk in the park. With his arms up like this, his sweater tickles his chin, but he doesn't mind because he can lift his shoes off the ground, and Tere and Pepa carry him until—he dashes to the pond!

The ducks, in a chevron, swim up. Tere gives Atín a piece of tortilla. He can't fling it far; it lands on the scum green. A duck waddles out of the water and gobbles it. The duck stands so close, Atín could thunk its head! Its yellow eyes want more tortilla. The glistening wet bill has two pinholes for nostrils.

"*Waahk,*" the duck says, and he shivers the water from his tail.

Pepa pulls him away from the duck and, with a flap of her shawl, shoos it back into the pond. Tere tosses bits of tortilla out far, the rest of the ducks quack and honk and stab their bills in the water. Too far for Atín.

There are people who want to watch Atín, but Horst keeps them back.

Atín has a hard time understanding Horst, but he hardly says anything anyway. But one time, Horst said, when Atín is big, he will show him how to shoot crows. Horst aimed his rifle at the trees and he said, "*Bak!*" Atín said, "*Bak!*" Horst said, "*Ja, ja. So.*"

And there are flamingos; they hide behind a bank of rushes. A pair of necks slither up, and those flamingos preen themselves. They toss around their bills, big as shoes. Near the far shore, a canoe glides by, its prow netted with gem green light. A man is rowing, his oars rising and then falling, *clap, swush.* A tiny lady sits in the back, trailing her hand in the green. Her bonnet makes her head look like an egg. The man growls at her; she turns away her face.

Here in the park Horst keeps his horse. In the stables, there are many horses. Pepa lets Atín give the gentle brown one a carrot. The piebald mare has died, "who knows why," Tere shrugs. It lies in the corner of its stall, covered with an army blanket.

Tere feeds the monkey. They watch its spidery fingers rip at the skin of the banana.

They all, except not the monkey, take a ride in Atín's pony cart. His ponies wear blue feathers on their heads. Their names are Pinto and Lola, and they both have chocolate brown tails that are nicely brushed and they swish. Many people wave at Atín when he goes by in his pony cart.

Afterward, with Horst following behind, Atín, his auntie, and Tere walk to the water tank where sometimes they find the lion man swimming laps. Sometimes there are dragonflies.

Always Atín looks carefully at the faces of the people in the park in case they might be his mamma or papa. Once, his heart leapt when he thought he saw his cousin Salvo sitting on a bench by the fountain. He was gnawing at a mango on a stick. But coming closer, Atín saw it was not Salvo.

Beneath the ahuehuetes, the air is gauzy; sunlight dapples the path as if someone has run ahead of them strewing coins. Pepa stops and rubs her hip.

Back in the carriage again, Tere takes Atín on her lap, and with her arms around him, she rests her chin lightly on his hair. He feels sleepy. Pepa says, "Pass him to me." As he is pulled over, a memory pricks him: the flowery scent of his mamma's hair, the soft seashell of her ear. Heavily, he lays his head on his auntie's shoulder, and he remembers how he used to feel his mamma's breath rise—just like this. Fall, like this.

"Don't cry," Tere says. She scoots close and tugs his little finger. "Whose is this funny worm?"

"Don't get him going," Pepa says. "He needs his nap." The carriage, with a jolt, begins to roll.

It is a long ride up the ramp around the mountain, and the two sorrel mares, as they always do, trudge slow. But Atín does not mind going back up to the big sky-house, not so much as he used to. After his nap, he can run with Tere through all the rooms, she'll call after him, "Where is Agustinito? Where is Agustinito hiding?" Wherever he goes in this big sky-house, people are delighted to see him. "So," the lion man always says, "how is my handsome little cousin?" The ladies coo at him and fondle his curls. As if he was a grown-up, the soldiers say to him, "Good day, sir." If Atín wants to see Horst's pocket watch, Horst takes it out and puts it in Atín's hand. That grandpa with the caterpillar eyebrows, just this morning, he bent down on his knee to let Atín peer through his eyeglass (everything went blurry). "I am your good amigo, Señor von Kuhacsevich," he said, but Atín cannot say that name, yet. "Kuha," Atín tries. And Atín knows Frau Kuha's room with its windup music box, so shiny that when he touches it his fingers leave prints. Frau Kuha has taught him to count: *Ein, zwei, drei*—what comes after that, Atín forgets sometimes.

"Vier," Frau Kuha says, holding up four fingers. "And then?"

Atín shows his bottom teeth.

"What comes next, now?"

"Fünf!" Atín says, with his whole hand.

"Ach," she says to Pepa. "He's already quite the linguist!"

He has lots of balls now, red and yellow, purple with stars, and a squooshy avocado green one that does not want to bounce, it just rolls. His new favorite is the red one. Tere takes Atín to the kitchen garden. One time his ball smacked the back wall and bounced out into the chili-pepper bush. The chef, Tüdos, wiped his hands on his apron and then, with a wink, tossed it back to Tere.

Tüdos wears a mushroom hat. His sleeves are rolled up to the elbows, and on cold days, too.

With Tere and Tüdos, Atín has seen the inside of the kitchen. He knows all the stairs, they don't frighten him the way they used to. He can take any stairs he wants, Tere showed him how to step down sideways. "One at a time," Tere says, "you can do it." At the bottom of the big stairs sit a pair of marble lions resting their beards on their paws. Whenever he wants her to, Tere lifts him so that he can put a finger in a lion's mouth and feel its smooth cold tongue.

At home he used to stretch his fingers for the bannister with its wood so smooth—he fell and his nanny Lupe caught him, or was that a dream? Sometimes he dreams about Lupe. He has had a dream of his mamma and papa, and his uncles, and Salvo, too, they were in a house on water. They looked out their windows, and all they could see was water.

Atín feels his auntie's hand heavy on his back. He puts his thumb in his mouth.

Sweet lamb, thinks Pepa. Sweet, innocent child of God. She loves him, and much more, she thinks, than his natural mother ever could have. Pepa has loved this child from the day he first opened his blue eyes, but in this past month and a half, her love has blossomed into something bigger than she has ever felt in her life. If she were starving, she would give him her last morsel; if she were dying of thirst, her last drop of water. He is all that she lives for now. The relation with her brothers and Alicia has been severed. Through no doing of her own—no, Pepa considers herself as innocent as the driven snow.

Isn't it always the same story? She is the one made to suffer! And when she acted out of patriotism and the fear of God. After having arranged everything for *their* benefit! Their pensions are more than double what they had hoped for. And that little American, she must have said a hundred times, *oh, to live in Paris!* That was all she could talk about. One had to put up with her endless nattering about the new wardrobe she would have made *à Paris*, after she had a chance to see what was, as she liked to say, *vraiment comme il faut.*

Alicia, Pepa concluded long ago, is like a child invited to help herself in a sweet shop. She has no control over her appetites or her emotions.

How very alone Pepa feels here. Carlota, half her age, is polite but cool. (Apparently, according to Frau von Kuhacsevich, this is her nature.) It has been nearly two weeks since the empress departed for Yucatan, taking with her an entourage of two ladies-in-waiting, Monsieur Eloin, His Excellency Fernando Ramírez, a passel of ambassadors, General Uraga, and what must have been more than half the servants. According to protocol Pepa is now the highest-ranking feminine personage in the Imperial Residence, and on the occasions Maximilian has condescended to include her at his table, he has seated her to his right. However, in the empress's absence, there can be no balls, no *tertulias*—court life has come to an abrupt halt. Dinners with Maximilian are a trial. His melancholy casts a pall over the entire party. He picks at his food, but the moment His Majesty sets down his cutlery, the footmen clear the table, no matter that the guests have not finished theirs.

Many evenings Pepa takes her supper on a tray in her sitting room. She understands some German but not enough to join the others in the billiards room. Frau von Kuhacsevich has kindly invited her to play whist and jack-straws with them, but Schertzenlechner cheats, and it is too tedious.

Tedious: this ramshackle castle, exposed to the ever-harsh sun, or the cold, and the biting wind. Annoyances are legion. One closes the drapes, well, one must put on a lamp, but these are filled with such inferior oil, they smoke and, within minutes, the room becomes the inside of a wigwam! The stench seeps into the upholstery, and one's hair and clothes. The footmen have no clue how to tend or clean a lamp properly, or else Frau von Kuhacsevich lacks the vocabulary to explain. Probably both. The only place to escape to is the park below, where one is a magnet for gapers and gawkers, so many malodorous Indians, and soldiers who seem to imagine one cannot see they are urinating into the bushes. And the Master of Ceremonies imposes one expensive nuisance after the other (diamonds for this event, pearls and silks for that), and one cannot blow one's nose without at least eleven footmen, a housemaid, and a bodyguard all to witness it.

A plague of busybodies! Starting with the empress, who, knowing no more about raising a child than she would a kangaroo, instructed the nursemaid to give Agustín cold baths and a daily dose of fish oil! No wonder he screamed. And Frau von Kuhacsevich, clearly, she is overburdened by her duties. The staff does not respect her.

With Maximilian's approval, Pepa has resolved to purchase a house, perhaps that one on the Calle Espíritu Santo with the charming blue-tile patio? This would have the added advantage of preserving her capital. Sending the bulk of it to New Orleans would be impolitic, and putting it all into jewelry, the same as depositing it in one of the local banks (even the vaunted Banco de Londres y México), unacceptably risky. It goes without saying that Pepa should continue to be included in court functions, but in her own residence she could take the reins, manage her own staff, receive her visitors with discretion, and in close consultation with Maximilian, of course, educate Prince Agustín without all this pointless interference.

This arrangement has not turned out quite the way Pepa had envisioned. Maximilian, who was so friendly, has become distant. He is dangerously distracted by his botanizing, his landscaping projects, trudging out to view the most recently unearthed Aztec whatnot—a cracked pot or some horrid idol with a necklace of skulls. One had to tag along with the ambassadors for the unveiling of the Sun Stone, sixteen metric tons of a pagan calendar, for all the fanfare one would have thought they were looking upon the Rosetta Stone. It is so typical of Germans to wax enthusiastic about these relics that ought to have been left right where they were found: in the rubbish pile.

This week, she has it from one of the chambermaids, Maximilian has been indisposed by another bout of—is it malaria, or just something he ate? His doctor has been dosing him with charcoal, salt, and egg yolk, a remedy of questionable value. Monsieur Langlais, the latest finance expert Louis Napoleon has deigned to ship over the pond, has yet to wrestle Mexico's treasury into any semblance of order—and how can he, when the French keep a throttlehold on the income from the customhouses and the mines? Rumors are—certain persons, among them very high-placed Frenchmen, have been shamelessly lining their pockets.

There is much that Pepa should like to put in Father Fischer's ear. Other than Maximilian, the German curate is her single trusted ally in this court. But with the difficulties Maximilian has been having with the church, after the papal emissary left the country in a high dudgeon, Father Fischer was sent to smooth feathers in Rome. Rome: the other side of the world. It could be weeks, even months before Father Fischer returns to Mexico—if he returns. It could well be that Pepa will have to fight her battles, and the battles for the future of this precious child, alone.

Things have so changed, only time will tell whether we shall all be here in another year.

Frau von Kuhacsevich dots this last sentence in the letter to her chum, and she startles: Princess Iturbide's carriage clatters past the window. Princess Iturbide would be bringing her nephew and his nursemaid back up from the park.

Frau von Kuhacsevich now considers adding a few more lines about the little boy, how he has grown, some of the funny things he says—and how very like Crown Prince Rudolph when he was that age. Agustín is one of those rosy-cheeked children, you just want to pinch their cheek all day! No angel, but what healthy two-year-old is? His presence, his gales of laughter, have made them all smile in these difficult days. But to think of this child cannot but also remind her of a disquieting unpleasantness.

Frau von Kuhacsevich heard about it from her coachman, who got it from Maximilian's coachman, who made her coachman swear never to repeat it (but, it turns out that Tüdos, the chef, of all people, was already in on it, thanks to blabby old Schertzenlechner). The child's mother, brokenhearted, rushed back to Mexico City and attempted to get up an intrigue with General Bazaine. Maximilian, with his typical generosity, did not arrest her but only had her detained and returned to her husband and his brothers, who were waiting for her out on the highway—as Maximilian himself supposedly put it, "with all the courage of a pair of hyenas." The latest is, their steamer departed Veracruz on October 2—more than a month ago. Probably, they are already in Paris.

Would that Frau von Kuhacsevich could live in Paris! Well, Trieste would be her first choice, and Vienna her second, but she would trade Mexico City for Paris in the twinkle of a crab's eye!

A wonder it was, to Frau von Kuhacsevich, that the parents, both in good health, had been induced to give up their child. But the mother, an American, was so young, apparently, her head must have been easily turned. Whose wouldn't, with such an offer from a Habsburg? The woman changed her mind, but too late, and that was a pity. Poor little boy, to have had such unsuitable parents. Frau von Kuhacsevich has heard, and finds it convenient to believe without question, that those Iturbides are gamblers and drunkards. She gives those ne'er-do-wells not another thought.

As for Princess Iturbide, her lizard eyes, her coiled-up hair, her sharptongued pronouncements on Prince Agustín's bath, Prince Agustín's naptimes, Prince Agustín's hot milk with sugared bread—Frau von Kuhacsevich feels dizzy with exasperation just to think of that woman. At the very first, Frau von Kuhacsevich remarked to her husband, wasn't it striking, how much Princess Iturbide resembles that steel-jawed Countess Haake, lady-in-waiting to the empress of Prussia?

"*Frau Furchterregend,* Madame Formidable," was Herr von Kuhacsevich's judgment.

Well, Frau Furchterregend had assumed her place in this court with the confidence of someone one would think had a family in the *Almanach de Gotha.* Typical parvenue. The housemaids and footmen were complaining about her by the first afternoon, but they hopped to her calls like frogs on a hot skillet, and when Her Highness was not satisfied, she took it upon herself, without the courtesy of consulting one, to dismiss them! A chambermaid who did not change the bedpans was one thing, but Princess Iturbide fired the nursemaid, Olivia What's-her-name, leaving one to scramble—another to be found and within twenty-four hours! *Lieber Gott*, it was excessive. In twenty-four hours, one has to take what one can get—which is the assistant pastry chef's teenaged sister.

All of this Frau von Kuhacsevich was tempted to write in this letter to her chum, but a wary hesitation has kept her hand hovering above the page. Or, perhaps, more than the cold stiffens her fingers. She thought to light the stove, but in these difficult days, one must set an example and economize with the charcoal. At last, she lowers her pen to the paper and pulls it across the page in tight little loops:

I beg you, burn my letters. God keep you. Your loving friend,

And she signs her name, with her quick practical scribble.

It will take a month for these words to arrive in Trieste; in another month after that, by God's grace, she might have her reply. In the long and lonely meantime, she must *fortwursteln*—slog on, with the strength of Job and the go-lucky concentration of a Chinese plate-twirler! The laundry, the pantry, the kitchen, the missing epergnes, and the problem of last Tuesday's delivery of tallow candles in lieu of seven kilos of lard, there is an impossible amount to do! But first, she slides open the desk drawer and reaches into the back for her secret stash of *Brombeeren mit Mandeln*. Her clothes being so tight, she should not eat one, but, she tells herself, she deserves two. They are so old, she has to use a blade of the scissors to scrape away the wrappers. But even stale, *ach*, how this chocolate sweetness brings back the good days . . .

As she does not have a handkerchief, and no one can see, she licks her fingers.

At this hour in the morning, the shadow of Chapultepec and the mount of basalt it stands upon reaches long into the park below. A little while earlier, that shadow was long enough to enclose, crouching and shivering in her rags, little Lupe.

"Ten thirty-seven," El Mapache said, and he shoved the watch in his pocket. He was proud to not only own a watch but know how to read it, for this, he believed, was the sign of a gentleman.

They had hidden themselves behind bushes. The ahuehuete trees, huge overhead and dripping with ghostly gray moss, made Lupe think of La Llorona. Her stomach made a fierce growl. She had not had a bite since yesterday morning, and she couldn't helping thinking that, had she stayed at Doña Juliana's, she could have been warming her bones by the fire and dipping her tamale into a steaming hot cup of *champurrando.*

But, in the past days, she has seen her Agustínito three times! Each time, her heart smashed like a broken dish.

El Mapache swatted dirt from his knees. "Get up, *abuelita.*" He pushed at her shoulder. *Abuelita* means little granny; grateful that he calls her that, she obeyed, though her body ached. She shuffled behind him on the pathway out of the park.

Two months ago, when his wagon was run into that ditch, El Mapache had grabbed the lantern and run. Why would he abandon the boxes of saints, the poor thrashing mules—why run? And into the downpour? Lupe had scrambled out after that light, her huaraches sucking mud, falling, picking herself back up, crying, "Father, I am alive! Father, do not leave me!" She'd thought he hadn't heard her, and then—this terrified her—she realized he had. "Keep up!" was all he said, as he kept on, his lantern swaying like a disembodied head.

After the rain stopped and the sun came up, he began to walk faster—she had to trot! "Father?" She tried again. In the daylight, now she saw that he had a meaty, sunburnt face, full of cruelty.

They came to a road, but he crossed that and took a narrow trail into the mountains. Shreds of mist clung in the trees. They saw a deer's tracks; there were quails, and jays, and hanging in midair, the little green-bodied flies. It had been such a long time since Lupe had been in the forest. She had forgotten the clammy air and the razor-like scent of pine. She wondered, were they not far from San Miguel de Telapón? Why was the father in such a hurry?

All day they had nothing to eat, and for water only handfuls scooped from a buggy creek. In the afternoon, they climbed over an oak that had been riven by lightning, and from there, she could see the snowy crest of Popocatépetl.

In the thin air, they were both breathing heavily. But on he walked, and on she followed. It was not until the sky began to pale, and a quarter-moon appeared above the trees, that finally, in the shelter of a shallow cave, he stopped. Bats swooped from the trees. He kicked away some pine cones and the carpet of soggy brown pine-needles, and when he had cleared a circle of earth, he allowed her to bring twigs in for a fire. The walking had kept her warm, but now, her skirts still damp from the rain, her thin blouse and her scalp wet with sweat, she shivered. Her feet were bloodied, and her arms and legs badly bruised when the cart crashed. Slowly, with a whimper of pain, she sat down next to him.

"Not so close," he said.

She scooted away.

"I said—"

He did not have to say more. She moved out to the edge of the cave. She hugged her knees, but she could not keep her teeth from chattering. Coyotes, or maybe they were wolves, began howling in the distance.

"Father?" she said in her tiny voice.

Instead of answering, he yawned.

He worked at the fire. When it was roaring nicely, he laced his fingers together, and cracked his knuckles. Then, he sang a song, a queer one with mermaids in it and rum and playing cards. His voice was rough and nasal. He wandered off key, and sometimes, it seemed to her, he was making up the words. As he sang, he poked at the fire with a stick, and every once in a while, he reached behind himself for a branch or twig and flung that on the pile.

"You sing one." His gold tooth glinted.

She sang a lullaby. He said he liked that. It reminded him of his mother.

"Father? Aren't we going to say the prayers?"

He spit into the fire. "I ain't no priest."

He said she could call him El Mapache, the Raccoon. She did not know what he meant. Was he making a joke?

He said, "You're looking at him."

She stared at him. Her teeth went on chattering.

He said, "You never heard of me? El Mapache?"

Mutely, she shook her head.

"Never heard of El Tuerto and Los Ciegos?"

"No," she said in her tiniest voice.

He hissed. That was all.

It was the first night of her life that Lupe could remember not saying her prayers. Well, she said them in her mind, and she wasn't sure that counted. She did not sleep at all, she was so cold, and afraid of wolves, and of La Llorona, and most of all that El Mapache might leave her here. She would not know how to get back to the highway. On her own, she had no way to get to San Miguel de Telapón.

The next day, she followed him along a trail by a stream. When they had to cross the water, El Mapache gave her his hand. They would eat at his camp where there was always *chito*, roast goat leg, and in the meantime, it helped to hold a sprig of wild sage to your nose. He stopped to let her rest three times, once by a telegraph pole, the first of a line of them that marched down the side of a hill. With his knife he carved a skull into the wood. From this place, they could see an open stretch of the highway, and alongside, a ribbon of pasture with mules on it. That was the entrance to Río Frío, El Mapache said, where the stagecoach stopped. But he did not go down there; they went on through the forest and into the dusk.

All the way up the steep trail to the clearing, she could smell, growing ever stronger, mouth-watering, roasting meat. There was almost no light at all when they arrived at what was only a clearing, a few thatched pine-log huts, a shed, and a hitching post. A rib-thin dog strained at its tether, barking and whapping its tail. All of a sudden, there were a dozen men around El Mapache, clapping him on the back. One of them had a lantern. Except for El Tuerto, their chief, they were even younger than El Mapache, and all dressed in a way Lupe had never seen before. One wore a blouse with lace cuffs, but his bare toes, dirt-black, poked out of his boots. Another wore breeches of that fine calfskin Don Manuel used to wear, but his coat was raggedy at the elbows and had no buttons. Several of the men wore earrings. They all swaggered around big-hipped with daggers and machetes and pistols. The ground, scorched in places, muddy in others, was littered with bottles. In the back of their camp, by the hitching post, another lantern cast a weak light upon a mountain of valises and crates and boxes and smashed-up baskets. They had a few sore-backed mules, a flock of chickens. She couldn't see the goats, but she could hear them, their anxious bleating, the clank of their bells. Behind the hitching post, another trail disappeared into the forest.

El Tuerto, a muscled monster, wore chaps so wide at the ankles they flapped when he walked, and his trousers had silver buttons all up the legs. His eye patch was fixed by a thong that disappeared into his greasy locks. His other eye was an irritated red. He flicked his hand. Except for El Mapache, the men melted away.

El Tuerto stood with his thumbs in his belt. "And the rifles?"

As if stung, El Mapache swung around and snarled at Lupe, "Get lost."

Lupe backed away until she could no longer hear what they were saying. El Tuerto threw his hands up, then crossed his arms over his chest, while El Mapache, it seemed, was trying to explain.

Meanwhile, a woman came out from one of the huts. It was the hut that, on the side of the door, had a wolf's pelt hung from its tail. "Who are you?" she demanded.

Before Lupe could answer, a second woman said, "*Ay, comadre,* what did El Mapache drag in?"

They looked at each other and sniggered. They had a wanton look; both wore pearl necklaces and earrings, but both were barefoot, and their serapes very dirty. The first one turned her head and scratched vigorously at the back of it.

Lupe thought to ask, "Is that the trail to San Miguel de Telapón?"

"It'll get you there."

The first one made a noise with her nose. "By the Second Coming."

They started to circle her. And a third woman came out, this one with a cannabis cigar in her mouth and a baby on her hip, and began without a word looking Lupe up and down as if she were an animal in the zoo. Later, Lupe would learn their names: Jipila, Chucha, and Ceci. These were the women of El Tuerto, Piojo, and Sabandijas.

The first woman put a hand on her hip. She tossed her hair. "Why do you want to know?"

"It is my village."

"It's not a village."

"You know it then?" When Lupe got no response, she turned to the second woman. "You know San Miguel de Telapón?"

"What's it to you?"

The light behind the treetops had turned purple. A smattering of stars winked overhead. Lupe looked at the ground; her shadow had melted into nothing. She was trying not to cry—from *susto,* from hunger. The smell, so good, of roasting goat made her feel faint.

She said again, in her tiniest voice, "I was born there."

The women looked at each other. The third woman shifted the baby to her other hip. It had crusty eyes. It seemed less asleep than unconscious.

Finally, the second woman said, "Listen, *abuelita.* Maybe you was born there and maybe you wasn't, but it was a couple of sheds and half a fence. When the war started, the French burnt what was there, and all the trees around it, down to the ground."

"*Comadre,*" the first woman said, "those were Austrians."

The second one gave a shrug. Then, looking down at Lupe, she said, "Don't think she'll eat more than a rabbit. I'd give her a carrot. If we had some."

"Come," said the first woman, taking Lupe by the sleeve. "There's *chito.*"

In Chapultepec Park now, El Mapache thinks, how strange is Lady Luck. It turned out this shriveled little apple held the seed to a golden prize that could bring him more than the good graces of El Tuerto, more than another chance to do business with the Juaristas. It could bring him unthinkable riches, and at the same time, genuine fame, for it would be he, by kidnapping Prince Iturbide, who would stab Maximilian in the heart. Or at least, make a jackass of him and get a pile of treasure for it! El Tuerto would give El Mapache his place then, wouldn't he? And the Juaristas, too. They'd know then, he hadn't double-crossed them about those rifles, eh? El Mapache could just see the look on that lieutenant's face when he would return the salute.

Respect, that's what it was.

Every day Prince Iturbide's mornings run like clockwork. The castle's chapel bells toll out nine, and not a moment later, his carriage starts down the ramp. At the bottom, in the park, they get out: the bodyguard, the nurse-maid, the prince, and the one Lupe calls Doña Pepa. She looks mean enough to skin a maggot, but she's got hip trouble, and Lupe says she's deaf in one ear. This pretty party winds down the path to the pond, where the tyke throws some tortillas at the ducks. Then to the stables; then to the caged birds and a monkey. Then a ride in a pony cart. Nearing the top of the hour, they're at the water tank—now, that's tricky there. When Maximilian is swimming, it's swarming with guards. With the bells of ten, they're in the carriage again, hauling back up the ramp.

In Chapultepec Park it's a snap to blend in. El Mapache wears a sombrero with the brim down to his eyebrows. Lupe keeps her shawl over her head. Passersby have a goggle at the prince, but none dares get close—the body-guard steps in if they try it. It was when Lupe first caught sight of the kid that El Mapache realized, for real, she hadn't been shitting him. She damn near screamed, "*Santa María!*" He had to pinch her to make her quit.

The other day, while the prince, his aunt, and the nanny were feeding the ducks, El Mapache went out in a canoe. The one he wanted to draw a bead on was the bodyguard. He was the tallest white man he had ever seen, a big-boned German with the plodding gait of an ox. At first, the bodyguard had seemed alert, constantly scanning the pathway, the bushes, the trees, but every once in a while, he would fall into a kind of a trance, staring as if he was watching something floating in midair. One time, he sat down on a bench, laid his pistol across his knees, and closed his eyes.

The wanker was taking his siesta!

This night El Mapache slaps down his decision. They will kidnap the prince at the pond. It is the farthest point from the carriage, from the stables, and from the water tank. On its rim, bushes give cover. The pathway curves as it approaches the water, so unless a person comes close in, he is blind to where the prince and the others are standing. This is no operation for a pistol; it needs knives—the sharpest of knives. There must be no more noise than a grunt. Lupe, he explains, will be kneeling in the bushes. When the ducks swim up to feed, and once the bodyguard looks drifty, she'll make a duck's honk. That's the signal for El Mapache to creep up behind that lummox and bury the dagger in his back. Lupe will have the butcher's knife, she can fend off the women. El Mapache will grab the prince and they will run like their clothes are on fire. Then, they'll hide behind a hedge where Lupe can calm him down—that's the trick. They'll all change clothes. And then, under her shawl, she'll carry the prince out of the park.

"What do you say, *abuelita?*" El Mapache grills her for the eleventh time.

Lupe holds the butcher's knife over her head; it gleams in the candlelight. They are in a shack in back of a barn, beyond the outskirts of the city, up a lonely, muddy trail. No one but a few skinny milk cows knows they are here. Lupe snarls—though her voice is still no bigger than a squeak—"Quit scream-ing or I'll cut!"

November 23, 1865

THE CHARM OF HER EXISTENCE

*T**he squeaking wheel is the one that gets the oil.* Yes, and the gears in the Tuileries are grinding too slowly; they want oil. But where, in which cog, to squirt the precious little that he has of it? John Bigelow, the U.S. Envoy Extraordinary and Minister Plenipotentiary to the Court of Louis Napoleon, knows himself to be an impatient man, and this, he believes, is his personal cross to bear. Tenacity of purpose: that is the French emperor's strength, but a brittle one, at least in the instance of this universally unpopular Mexican expedition.

This chill and sluggish late November morning, near waking, Bigelow had dreamt that, with his tin can of oil, he had run up to the gates of the Tuileries and emptied it into a bed of tulips!

Now, at his breakfast table, he pulls at his graying mutton-chop beard, bemused at his own childishness.

"What are you grinning about, old man?" Mrs. Bigelow reaches over the breadbasket for the teapot.

"Hmm, nothing. The preserves?"

"At your elbow."

"Ah."

He spreads orange marmalade over his brioche. Across the table, Mrs. Bigelow, a petite, round-faced, and congenitally pleasant woman with a dimple on her chin, steadies her cup on her saucer. Her nut brown hair, combed over her ears, is just beginning to gray.

"Mr. Bigelow?"

"Mrs. Bigelow?" He raises his brioche as he would a flute of champagne.

He is about to tell her his foolish dream, but the children—Grace, Johnny, Jenny—charge in, and the breakfast room is a hubbub of scraping chairs and chatter and forks on plates, Johnny up on his chair shouting, though his mother shushes him, "pass me *du jambon!* Pass it to me!" Since Poultney's gone off to school, the little ones seem only more rambunctious. Lisette, their French girl, lowers the squirming Annie into the highchair; Annie, her face a little sun, begins banging her spoon.

Bigelow is facing Johnny and Jenny. The empty chair between them, which no one has the heart to move nor sit in, belonged to Ernst. This is the 126th day since the poor child, only four years old, died of the fever in his brain. His father counts those days like a beggar his dwindling coins, for with each one, the angel's face grows dimmer in his mind. How cruelly little his father remembers of him. Bigelow is trying, as he does at many odd moments in his days, to conjure a memory of that dear shy child. Ernst would have been sitting here, his mother telling him, *elbows off the table, darling,* his fingers in the mess of his runny eggs on toast. Mrs. Bigelow interrupts his reverie:

"Are you going to eat your breakfast, Mr. Bigelow, or just moon at it?"

Bang, goes Annie's spoon. *Bang, bang!*

Bigelow places his brioche on the plate. "Annie, sweetheart, stop that."

Mrs. Bigelow reaches across the table and pours him more tea. "Won't you have an egg?"

Jenny cries, "I want juice, too! Grace took it all!"

"Did not!"

"Did too!"

"I've got to go." Bigelow folds his napkin. He kisses his wife and then, going round the table, kisses each child, Grace, Johnny, Jenny on her fat peach of a cheek—and last of all, little Annie, whose cupid's bow of a mouth is already smeared with chocolate, he kisses on the top of her golden head.

In the foyer Lisette holds his coat open for him. *"A bientôt, Monsieur Bigelow,"* she says and makes a curtsey he does not notice. He grabs his umbrella and hurls himself out the front door.

• • •

From Bigelow's carriage window, the buildings, swirling in mist, float past like ghosts. How he loved this city once. He used to be fond of quoting Sainte-Beuve, *O Paris, c'est chez toi qu'il est doux de vivre*—at home with you, life is sweet. Now its streets depress him and especially on days like this one. To see blackened gutters clogged with trash, those pissoirs like standing coffins, he cannot help but sink into morbidly vivid thoughts of Robespierre and guillotines.

To Paris, to this legation, he has given the best years of his career, lobbying against the Confederacy. When the wire came last spring that General Robert E. Lee had finally surrendered at Appomattox Courthouse, he felt as Hercules must have felt after having cleaned the Augean Stables. He took to his bed with the worst grippe of his life, unable to do anything for three days but sip weak broth whilst Mrs. Bigelow read to him from Swedenborg. Only on the third day was he well enough to prop himself on pillows and read his *Poor Richard's Almanac.* It took him a month to recover his health, and then in July, on a day so hot that the flowers wilted, and Lisette had to close the shutters against the sun, Ernst died.

And alas, there is one more filth-encrusted stall in this stable: this Mexican imbroglio. He cannot go home, he must shoulder the shovel again. It is November already. When, Sweet Jesus, will it be finished?

French intervention in the Americas, he has made it very clear to the foreign minister, will not be tolerated. *Was this not made plain when Washington recalled its minister, Mr. Thomas Corwin, from Mexico?* The United States will never recognize an imperial government in Mexico.

"Nonetheless," Drouyn de Lhuys answered, "you recognized the empire of Iturbide, did you not?"

"That is true," Bigelow replied. "However, Iturbide was a Mexican, supported by the Mexican army and the Mexican people." Drouyn de Lhuys seemed to have no parry for that, so Bigelow rammed it in: "Furthermore, Maximilian permits slavery, witness his decree of September 5, forced labor by former slaves on lands colonized by immigrants from the Confederacy, *AND*—" (Bigelow had to raise his voice to forestall the French minister's interruption)—"in this Black Decree of October 3, the summary execution of any individual found with a weapon—why, you must agree, sir, these are barbarities against the LAW OF NATIONS!"

"Why do you tell me?" Drouyn de Lhuys examined his fingernails. "What concern is it to France what the government of Mexico decrees? Anymore than—" like a saint engulfed in flames, he rolled his eyes ceilingward—"the decrees of China, or Lapland?"

"Monsieur Drouyn de Lhuys. Does the French Imperial Army have thirty thousand men stationed in Lapland? Has the French Imperial Army backed a new emperor of the Laplanders, shall we say, a younger brother of the king of Poland?"

Drouyn de Lhuys put his thumbs in the pockets of his vest and burst out in loud laughing. "Oof," he said, "You should be writing novels!"

To think of that scene, the French minister's arrogance, it makes the bile rise in his throat. *Well*—Bigelow relaxes his grip on the neck of his umbrella—that's all there is to it: the United States and France are, *à contre-coeur*, in a standoff, pistols drawn. Intelligence reports are that the French still have thirty thousand men in Mexico. But in the United States, the same number remain massed at the Río Grande, along with all their artillery, rifles, ammunition, tents, mess wagons, and Lord knows how many hay-munching mules.

Then two weeks ago came tidings of a truly peculiar complication. Seward's cable from Washington had directed Bigelow to receive Madam de Iturbide, née Alice Green of Georgetown, D.C., who claims that the Archduke Maximilian, soi-disant Emperor of Mexico, has kidnapped her child! Her case revolted him. In sober fact, she had signed away her own child for rank and lucre. But, Seward's instructions still trembling in his hand, Bigelow had chided himself: *Judge not that ye not be judged.*

The advice this father gives his own children! To Bigelow, moral snobbery is as offensive as social snobbery. As his wife, who is of the Quaker persuasion, likes to say, You must give everybody *one* chance!

A light rain has begun falling. Umbrellas bloom along the Champs-Elysées. Madam de Iturbide is expected in his office within the hour. What vulgar class of person might she be? Already Bigelow is steeling himself for the tawdry scene. The gas lamps flicker inside that pastry shop; in its window, a hillock of that red and green *bombe mexicaine*. Last year, in the more elabo-rate dinner parties, that was *comme ça*. No one in Paris would serve that to him. Mrs. Bigelow reported that it is an atrocious concoction sopped through with rum. No, she has not looked well since Ernst died. As soon as this Mex-ico question has been resolved, he should like to take Mrs. Bigelow and the children home to New York, to their farm at Buttermilk Falls. In the long summer days, he could work on his memoirs, re-read Gibbon and de Toc-queville, this time in the original French. The children could play in the for-est, fish, and ride ponies.

Man proposes, God disposes. Patience, Bigelow reminds himself as he steps down from his carriage. He feels the cold drizzle on his face before he raises his umbrella.

He tells himself once again, *Patience.*

At eleven, just as the clock on his bookcase *tings*, Madame de Iturbide is ushered in. To his surprise she is dressed most tastefully in dove gray with a black velvet collar. Modest pearl earrings. He rises from behind his desk and comes around to take her gloved hand.

"Oh, I am very much obliged to you, Mr. Bigelow," she says breathlessly. *Does he detect a hint of a Virginia accent?*

"Do be seated."

"Where?"

He thinks, *why, she's frightened as a rabbit. What was she imagining, that he would have her perch on the edge of his desk?* "There, Madam. Either one of those chairs will do."

Her fine fair hair and the way she sits nervously pulling at the fingertips of her gloves, reminds him of a friend of his sister's, with whom he had once gone strawberrying.

But he returns his attention to his desk. The blotter, the inkpot, his spectacle case: these he aligns with the precision of a surgeon preparing for an operation.

"Yes?" He signals.

She begins in rush, "It is not *at all* what Maximilian has made it out to be, it is a *fraud*, you see, it—"

"A fraud?" Bigelow interrupts. He leans back into his chair and makes a tent with his fingers. From across his enormous oak desk, he regards her coolly. "Are they *not* your and your husband's signatures on Maximilian's contract?"

A flush of crimson appears on her forehead. She begins, silently, to weep. "I admit," she brings out a lace handkerchief, "I had allowed myself to be dazzled, maybe a little, by the prospects held out to my child, but I—I had *never* imagined that a *mother*, would be separated from her *child* in his *infancy!* And—"

"AND," Bigelow says, "the indemnity the Iturbide family has been paid?" Like a coon cat in wait for a chipmunk, he stays very still in his chair.

"It has *not* yet all been paid, but more important, the majority of these assets and pensions had been granted long ago to the Iturbide family and were in arrears. I mean, they were not honored by *previous* governments."

"By the Republican government of Benito Juárez."

"As well as others."

"But Madam. Pray tell. Why should Maximilian wish to keep your child when you so evidently want him back?"

"Because my son is an Iturbide. Had my father-in-law, the Emperor Iturbide, lived, had his government survived, I mean, you see, my son would be in line for the throne. My son is very popular in Mexico, and he is likely to become more popular when he comes of age, and that is why Maximilian considers him a threat."

"Your two-year-old babe is a threat to Maximilian?"

"Yes!"

Bigelow closes his eyes, taking this fully in. How ridiculous is the monarchical form of government, he thinks. Out of the age of moated castles and knights in shining armor—bah, the stuff Southerners and women want to read novels about. If they really had a handle on what went on in a European court . . . the interbred mediocrity and sycophancy, the waste, cronyism, despotism, the bald corruption that could make a Boss Tweed blanch!

"But." Bigelow opens his eyes again. "Tell me, Madam. Exactly. Why did your husband's family agree to this un—" He was about to say, *unnatural intrigue,* but he clears his throat. "Arrangement?"

"My sister-in-law is not on good terms with her brothers, she is very ambitious, and has been bribed by the title of princess and a place in Maximilian's court. My brothers-in-law are here in Paris also, and they and my husband *completely* support me. Agustín Gerónimo, my husband's older brother, wrote Maximilian a *strong* letter of protest."

"But you and they signed Maximilian's contract?"

"But not entirely by choice! You see, Maximilian made us to understand that our son could be taken from us by force! Last summer, the order was thrust upon us, with no explanation, to quit Mexico and—"

"Madam." Bigelow places his hands flat on his desk. He feels a headache coming on. "It would be better, I think, if you were to make a formal statement." He taps the buzzer on his desk. In an instant his secretary, a stooped young man with the hard-boiled demeanor of a Vermont parson, slides himself onto the chair to Madame de Iturbide's right.

Madame de Iturbide is still on the edge of her chair, but she speaks now with a voice so sure and clear, it seems to Bigelow as if her throat were lined with polished jade:

"I had sent some of his playthings and a note to the empress commending my son to her protection. I had been promised news every day, but other than a telegram the first night, that he had slept well, nothing. Not *one* word!" She raises her chin and blinks back tears. "This past summer we were made to understand that our child could be taken from us with or *without* our consent, and when the invitation to this arrangement was made to us, I *never* imagined that my son would not have a mother's care—I had understood that in some years, he would go to Europe for his education. But no sooner had we signed it than we were informed our departure from Mexico was not to be delayed by *even one day*! We threw together what belongings we could and took the stagecoach to Veracruz, where we were to board a steamship, but when we got to the city of Puebla . . ."

Bigelow waits for her to compose herself.

"I knew," she said quietly. "I could not continue without my child. I returned to Mexico City in great haste."

Bigelow keeps one finger over his lips. "Alone?"

"Yes, for my husband and his brothers would have been arrested. I traveled under my maiden name, Miss Alice Green, and in Mexico City I took asylum in the house of my landlady, who is the widow of Gómez Pedraza, a loyal friend of my father in-law." She pauses here, it seems to Bigelow, for him to take special note of this name.

"Doña Podressa?"

"Exactly. She took me in her carriage to see General Bazaine. He had just received a note from Maximilian, that a solemn contract had been signed and that he should take no notice of my suit. But I pleaded with General Bazaine, I said to him, as a brokenhearted mother, I *beg* you to write to the emperor again, and enclose my letter to him with your own."

"General Bazaine agreed?"

"More than that. He sincerely regretted that he did not have the authority to take direct action, but that he would do all in his power to induce Maximilian to give back my child." She snaps opens her handbag. "Here is a copy of the letter." She unfolds the letter and hands it across the desk. "It is my own translation from the Spanish."

Bigelow hooks his spectacles around his ears and begins to read, but not without difficulty, because the handwriting is sharp with pike-like "t"s and cramped, spiked "s"s. He recognizes at once that, naive a creature as she may be, Madame de Iturbide is not a person to be trifled with.

Mexico City, September 27, 1865
Calle de Coliseo Principal No. 11

To His Majesty,
The Emperor of Mexico

Sir:

After my despatch from Mexico the 16th of September, my presence in this city will appear strange to your Majesty, but a grief that has no bounds, a feeling the most intense known to man, has guided my steps in search of a son who is the charm of my existence.

There is in the life of parents a constant thought, the welfare of their children, and I—poor me—who enjoyed life so much in looking at my child, thought always of his future; his education occupied me as the only mission to be fulfilled by me on earth, and in one of those moments in which I vacillated in regard to the position of my dear Agustín, I came to separate myself from him, thanking your Majesty for keeping in mind the Iturbide family, in which you distinguished very specially my son; but I have wept so over this separation, I have undergone such bitterness during these nine days, that I have no words with which to explain to your Majesty all the magnitude of my trouble. I thought that if I did not see my child, I would lose my mind, and all my family was obliged to take part in that idea, permitting me to return to address the prayer, which I make with a heart full of grief, with a heart that needs a ready consolation; this prayer is to see my child and not to be separated from him in his infancy.

In my dreams as a mother, I never thought that my son should be a prince who would aspire to a crown; my passion was to educate him as a good Mexican, who, brought up with good ideas, might one day become useful to his country; but, very contented with the humble position in which I lived, my happiness knew no limits, and now that your Majesty honors in my child a national memory, am I to separate myself from a child who stands in needs of all my solicitude? What remorse, if I survived this separation, would not the least mishap in the life of my child create in me!

This black thought has followed me everywhere, since my child was no longer at my side, and I have nothing either in my heart or in my head to render me tranquil; each passing hour increases my grief; and if your Majesty is convinced of the sincerity of my words, it is not possible that your Majesty would prolong any longer my sufferings.

No longer to see my child! To separate myself from him, perhaps forever! To abandon him when he most needs my care! There is no agony comparable to this sad thought. Your Majesty cannot insist on a separation that puts in danger my existence, and I hope that, doing justice to my feelings, your Majesty will accept my gratitude for your affectionate treatment toward my child, and will order that he return to the side of a mother who ought not for one moment to abandon him, no matter what might be the expectations of his future.

I am confident that her Majesty the Empress, who has shown her-
self so kind to my son, will support my prayer. The good heart of Your Majes-
ties cannot permit that the profound affliction of your servant be prolonged.

Alice G. de Iturbide

Bigelow's heart has softened like a pat of butter left in the sun, but he does not reveal this. He passes the letter to his secretary. "Make a copy of this also."

"Yes sir."

Bigelow removes his spectacles, folds them into their case, and tucks it inside his breast pocket. Heavily, he leans back in his chair and again makes a tent with his fingers.

"And what, precisely, was the archduke's reply?"

"He did not reply. The empress sent a messenger with my own letter, the one I had written to her commending my child to her care, and a note saying that it would take some time for Their Majesties to reflect on whether either of my letters required a reply. After two days, an officer of the Palatine Guard arrived and said that Their Majesties wished to confer with me about my child in person, rather than by correspondence. The officer said that he had seen my child, that he was—" Her chin trembles, and she has to stop for a moment and dab her eyes.

After a deep breath, she resumes. "This officer told me that he had seen my child and he was well. He spoke so *kindly,* he seemed *such* a gentleman! I went with him downstairs and there, waiting, was a palace carriage. I stepped in and we drove off. When we should have turned to go to the Imperial Palace, we went straight on, and I said to the officer, 'Oh, I suppose the court is at Chapultepec Castle?' 'Yes,' he said, but he wouldn't look at me, and I knew then it was a trick! On the outskirts of the city a coach with another Palatine Guard and two soldiers were waiting for me. Their idea was to take me to the city of Puebla."

"Pueblo?"

She nodded. "I refused to get in, I was *not* going to abandon my child! On the side of the road, I sat down on a stone. Well, they picked me up and with no more ceremony than if I were a sack of potatoes, they shoved me into the coach! We rode all that day and all that night. I was dressed for an audience with the emperor. I had no coat, only a mantilla to cover my head, no food, or water to drink, not a peso to buy any! We were told to take the first steamer out of Veracruz. An armed escort made certain that we did."

"By Jove."

For a moment more the scribbling continues. When the secretary looks up, his eyes behind his spectacles are as wide as silver dollars.

"What I so hope with all my heart," Madame de Iturbide says, "is that you, sir, might be so kind as to recommend to Monsieur Drouyn de Lhuys that he receive us, because if we could make Louis Napoleon understand, then he might persuade Maximilian—"

"Madam," Bigelow cuts her off (he is afraid, perhaps too severely). "I am sorry for your misfortune. And, personally, I assure you that I should like nothing better than to help you, but understand, the United States do not recognize Maximilian's government."

"Oh, *please*, sir—" Her eyes well with tears.

"As the minister representing the government of the United States, it is awkward. In any event, I must speak with your husband and his older brother."

He ends the interview here, because *considered caution* are his personal watchwords. And, of course, he reminds himself, there are limits to what a woman can be made to understand.

That evening, after the children have all been tucked into bed, Bigelow tells his wife everything. For a long while she gazes into the crackling grate. This is her way, silently, carefully to stitch her thoughts together. She holds her cup of anise tea with both hands. Her round, double-chinned face, lit by the fire, reminds him of a Flemish madonna's.

He reminds her of the *Saint Paul* by Michelangelo.

She knows, in her secret heart, that she is not the paragon of moral virtue her husband believes her to be. Nonetheless, she aspires to that—though, what she really feels, listening to him talk about Madame de Iturbide's tiny son, is a curl of envy. Her own darling, four-year-old Ernst, is lost. And their first child, also, not yet two years old, shortly after a ghastly fall from the top of a book cabinet. One day, on the other side of the veil, they shall all be re-united. But that takes away none of the pain.

Having composed her feelings, Mrs. Bigelow takes a sip of her tea. "Pity," she says, finally, setting down the cup. "Pity is what I feel for those poor parents."

Bigelow is tempted to take her hand, but he does not, yet.

Shaking her head, Mrs. Bigelow says, "What a propaganda gift for Juárez."

"Yes, isn't it."

"*If—*" she raises her face to him—"if, and only if, the father's story matches the mother's, in each and every particular, I think you should skate out, though it be thin ice, to the very verge of official propriety to assist her."

"You think so."

"She is our countrywoman."

"Yes."

"You must speak privately with Drouyn de Lhuys."

"Exactly."

"You must urge him to help her."

"As soon as possible."

Mrs. Bigelow's expression has turned fierce. "It is the only Christian course of action."

"Of course."

A wise and compassionate wife, is there any greater blessing? This is Bigelow's favorite time of day, by the quiet, gentle, soothing crackle in the grate. His wife leans into his shoulder, and slowly, he strokes the mane of her loosened hair.

Bigelow says, "Maximilian has shown himself a cruel tyrant."

Mrs. Bigelow says, "And quite the bumbler."

"Quite."

"Yes," Mrs. Bigelow agrees, closing her eyes. Her head is heavy on his shoulder, and it smells of flowers. "That is how they will make it out in the newspapers."

"Things fall of their own weight."

"They do," Mrs. Bigelow says, taking his hand.

Bigelow says, "That ridiculous monarchy, just as soon as Louis Napoleon withdraws his troops, it will fall—"

"A rotten apple from the tree."

November 25, 1865

PAS POSSIBLE

*I*n the office of the French minister of foreign affairs, Bigelow wonders, was it so much, was it so very much, to have hoped he could prick his French counterpart's conscience? As was his own, as would be that of any father, indeed, that of any honorable gentleman. Bigelow had imagined his message a shuttlecock batted over a series of nets: to Drouyn de Lhuys, to Louis Napoleon, then to Maximilian—and Maximilian, mortified. *Et voilà!* the boy reunited with his mother and father. But smack into the first net: from Drouyn de Lhuys, not a flinch of compassion!

And, as Bigelow knows full well, it is no given that this conversation will go beyond these four walls. Drouyn de Lhuys holds his cards close to his vest, which is one of the reasons, Bigelow supposes, Louis Napoleon has kept him in his cabinet as long as he has. Drouyn de Lhuys knows too much. Louis Napoleon should have dismissed him long ago. In fact, Mrs. Bigelow pointed it out, how very telling that Louis Napoleon did not cut Drouyn de Lhuys back in 1851, when he threatened to resign should the emperor marry the countess of Montijo. Shortly thereafter, Louis Napoleon had a second opportunity to ask for his resignation: at a ball here, Madame Drouyn de Lhuys snubbed the countess of Montijo, who, though not yet formally engaged to the emperor, was attending as His Majesty's personal guest. As all the world knows, the countess of Montijo, "a little Spanish nobody," as Madame Drouyn de Lhuys went about saying, is today the Empress Eugénie, mother of the Child of France.

Bigelow can scarcely endure the Tuileries' frou-frou decor, though he has warmed, personally, to Louis Napoleon. For all the emperor's vices (impetuosity, womanizing, mirror-gazing), Bigelow cannot help but feel fond of him. After their mutual dentist, Dr. Evans, Bigelow would be the first to admit that he has joined the legions of Americans who have succumbed to the charisma that big-hearted adventurer. Nonetheless, Bigelow's years in Paris have by no means changed his republican proclivities. Son of Connecticut Presbyterians, Bigelow is a strict abolitionist who has strived his whole life to be the sort of man who, as he puts it to his children, does not eat his pie first. And that would be plain apple pie, thank ye.

Many a time Bigelow has told his children that it was when, as a child, he had the task of driving the cows from the milking shed to pasture, because the beasts were very slow and he was small, he learnt his first lessons in patience. As the cows would stop to pull at the weeds by the roadside or simply stand, working their cuds, he would notice the shape of a cloud—how like a giraffe it was, or a hippopotamus, or a castle turret. He would notice that the clover was just beginning to come in, that the dandelions had sprouted their first gossamer globes, that the oak leaves had been kissed with autumn flame. As now, standing in the office of Drouyn de Lhuys, he notices that on the Aubusson carpet in front of the ormolued méridienne's left leg, there is what appears to be a coffee stain. It was not there yesterday.

Everywhere in this office there is some trivial thing in want of repair: a hairline crack in the window glass, a chip in the crown molding. Outside, the fountain is misfiring. The mulberry trees have been indifferently pruned, and one appears to have a rag, or is that a scrap of paper caught in its twigs?

Bigelow's mind does tend to wander when Drouyn de Lhuys rants, for this rant, he has heard it before, indeed he knows it almost word for word. How many times has Bigelow been obliged to endure it? And, right on cue:

"You apparently believe, that the *whole* of the Americas are *your* property, and that the institutions and forms of government must conform to *your* philosophies and *your* designs. These enormous pretensions—"

As if France's sending an army into Mexico were a work of holy charity! Bigelow has been in Paris for too many years; he is beginning to feel like an actor in an opéra bouffe with an over-long run. Stage left, the U.S. minister looking grim as an undertaker; stage right, exuberantly gesticulating, his counterpart, a soaped trout of an aristocrat with curls over his ears and ruffles on his cuffs.

They are *bons amis,* good friends, so they insist to one another in front of others. Tomorrow evening, as he did last Tuesday, Bigelow might well find himself seated to the left of Madame Drouyn de Lhuys, who would be sparkling with sapphires and in prodigious (so terribly distracting) décolletage. Over the *carré d'agneau aux fleurs de lavande,* they might converse about the weather.

Bigelow has, at least, eased his conscience by mentioning (and he did stress that this was in a purely private capacity) the plight of his countrywoman, Madame de Iturbide. He has presented Drouyn de Lhuys with copies of the transcript of her interview, her letter to Maximilian duly translated into French, and his notes from his subsequent interview at the Grand-Hôtel with her husband, Don Angel, and his older brother, Don Agustín Gerónimo. We do reap as we sow. This tirade is the consequence.

"*Vous venez en France avec vos plaintes* . . . You come to France with your complaints against a government that you—" with a wounded sigh, Drouyn de Lhuys puts the heel of his palm to his forehead—"*refuse* to recognize! And now!" Drouyn de Lhuys gives his most Gallic, eye-rolling shrug. "*Now* you come to tell me about an *American* child!"

Arms across his chest, Bigelow rocks back on his heels.

Drouyn de Lhuys says, "Why do you not take the matter to President Juárez, the Mexican authority that you *do* recognize?"

Bigelow finds himself staring at that wretched coffee stain.

"Ah . . ." Drouyn de Lhuys makes a malicious smirk. "Perhaps you cannot find President Juárez? Perhaps he has sought refuge in your republic, and perhaps you have given it to him. But surely you would know much more about his whereabouts than I would."

Maximilian is claiming that Juárez has abandoned Mexican territory, and therefore, the republic's sympathizers, if found armed, can be considered not enemy combatants but criminals, who may be shot.

Bigelow clears his throat. "Our intelligence is that President Juárez is at the Texas border, but he remains resolutely within Mexican territory."

"Ah, oui?" Drouyn de Lhuys moves his jaw, as if chewing this choice morsel of information, his tongue delicately disjoining flesh from seeds. He cricks his neck. *"Bien sûr,* we are not and we have no pretensions to be the government of Mexico, you do France too much honor to treat us as such."

"I take it then that you will not receive Madame de Iturbide."

"Pas possible. Impossible."

"Even as a private matter?"

Drouyn de Lhuys shows his long yellow teeth, and, placing one ruffled cuff across his waist, dips his head. *"Au revoir,* Monsieur Bigelow."

The Imperial Palace of Mexico: In the office of His Majesty, the desk, an expanse of leather-topped mahogany, is awash with a pinkish cold morning light—and the balance sheet of the Mexican Imperial Treasury, which is to say, an undone sheaf of papers all of them dense with pencil scribblings. The sight of this mickle makes Maximilian sink his head into his hands. As Bonaparte famously quipped, "You need three things to win a war: Money, money, money." Where is it?

Evaporated.

Would that at this moment he could be in a toasty salon, sprawled on the carpet with the little cousin, building a castle out of blocks—oh, to be a child again, without a care! Instead, one confronts this specimen, in a cravat of the sort a petit bourgeois would have been wearing a decade ago. His head—a phrenologist's wonder!—is reminiscent of a cantaloupe, and his upturned nose too short. This disproportion plunges one into the despair one feels in a room where the furnishings—

Why is it so damnably hard to focus? One's thoughts jerk and blur. Enough with this number blather:

"Monsieur Langlais, a final diagnosis. Can one avoid having to take out another loan?"

"Pas possible."

Pas possible! Those poison words! One should like to solder the letters together, p-a-s-p-o-s-s-i-b-l-e, into an iron-tight chain, wrap it around this bean counter's neck, and strangle him until his eyes bulge. It is over the edge to be informing one at this late a date that, after the payments to the holders of the Jecker Bonds (cronies of the duc de Morny), and now the Iturbides' excessively generous pensions, never mind this Sisyphean attempt to build a Mexican Imperial Army, there is nothing for one's civil list. One has sliced, chopped, filed, chipped, grated, pared the budget down, not *to* the bone but *into* the bone—and General Bazaine diverts the pathetic trickle of income from the customhouses and rains it over his moronic rabble—oh, with their galling incompetence, their arrogance, senseless brutality, these French are a millstone around one's neck. But one takes it coolly. One massages the bridge of one's nose. One speaks through one's teeth:

"Thank you. That will do for today, Monsieur Langlais."

"Your Majesty." Monsieur Langlais bows. He gathers his papers and, from the secretary, takes the copy of the schedule of the debits to be made on the account of the Mexican Imperial Treasury in Paris. This is the fifth wandless Merlin Louis Napoleon has sent over the pond, all with sumptuous salaries paid by the Mexican treasury. Maximilian chews his thumbnail—and rips it to the quick. A bud of blood appears.

"Bollocks!" Maximilian says under his breath.

"Excuse me?" his secretary asks. A swarthy boy, clean-shaven and wearing spectacles, José Luis Blasio sits to the side of the desk, ankles crossed.

Maximilian places a fist on his hip and regards the stove, a squat iron contraption installed in the far corner. "You are hot?"

José Luis puts a finger in his collar and stretches his neck. "It's broiling in here, sir."

"Nonsense! One needs more furs than in Milan in winter."

"I wouldn't know, sir. I have never been to Milan."

Maximilian throws back his head and laughs. But having seen the window ajar, his smile drops. "You opened that window?"

"Er, yes, sir."

"Be so good as to close it."

José Luis closes the window.

"Hot-blooded boys cannot understand that old duffers, such as my thirty-two-year-old self, have ice-water running in our veins. Open that window again, and I shall send for a carpenter to nail it shut. Well, what is the next nuisance in the dispatch box?"

José Luis picks up a letter. "A complaint from the mayor of Tampico."

Maximilian sighs and then lights a fresh cigar. Elbow on his desk, he rests his ear in his hand.

José Luis speaks to His Majesty's bald spot. "French, um, atrocities, sir."

Maximilian turns the cigar in his fingers. "Specifically?"

"Er," José Luis peers closely at the letter. "It says here, six guerrillas were shot, mutilated and, um, left hanging by their feet from the trees in the plaza."

"And?"

"This was in front of, er, it says, 'the café owned by Don Rogelio' something."

Maximilian puffs his cigar. "Something? That is an original surname."

"Difficult to make out the handwriting, sir."

"So . . ." Maximilian still has his ear in his hand. He exhales toward the ceiling and watches the smoke swirl. He closes his eyes. "The café owned by Don Rogelio something, the mayor's colleague, has been enjoying less custom than usual?"

"Seems to be the slant of it, sir."

Maximilian stabs his cigar into the ashtray. He drums his fingers. Then, suddenly, with a long arm, he slides the fire orange Totonac bowl across the desk. "Bonbon?"

At this very moment, a few blocks away, Princess Iturbide is heading to a crucial appointment—to see Count Villavaso's Number 12 on the Calle de Coliseo Principal, a mansion that, it so happens, stands opposite the widow de Gómez Pedraza's. Over the past month, Princess Iturbide's search for a residence has been an exercise in increasing frustration. She has not seen the inside of Count Villavaso's house, but from Mrs. Yorke's descriptions, it is the single house in Mexico City of a size and style suitable for the residence of a crown prince that is not a mice-infested wreck. (There was one other, but its best rooms have been requisitioned by French officers, who will not be leaving, and no, it does not matter a straw to them who the new owner might be—the cheek!)

Princess Iturbide is at the end of her tether—every day another pettiness imposed by the Master of Ceremonies, who has grown bolder in the empress's absence. Last Saturday, four of the little boys invited to her children's party were turned away at the gates to Chapultepec Castle because, that martinet declared, their shoes were the wrong color. Not brown; shoes had to be black. The *wrong shoes!* On two- and three-year-old babes! It turns the mind to taffy.

Princess Iturbide sees Maximilian only rarely, while everyone else and their third cousin's monkey, all assume they have a standing invitation to nose themselves into the nursery. Some footman painted Agustín's toy blocks purple; the cheap paint flaked off and discolored the carpet. Without the courtesy of requesting one's permission, Frau von Kuhacsevich teaches him to count in German, Hungarian, and some Balkan language! Last night, while one was at the theater, Tüdos took it upon himself to feed Agustín a heaping bowl of veal goulash, and the consequences of that kept the nursemaid up half the night. Puppies have been turned away, a tortoise, an albino squirrel!

And the pilfering! Lingerie disappears from the drawers; overnight, a half-bottle of one's orange-flower cologne evaporated. The darling came to Chapultepec Castle with a favorite toy, a blue ball, and someone stole it. What other conclusion can she come to, after asking five times, has someone, anyone seen it? She did not put it past that nursemaid she dismissed, Olivia What's-her-name, to have taken it away with her, out of spite. One must live with every cupboard, drawer, and trunk locked.

In a word Princess Iturbide is wild to be out of the Imperial Residence. Count Villavaso has determined to go live with one of his daughters in Querétaro, and according to Mrs. Yorke, having lost their hacienda in Guerrero to the insurgents, they are keen for cash. God willing, she will get his house.

Taking the lackey's arm, she steps down onto the cobblestones. Across the street the windows of the widow de Gómez Pedraza's house are shuttered. Her cedar doors, sunbleached and battered, are nothing special; Count Villavaso's, however, are carved with acanthus leaves and bare-breasted caryat-ids—all in need of a coat of varnish, but superb. The stone escutcheon with the count's coat of arms: that, of course, will have to be chiseled out. The brass knocker, in the shape of a lion's paw, has been nicely polished. She lifts it as high as it will go and lets it drop with a definitive *klak*.

Furious barking. What must be a horse of a dog throws itself against the inside of the door. Footsteps hurry. Groaning, the great wooden door opens just enough to reveal the mastiff's slavering snout, and above it, the porter's pocked cheek. Pepa wrinkles her nose at the smell that seeps out, of liver fry-ing in lard.

The eye regards her.

"Pas possible!"

"I am not French. I am Princess Iturbide."

"No se puede pasar. You cannot come in."

"Excuse me?" She thought, perhaps she had not heard him correctly. Never has she been treated thus by a porter. "I tell you, I am Princess Iturbide."

The mastiff gives an ugly growl. The porter says in the same rude tone, *"No se puede pasar."*

"I am expected! I have come all the way down here from Chapultepec Castle to see this house, and at considerable inconvenience!"

In a frenzy, the mastiff lunges, but the porter, one hand on the latch, keeps his grip on its collar, and the door closes. With a clank, the bolt comes down.

Stunned, Pepa turns and nearly collides with a beggar. And an Indian car-rying a stick with a string of wee paper piñatas; he breaks into a toothless singsong, the *piñatitas* dancing in her face, "Two pennies, one for two pennies."

Foolish, she chides herself. Why did she not bring the bodyguard? But these Germans gossip like magpies; she has had quite enough of their big noses in her personal business.

"Stand back!" she says, shooting the lackey a venomous look for not hav-ing said it first. Bracing her hip, she limps to the curb where that lackey, ash-ine in his palace livery, face slack with indifference, holds open the carriage door. More beggars and a threesome of shoeshine boys crowd around. As Pepa settles inside, grubby faces appear in the window. One of those boys hops up, and up, trying to see her.

"Go away!" She raps her ring on the glass.

One says to the other, "She's the witch."

There is a pleated silk curtain. With a fierce tug, she pulls it closed.

On the interminable ride back to Chapultepec Castle, it occurs to Pepa that the porter may have mistaken her for someone else. This is a wounding idea, because she believes herself to be a singular individual. In shops, of course, she is recognized at once and attended with elaborate courtesy. The best people have been collecting her carte de visite. The wife of the British ambassador has pasted it in her album, after the duc de Morny (Louis Napoleon's half-brother), and right next to one of the Murat princes.

But then, a little while later, another explanation occurs to her: that something fearsome had just transpired in that house. Robbery, a murder? It has gotten so that one can travel only a mile or two beyond Chapultepec, and risk encountering terrorists and their sympathizers. Since the empress departed for Yucatan, things have gone from bad to worse. As Madame Almonte says, "Maximilian needs to take the velvet glove off his iron fist." By God in Heaven, he had better do it!

Nothing to do. Nothing to be done. Grain by grain the sands have slowed. The hourglass is spectacularly jammed.

On a folding chair outside the door of nursery, with his elbows on his knees and his chin stone-heavy in his hands, Weissbrunn, the bodyguard, slumps.

Prince Agustín is having his nap.

Was it an hour ago—it seems a year—Princess Iturbide came back from the city with a face that could have shriveled the testicles of an elephant. She'd gone to see some house she's got the butt-headed notion to buy. There is no house he's heard of that doesn't have several officers quartered in the best rooms. Why she would want to leave Chapultepec Castle, he can't figure. Nights, Weissbrunn wouldn't walk anywhere in Mexico City unless he was blind drunk, or absolutely had to, and then, he'd take the middle of the street and armed with a pistol, saber, and brass knuckles.

Frau Furchterregend, Madam Formidable, that's the Germans' nickname for the Princess Iturbide; in the residence, they all use it behind her back. Before, with the click of his fingers, Weissbrunn could have tossed off ten nicknames for a self-important battleaxe like that one. But here in Mexico City's thin mountain air, or maybe it's all the cannabis he's been smoking, his head feels like it's got sawdust in it, and glue. The little Iturbide, Weissbrunn just calls him by his Christian name. *Agustín! Agustín, come away from the horse.* Tere, his nursemaid, she's a treat for the eyes, but such a little cabbage-head. She let Agustín walk right by a horse's hind legs. They were outside the stables in the park. *"Das Pferd!* The horse!" Weissbrunn cried, unable to think of the word in Spanish, but Tere froze. He roused himself from the bench, and grabbed the nipper by the back of his jacket, and swung him up over his shoulder. Agustín started screaming, Christ, a bullhorn in his ear.

Yeah, here's the big-fuck adventure of the New World: Lieutenant Horst Weissbrunn's turned into a goddamned baby-minder.

Weissbrunn may have a sharp-looking uniform and a splendid mustache, but this bodyguard duty makes him feel lower than a stomped-on cow patty. The prince—he's a beautiful boy—just makes Weissbrunn think of his own lousy self. He could have been a father by now. Why isn't he married? He's made a dog's breakfast out of his life, beginning with the gambling. Slap-stupid wagers he made when he was drunk, so! Conduct unbecoming to a gentleman, his superior officer stuck that in his file. So, he had to ship out with the volunteers. For Archduke Max, yeah, Viva Max! And all that cart-load of Mexican flag-waving crap.

Austria is about to lock horns with Prussia, and where is Lieutenant Horst Weissbrunn of the ulan (cavalry) regiment number 10? Cooling his heels in this piss-ant setup. And he's no longer in the ulan regiment number 10 because he's gambled away his mount, four pairs of boots, his watch, and his signet ring, and after that he got drunk, and he said something idiotic, he can't even remember what, that got him slapped on the cheek by a pretty French girl, probably the only pretty French girl in the whole fucking country, and in front of his commanding officer, who laughed, a big jiggling gutbucket of a laugh, "Weissbrunn, what an ape you are!"

"Who's the ape?" Weissbrunn glared at him.

The officer, being stupid with beer, said, "If I'm the ape, Weissbrunn, you're the ape's prick."

And so, Weissbrunn, being even more stupid with beer, and some more of that cannabis, yeah, barely able to stand, challenged him to a duel. In Austria this would have got him clapped in handcuffs and to a court-martial, but this is Mexico, where in the wind of such strong need, yes! Turkeys fly. And the ostriches, too! Hell, take some of that Oaxacan mezcal, and you'll find the furniture flying right out the window. So, he got demoted and sent to the Imperial Residence, Chapultepec Castle. He was pulling sentry duty for the whole fucking raining summer.

And did it rain? Like a cow pissing on a flat rock.

Volunteering for Mexico would have looked a sight smarter if he could have seen some real action. He'd give his right arm to be one of Fünfkirchen's ulans roaming the sierras—ambushes, gun battles, hand-to-hand combat! If he'd stayed with his regiment, by now, he would have seen combat at Tetela de Oro, at Zantla, and Ahuacatlan. Combat is the golden chance to distinguish oneself, to redeem oneself. Battle can be alchemy, in a flash a heap of dung turns into a mountain of gold, that is, a chestful of medals. Of course, instead, you could get a bayonet through your guts.

But in Weissbrunn's case, that would not be likely. If his head is a mess, his body has a mind of its own, and his reactions, when he's sober, are lightning-quick.

He packs a .36 caliber pistol six-shooter with a seven-inch barrel. It was issued to him last month when he reported to work inside the Imperial Residence. Other than in target practice, he's fired it twice, both times off-duty. He hit a goose. *Bak*, it fell out of the sky and splashed into Lake Texcoco and sank. The second time, behind the stables in the park, he popped a squirrel as it went leaping along a high wall—*Bak*, a fluff of fur. The rest of the critter disappeared, over the other side.

In Austria, he'd packed a .44 caliber six-shooter with an eight-inch barrel, and in Italy, in '59, he used the hell out of it. He doesn't remember most of the Battle of Solferino, except that when he ran out of bullets, he picked up a rifle, and when that was out of bullets, he was bashing in their skulls with the butt. And then, he's not sure when this was, he was running, stumbling through drifting smoke over bodies, legs, pieces of flesh, there were pools of blood on the rocks, crows were circling, and the *boom-boom* of the artillery. It was all a jumbled, crashing blur except for one thing, and this remains in his mind, as clear as a photograph: curled atop a fence rail, perched there like a creature, a severed hand. That image sears into his mind, oh, about 2,779 times a day and in his dreams. *That hand.* His own big-knuckled hand—to see it there, resting on his thigh . . . he slips it inside the front of his jacket. The way he makes the memory stop, until it pops back, is to hum, *Ein, zwei, drei und der Hündschen . . .*

Fuck no, he isn't going to report what happened this morning down by the duck pond.

Frau Furchterregend had gone to the city, so it was just the three of them, Weissbrunn, Tere, and the prince. They left the carriage, they walked along the path to the pond. Weissbrunn was feeling nasty. He had cramps. Maybe he'd eaten bad fish. Tere set her basket of tortillas upon a tree stump. She tore one up, and Agustín began to toss the shreds. Whenever the ducks crowded too close, Tere would sling a piece out into the pond, and the ducks would tail after it, and then Agustín would ball up his fists and stamp his shoe. So Tere would give the nipper a bit of tortilla, he'd drop it near his feet, and the ducks would swim right back, the water rippling and sparkling behind them. It went on like that, ducks swimming out, ducks swimming back. Once in a while a mallard rose up, flapping his wings, as if to announce, *No, you fuckers, the tortilla belongs to ME! ME! ME!* The mallards went pecking at each other and splashing, but the others milled near the other shore or went to perch on a rock and preen their feathers.

Once, when he was about six years old, in Ölmutz, his uncle showed him his kaleidoscope. Horst held it to his eye while his uncle turned it so that the colored glass went to diamonds, to ice-crystal shapes, flowers, scarlet, purple, dazzling blue. It was like watching the stained glass of the cathedral come to life, magically form itself and reform itself. And Weissbrunn was thinking how it was like that in a way, the patterns of the ducks forming and reforming on the water, so green as glass, leaves and ribbons of foam floating along its surface; through the wavering, mottled reflection of the ahuehuete trees, and near the sandy edge, close to where they were standing, there were rocks on the bottom, furred with moss and water-grasses, gently waving. In the hedge a rustle: A tiny Indian in a shawl, a face like a raisin. Her eyes darted to something behind Weissbrunn. He swung around; a knife-blade ripped through the side-flap of his coat. He grabbed the wrist, and before he could see the face, with his other fist, he socked and socked it and punched, Weissbrunn kicked him in the ribs, he kicked the knife away, and he threw him face down, and landed a knee in his spine, grabbed his hair, and smashed that face into the dirt.

"*Schwein!*" Weissbrunn shouted into his ear.

Weissbrunn smashed his face down again, then pulled him up by the hair. What was this asshole trying to do? But Weissbrunn couldn't think what to say, not in German, least of all in Spanish. His heart was racing, but his skull felt like it was full of mud. He slugged him in the mouth.

The Mexican groaned and then lifted his head and spit out a bloody gob. It had a gold tooth in it.

Weissbrunn took his knee off the Mexican's back. "Get up," he ordered, and as he stepped back, he slid out his pistol.

Cringing, the Mexican stood. His face was pulp. His nostrils quivered, he was breathing raggedly. His frock coat was a gentleman's, but its collar gaped and the sleeves were too long, rolled up. The boots looked stiff and misshapen, the toes curled upward, and the tops came up to his knees he was so short. Weissbrunn loomed two full heads taller; his shoulders were almost twice as broad. A feeling he recognized came over him: a peculiar, deadly calm. It was what he felt when he had to slaughter an animal. It was what he felt when he'd been in the beautiful thick of battle.

He said, "Put your hands up."

The Mexican's hands went up, shakily, but not high; the fingertips almost touched his earlobes.

Weissbrunn cocked the hammer. "Higher."

Blood was streaming from the man's nose onto his shirt. Droplets, bright crimson, splashed the sand.

Aiming the pistol at the Mexican, Weissbrunn checked left, checked right. At the commotion, the ducks had scattered to the other end of the pond, and Tere was sitting on the tree stump with Agustín on her lap. She was trying to wrestle his arms down and wrap him into her shawl. He was crying, "Lupe!" Some baby-prattle.

Weissbrunn stood there with his finger on the trigger. What was he supposed to do? He couldn't think. Nail the fucker between the eyes? Not in front of the baby.

He had not been issued handcuffs.

He'd had a silver whistle, but where was it? He patted at his pockets . . . *Ach, ja,* he'd lost that at cards also.

Firing shots into the air? Could bring help, but more likely, with these idiot Mexican park police, a crazy shoot-out.

He had one thing straight: Protect the prince. He'd told himself a hundred times: *fuck that up and you're fucked.*

He could feel the sweat running down the sides of his nose, and between his shoulder blades. His intestines were cramping again. Suddenly, he needed . . . Christ on his Throne in Heaven! And it wasn't going to wait until he could get all the way back up to the residence. He'd been lusting to kill, but now, he wanted nothing more in the whole world than to run into the bushes and drop his trousers.

Weissbrunn said, holding himself firmly, "If I see you here again, I will kill you." He lowered his piece.

The Mexican, trembling, leaned forward and spat out another gob of blood.

"Go!" Weissbrunn said, waving his pistol toward the path back into the park. "Get out of here!"

The Mexican still had his hands up, and he stared at Weissbrunn with stark terror.

"Go!" Weissbrunn shouted.

"You will shoot me in the back."

"If you do not go," Weissbrunn said, "then I will shoot you in the face!"

The Mexican fled, his arms jack-knifing up the path, and Weissbrunn ran the other way, crashing through the bushes.

Afterward, when he came back to the pond, Weissbrunn found fresh sand sprinkled over the blood. The gold tooth that had fallen there was gone. Tere and Agustín were feeding the ducks again, as if nothing had happened. Weissbrunn came up behind them. He dimly realized, this little nursemaid now held his career in her hands. For this elephantine fuckup, he wouldn't get sentry duty, it really would be a court-martial. Beneath her nursemaid's cap, Tere wore her hair in coiled braids. Her hair was so dark it almost seemed blue. Many times, Weissbrunn had wanted to tell her that.

"Um," he began, and then he held his breath.

He wasn't sure how to say what he wasn't sure he should say in the first place. Besides, what a dumb-fuck thing to say at a time like this. *I like your hair. It looks almost blue.*

Tere flicked a piece of tortilla into the crowd of birds. Frau von Kuhacsevich had said she was the assistant pastry chef's cousin. Christ, she'd know everyone in the kitchen, all the Mexicans. And Tüdos, that magpie, he talked to Frau von Kuhacsevich, and she talked to everybody.

Keeping her eyes on the pond, Tere spoke as she always spoke to him, in a shy voice, as if to someone else.

"I won't tell."

What was he supposed to say to that? The breeze riffled the ahuehuetes and brushed over the water, erasing their reflection. He thought to himself, *You stupid, stupid fuck.*

Tere bent down to hand Agustín another shred of tortilla. "Don't eat it, sweetie, it's for the birds."

Weissbrunn fumbled out a cigarette and put it in his mouth. And then, Tere came up to him and boldly put her hand on the case.

Weissbrunn said, "I didn't know you were a smoker. Be my guest. But I warn you, they've got kick." He meant the cannabis he'd crumbled into the tobacco.

She kept her hand on the case. (*The hand.* The hand. He tried to blink it out of his head. *Ein, zwei . . .*)

"What?" Weissbrunn opened his eyes. "You want one? Take one."

She pulled the cigarette case.

"Hey," Weissbrunn said, pulling it back. It was silver, it had his father's monogram on it. This was one of the last things he owned that he hadn't lost at cards. She tugged with a fierceness that so surprised him, he let go. She hid it in a pocket deep within the folds of her skirt.

Weissbrunn took of his hat. He plowed a hand though his hair. Under his breath, he said, "Eh, ffff."

Still cooling his heels outside the nursery, Weissbrunn can tell by the angle of the sun puddling by his boot, another ten minutes killed. He yawns and shifts in his folding chair. If he'd give his right arm to be with Fünfkirchen's ulans, he'd give his left for a cigarette.

A goddamned cigarette!

He slides his pistol out of its holster. He lays it across his lap. He drums his fingers along the barrel. His finger, almost by itself, curls around the trigger. He lets the pistol swing; he twirls it. Then—it always flares into his brain out of nowhere: *the hand, the hand, that fucking hand* on that fucking fence rail, *Ein, zwei, drei* . . .

What if he just blew his brains out?

The end of the barrel: He presses it into his temple. He can feel the steel ring of the trigger against the flesh of his finger. With his thumb, he cocks the hammer. One squeeze—one little squeeze would do it. Now?

Not now. Not yet.

He lays the pistol back across his knees, just in time to touch the visor of his cap. *"Grüss Gott!"*

Frau von Kuhacsevich answers, "Good afternoon!" as she swishes by, her keys jangling.

And in her wake, Frau Furchterregend throws open the nursery door. "Weissbrunn!"

He's already snapped to attention. "Your Highness." He shoves the pistol back in its holster.

"We will be attending a children's party on the Calle de San Francisco." "Yes, ma'am."

Weissbrunn follows her and Prince Agustín, grumpy-faced in his starched white-lace frock, and Tere, who has sprayed herself with orange-water to conceal the smell of what she's been smoking. Her eyes are red.

They amble down the corridor slowly, because Frau Furchterregend's hip is bothering her. All the same, Agustín falls down on the slick marble and cries. He reaches his little arms up for Weissbrunn. Weissbrunn wants to pick him up and carry him, but he cannot do that in front of Frau Furchterregend.

Slow, slow, to have to move so fucking slow, and behind a screaming two-year-old, Weissbrunn feels sure, any day, any moment, his skull is going to explode.

❦

THE WIDOW DE GÓMEZ
PEDRAZA, AT-HOME

La Sociedad—that newspaper, as Doña Juliana de Gómez Pedraza likes to say—is little more than adverts for over-priced flubdubs and a dose of sugar-coated fantasy. Anyway her cataracts make reading well nigh impossible, and so, as she hasn't the vim to get about, Tuesday, her at-home day, is "newsday"—though the idea of news puts hummingbirds in her stomach. Public security appears to be going from troubled to catastrophic. A neighbor may have been murdered. The French are no longer trusted. Last week Madame Bazaine, her niece, warned, "Do not expect to see us here at this time next year. That is all I can tell you and you mustn't repeat it."

Moreover, in addition to the smaller aggravations of wartime, which to Doña Juliana are not small, three times Chole has burnt something since Tuesday last. This morning it was a batch of date-and-walnut cookies—with dried fruits and nuts at four times the price they were last year this season! The smoke has been fanned out of the kitchen—but not the stink, and it will be hours after the last of the visitors will have left before the windows in the drawing room can be shuttered.

Dressed in black, perfumed, and her gaunt face rouged and powdered, Doña Juliana glides on velvet slippers into her drawing room. The chairs, the chaise, and the two sofas have been arranged in a circle. She fluffs a cushion, straightens an antimacassar. Then she inspects her sideboard laid out with cups and saucers, and, proud upon a China stand, protected by a dome of glass, her famous pine nut-studded chocolate cake. She then eases herself into the wing chair by the window—the window with the crack she dare not grudge a peso to replace. And its frame wants a coat of paint. And the *mozo* has been conscripted into the army, she supposes (Pablito simply disappeared one day last spring), and so, it is Chole who shall have to scrape the bird droppings. She's been reminded twice, and she's yet to do it.

Doña Juliana reminds herself: *Al bien buscarlo, al mal esperarlo.* Look for good things, wait for bad things, as Don Manuel used to say.

This wing chair is the one in which, fourteen years ago, Don Manuel breathed his last. In the embrace of its cushioned, red-leather depths, his widow used to spend her days embroidering cloaks for the Templo de la Profesa's effigy of the Virgin, but since her seventieth birthday her eyes have been ruined for fine work. The Almighty in His Infinite Wisdom has taken this pleasure from His servant, as He has taken so many things, so many dear ones. She leans over the arm of the wing chair, her mantilla draping her elbow, and peers down into the street: a canyon of shadow. Her vision may be fogged, but she can make out that it has not been swept. "*¿No toman chícharros?* Won't you have peas?" A woman with a basket passes below; her lilting call fades. There are fewer *ambulantes*. The lard-seller has not come by in over a week. Opposite, over Count Villavaso's *porte-cochère*, the black bow and ribbon has been knocked askew; a length of it trails to the flagstones.

She is hoping to see her niece's carriage—it always scatters traffic and, once parked, attracts a crowd. A good six months have gone by since the wedding, but Doña Juliana is not yet accustomed to hearing Pepita called Madame Bazaine. Pepita has been going around with no less than three bodyguards, sometimes as many as four, an ostentatious number it seemed to Doña Juliana until Pepita explained, the general insists upon it. And the general, Doña Juliana knows, is not an ostentatious man.

Tsk, Doña Juliana clucks her tongue: there, hurrying past in the street, goes Lupe—again. Doña Juliana would recognize her ex-*galopina* anywhere: the pigeon-toed gait, the skinny white plaits bouncing on her tiny humped back. She's up to mischief, but what? (Where can Lupe be eating?) That little ingrate was the bane of Chole's days. Poor old Chole, who hard to believe, is now even more frail than her mistress.

Such has become the once grand house of the Gómez Pedrazas: a cold cave for a widow and her arthritic, bad-tempered, increasingly forgetful cook. In these nearly three months since Angel and Alicia's departure, it has been sheerly by the resources of her rapidly dwindling bank account in New Orleans, and her niece's intervention, that Doña Juliana has managed to keep the third floor of this house vacant. Everyone else in Mexico City—Mrs. Yorke, even Conchita Aguayo, one of the empress's ladies-of-honor—has been obliged to billet officers. Some may be gentlemen, Mrs. Yorke claims her are, but Doña Juliana can imagine the uncouth characters they would have visit, their women, drinking, card-playing, language she would not wipe the floor with—*Tsk*, Doña Juliana clucks her tongue again. In all her years, Doña Juliana has seen more soldiers than she could shake a knitting needle at: Spaniards, royalists, revolutionaries, liberals, for the empire, for the republic, legions of bugle-blowing Yankees . . . Why, last Tuesday, one of her elderly visitors, after one too many tequilas, declared that it no longer mattered a pin to her which uniform a soldier wears, be it blue or green or gray—a soldier makes war. And what is war? It is the making of widows and orphans.

The Demon's work: that is what Lupe must be up to. Twice last week, from this window, Doña Juliana has spied her tagging after a ruffian in a cutaway coat so big on him the tails were dragging on the ground. He wore his sombrero low over his forehead. Too low. He was hiding his face. At once, Doña Juliana rang the bell for Chole.

Had Lupe come by?

Chole mumbled at the floor.

"Don't be shy with the truth. Did Lupe come to this door?"

More mumbley-mumble.

Doña Juliana had not run a household all these many years for nothing. Servants, she knew perfectly well, tried to protect one from whatever they fancied might be upsetting. The better to gauge things, Doña Juliana put her lorgnette to her eye. "*Tsk*. Out with it."

"She came to the door, yes."

"When did she come to the door?"

"Yesterday."

"When yesterday?"

"Before the coal was delivered."

"What did she want?"

"I saw it was her from the judas window. I did not open."

"You did not speak to her?"

"Señora, I did not."

"Not one word?"

"Two. I told her, *Go away!*"

Doña Juliana leaned in close and, through that lens, narrowed her eye. "Do you swear it?"

"Before Jesus Christ Our Savior."

"And before all the Saints?"

"So help me." Chole crossed herself.

The lorgnette went back into Doña Juliana's pocket. "Good. That is what I want to hear."

One had to drill it into servants, the new, the old, the trustiest, that never, ever were they to open the door to anyone other than the master's family and recognized friends. One could not repeat the warning often enough; for a servant to open the door heedlessly—but once!—could be the very invitation to mayhem and murder. Such has been the disgraceful situation of this country in every one of Doña Juliana's years, and it is getting worse.

On no account is an ex-*galopina* to be allowed into this house. Least of all Lupe, that silly rabbit. How her head swelled up like a soufflé when Pepa de Iturbide had the absurd idea to make her the nanny to the grandson of the Liberator! "What do you know about babies?" Pepa had asked that little mosquito. "All that God wants me to," Lupe answered, an answer that described the grass the Goliath of Truth was standing upon—but left out the Goliath, which was that Lupe knew nothing whatsoever. She could peel and chop, and if pressed, pluck birds (she was too squeamish to wring a chicken's neck, Chole always had to do that work).

Of all the servants in all the years in this house, Lupe was hands down the most insolent, fork-tongued, and conniving. There were the disappearances over the years: a silver thimble, a pearl earring, one of the cuff links Don

Manuel swore he had left in a dish on his bedside table . . . a cigar or two . . . a sock . . . a spoon, small things one might have misplaced, but then it happened a time too often. Chole complained Lupe stole her soap slivers. It was out of God-fearing charity that Doña Juliana first gave that orphan a job in her kitchen and kept her all those years—what had it been, over fifty years? Doña Juliana had warned Alicia when she sent Lupe to cook for her: "She'll do, but keep her in the kitchen." And then, when the Iturbides left, once again Doña Juliana offered to keep a roof over Lupe's head. And what was that one's answer? To run off, just as that *mozo* probably did, with who-knows-who.

"*Shuh!*" she shoos a pigeon from the ledge.

Sitting by an open window in December invites catarrh, Doña Juliana's doctor would scold her—the doctor she has now. She has outlived three. She likes to say, the reason is, she's not let one grain of tobacco cross her lips. She luxuriates in fresh air—the freshest possible. In fact, she used to take her sewing and a parasol to preserve her complexion up to the flat-roof. From there, she could see what seemed to her the whole world: the volcanoes in the distance, and closer, the sun-rinsed towers of the cathedral. One had to come around to the side of the maids' quarters to see it: yonder west, past a stretch of fields, rose the rock crowned by Chapultepec Castle. With the setting of the sun, the façade turned a marvelous tufa pink; it brought to mind a box of Spanish nougat-candy. Before Maximilian, it housed the Military College. If the wind happened to be blowing her way, she might catch the *tat-tat* of drums.

From the wing chair Doña Juliana peers down into the street again. A page of *La Sociedad* skids along the cobblestones, like a bird with a useless wing. Not in years has her first visitor been so tardy. When Don Manuel was alive, on Tuesdays she would receive as many as two hundred—countesses, wives of bankers, of ambassadors, of cabinet ministers and generals. This drawing room was often abuzz with twenty, thirty, forty of the most important ladies in this country. Sure as the moon calls forth the tides, with power and influence come swells of well-wishers, gossip-hunters, the favor-seekers—you can never satisfy them all, and though you try, and though they offer you a face of sunshine, Lord knows what thunderbolts are hurled behind your back.

As Don Manuel often observed, it is when you are out of office that you learn which are your true friends. Of course, last year, when General Bazaine began courting Pepita, and she, Doña Juliana, served as chaperone, all of a sudden Tuesdays got busier. Madame Almonte showed up, that was a first . . . but the most familiar thing. Doña Juliana warned her niece, take care how you treat people, for when you are perceived as powerful, it is easier than you imagine to offend. *Mi querida,* one day, away it all will flow. And we shall all, whether queens or beggars, have to answer to Saint Peter at the gates of the Hereafter.

Doña Juliana gets up and goes over to her harpsichord. Hesitantly at first, then swiftly, her still nimble fingers dance up and down the scales. Her shoulders sway as she loses herself in the minuet. And so she does not see or hear her first visitor's coach sweep up to the curb. The lackey, in full livery, hops down and snaps open the door. Out comes the last person on earth Doña Juliana is expecting to see today—Pepa, that is, Princess Iturbide.

As for Princess Iturbide, this December morning may be bright as the beginning of the world, but she is sorely troubled by a black cloud of worries, resentments, disappointments, and outright fist-clenching fury. She did not sleep well, and from the moment she got out of bed this morning, her mind has been churning. Would that Father Fischer were here! And the empress and half the cabinet not yet returned from their hair-brained expedition to Yucatan! Most confounding are Maximilian's absences. He does not show himself in the theater, he does not ride, he does not drive. He squanders entire mornings being instructed in the Nahuatl language! For days at a time he meanders off to whatever flea-infested Indian village and, with his personal botanist, traipses about the countryside with butterfly nets. And, complaining of the cold in Chapultepec, he has taken to sleeping downtown in the Imperial Palace, where, according to Frau von Kuhacsevich, he keeps a stove going as if he were in the snowbound Hofburg! In Chapultepec Castle, Princess Iturbide and her tiny godson might as well be marooned on an island of savages. The von Kuhacseviches have lost control of the staff—to the point where, after dinner, whilst the Mexican footmen clear dishes and platters, an

Austrian must pick each piece of silverware off each tray as it goes by—oyster fork, salad fork, cream-soup spoon, and etcetera. He lays the pieces upon a napkin he has spread on the floor in the corner, and then wraps it all up and carries it off to wash the silver himself. This in full view of all present! Such is the extent of pilfering: next the malachite urns shall have to be chained to the floor!

The single sunny spot in her life is that she has wrested control over her own and Prince Agustín's schedules. When the empress was in residence, mornings were taken up with interminable tours of orphanages, hospitals, schools for paupers, and then, the *tertulias,* state dinners, balls; for herself, Pepa was left with only the most niggardly portion of the day. Over the past month, however, she has had her mornings free to search for a residence and, also, to go shopping and visiting. She is much in demand. But if she has very naturally slipped into being treated as if she were a priceless and fragile sculpture, by no means has she forgotten her friends. This morning she dedicates to visiting the widow of one of her late father's most loyal supporters. Yes, Doña Juliana, widow of Don Manuel Gómez Pedraza, the aunt of Madame Bazaine, and, it so happens, Angelo and Alicia's ex-landlady.

Alas, it was Doña Juliana who in her carriage took Alicia to see, or rather, intrigue with General Bazaine. But from the moment Pepa heard about that (from Frau von Kuhacsevich, who got it straight from Maximilian's coachman, the horse's mouth, as it were), she concluded that Doña Juliana, caught off guard by the little American's hysterics, must have merely thought to go first to her one relative with an "in"—that most unlikely Madame Bazaine, her niece Pepita. They called it a December–May relationship, but it was more December–January—the groom robbed the cradle!

Well, why, in Heaven's name, did Alicia not first contact her own sister-in-law? That was an "in" if you wanted one! Why did Alicia not think of that?

It was the grossest humiliation to have been subjected to Their Majesties' consternated questions. Over the past months it has become increasingly clear to Pepa the injury, possibly irreparable, that the scandal made to her reputation at court. But should she have been surprised? From the very first, she did not approve of Alicia. Miss Green was "green" indeed. A Washington belle with a head full of air could hardly be expected to adapt to Mexico, and she was too young for Angelo—half his age! Angelo must have been bewitched. Pepa told their mamá (and she half-believed it herself) that the cook at Rosedale, Aunt Sally, a Negress the size of a house, must have slipped an aphrodisiac in his chowder. True, in the past two years, one's estimation of Alicia had improved, marginally, but as her recent irresponsible behavior has abundantly revealed, first impressions were not mistaken. Princess Iturbide is only sorry that Doña Juliana has been embarrassed. To this sweet, gentle, devout old family friend, Princess Iturbide has no intention of mentioning the episode, any more than she would if, say, someone passed gas. A highness's mere presence at Doña Juliana's visiting day will convey that her hostess is restored to favor. Yes, in paying this first visit, she descends from her proper level. But information is currency; a peso of it might be exchanged for larger coin from Madame Almonte, Frau von Kuhacsevich, Count del Valle, Tüdos, who knows?

Chole, with labored breathing, leads her up the stairs. The stairwell stinks of burnt molasses. The stone steps are worn and chipped. Princess Iturbide grips the railing, favoring her left hip. She turns her good ear to the tinkly buzz of the harpsichord. The parlor stinks of not only burnt molasses but, as ever, mildew and rotting leather, never mind that the window has been left wide open. Beneath the portrait of Don Manuel, there on a dusty scrap of velvet sprawls a sorry-looking crèche, all ajumble, the roof of the straw manger listing, and some of the angels missing wings, or arms. Over the sofa the same worm-eaten painting that must have been hanging there since the last century: Our Lady of Guadalupe, and, kneeling before her, church officials in lace and scarlet robes, the viceroy in a blue coat—a long-faded blue that quite clashes with the upholstery.

Doña Juliana, touching the diamond brooch at her throat, rises from her bench.

She comes around and embraces Pepa. She pats Pepa's cheek, just as she did when Pepa was a little girl.

"So good to see you, my dear, wherever have you been? I thought—"

"And you." Princess Iturbide breaks away, irritated at her hostess's ignorance of protocol. Wasn't it all over Mexico how foolish Madame Almonte had made herself in receiving Carlota at Veracruz with an abrazo?

"Ah!" Doña Juliana says sadly as her hand disappears into the folds of her shawl. "You have not brought Agustinito?"

Pepa does not answer as she arranges herself on the wing chair, which protests her bulk with a dangerous-sounding creak. Doña Juliana has the eerie sense that she is treating with an apparition. After the fiasco with Alicia, Doña Juliana assumed she had been cut. Pepa seems to have changed. Is it her bearing? She has put on weight. She's had to move her black pearl ring to her pinky. And what an exotic crust brown loaf of a hat. *Chapeaux*, the French call them. Doña Juliana herself would sooner go out of her house with a cookpot on her head!

To Princess Iturbide, her hostess seems of a piece with the ancient furnishings, awaiting, with passive and pious stolidity, the indignity of further deterioration. Dust clings to absolutely everything.

Doña Juliana repeats: "You have not brought Agustinito?"

"Pardon?" Pepa says, turning her good ear.

"Agustinito. How is he?"

"In the park."

Doña Juliana claps her hands. "A splendid day to be in the park! Though a bit chilly for my old bones. And tell me—" she leans closer to Pepa's good ear—"*how* is the little darling?"

"Plump. Rosier than ever."

Pepa seems unusually distracted. Doña Juliana is uncertain what more she might ask about the little one whom she has missed as if he were her own grandchild. Oh, with such heartache. Every morning, she used to lean over his pram to tickle his chin, or squeeze a chubby leg. *Who is this* pollito? *Is he Agustín* chiquitín?

The Gómez Pedrazas have always been close to the Iturbides. Her husband's friendship with the Liberator and in recent years her friendship with his children had been a wellspring of pride. She had been devastated when Angel and Alicia left—and hurt, though not surprised, when, once she joined the court back in September, Pepa sent no invitations and stopped coming to her at-home days. Princess? Your Highness? What should Doña Juliana call her? "Pepita" is what she once called her, the same as her niece. Oh, but that was fifty years ago.

As far as the baby is concerned, as Don Manuel used to say, *Don't be a dog between two tacos.* In other words, if you don't want to end up hungry, choose. Don Manuel chose Iturbide—and, though that almost cost him his life, he had made a sacred oath to his emperor. But there was something else Don Manuel used to say, and in this peculiar circumstance, it seems to Doña Juliana the wiser: *if you can do nothing, say nothing.* Though her heart belongs to Alicia, who had been so frantic with grief—a mother's grief, and what would Pepa, a spinster, know of that?

This is what happened on that horrid, rain-soaked middle of the night back in September: Doña Juliana heard such a violent clanging it took her a moment to recognize her own doorbell. Who would jerk its rope like that? Chole ran down to see through the judas eye: a woman in a hooded cloak, dripping wet—Alicia! Looking wild, her hair disarranged, her face stained with tears. Chole brought her a cup of *té de tila*, linden flower tea, to calm her. Alicia spilled it down the front of her dress. Where was her husband, and her brothers-in-law? Waiting near the city of Puebla. It made no sense, and then all at once it made perfect sense.

"If I cannot see my child—" Alicia let out a sound that could have come from a wild animal.

Doña Juliana took her into her arms. "I know, I know." And she did know: Doña Juliana had lost her only child in a miscarriage. "You are not alone," she said, smoothing Alicia's damp hair. "And remember, Our Mother Mary also lost her son, Jesus."

Doña Juliana did not question what she was to do: help in any way. Alicia spent the rest of that night pacing. Doña Juliana could hear the floorboards creaking, and her muffled weeping. After breakfast, which Alicia did not touch, at once Doña Juliana took her to her niece, Madame Bazaine. From General Bazaine it would be a straight shot to Maximilian's ear—no need to go through twenty-seven layers of flunkies. As the widow of a man who had been a cabinet minister and briefly president, Doña Juliana was no stranger to these backdoor strategies. And, having chaperoned her niece during the recent courtship, Doña Juliana had, despite her prejudices (above all, that he was too old and also French), grown to esteem General Bazaine as a man of honor, with both good sense and a good heart.

Pepita's reaction to Alicia's story was to cover her mouth. With a gravity far beyond her seventeen years, she grasped Alicia's hands and said, "My dear friend, I will do all in my power to help you."

Without delay, Alicia was ushered into the general's office. Doña Juliana and her niece waited in the anteroom on two of the several straight-backed chairs lined up against a wall decorated with a bristling array of sabers and muskets and pikes. It was stale-smelling with ashtrays and a spittoon; Doña Juliana got up and, with some trouble, forced open the window. She had just sat down again when his aide-de-camp, Captain Blanchot, came out of the general's office and, uncertainly, pulled the door closed behind him. *"Bonjour,"* said the two señoras. But Captain Blanchot—whom they had seen at innumerable dinners and balls and, recently, at his own wedding to one of the Miss Yorkes—did not recognize them. He brushed his fingers at the back of his collar and then, as if he'd decided something, slapped his thigh, and stalked off into the garden.

Doña Juliana said in a low voice, "The general is only trying to protect him."

Pepita whispered, "How I *hate* Maximilian."

Doña Juliana patted her niece's hand. "The less said, the sooner mended. Remember who you are, dear. Your husband has been put in a delicate position."

Doña Juliana then brought out her rosary beads and worried them for twenty minutes that felt to her like twenty hours.

Afterward, Alicia told her that as soon as he had sent his aide out of the office, the general informed her he had just received a message from the palace—that Maximilian was aware she was in Mexico City and that, as she had of her own free will signed a binding contract, Bazaine should take no notice of her suit. She had dissolved into tears. The general, very much the gentleman, invited her to be seated, and with his own hands, he poured and brought her a glass of water. Her story spilled out of her, and tears, and she didn't really remember it all, but when she had finished, she found him looking at her from across his desk with an expression of deep sadness. She gave him the letter she had written Maximilian. He put on his spectacles to read it. Then he lay the letter flat on his desk and put both of his bear-like hands on top of it. His Spanish, though oddly accented, was impeccable.

"*¿Y qué, su señoria, desearía que yo hiciése?* And what, Madam, would you have me do?"

"Send my letter to Maximilian."

"Consider it done."

Over the next two days, the tenderest hopes were nurtured . . . above all, in fervent prayer to Our Lady, to Jesus, and San Judas Tadeo, or Saint Jude Thaddeus, the patron saint of desperate cases. Day and night Doña Juliana kept the wax tapers burning before the altar in her drawing room. Then, on the second morning, a Palatine Guard appeared at her door. He said that Their Majesties wished to confer with Doña Alicia about her son's future. The officer was one of those Austrians, crisply polite, but there was a deadness in his blue eyes; Doña Juliana felt very uneasy. The coach he had come in, parked directly in front, blocked her door. It was the size of a wine merchant's van, and its curtains drawn. On its gleaming black side, stenciled in gold, was the spider-like monogram MIM, for the Latin, *Maximiliano Imperator de Mexico*.

"Please," the officer said, and with a gesture, made Alicia understand that she was to climb in.

"No, no," Doña Juliana said, "Let me lend you my carriage." As a signal, she squeezed Alicia's elbow. Later, looking back on it, Doña Juliana realized she could not have prevented Alicia's arrest. Maximilian must already have given the order. It could not have mattered which coach Alicia climbed into. But at the time, Doña Juliana did not know this. She waited all morning for Alicia to return, and then she waited all through the afternoon.

That evening Father Fischer came to the house. By this time, Doña Juliana was so sick with worry she could scarcely breathe. Father Fischer explained that yes, Princess Doña Alicia had been detained but no, nothing untoward had happened, she had not been thrown in a dungeon (he laughed gently) nor anything of the kind. What on earth did Doña Juliana take Maximilian for? Alicia would be reunited with her husband and brothers-in-law in the city of Puebla, they would continue on to Veracruz, board the first steamer out, and reside in Paris, generously provided for—

"Oh! But the heartbroken little mother!" Doña Juliana sniffled into her handkerchief.

Well, Father Fischer countered, it was surely very painful, but there were matters of a higher interest for the nation. This was a time when many people were making many sacrifices, and as Doña Juliana knew, Their Highnesses Don Angel and Don Agustín Gerónimo and Don Agustín Cosme, and Doña Pepa and, indeed, Doña Alicia herself, had signed a very (he swung his head), very solemn contract.

When Doña Juliana could not stop shaking, Father Fischer sat with her and together they recited the Lord's Prayer. His soutane smelled of cabbage, and his breath of beer, but his voice, so smooth, soothed her. Then, with three graceful flicks of his hand, her confessor blessed her. Doña Juliana should not trouble her mind, he said. This was what God wanted.

On this Doña Juliana and Pepa agree heartily: it will be a gala day when Father Fischer returns from Rome. He shall reconcile His Holiness with Maximilian, neither has the least doubt, for Father Fischer is a man of the firmest integrity, the utmost perception, and a charm that could make the Devil give up his horns. Doña Juliana has written to Father Fischer, though she has not yet received an answer. "And you?"

Pepa cups a hand to her ear. "Pardon?"

"Have you had any mail from Father Fischer?"

"Ah, mail. Have you heard—I'm sure there's been no report in the newspapers, but last week, renegades captured the mail coach twice."

It seems that Pepa misheard her question, but Doña Juliana follows this new tack. "Twice, you say?"

"My sources are in the Palace Guard. The mail bags were slashed open and their contents dumped over a hillside—within sight of the fort at Río Frío."

"Brazen they are!"

"Quite." Pepa takes a large forkful of cake.

"You've no news of Father Fischer then?"

"Who?"

"Father Fischer.

"Not yet."

"God willing, soon."

Pepa closes her eyes. "God willing." She accepts a freshened cup of *café de olla*. "Madame Bazaine, is she well?"

"Very." But Doña Juliana is in no mood to offer up tidbits about her niece. Whatever she says about Madame Bazaine will be repeated as on a bullhorn. "I have terrible news. My neighbor, Count Villavaso, across the street, may have been murdered."

Princess Iturbide gasps. "Murdered, you say?"

Doña Juliana explains: Chole got it from the count's cook that in the night a thief had broken into his kitchen. "Apparently, the count heard the noise, grabbed his musket and, as he ran down the stairs, slipped and cracked open his skull. Either that or someone hit him with a brick bat."

"A what?"

"Brick bat."

"What?"

"Brick bat. Someone hit him with a brick bat."

"Ah."

"The cook found him in a heap at the bottom."

"God save his soul!"

"All that went missing was a bag of cornmeal."

"That is the price of a man's life these days."

It seems to Doña Juliana that her visitor is giving her crèche a ferocious stare. "What is the matter?"

"His son will agree to sell it?"

Doña Juliana blinks. "Whose son?"

"Count Villavaso's. It is my object to buy that house."

"My dear, you cannot live where something so evil has happened!"

"Where else am I to go? Unless I am to live in what has been turned into an officers' barracks, or wait an eternity for repairs to be made. Other than Count Villavaso's, there is not a suitable house to be had between here and Timbuktu."

"My dear." Doña Juliana leans forward to pat Pepa's hand. "You would give me the happiness of my life if you would take the upper floor of my house."

"If that were possible . . ." The Heir Presumptive in rented rooms? *Une idée affreuse.* But Pepa is a disciple of discretion when it comes to other people's feelings. "I've a nest egg to invest. Property, that's the thing."

At the mention of money, Doña Juliana feels a sudden attack of indigestion. She puts her hand to her ribs but, with some effort, arranges her face into an agreeable expression. She holds out the plate of date-and-walnut cookies. "Have another?"

"I couldn't."

Doña Juliana raises the coffeepot. "More—?" The clock on the mantel interrupts her with ten *tings.* Or rather, as its ancient mechanism has begun to fail, *ting, bong, b-B-b-bong, brrrr-ong, bing, ting.*

Pepa brings herself up, using the arms of the wing chair to brace herself. "Prince Agustín will have returned from the park." She makes no move but allows herself to be embraced.

"Bring Agustinito with you next time?" But Doña Juliana's voice so quavers that Pepa does not hear her.

On her way out, passing the last little table, Princess Iturbide happens upon the the carte de visite of her godson. She picks up the silver frame and gazes upon his small person as if for the first time, her eyes softening the way a mother's would. Prince Agustín stands with one pudgy hand on the cane seat of a chair. He wears those shoes the Master of Ceremonies had so strenuously objected to, and a lace-trimmed frock. That helmet-like hat he refused to put on is on the chair. His lips slightly parted, his expression is at once innocent and frank. Princess Iturbide has given out some two dozen of these cartes de visite—she wonders, who passed theirs on to Doña Juliana, or did she purchase it, and in which shop?

Doña Juliana says, coming up behind, her lorgnette to her eye, "The intelligence, it shines right through."

"Oh, he is in charge," Princess Iturbide agrees.

"He reminds me so much of his—" Doña Juliana was about to say "mother," but she catches herself and says, instead, "grandfather."

"Indeed." Princess Iturbide sets the picture back on the table, upon the moth-eaten altar cloth with the other little portraits, dusty photographs of

Doña Juliana's nieces and nephews, General and Madame Bazaine's wedding portrait, dusty miniature oils of long-dead sisters, Don Manuel . . . And, amongst a collection of dusty snuffertrays, that atrocious ivory of a Madonna. Its eyes, Pepa judges, are squeezed-looking and the fingers those of a monkey. Pepa's mamá had inherited a collection of ivories, including an exquisite Virgin of Loreto, a Santa Rosalía, and a Saint Francis of Assisi with an open-winged sparrow—an Oriental marvel—attached to the hand. In Mexico, Mamá had kept them in her boudoir, and been heartbroken to have had to abandon them. Compared to those ivories, this is pitiful. If she were Doña Juliana's daughter, Princess Iturbide thinks, she would advise her to put it away. Or at least clean the thing! A handy recipe is to dissolve rock alum in soft water, then boil the ivory for a minimum of a quarter-hour. One can take a hogs-bristle toothbrush to it. When clean, it must be wrapped in a damp cloth, to keep it from fissuring. But, as Mamá used to say: *El consejo no es bien recibido donde no es pedido*—Advice is not well received where it has not been invited. One must have patience with the elderly, Pepa reminds herself. There, but for the Grace of God, go I, and shall I go. A dim golden glimmer of what she imagines to be her future: herself in a sumptuous salon, receiving her godson, a beautifully educated young man soon to be, if not already, emperor of Mexico: Agustín III, a man with a vision for his people and the fear of God.

Doña Juliana takes both of Pepa's hands in hers. "Bring him with you next Tuesday?"

"If God wants it." Princess Iturbide pulls away.

In the hall mirror, as Princess Iturbide adjusts her chapeau and pins it to her thinning hair, Doña Juliana yearns to ask if there has been any news of Angelo and Alicia—have they arrived safely in Paris? Did Alicia see her mother in Washington? The poor dear, is she feeling steadier? And Angelo, have the Parisian doctors cured his gout? Agustín Gerónimo, the eldest, was coughing so violently the last time she saw him. Is he—? But Doña Juliana dare not presume. She can hear the shade of Don Manuel whisper, as he so often did in the days when Don Agustín was their emperor, and he walked at his side through the hallways of power: *Let discretion be our guiding star.*

Princess Iturbide picks up her purse and fastens it to her belt. "You need not accompany me to the door."

Doña Juliana cannot help herself—after a stitch of hesitation, she calls after Pepa, "Next week, if you can come, do bring Agustinito?"

But too late; Princess Iturbide, halfway down the stairs—greeting Mrs. Yorke and her daughters, who are on their way up—does not hear.

December 11, 1865

❦

THE BOOK OF THE SEA

*I*n the Grand-Hôtel in Paris, Angelo sleeps into the meat of the morning, dreaming: the king is dead. The roar rises from the crowd, *who then?* He lifts his palm and the sea cleaves. He strides—a Moses—onto the sand, the rock-strewn bottom. On either side of his path rise walls of water. They are crystalline; he can see the fishes swimming within. He strides on, swallowing planetary distances. It is so simple to bring forth a path through the sea. Why, he wonders, had he not understood this?

But another dream comes more often, indeed nightly, and again this morning upon the cusp of waking: in which he is being backed at saber point to the edge of a cliff. He wakes with his heart racing and his skin gone cold. Once, last week, he had woken up, thrashing the blankets, shouting "Pepa!" and woke Alicia.

Alicia rages that Pepa tricked her. *Pepa could have convinced Maximilian to give back the baby. Pepa was always bragging that she had Maximilian's ear. Maximilian has a good heart, doesn't everyone say so? So, if he won't give back the baby, it's because Pepa . . .*

Her accusing words are knives in his heart. Her misery is the fault of his family's glittering burdens. He never should have allowed her, so naive and headstrong, to make, let alone influence, such a decision. Teeth clenched, he accepts this.

From the start, he had resisted it. Such costly honors, he should have— God, he could have!—held his ground. On the long crossing to Europe, his mind circled and circled until one day it stumbled upon the trapdoor of a horrifying realization: last summer, when Maximilian first ordered the family to quit the country, they could have turned to General Almonte. That was the lifesaver, right under their noses! Almonte, when ambassador to Washington, had been the guest of honor at their wedding, in the front parlor at Rosedale. A member of the delegation that offered Maximilian the throne, Almonte had served as regent under the French Occupation and now, if Maximilian had sidelined him, his wife was chief lady-in-waiting to the empress. But, the bastard of Father Morelos had obscure loyalties—perhaps, still, to Santa Anna? In no wise of the Iturbide's social rank, this was not an individual to whom one would want to be beholden.

The head of the Iturbide family, however, is not Angelo. Agustín Gerónimo would sooner deign to oblige himself to a pickaninny.

But, God, Angelo thinks now, if they could have put aside their scruples! Anything, to accept a minor position in any European legation, even South American, anything, dear Jesus, would be better than to live like this.

Every day Angelo listens to his wife rail, for as long as he can stand it, which isn't long: he has to go out. He unspools hours over newspapers in cafés, trolls the bookstalls, and the echoing galleries of the Louvre where he looks blearily at the same pictures again and again. What can he possibly say that Alicia would be able to hear? She has reason to insist that Pepa was overly persuasive, but it is not so simple. Maximilian is hardly Pepa's puppet. Nor Father Fischer's. If there be a puppeteer, it is Louis Napoleon. The irony is, Maximilian has exiled them to Louis Napoleon's doorstep.

Patience, Mr. Bigelow had counseled when he'd come to call on the Iturbides at the Grand-Hôtel. Mr. Bigelow reported that he had mentioned their plight to the French foreign minister and requested that, as a purely private matter, he receive the Iturbides. Drouyn de Lhuys's answer had been a resounding, *"Pas possible."*

It has now been more than two weeks with not a word.

They had so tightly grasped the hope that Drouyn de Lhuys might receive them, and then, having heard their heart-wrenching story, that he might speak to the emperor, who might then urge Maximilian to return their child.

Oh, would that it were, as Mamá used to say, *flan frío, caliente el cuchillo,* for a cold flan, a hot knife!

Angelo would have harbored no hope at all, but back in October, when they visited Washington, the secretary of state received him in his home—a rare honor, as Seward was still recovering from having been stabbed in the throat on the night of President Lincoln's assassination. Angelo knew him from the early 1850s, when Seward was the senator from New York and Angelo was secretary and, as the ambassador had not yet arrived, acting head of the Mexican legation. (In conversation once, Mr. Seward had said that, second to the U.S. Constitution, his father's Plan of Iguala was the most important political document of the New World. Seward had been showing off; nonetheless, Angelo, accustomed to so much casual disregard for Mexico, could not help but have been flattered.) By the end of this meeting with Mr. Seward, they had become more than acquaintances. As another of Mamá's rhyming sayings went: *el enemigo de mi enemigo es mi amigo,* the enemy of my enemy is my friend. It was a dangerous game to be getting into, but Maximilian left them no quarter. With Mr. Seward's letter in hand, the Iturbides raced to Paris . . .

And after all these weeks on tenterhooks, to hear Mr. Bigelow counsel patience, Alicia had buried her face in her hands. Angelo had wanted to bellow out of despair. Instead, he said quietly, "We remain much obliged to you, sir."

"Yeah," Agustín Gerónimo said, "patien', uh."

There had been something lewd in his older brother's expression, but it turns out he is suffering from an abscessed molar. He has such a holy terror of dentistry, he has been suffering in silence—swearing he isn't hungry, or he's trying to quit his pipe. Now there is no disguising it: the entire left side of his face is red and swollen. His neck is tender. This morning he's taken such a quantity of laudanum for the pain that Angelo has to help him into his clothes. Dressed, Agustín Gerónimo staggers toward the chaise, steadies himself on the back of the bergère, then grabs at the doorknob, misses—Quite the drama, and all before the waiter arrives with the breakfast trolley, which perfumes the room with mint and fennel and alcohol. Always the alcohol, and now that the youngest, Agustín Cosme, has used his first payment to buy himself a tavern in Montparnasse . . .

"What's this? Absinthe with your egg?" Angelo softens that comment with a small laugh.

From the chaise, where he is stretched out with a blanket over his legs, Agustín Gerónimo says, "You hav' th' egg."

"I have eaten. An hour ago." A wheezing cough.

"I shall fetch Dr. Evans."

"God, no."

"Brother, you ought not go on like this, putting nothing in your stomach. I really do think that a dentist—"

"Y' deaf?" Agustín Gerónimo gives him a lidded, yellow glare. "Gimme that glass."

Stiffly, Angelo complies.

"Spoon," Agustín Gerónimo commands.

Using the silver sugar tongs, Angelo places a lump of sugar on the slotted absinthe spoon. He hands it into his brother's trembling grasp. "I'll pour for you." Angelo trickles the water over the sugar. As it falls through the slots, the absinthe louches, turning from emerald green to a milky brownish green.

Shakily Agustín Gerónimo brings the glass to the right side of his mouth. He winces hideously. Angelo, meanwhile, wrestles himself into his cashmere coat. (Before crossing the Channel, they had outfitted themselves at Hill Brothers Tailors on Bond Street.) He picks up his beaver-fur top hat, but instead of putting it on, he holds it by the rim.

"Brother?" Angelo taps his hat lightly, as if it were a drum. "Let me fetch Dr. Evans."

"Dammit!"

They begin arguing, and Alicia, in her dressing gown, rushes in from the bedroom. "What is it?"

Having opened the door to the hallway, Angelo says, *"Adieu."*

"Darling, where are you going?"

From the end of the hallway come voices and the bumps of luggage being moved. These days, he's so easily distracted. Alicia's dressing gown is one he has not seen before: pearl white silk painted with—what are those, peacocks? It is, he considers, in questionable taste. Her turquoise slippers with orange tassels, also new, are ridiculous.

"Out," Angelo says, pulling on his fur-lined gloves.

Agustín Gerónimo lifts his terrible head from the chaise. "I forbid you to bring that quack!"

Angelo slams the door.

Angelo makes his way down the Avenue de l'Opéra, and the sober moon gray edifice of the Grand-Hôtel disappears behind the crowds. He has no plan but to steady his mind. He will not go to any tooth-puller. In all his forty-nine years, Angelo has never disobeyed his brother. It is the way they were raised, to obey their father and, after his murder, to obey Agustín Gerónimo. Angelo is brusque with his wife only because he does not know how else a husband could be. Her happiness is his sun and moon and every star. Alicia, who was so vibrant, so bubbly, now has the permanent expression of someone who has been slapped. She bursts into noisy tears in a café, in the hotel's hydraulic lift, and the other day as they happened by a toy shop. What did it was the sight of a little boy holding his mother's hand as they came out; the child had a toy horse in his other mitten and he dropped it. Alicia picked it up from the pavement and ran after them. *"Mercy bo-coop,"* the woman said. (Now the war was over, Americans were arriving in droves.) From beneath a mop of straw-colored curls, the child looked up at Alicia and said, "My name is Michael!" "That is a fine name." Alicia's voice strangled in her throat. And there was the day last week when, as they were coming out of the Louvre, the Prince Imperial's carriage sped past. Now anything, everything sets her off.

It has crossed Angelo's mind that his wife may have become permanently unhinged. This provokes his impatience, rage even, but at other times a knee-weakening grief. He'd had such pride in her. She was no *ñoño*, whiner. Had Mamá lived, he feels certain, she would have rescinded her harsh judgment about Alicia. In Mexico Alicia had learned Spanish so quickly. He would give her books to read, and she read every one and asked questions about the words. Right away, she took to wearing a mantilla, and eating tortillas, beans, *pico de gallo.* She sipped tequila with salt on the rim of the glass and a squeeze of lime, and she did not hesitate to try jalapeño chiles, *chiles de árbol,* poblanos, eggs with *machaca,* tamales of all flavors. As for bullfights, his Alicia was not one of those wilting Anglo-Saxons; she wanted the best seat in the ring, and she cheered, "Olé!" with the rest of them. But that now seems an aeon ago, and Alicia a different woman. Confused, Angelo veers between treating her as a mulish child, or a vengeful goddess. How much easier it would be were Alicia's wound in her body. A broken bone, he could bind up. To a cut, he could apply a salve. But for a mother's broken heart? He does not have a clue what to say, and the wrong word, however well intentioned, is acid.

If Drouyn de Lhuys will not grant them an interview, so be it. The question is how Maximilian will react to their having met with Mr. Bigelow. Maximilian has his spies, and no doubt Louis Napoleon and Franz Joseph lend him theirs. The Geheim Polizei, Vienna's secret police, has the biggest intelligence network on the continent. Very possibly, Angelo considers, when the Iturbides arrived here in Paris, Maximilian had already been informed of their meeting with Mr. Seward in Washington, for there was no one at the station to receive them. The following day, José Hidalgo, the Mexican ambassador, accompanied Angelo and his brothers to the bank—but with such insouciance, it crossed Angelo's mind that Hidalgo would have sent a flunky had he not been greedy for news.

Once the business of signing the accounts and taking receipt of the funds had been completed, in the bank's foyer, Hidalgo pressed Angelo, what was his view, when would U.S. troops cross the Rio Grande? Or, did Angelo think that, with Lincoln gone, the United States would recognize the Mexican Empire?

The answer to the first question would have been, no, sending troops to the border was a bluff, and to the second, never, or at least, not while Seward remains secretary of state. But Angelo, peeved at this affront to his brother's dignity—the ambassador should have addressed himself to the head of the family—said only, "It is anyone's guess."

Hidalgo wanted to understand, what was this so-called Monroe Doctrine? Angelo gave a curt explanation.

"But what is a 'monroe'?" Hidalgo asked.

Agustín Gerónimo guffawed. He tried to disguise it with a cough, but too late.

Angelo had felt his stomach sink. He had thought, for a moment, that the ambassador was jesting. The pudgy-faced son of Spaniards, with pale skin made paler by a black beard, the ambassador had the visage of a Jesuit: deadly earnest.

Angelo answered, "James Monroe was president of the United States from 1817 to 1825."

"Ah." Hidalgo pressed his lips together.

They had embarrassed the ambassador. This was very stupid. Hidalgo was a personal friend of Eugénie's; now that avenue of appeal, before even being looked into, was blocked. Hidalgo took leave of Angelo and his brothers on the street outside the bank, without having asked after their family or offered any service whatsoever.

The next morning, Alicia went to her interview with Mr. Bigelow. (For himself, a Mexican subject, to be seen going into the U.S. legation was unthinkable. It was risky, but he accompanied his wife as far as the café on the opposite side of the boulevard.) Alicia's interview went well, and the following afternoon, Mr. Bigelow called on them at the Grand-Hôtel. Mr. Bigelow ended by declaring that, in all frankness, he did not expect the archduke's government to survive the year.

Agustín Gerónimo smirked. It was already the end of November. "What, you think Maximilian'll abdicate 'fore the end of next month?"

"It would be in the archduke's best interest to do so," answered Bigelow.

Angelo had also found it amusing to hear Maximilian referred to as "the archduke." True, on coming to Paris, they had been surprised to learn how unpopular the Mexican expedition was, as evidenced by the graffiti in the streets and the rabid speeches coming out of the Legislative Chambers (*French blood shed for a foreign prince*, and so on). Nonetheless, Angelo did not alter his conviction that, despite the challenges, Maximilian, as the only realistic alternative to anarchy, could reign in Mexico for years to come. For the sake of conversation, Angelo had ventured a mild query. "But is not Louis Napoleon committed to staying in Mexico by the Treaty of Miramar?"

"Of course." Bigelow picked up his umbrella. "Until he no longer finds it convenient."

So, Angelo thought, the United States will make it "inconvenient"? That is a limp threat. Now, as Angelo is nearing the end of the Avenue de l'Opéra, the arcades of the Palais Royale coming into view, he could laugh out loud. In fact, he does, and the sound startles a woman with a basket on her head, who steps away wide, scattering chestnuts. Angelo does not see her, nor any of the crowd; the cocoa-seller with the barrel strapped to his shoulder; the hacks lined up at the curb, the horses' breath coming out of their nostrils in puffs. The sky is a gathering tent of felt. He strides right by the corner of the Rue de Richelieu and the gypsy in a sheepskin coat, smacking at a tambourine.

Manifest Destiny? Angelo rolls his eyes. Yankees are overconfident by nature. They blunder in without a notion of the first switchback in the labyrinth of Mexican politics. On the one hand, there is Mother Church (what would Protestants know about that?). On the other, there is the Mexican Imperial Army's officer corps (some rigidly ultramontane, others, ever mercurial, for or against Santa Anna). Then the caciques with their peons and thugs. Then the conservative landowners. And those Yucatecs keen to secede . . . And Santa Anna, that old one-legged lion with nine lives—at least one or two left to live—he must be skulking around somewhere, on Saint Thomas? New Orleans? New York?

As for France, it is entirely too much for Angelo to swallow the idea that Mr. Bigelow, this New York lawyer, friendly as he may be with Louis Napoleon, could persuade the latter to sully French prestige.

Maximilian von Habsburg abdicate? Just as soon as Bigelow was in the corridor and the door closed, Agustín Gerónimo remarked, "Eh, takes the biscuits!"

Agustín Cosme spoke at last. "But people say that in the tavern."

"What?" Angelo had said.

Agustín Cosme said, "That Louis Napoleon will slough off Mexico and get rid of Maximilian."

Agustín Gerónimo had the last word. "Louis Napoleon would sooner stand up in his box at the opera, turn 'round, and show the house his bare buttocks."

. . .

Head down and collar up, Angelo starts across the Pont Neuf. The sky has dulled the Seine to rippled lead. A barge, trailing a chevron, disappears beneath his feet. His nose smarts from the cold, yet in this cashmere coat, he is sweating. He unwinds his scarf, then he stuffs it in his pocket. He crosses over the to Île de la Cité; to his left, the grim towers of the Conciergerie press against the water. In the past two weeks, he has crossed this bridge so many times, he no longer glances at the buildings nor meditates on their meanings. He does not hear the clang of the bells of Notre Dame, nor notice the snow-flakes, one, then three, wisp-like feathers, beginning to float down.

He thinks: Moreover, Maximilian's father-in-law would not permit Louis Napoleon to wiggle one inch. According to yesterday's newspapers, Leopold remains gravely ill. But Leopold has been ill before and recovered; what man over the age of twenty-five has not? The other day, in the tobacconist's, Angelo happened to see, among the cartes de visite of opera singers, the Prince Imperial and his two spaniels, and Queen Victoria, and Leopold's most recent: a Saxe-Coburg with the constitution of an ox.

It boils down to this: If they cannot get through to Louis Napoleon, the baby could grow into a little boy who loves Maximilian—the thought makes Angelo sick. He covers his mouth with his glove.

The crowd, a sour-smelling woollen river, pushes and jostles around him.

Angelo may have a delicate stomach, but he is not squeamish. He was just two years older than his little son is now when he yodeled with delight to see cocks shred each other with the razor-sharp knives on their claws. His body-guards took him to bullfights. When the matador plunged the *estoque* into the heart, and the beast kneeled before him, blood dripping from its snout onto the sand, Angel would toss up his sombrero, his high-pitched child's shout into the roar: "Olé!" He was six years old when, from a balcony, he and his sister Pepa saw a sentry shot in the chest. It was so queer, the way the soldier spun and then, like a marionette, sat down on one leg. Then he tipped over, and his shako tumbled into the street. As the sentry lay twitching, the blood bloomed, a rose on his chest. Angel had wanted to watch, but a bodyguard picked him up and carried him kicking into the nursery.

His favorite book was one his father had given him: X. Salvatierra's *Los conquistadores del mar* (The conquerors of the sea). Its every page was soaked in blood. Men-of-war lowered their cannons. The enemy swarmed onto the decks, slashing sabers, blasting muskets! In the island jungles, men in feathers loosed arrows dipped in toad venom; the survivors mowed them down with mortars and buckshot. But more than savages, more than sandpaper-thirst, more than hunger "fiercer than wild beasts gnawing their innards," their mortal foe was Sir Rupert, whose final outrage was to loot the mission's chapel and, using his necklace of dog's teeth, scrape the pearls from the cloak of the Virgin's effigy. In the end, Sir Rupert's arms were roped behind his back. A pistol at his kidneys, he walked the plank. Many times Angel had squinted in gruesome fascination at the minuscule typeface:

Below the scuffed toes of his boots, in the ice-cold ocean, the sharks' fins, those arrows of obsidian, went churning in hungry circles. His appointment with Destiny had arrived, but know ye, Sir Rupert did not flinch.

Their father had read the beginning of *Los conquistadores del mar* to the family and servants when, after his abdication, they sailed to Leghorn. Below deck, swaying on their hooks, the lanterns shed a queasy light. The ship creaked and groaned. The children sat around their father, rapt. But Mamá protested, this novel was too violent. Agustín Gerónimo laughed at the wrong places, and their sisters, and especially the eldest, Sabina, cried at the part where the marooned men, having eaten their mules, had to butcher their dog. Or else it was cannibalism!

"Hang on," Papá said. "You'll get that chapter tomorrow."

To Angel, it was all so wonderful, and forever after, whenever he read his book, he imagined his father's voice in his head, rich like whiskey, telling the story to him, and him alone.

That their father had been murdered on his return to Mexico was something no one spoke of; all Mamá would say, apropos of one thing or another, was "before God took him." As the book's hero, Captain Calderón, told his men:

A warrior turns to death, as a sunflower to the sun.

They had not been in Georgetown long when, after Christmas, their next-door neighbor on N Street began to waste away. Miss Fitzgerald's skin turned ashen and her eyeballs yellow. It was springtime, and the air smelled of lavender and damp earth as he watched her casket being lowered into its grave in Dumbarton Oaks. The sounds—shovelfuls of earth hitting the casket's lid—the women crying—birds singing—this—death—was stunning to him. He had known infants to die of measles, or fevers, but that the body of a grown-up could turn against itself? And that he, who was all of nearly nine years old, had not understood this—how, he asked himself over and over, could he have been so stupid? That night, he burned three candles re-reading *Los conquistadores del mar.* He tallied the deaths with his pencil. One hundred and thirteen men were killed by, variously, cannonballs, machetes, an axe, arrows, a boa constrictor, two-headed cobras, a python, a pit viper, a tiger, a poisoned Manila cheroot, Foo Chong Ta (the most excruciating kind of water torture), and a category he labeled "falling objects & misc." No one had expired of something so boring as a tumor. Well . . . he sighed when the dawn seeped through the thin curtains, his destiny was not his father's. As Angelo (he'd added the "o" lest he be teased), his schoolboy's existence in the United States had a blandness to it—but a dash of style, if he could help it.

Over the years, he devoured *The Last of the Mohicans, Ivanhoe,* everything by Dumas, Dickens, and Edgar Allan Poe (whom he once happened to see coming out of a Pennsylvania Avenue barbershop with his cloak on inside out). But it was his book of the sea that Angelo read again and again, until the binding began to fray, the once bright turquoise morocco leather took on a dark sheen. There was something magical about this little tome, printed so long ago in Mexico City. In the story of Calderón, captain of the most magnificent galleon that ever sailed the Seven Seas, he could open it to any page and lose himself, all his fears and worries gone, like the breath from a mirror. Merely holding this book in his hands steadied his mind. It was the connection to his father. It was the triumph, always, over dangers, over evil, and more: Angelo, too, knew what it was to stand on an open deck, feet splayed wide for balance, and take the salt spray. He knew the dawn, a sun so huge there is no hiding from it; and the moon brighter than any seen from mere land. To be upon the open sea is like being inside the sky. He knew the sea's miseries, hammering nausea, the last despairing days of having to drink brackish water from the bottom of the barrel and gnaw hardtack crummy with worms. Now with steamers, an ocean crossing is not the hardship it once was. But always there is the sea's huge rage, its beauty, and the realization that steals upon one, especially at sunset: what dazzling hubris it is to have sailed into the heart of it.

Yes, it had impressed him that Maximilian had been commander of the fleet. He had forgotten that. *How could he have forgotten that?*

"I am at a total loss as to why you should have involved yourselves in such a scheme." That was what Mrs. Green had said about the contract with Maximilian. And then, having said her piece, as was her way, she said no more. Last month, when they passed through Washington on their way to Paris, he and Alicia stayed in her farmhouse, Rosedale, in the heights above Georgetown and just south of Fort Reno. Mrs. Green had managed to save her orchards, while others in the neighborhood had been chopped down for firewood for the soldiers. The whole hill to the west, in years past ablaze with autumn colors, was bald. In the District of Columbia, the slaves had been freed at the beginning of the war, which Mrs. Green had accepted without protest. She had often stated that emancipation was inevitable. But now, what was she supposed to pay the Negroes with? She could feed them, but that wasn't good enough. An acre of pumpkins was rotting on the ground.

As always at Rosedale, Angelo wore long underwear, spoke as little as possible, and avoided the pickled asparagus.

"Creamed turnips?" Alicia passed him the chipped dish and wooden spoon. Mrs. Green had Wedgwood china and good silver, but she certainly wasn't going to take it out for this son-in-law.

"Thank you," Angelo murmured, grateful that Alicia had indicated what the vegetable was. Mrs. Green was a skinflint with the candles; in this light, the food all appeared the same unappetizing gray.

His brothers had not been invited to Rosedale. They stayed at the Willard Hotel, where they ran up staggering bills for oysters and beefsteak dinners with champagne.

The bitter fragrance of roasting coffee brings Angelo back as he arrives on the Rive Gauche, into St-Germain-des-Prés. The snowflakes are coming down thicker, leaving his cashmere coat damp and his boot soles gummed with slush. In Mexico City, on this day, the streets would be streaming with pilgrims, Indians bent double under their loads of rolled-up straw mats and clay pots, some wearing an image of the Virgin on their chest, and many making a good part of the journey on their knees. Tomorrow is the Day of Our Lady of Guadalupe—and the night will crackle with fireworks. What he would give to taste a mango, a *chirimoya*, a steaming mug of *champurrado* . . . he would trade these oily omelettes and toast points slicked with foie gras, this watery coq au vin for the smell—just the perfume!—of tortillas warming on a *comal*. Or to hear, sweet caress, the strum of a Mexican harp.

He buys an umbrella, a fine one of silk and with an ebony handle. He turns off the Rue Dauphin and into a crooked street of little shops, antiquarians, and book dealers.

He has always had a weakness for bookshops. But in Washington, Philadelphia, New York, London, Mexico City, never in all his forays has he come across another copy of *Los conquistadores del mar,* nor anything else by X. Salvatierra. No, the book dealers all say, they have never heard of X. Salvatierra.

Before leaving Mexico City, he had his library packed pell-mell into crates. The single volume he brought with him was the X. Salvatierra. He keeps it wrapped in a flannel nightshirt at the bottom of his steamer trunk, along with his medal of the Order of Guadalupe and a miniature of his parents. Years ago, in Washington, a British diplomat had told him about Hafiz, whose poetry the Persians use as an oracle. Often, when alone, Angelo holds his little blue book on his lap and then, eyes closed, allows the pages to fall open. Yesterday he placed a finger on this passage:

Sir Rupert said, "The coconut is the most useful fruit in the world. Un-milked, it makes a mighty projectile."

"I'll make us a catapult!" the carpenter shouted.

"Aye!" Sir Rupert cried, holding up his fat green trophy. His rabble hooted and clapped. One banged the barrel of his musket against his drink-ing cup. Another, a grizzled old one-armed mate, clashed his cutlas against his hook. Such was their happiness, for though shipwrecked, with the bounty of these coconuts, they believed, they could save themselves from being utterly annihilated by Captain Calderón. But all of a sudden, there was a rustling in one of the trees and,

THUK!

The smallest cabin boy's skull had been split by a falling coconut. The boy, Jesus in his mouth, fell into his own shadow. His brains oozed into the hot sand.

"Stop it!" Sabina had cried with her fingers in her ears.

Pepa, indignant, said, "Papá, please, read us something nice."

The boys groaned.

"Well," their father said, closing the book—though he'd kept his place with his thumb. "The best part of the story is coming up."

This was after the cannibalism chapter and the Foo Chong Ta.

"Go on! Keep reading!" Angel had urged.

"No!" cried the girls.

"Yes!" said the boys. Unsteadily, for the ship was rolling heavily, Angel had gotten up from his place on the floor and gone over to his father and pulled at his sleeve. "Please, Papá. Please, the part that happens next."

His father, having received an imperious glance from Mamá, placed the book back inside the trunk. "Another time, son."

But there was not another time. In Leghorn, his father set to work, began traveling, and after depositing Angelo and the older children in school in En-gland, returned to Mexico. It was later, after England, when he was sent to the Sulpician Brothers in Baltimore, which did not feel to him any nearer to his mother in Georgetown, that Angel, the boy who had become Angelo, read the rest of *Los conquistadores del mar*, whispering the Spanish words, incandescent music, to himself alone.

Paris is his Purgatory, shuttered city under mansard roofs, its patches of dirty winter sky stitched with crows. A *chiffonier* works the alleyway with his hook.

The English bookshop: for the second time this week, Angelo pushes in the door, tinkling the bell, a Hindu contraption made of brass. From the counter the marmalade cat leaps down and brushes past his leg. Only then does Mr. Silvius Mackintosh lift his nose from his newspaper, *Le Moniteur*.

"Ah, Prince Iturbide. The Dickens has come in."

"Our Mutual Friend?"

"Aye. I can recommend it."

"My wife hasn't—" Angelo realizes, by the puddle on the floor, he should have wiped his boots. He returns to the doormat.

Mr. Mackintosh says, "When the Princess asked for it the other day, it wasn't in yet."

Angelo hangs his hat and coat on the pegs by the door. He smooths the top of his hair. "She's been reading *Bleak House.*"

"Has she now?"

"It's depressing, she says."

"Well, the tonic might be *Our Mutual Friend.*"

Angelo runs a finger over the spines of the Shakespeares: *MacBeth, Hamlet, As You Like It.* "Don't tell me the ending," he calls over his shoulder, "but is it uplifting?"

"Pooh!" The Scotsman puffs out his cheeks. "It's Dickens."

"Right."

With a rustle, Mr. Mackintosh returns to his newspaper. It's a good sign when a customer not only removes his coat and hat but helps himself to the ladder. Last week when this one came in, Mr. Mackintosh had taken him for an American—until he gave his name, to have a package sent to him at the Grand-Hôtel. Already, most of the English-speakers resident in this city have heard that Prince Iturbide and his American wife are here to procure the return of their child, who has been kidnapped by Maximilian von Habsburg, so-called emperor of the Aztecs. Some, such as himself and Mrs. Macktintosh, are of the opinion that Queen Victoria ought to step in, and shame those German cousins of hers into a sense of decency. Taking a child from its parents, what is this world coming to? Others say those Iturbides are ne'er-do-wells. The youngest son of the emperor has become the proprietor of a tavern! But stones and glass houses, eh? What will happen? No one claims to have a crystal ball, except Mrs. Bigelow, it seems. After church services last Sunday, at the coffee urn, Mrs. Bigelow told Mrs. Macktinosh that, before the new year, rely on it, the "archduke" will be on the boat back to Europe.

The front-page news today is that King Leopold of the Belgians, father of the empress of Mexico, has died. Mr. Mackintosh is curious to know what Prince Iturbide would have to say about that. But he would not presume.

"Finding everything?" he calls out, but Prince Iturbide, at the top of the ladder, is engrossed in what appears to be—is that Gibbon's *Roman Empire*? Wouldn't that three-volume set be a nice one to sell, and at full price? The cat lands on the newspaper, making a loud meow.

"Naughty Ginger," Mr. Mackintosh scolds, pushing her away.

FLOWERS & FISH & BIRDS
& BUTTERFLIES

*D*epend on it: Maximilian is shepherding Mexico into the modern world—so José Luis Blasio, His Majesty's secretary, has told his family and tells himself. And this is no small task when His Majesty must grapple not only with our backwardness and ingratitude but suffer that thorn in his side, General Bazaine. The rumor is that, abetted by his Mexican wife's family, Bazaine schemes to push aside Maximilian; they aim to have Louis Napoleon make Mexico a French protectorate, with himself in charge—not that José Luis would give that a peso of credence. But José Luis does consider it an outrage, the latest of many, that Bazaine would wire a complaint that Maximilian has removed his court to Cuernavaca, rather than "attend to business in the capital."

Yes, they are here in the Casa Borda, among gardens and fountains, fruit trees, palm trees, parrots of every size and color—a world away from Mexico City. But does not Louis Napoleon go to Plombières and Biarritz? Queen Victoria, who has sterner blood, travels as far as Balmoral in the Scottish Highlands. Dom Pedro II of Brazil retires to his villa in Petropolis. And did not the empress's late father, Leopold, absent himself from Brussels in the Château Royal at Laeken? It is natural that for the winter, His Majesty should hold court in a healthier clime. But even here where he siestas in a hammock, drinks limeade from a coconut shell, and wears an ecru linen suit with an open-necked blouse, Maximilian's work never ceases. It is a wide rushing river that José Luis can only hope will not overspill its banks. In the past year,

José Luis has come to appreciate the uncompromising necessity of working long hours (indeed, his eyesight, never strong, has deteriorated from so much reading in the dim of early mornings). Maximilian arises at four; his valet attends him, and though he might linger over breakfast, by no later than six, he is at "the bridge," as he says, that is, at his desk—or, as here in Casa Borda, a folding table on the veranda. His Majesty's dispatch box is heavy, and growing ever heavier . . .

José Luis carries it across the damp lawn. Birds sing. The sky is the color of fruit.

Not so long ago, José Luis imagined that an emperor simply, well, sat on his throne, one serene hand extended to receive kisses. An emperor, he supposed, dressed every day in a sumptuous cloak and carried a scepter and orb studded with diamonds. His was a life of adoration and glory—*ha!*

The legs of the folding table groan.

"That is a heavy one."

"Yes, sir." José Luis pries open the lid.

"Bonbon?"

"Thank you, sir." José Luis dips his hand into the Totonac bowl. Until he came to work for Maximilian, José Luis never could have imagined a gentleman making use of such a thing. The first time he saw this earthen bowl—the eye-popping fire orange, the black caterpillar carved around its circumference—right by the Imperial inkpot, and filled with fancy bonbons, he was perplexed. Why, when His Majesty could have the finest porcelain, the most exquisitely wrought silver, would he want this barbaric pot? At Maximilian's side, José Luis is learning every day to see with new eyes. The Totonac bowl, for instance, is a superbly proportioned antiquity, its exquisite color, as Maximilian put it, "fiery as the flesh of a Sicilian blood-orange." Not that José Luis has yet seen such a gruesome fruit (which he is sure must be delicious). One day he hopes to see Sicily, and also Naples, and Rome, and Paris—Europe, not in a picture book, but with his own eyes. That is the dream of his life.

José Luis is about to bite into the bonbon when Maximilian says, "You'll want to dunk it in your coffee." Maximilian clicks his fingers; the footman steps forward and pours. The cup, Sèvres porcelain, has a gold rim and monogram, MIM, for the Latin *Maximiliano Imperator de Mexico*. The footman's snow white glove presses on the silver lid. It is the last coffee in the pot, dribbling out thick and grainy.

José Luis plucks the telegram from the top of the pile. "This just came in, sir—"

Maximilian interrupts, putting up a finger. "What is the name of that bird?"

José Luis holds his breath. Above the usual racket, there is one high-pitched *hiyee, hiyee!*

"Er, I wouldn't know, sir."

A curtain of boredom comes down over Maximilian's face—or, more likely, José Luis thinks, disappointment. For a Mexican, José Luis has beautiful penmanship, more than passable Latin (and some Greek, too), but he was not taught one blessed thing about botanizing. With an inward sigh, he reminds himself, yet again, *We Mexicans are so backward.*

"Perhaps," Maximilian says, clasping his hands (a knuckle cracks), "you might be of more help with the dispatch box?"

Hiyee, hiyee! The nameless yellow-breasted bird alights on the topmost branch of the jacaranda in the next patio, which happens to stand directly outside the door to Princess Iturbide's bedroom.

Hiyeeeeeeeeeeeeeeeeee!

Just when she was beginning to drift back to sleep! Pepa pulls the pillow over her good ear. But the bird's cry is too shrill to muffle:

HIYEEEEEEEEEEEE!

This (she grits her teeth), after she has been lying awake since four in the morning—an hour Maximilian and a few hard-bitten sailors might accustom themselves to but one that she, as would anyone with a squib of sense, considers a perversity. It is a holy miracle that she got a wink of sleep at all! So appalled she is by Maximilian's whim to uproot the court to this hamlet, two bone-jarring days' travel up and down the sierra—good gracious, this is no time to abandon the capital and go gallivanting about with butterfly nets and beetle jars! Matamoros is under siege; the whole state of Guerrero, from Acapulco to Iguala, is in thrall to guerrillas. And Pepa got it from Frau von Kuhacsevich, who got it from Lieutenant Weissbrunn, that whilst the empress was in Yucatan, Maximilian fancied a visit to Acapulco, but General Bazaine nixed it because it would have been impossible to maintain security for his person. That is the sum of things!

Oh, but in Mexico City Maximilian felt cramped, "an oyster in a bucket of ice," he said. Over the past two months, the few times Pepa chanced to see Maximilian, he spoke of the empress's dispatches from Yucatan proudly but with—Pepa recognized it when she saw it—a glint of green. If Maximilian could not have his expedition to Yucatan, by Jove, he was going to go some place tropical! And Maximilian would not be outshone by his consort. Oh no . . . A mere visit to Cuernavaca would not do; he had to serve himself the whole enchilada with the big spoon: an Imperial Residence with landscaping, fountains, an ornamental pond stocked with exotic fish, and furnishings and flubdubs aplenty, *comme ça* and *de rigueur*. Whom did he imagine he was impressing with this caprice? And poor Charlotte, so exhausted after Yucatan . . . And as if the von Kuhacseviches were not already floundering in their attempts to manage the Imperial Household in Mexico City! As if the Mexican Imperial Army could offer its officers anything approaching a living wage! Or keep its depots stocked with gunpowder! It is a monumental waste of time, of effort, of money, and to boot, Casa Borda is crawling with cockroaches, beetles, earwigs, and moths—a bonanza for Professor Bilimek!

Furthermore, uprooting herself and Prince Agustín to Cuernavaca could not have come at a less convenient time. She had just taken possession of her new house, and this itself was a small disaster. The week before Christmas, the son of that unfortunate Count Villavaso finally put the house up for sale again. He apologized for offering it at such a price, but prices had gone up generally, and as his family was removing to Spain, he could not accept one peso less. Pepa, by then a veteran of three exasperating months of searching, agreed to pay the full price—and right away, before the place could be overtaken by one army or another desperate to billet their officers. But then the day after the bank transferred the funds, a letter arrived at Chapultepec Castle, that Doña Juliana de Gómez Pedraza had been robbed—her silver cleaned out, all her ivories, jewelry, clothing, half the pantry, and her old cook, Chole, murdered—and she was so beside herself she had determined to quit the city. Querétaro, that was her plan, and she offered Pepa her house, a far finer residence than the count's, at a price that was—Pepa squeezed her fists and nearly wept—one half what she had just paid.

And the new wallpaper is being hung, and she is not there to supervise it, nor the delivery of the Parisian gas lamps from the Emporio de Luz, nor the pair of Christofle silver-plate epergnes, nor the Steinway piano—Lord knows where those furniture movers will set it down, never mind that one has marked the floor with chalk. One cannot rely on footmen to supervise, and certainly not on chambermaids lent by Frau von Kuhacsevich (though that was very kind of her). She might have entrusted Lieutenant Weissbrunn to do that job, though he is an odd duck . . . But Weissbrunn's orders were to accompany them to Cuernavaca. No, the head of the Palace Guard said, this could not be countermanded except by the "highest authority"—in other words, Maximilian—and as that Austrian officer's tone made clear, if Pepa dared try that avenue, it would cost her.

Pepa had already reached her limit when she arrived here in this buggy country house to find that she and Prince Agustín had been assigned rooms that front the street! Frau von Kuhacsevich threw up her hands; she was truly, terribly sorry, but nothing could be done because the rooms had been assigned by His Majesty. One was forced to endure the concert of carts clattering over cobblestones, drunken Indians, barking dogs, all this in addition to nonstop crickets and frogs and tomcats yowling and spitting and scrabbling over the rooftop—and then, at what must have been three in the morning, an entire burro train—burros enough to outfit the siege of Troy! And the driver pelting rocks at the beasts (one rock hit the wall right outside her bed!), and he went close by the window, as slow as you please, bellowing at the top of his lungs, "Brrro! Brrro!"

HiyEEEEE!

What more, then, is a bird with a blood-curdling screech? Pepa hurls the pillow to the foot of the bed. "May Maximilian shoot it and stuff it for Professor Bilimek's museum!"

And this is exactly what Mathilde Doblinger, the empress's wardrobe maid, is thinking. She'd spied it earlier: a witch-black thing no bigger than a robin, with a stub tail. Then it opened its beak in a cry that could make your hair stand on end! From the sound of it, the creature must have flown over to the other side of the garden, where the Iturbides' rooms are, thank God.

She pulls tight the stays in Charlotte's corset.

Charlotte says crossly, *"Tighter."*

"But ma'am, you won't be able to breathe!" Instantly, Mathilde lowers her eyes, for that was an impudence. With as gentle a tug as she can manage, she tightens the stay. Charlotte is insisting on wearing her corset so tight, it leaves welts over her ribs. She has been chewing the lace off her handerchiefs. And she has not stopped this hideous habit of pinching the insides of her arms.

King Leopold has been with God since early December, but the cruel news did not come to his daughter until sixteen days ago—January 6, the Feast of the Epiphany. It crushed her. Already she was in a delicate state, for she had just returned from Yucatan, where she had been made to eat brew-like foods and endure inhuman heat. They ran her like a slave with tours of schools, orphanages, rope factories, audiences, dinners, balls, every day from morning to night—and then, alone in her room, by a guttering candle, or a lamp if they thought to provide one, Charlotte would write letters and reports, pages and pages. And the next day she would be put through the same, and the day after that, it was a merciless treadmill, and they drove her deep into the jungle—Lord in Heaven, those lizards *were* the size of cats—and she marched to the top of a pyramid in heat that could make a combat soldier faint. In Yucatan, death came close enough, if not to take her, at least to pull her sleeve. Two of the footmen, one an Austrian, the other a Mexican, died of yellow fever. Arriving in Mexico City, Charlotte had circles under her eyes, dust thick in her hair, dust behind her ears, dust even in the creases of her palms. How heartless of Maximilian then to drag her to Cuernavaca.

He took her down a notch, that's what Frau von Kuhacsevich says—that Maximilian told Charlotte she should not feel too satisfied with her tour of Yucatan, because elsewhere in Mexico, General Bazaine is not doing his job, his men are lazy, or else stupidly cruel, that is why the guerrillas have been gaining ground. That old lecher—*ach,* there is much that has come to Matihlde's ears about Bazaine. For instance, that he is the secret partner in a Mexico City shop that sells imported French laces, ribbons, buttons, silks, stockings, and all the like—and does Bazaine pay duties? Not when he can slip his merchandise into boxes labeled ARMES ET MUNITIONS. As for the Yankees, those vultures, five days after the new year, a gang of drunken Negroes crossed over the Rio Grande, sacked the port of Bagdad, ravished the women, slaughtered the garrison, and Bazaine did nothing. Nothing! He sat on his fat rear end!

Frau von Kuhacsevich has let slip that she suspects they may all be home in Trieste by year's end, perhaps sooner. Which would be welcome news for Mathilde, except, she knows, to have to go back, after all this, would send Charlotte over the edge. Frau von Kuhacsevich is not the only one who, back in Trieste, overheard Charlotte say, "I would rather die than spend the rest of my days with nothing to do but stare at the sea." Trieste is such a windblown provincial town. At low tide, the air out by Miramar Castle smelled fishy. Mathilde had not particularly liked it, either.

Now, to see Charlotte left an orphan and in this godforsaken situation, Mathilde could weep. But in front of her mistress, Mathilde must be strong. She prays to Mother Mary, *Give Charlotte the grace of Your strength.*

Mathilde lays the hoopskirt flat on the floor. Charlotte steps into its circle; Mathilde pulls it up and fastens it around her waist. Then the frock: black crêpe de chine edged with a trim of scalloped black satin and moiré panels with black piping. At the news of her father's death, Maximilian and Charlotte had raced back to Mexico City, where the court went into strictest mourning. In the Imperial Palace, among heaps of flowers, Maximilian received the condolences of his ministers, the diplomatic corps, the Austrian and the Belgian volunteers, and Bazaine and his ilk. Charlotte would speak to no one; Mathilde brought her food, but she scarcely touched it. Charlotte wanted the shutters closed. She kept a candle flickering before the image of Our Lady of Guadalupe, and knelt—not on her prie dieu, but on the bare floor, and bolt upright—her gaze fixed upon that strange, dark face. Outside, the sun-shocked streets were draped in black. But after a mass had been said in the cathedral, there was no rest for Leopold's daughter. At once, Maximilian, as was his whim, ordered that she pack up and haul herself once again over the mountains to Cuernavaca, and this time with the entire court, including "Princess" Iturbide and that caterwauling brat.

Afternoons, when Charlotte comes out onto the veranda, what does she see? Maximilian in his white suit, tossing a ball to another woman's little boy in his white frock. Charlotte turns a corner and finds Professor Bilimek down on one white knee, showing that boy some bug he has picked up off the ground. That's right, the Master of Ceremonies has decreed that, here in Cuernavaca, everyone, except the empress, shall wear white. The dirt is still fresh on her father's grave, and her husband and his court display themselves in white!

And Maximilian and "Prince" Agustín have grown so fond of each other. "Little cousin," Maximilian calls him. It is revolting. Princess Iturbide, an elephant in her white clothes, takes up space at every dinner, every tea. She's scavenged a bit of German now, and in the evenings after dinner, she joins the von Kuhacseviches in games of whist and jackstraws.

If Maximilian abdicates, will Charlotte be made to play hostess to these people in Trieste as well? Or, is the idea to leave Princess Iturbide in Mexico as regent? But the moment Mathilde begins to wonder about such matters, she feels as if she were bumping around in a dark closet full of dangerous things.

Mathilde buttons up the back of Charlotte's frock, and then—Charlotte lifts her arms—Mathilde brings the black silk sash around her waist. With deft fingers, Mathilde ties the bow.

Now the coiffure. The hairdresser has done so badly, it must be redone. Frau von Kuhacsevich says, to try to find a skilled hairdresser here, one might as well expect to fish a dolphin out of a turtle pond. Having unpinned Charlotte's hair, Mathilde brings the brush down the length of a chestnut-dark strand. In the mirror Charlotte's eyes follow the brush. Mathilde knows that the Empress Sissi's hairdresser keeps a strip of tape along the inside of her apron pocket, so that, when the brush is full, secretly, she swipes it there. Sissi says, "Show me the dead hair." This hairdresser always shows her the brush clean—therefore, no one else may touch Sissi's hair. Such are the wages of vanity, to attract, as moths to a flame, deceivers and flatterers. Maximilian, too, is vain. In a hundred ways, but especially with his beard, which he has his valet, Grill, tend with lotions as if it were a woman's tresses. Maximilian cannot pass a mirror without throwing back his shoulders and regarding himself.

"Ouch!" Charlotte says.

Mathilde picks apart the knot. She pins the hair up with tiny hairpins, pulling them one by one from her lips. The sides of the coiffure, combed loosely over the ears, she stuffs with handfuls of lamb's wool dyed to match. Now (and she hands Charlotte the sandalwood fan to protect her face) the mist of lacquer to keep it set. The finishing is a wreath of black silk rosettes. Mathilde fixes this to Charlotte's coiffure with another multitude of tiny pins. Once she's finished, Mathilde hands her the silver hand-mirror. In this way, Charlotte, tilting her head slightly, inspects the back.

The light has gone out of her eyes. Frau von Kuhacsevich says Charlotte is arrogant, unfeeling; but Mathilde understands: it is, rather, that she has so much feeling. She is a brave soul in suffering. If not for the unbridgeable moat of difference in their rank, Mathilde would embrace her mistress, kiss her, tell her, *You are not alone. Have faith in Our Lady. Have faith in God's mercy.*

On the tray lined with dark blue velvet, Mathilde presents the earrings: black pearls. Mathilde then brings the little box with the live beetle. The insect is chained to the pin, and on its back is a pasted-on jewel. A souvenir of Yucatan, it is worn as a brooch. Mathilde dislikes having to touch the thing; it wriggles.

The black pongee parasol trimmed with black ostrich feathers.

"What?" Charlotte seems confused.

"Your parasol, ma'am."

"I will not be going into the garden." Charlotte closes her eyes and touches her eyebrows with her fingertips. On the shoulder of her blouse, the jeweled beetle crawls to the end of its chain. "I have such a—" Charlotte's voice quavers, "*beastly headache.*"

"May I bring you a linden flower tea?"

In barely a whisper: "No."

"A cool cloth?"

Charlotte says no more; as she sweeps by, Mathilde sinks into her deepest curtsey. Charlotte's footsteps fade down the long veranda. The room feels suddenly hot. The furniture all too large, the mirror greasy. A horsefly swings past, and out the door.

Mathilde stays, picking the hair out of the silver brush, and then a few strands more off the floor tiles. It is her duty to keep the brushes clean. It is her self-appointed duty to make certain that not one single hair is lost. There are witches in this country.

Hiyee! In the garden, as she descends the stone steps from the loggia to the ornamental pond, Frau von Kuhacsevich ducks. *Hiyee!* The yellow-breasted bird swoops low and alights on the rim of a canoe that has drifted into a mass of lily pads. Then, with another ear-splitting cry, the bird darts up and over the wall.

"*Grüss Gott!*" Lieutenant Weissbrunn greets her, touching his cap.

Frau von Kuhacsevich returns the greeting, but coldly. She has heard, through the grapevine—from Tüdos, in fact—that Weissbrunn has requested a transfer. Why did he not tell her? She minded that he did not; she minded very much. Well, he is not a talkative fellow, this ox. He is from Ölmutz; that alone would make her dislike him.

"*Hola!*" Agustín says. His nursemaid, Tere, holds him in her arms; he was pulling limes off the low-hanging branch. He's in a white cotton frock and sandals and his legs are tanned.

"*Hola!*" Frau von Kuhacsevich answers kindly. She squeezes a chubby knee. "You are going to give the ants and beetles quite a feast."

He laughs, and another lime thunks to the ground.

Frau von Kuhacsevich is intentionally cool with the nursemaid, because she suspects that some hanky-panky has been going on with Weissbrunn. Tüdos, the chef, alerted her. Frau von Kuhacsevich has not yet witnessed anything worthy of report, but she has seen the way those two steal hot little glances at one another.

Glacially therefore: "Where is the princess?"

"In her rooms, ma'am."

Frau von Kuhacsevich shoots Weissbrunn a look that says—well, she hopes it says, *Don't think I'm not keeping an eye on you two.*

Frau von Kuhacsevich has come to feel protective toward the princess and this dear little boy. Her friendly feelings had surprised her, because at first the princess was so demanding—a bit of a parvenue, really, but in time Frau von Kuhacsevich found that not only was the princess's etiquette scrupulous but it was very interesting to converse with her. They both spoke French, and between the smatterings of Frau von Kuhacsevich's Spanish and English and the princess's admirable efforts to improve her German, they made themselves understood. Father Fischer, he was the first topic of conversation that endeared them to one another. They were both rock sure, if anyone could reconcile His Holiness to His Majesty it was Father Fischer. Maximilian had been absolutely right to select Father Fischer for the mission to Rome, and oh, were he here, what wise counsel he could give in these trying times!

Unlike Frau von Kuhacsevich's husband, Princess Iturbide was a willing audience, fascinated in fact, by anything Frau von Kuhacsevich might happen to say. Who favored whom, and how they'd worked together back in Vienna, or Trieste, and what it was like to run the viceregal household in Milan (where they had blackamoors serve the gelato), and why it was that Maximilian always ate those same bonbons, and why Schertzenlechner, Maximilian's oaf of a chancellor, had left Mexico in a huff. He had a showdown with Monsieur Eloin, who proved, with documentation, that Schertzenlechner—it was true!—had been continuing to draw his salary as a Hofburg valet! "The Big Moo" was what the Germans called Schertzenlechner behind his back, and Princess Iturbide thought that the most amusing nickname, "Apt, oh, very apt!" she said approvingly.

And the princess was herself a fount of information. She had unending friends in Mexican society; she was frequently off visiting with them. These people mixed with the better class of American colonists (exiles of the vanquished Confederacy, for the most part), and as those people had been obliged to billet officers in their houses, their little soirées more often than not included high-ranking men, some very close to General Bazaine. One had big ears for what they had to say!

"And what was your father like?" Frau von Kuhacsevich had asked Princess Iturbide.

"Tall, very tall. And he had red hair."

"Did he really!"

"It was quite red."

"Red as a Scotsman's?"

"Yes."

"Oh, wonderful. And do you think Prince Agustín will also be red-haired?"

"I do not think so."

"He will stay blond?"

"For his babyhood, but they grow up, you know . . ."

Nothing pleased Princess Iturbide more than to talk about her little godson. Prince Agustín was so bright, such a handsome dumpling, and clever as the dickens (and one was going to have to make sure, the princess said severely, that he would not turn out too clever for his own good). Clearly, at not yet three years old, he was showing a talent for languages . . . he could count to twenty in Spanish, and to ten in German, French, Hungarian, and Nahuatl.

From Princess Iturbide, there was much to learn about Mexico, for instance, that the Emperor Iturbide's palace was not the Imperial Palace of today but the more compact and elegant palace that is now the Hotel Iturbide, where the stagecoaches arrive and depart. And the princess had many helpful tips about Mexican cuisine, all excellent to pass on to Tüdos. *Cuitlacoche,* for example, Frau von Kuhacsevich had thought disgusting, on a par with roasted maguey worms, mosquito paste, tacos of ant eggs, and the like.

"No, no," the princess had advised her, "you must not think of *cuitlacoche* as corn smut, but as a kind of truffle."

"A truffle!"

"It is a mushroom."

"Yes!" Frau von Kuhacsevich had clapped her hands. "Truffle hunting in the autumn, what joy, oh! You know, once near Innsbruck—" And Princess Iturbide listened to every one of her many happy reminiscences about Bad Ischl and the mushrooms there, the big spicy *Herrenpilze* that could also be gathered in the Vienna Woods and which were the favorite of Maximilian and oh yes, all the archdukes, they took them sautéed in butter and then simmered in brandy and cream. Franz Joseph, he wanted the broth only, and Sissi, it was a scandal the way she took hers, steamed, no butter.

"No butter!"

"Not a drop."

They were both women of a certain age, both despairing over the ruin of their figures.

"I cannot help myself when there's bread on the table."

"I'm that way with chocolate, anything with chocolate in it, I'm done for."

"I know exactly what you mean."

On her birthday, Princess Iturbide sent Frau von Kuhacvsevich a bouquet of violets in a monogrammed silver vase. For the princess's birthday, after careful thought, Frau von Kuhacsevich decided on giving her new friend the rosary beads she'd had blessed by His Holiness when she visited Rome with the imperial entourage, en route to Mexico.

"Blessed by His Holiness!" The princess took in a sharp breath, and her face turned grave. She embraced Frau von Kuhacsevich and kissed her on both cheeks. She then pressed the rosary beads to her heart. "My friend," she said, "I shall treasure these for the rest of my life."

For Christmas, Frau von Kuhacsevich received, in an exquisite silver and polished-bone frame, a carte de visite of Prince Agustín. Proudly, she put it on the shelf in her office, beneath the watercolor of the orchids by Professor Bilimek, and next to the pie basket for the receipts.

Midmorning, making her rounds, Frau von Kuhacsevich minces along the veranda outside the empress's rooms, the pendulum of her ring of keys swinging alongside her skirts. She greets the gardener clipping the hedge; she steps around a chambermaid, who looks up from scrubbing the tiles, to answer her mistress:

"Buenos días, señora Kuhaes." (Not a one can manage the pronunciation of her name.)

The laundress with a basket of folded linens.

Frau von Kuhacsevich thinks to turn around and ask, "Have you put clean bed linens in the room for the Austrian ambassador?"

"Sí, señora Kuhaes." A toothless smile.

"And clean towels for the washstand?"

"*Ahorita,* in a little minute."

And that one was imported from Mexico City! It is a task for a Hercules to set up an Imperial Household in the tropics. There are no servants to be hired in this village, unless one wants those whose feet have never known shoes and whose hands would not know from Adam what to do with a fork (and whose concepts of cleanliness are best left uncontemplated).

On the steps to the next patio, Frau von Kuhacsevich must pause to fan herself. Cuernavaca is not the Turkish bath of the hot lands, but more, as Maximilian put it, of an Italian May. Pleasant for the men, and Prince Agustín, perhaps, but a trial for those who must encase themselves in corsets and crinolines. Oh, poor Charlotte that her father has died, but Blessed Jesus, what would Frau von Kuhacsevich have done had she been obliged to wear mourning black! The thought simply wilts her. She is afraid her face has gone red as a beet. Her back feels sticky, and under her bonnet, she can feel her scalp sweating. Taking the bonnet off is out of the question: her roots have grown in nearly an inch—in all the rushing to and fro, there has not been a snatch of time to touch up the color.

An Italian May: in that spirit, for luncheon, Tüdos has concocted an *amuse-gueule* of olives, basil, and *requeson,* a cheese too strong to pass for mozzarella, but toothsome. In addition to coffee, he will be making a big pot of *canarino:* simply, the zest of lemons steeped as tea. Well, here it has to be made of limes—*ni modo,* no matter, as the Mexicans say.

Frau von Kuhacsevich makes her way across the blossom-strewn patio to the veranda where the luncheon will be held. Out on the lawn, in the speckled shadow of a Brobdingnagian ficus, the orchestra is setting up their folding chairs and music stands. She has had to ask the conductor, Sawerthal, to move the chairs twice; Maximilian wants the music to be heard clearly, but it must not overwhelm the table conversation.

Earlier this morning, in her office, she had reviewed the seating chart with the Master of Ceremonies. He had bristled at her interference, but the problem was—Frau von Kuhacsevich tapped her pencil on his chart—it would not do to seat Princess Iturbide to the right of His Excellency Don Fernando Ramírez.

Sotto voce: "Is there something I ought to know?" The Master of Ceremonies was practically smacking his lips for a juicy morsel.

Frau von Kuhacsevich ignored him; she was not about to betray her friend by explaining that, in her left ear, the princess is hard of hearing.

"Better this." Frau von Kuhacsevich tapped her pencil, making a dot on the paper. "Put Princess Iturbide on the *left* of the Austrian ambassador."

The Master of Ceremonies pursed his lips and exhaled loudly through his nostrils. The intensity of their concentration was that of a couple of generals at their maquette.

"Well," he said finally. "If you must move her, it would be easier to switch her with the American's wife. Here, you see, put Princess Iturbide next to Monsieur Langlais."

Frau von Kuhacsevich shot out her bottom lip. One finger alongside her chin, she considered this many-faceted idea. (Monsieur Langlais, the finance wizard . . . man of the moment . . . her husband, for one, suggesting he may yet perform wonders . . . but Maximilian finds his conversation tedious . . . plebeian . . .) Her eyes roved over the chart. The Belgian ambassador here, General Uraga's wife there, and then the Spanish ambassador and General Almonte (that toad, but he does speak English), the Marquis de la Rivera (trilingual, but an impossible snob) . . . This required the highest degree of *Fingerspitzengefühl* . . .

By her silence, she had stuck to her guns.

"All right," the Master of Ceremonies said. "I'll leave Princess Iturbide on the left of the Austrian ambassador. But I cannot leave the botanist where he is."

"Professor Bilimek? Oh, put him next to that lady-in-waiting."

"Señorita Varela?" The Master of Ceremonies raised his eyebrows. "Hmm."

"He does not speak Spanish and she does not speak German."

"Let them speak French."

"Her French is very bad."

"Why worry?" Frau von Kuhacsevich threw up her hands. "Professor Bilimek never says anything anyway."

• • •

Now, on the dining veranda, to the cacophony of the orchestra's warm-up, the yowling violins, the swirling trills of flutes, Frau von Kuahcsevich inspects the table, to ensure that each place setting has its name card according to the chart; each its menu, and its salt cellar with miniature mother-of-pearl spoon; each its array of forks and of spoons and of knives; the lineup of water and wine goblets (a Chablis to begin, then a rosé, then a red, then a sweet wine, and finally, a flute for the signature pink champagne); the knife-pleated serviette folded into the shape of swan; tucked into each, a bread roll (one was missing at Madame Almonte's place; thank God she checked). Using her middle finger, Frau von Kuhacsevich measures the precise distance of each plate from the table's edge, and the distance of each water goblet from each plate. Next to General Uraga's water goblet is a dead bee. She plucks a leaf from a tendril of the nearby bougainvillea and uses that to scoop it up.

In Milan and in Trieste, she had been able to delegate this task of inspecting the table, but not in Mexico—most certainly not in Mexico. It all falls on her, and sometimes she feels she's being buried beneath an avalanche. She has been on her feet since breakfast! And after luncheon, while everyone else enjoys a siesta, she, swollen feet or not, still has a long day's work ahead of her. Right now, she would like nothing better than to go into her bedroom, shutter the windows, and peel off her clothes.

After securing the extra serviette for Madame Almonte's place setting, and checking that the laundress has left fresh towels in the Austrian ambassador's room, Frau von Kuhacsevich permits herself a break. She goes to the garden to look for the princess, whom she finds on the far veranda, sitting all alone in an *equipal* chair. Out on the lawn before her, the little boy is playing with his nursemaid. At Frau von Kuhacsevich's approach, a small snake slinks out from behind a potted palm and disappears around the corner.

"Your Highness!" she salutes her friend.

The princess answers with a radiant smile and, with a tap of her fan, indicates the chair next to hers. "Do you smell those orange blossoms? I was just thinking of Goethe. *Kennst du das Land, wo die Zitronen blühn?*"

"So lovely," Frau von Kuhacevich says, putting her swollen feet up on a footstool. "I hope you do not mind?"

"Pardonnez-moi?" Princess Iturbide turns her good ear.

"I hope you do not mind I put my feet up."

"Not at all," the princess murmurs and continues fanning herself.

From the middle of the lawn, the bodyguard pitches the prince's red ball; it sails through the air in a slow, easy arc. Tere, in a wide-skirted pirouette, leaps up and catches it. The prince toddles after her, away toward the stone steps that lead down to the artificial pond. From the edge of those steps, Tere tosses the ball across the lawn, to Weissbrunn. And the dainty scene is repeated.

"A grand time the young ones are having," Frau von Kuhacsevich says.

The princess half rises from her chair and calls out, "Let him have the ball!" Turning to Frau von Kuhacsevich, she says, in a lower voice, "I don't know about this nursemaid."

"Yes, well." Frau von Kuhacsevich clears her throat. "By the way—are you hungry? We've another hour before luncheon."

"Famished, now that you mention it."

A footman brings a pitcher of limewater and a dish of jicama slices with chili powder and salt. The two fan themselves and, refreshed, chatter just as happily as the canaries in their mosque-shaped cage.

Out on the lawn, Prince Agustín's red ball lands in the grass. He wants Weissbrunn to throw it again, but Tere says, clapping her hands. "Time for your lunch."

The prince shakes his curls. "No!" He kicks it: the ball rolls over Weissbrunn's boot, *bup,* and it roll-a-rolls . . . down the slope of the lawn toward the bricks . . . toward the stone steps down to the artificial pond . . . Tere calls out, "Agustín!" But he toddles after his ball. She gathers her skirts and chases after him as he goes, faster now, toward the steps, and Weissbrunn chases after them both, his saber and pistol clanking. They are all three giggling when—from her *equipal* chair Princess Iturbide gasps—Agustín tumbles down the steps.

But they are shallow steps and only a few. Prince Agustín has not even scraped a knee, only banged his arm and had the breath knocked out of him.

Tere swoops down and covers him with kisses. Weissbrunn pats his heaving back. At the ruckus the macaw in its cage begins screeching. "*¡Ay, qué susto!* What a fright!" Tere says, hugging Agustín tight—but to see his bodyguard's face twisted with fear, Agustín bursts into screams, and this puts not only the parrot but Princess Iturbide and Frau von Kuhacsevich in a complete kerfluffle. The empress comes, trailed by Señorita Varela and Madame Almonte and four chambermaids. Princess Iturbide hovers so close to her godson, the child can scarcely catch his breath. Don Fernando Ramírez and the Austrian ambassador, who happened to be strolling by the pond at the time, look on with stricken expressions. Maximilian, his secretary, his botanist, and his doctor, race in.

Princess Iturbide, her hands gripping Agustín's shoulders: "Is it broken?"

Gently, as the child sobs, Dr. Semeleder takes his arm.

The empress, with glassy-eyed strain: "Will he need a splint?"

Dr. Semeleder folds the arm in again and then straightens it out. Agustín has stopped crying. For the first time, the child seems aware that he is the object of intense attention. At some point in the commotion, he has been set on top of the table that, but a moment earlier, held the tray of jicama slices. His eyes widening, he looks at everyone looking at him. It seems he is deciding whether to start crying again. Maximilian squeezes his knee.

"Little cousin, so! You are quite fine."

Agustín laughs.

"Ha ha!" Maximilian says, which encourages Agustín to laugh more. Frau von Kuhacsevich claps for joy, and the others join in, a sound, all up and down the veranda, like rain pelting a window. From its cage, the macaw lets out another ear-piercing squawk.

"What?" Maximilian says, turning around to face the crowd. "Would you have him take a bow?"

A wave of gentle laughter answers him.

Maximilian then hoists Agustín to his shoulders, and with a long-legged stride, takes off in a bouncing jog across the lawn in the direction of his office. José Luis and Professor Bilimek, holding both his own and Maximilian's butterfly nets, follow—the one behind the other.

From the veranda, the crowd disperses: the empress to her boudoir, the princess to hers, the ladies-in-waiting arm-in-arm out into the gardens; Frau von Kuhacsevich, with a voluptuous sigh, to inspect last-minute matters in the kitchen; and Tere and Weissbrunn—well . . . let us draw the veil over that pair . . .

"Grab hold!" Maximilian says to Agustín. "No, not my neck!" They fly over the greenest part of the lawn, Maximilian zigzagging around the croquet hoops, then past the orchestra, the butterfly nets fluttering behind Professor Bilimek, white and pillowy. A flock of swallows bursts overhead; a crow caws from the top of the jacaranda; and over the dappled lawn beneath the ficus tree, just as the last of this little parade, José Luis, clears the final cornetist, a one-legged hussar in a sun-faded captain's jacket, Sawerthal's baton swings the orchestra into "Wiener Kinder."

Maximilian feels a special affinity for children. It is not so much that he wants one of his own, but that he identifies with their unblemished beauty, their innocence, and above all that natural ability to lose themselves in the joy of a moment. Or is it really a natural ability? He wonders. In an adult, certainly, it can be a talent cultivated as artists do, yes, as must any of those who, by profession or inclination, call upon the Muses.

When he was a twelve-year-old boy, there was a distinct moment one gray winter's day in the Hofburg when he looked up from his schoolwork, the endless hieroglyphics of trigonometry, and caught sight of his reflection in the window. Four o'clock and it was nearly dark outside. He had been horrified: how old he looked. The life drained out of him! In a whisper that neither his older brother, Franz Joseph, nor Charlie, could hear, he solemnly swore: I shall not forget who I truly am.

Adults, it seemed to Max, were as butterflies in reverse: they, too, had been beautiful and free, but they had folded in their wings, spun themselves into a cocoon, and let their appendages dissolve until what they became was hard, ridgid, little worms. One's tutor, for example, reminded one of a nematode.

Twiddling concern with numbers, "practicality" in all its Philistine guises, makes Maximilian stupendously bored. He needs vistas of sky, mountains, swift-running and sun-sparkled water; he needs—as a normal man must eat—to explore this world, to see, to touch its sibylline treasures: humming-birds; the red-as-blood breast of a macaw; the furred and light-as-a-feather legs of a tarantula. God in all His guises: mushrooms, lichens, all creatures. As a boy Max had delighted in his menagerie: a marmoset, a toucan, a lemur. The lemur escaped and, outside overnight, died of cold. A footman opened the door in the morning, and there the thing was, dusted with snow and stiff as cardboard.

"I detest winter," Max declared. Franz Joseph, Charlie, and the little brothers, bundled in woollens and furs, they could go ice-skating or building fortresses for snowball fights. Max preferred to stay inside with his pets, his books, and the stoves roaring. The one thing he relished about winter, for it was a most elegant way of thumbing his nose at it, was to go into the Bergl Zimmer and shut the door behind him. Its walls and its doors were painted with murals, trompes l'oeil of the most luxuriant flora and fauna: watermel-ons, papayas, cockatoos, coconut trees, hibiscus. Where was this, Ceylon? Java? Yucatan? Sleet could be falling on the other side of the Hofburg's win-dows, but this treasure of the Bergl Zimmer, painted in the year 1760 for his great-great-grandmother the Empress Maria Theresa, never failed to trans-port one into an ecstasy of enchantment.

His mother had counseled her sons, many times: "Make up your mind to be happy. Then you will be."

Here, this moment in Cuernavaca, one is happy: perfumes in the air, col-ors from the palette of Heaven, birds, flowering trees, and vines and or-anges, the music of the orchestra and of the fountains, this bone-warming sunshine . . .

"Hurrah! Professor Bilimek, what have you to show us?" Maximilian sets Agustín on the grass. They have arrived at the veranda outside his office. The professor has a clipped white beard that makes his face appear both rounder and ruddier than it really is; his eyes are small and watery behind wire-rimmed spectacles. He removes his straw hat, mops his bald head, and then, from one of the many bulging pockets in his smock, he brings out a small jar.

"*Etwas wunderbar.* Something wonderful," Professor Bilimek says. Switching to French: "*Un petit bête du Bon Dieu.* One of the good Lord's little creatures," he says, putting it into Agustín's hands.

A Capuchin, Professor Bilimek is profoundly shy around adults, especially about his Spanish, which is why he lapses into French with anyone who cannot understand German. Years ago he accompanied Maximilian to Brazil and managed the entire expedition with nary a word of Portuguese.

The jar imprisons a ladybug. Agustín watches the ladybug crawl up the inside of the glass; then he sets the jar down on the bricks.

Off to the side, in the lime green shade of an espaliered fig tree, Maximilian reaches past the aphalandra to finger a leaf the shape of an elephant's ear. To his secretary he says, "*Monstera*, or the Latin name is *colocasia esculenta*. In Brazil, however, the leaf is distinctly larger and more reniform. The natives use them as parasols."

"Extraordinary!" José Luis leans in for a closer look at the very same plant his own mother keeps in a pot on the laundry patio of her house in Mexico City.

"But they are of no use in tropical downpours."

"Goodness, yes. Yes, I can imagine!"

Grasping it low down on its stem, Maximilian snaps off the leaf. "Little cousin?" Agustín comes close and Maximilian bends down. "For you, a parasol just your size."

Agustín giggles, but unsure what to do with the big leaf, he drops it on top of the jar with the ladybug. He runs out onto the lawn, into the shadow of the ficus tree, past the mango tree, and into the sunniest part. Here he bends his knees, puts his bottom in the air, and plants the crown of his head on the grass. After a pause in this awkward position, he flops over.

"Bravo!" says Professor Bilimek.

Agustín makes another somersault.

"Bravo! How many can you do?"

Agustín holds up three fingers.

"*Drei?* Three?"

"*Drei!*"

"*Encore une fois!* Once again!" Professor Bilimek says.

From the veranda, with his arms crossed over his chest, Maximilian watches the little boy with a glower of envy. To be an adult is to live in a kind of jail. To be a sovereign is to live in that same jail, but in iron fetters, and the key tossed out through the bars. He had so envied his elder brother's having a throne, and been so angry at being bullied into signing that Family Pact . . . but his feelings toward his brother are beginning to soften a little. In this job he has grown old so quickly. As a matter of fact (he puts his hand to the top of his thinning hair), he is well on his way to going as bald as Professor Bilimek. In another year or two, Maximilian's head will be a billiard ball—no, worse, a freckled egg. And from all the coffee and tobacco, his teeth have turned brown. He is no Romeo. Though his beard is looking fine. As a kind of compensation, he has been letting it grow. Proudly, he gives it a smooth.

"Little cousin, come!"

When Agustín runs back to him, Maximilian takes him by the hand and dismisses the others.

To abandon the sunshine for his office, even with the little "cousin," is to come crashing back into a waking nightmare. Maximilian has granted the Austrian ambassador an interview before luncheon, in which he must steer his leaky craft between a Scylla and a Charybdis, that is, between impressing Vienna with his good governance of Mexico and opening the road to his possible return to Austria, upon which depends the renegotiation of the Family Pact.

The Kaiser was the one who had acted in bad faith, Maximilian believes. But now, nearly two years gone by since he was forced to affix his signature to that accursed scrap of paper, he realizes, the bitterest cup was the one he drank of his own volition, thinking it sweet syrup, whilst on board the *Novara*. That is, it was a grievous, possibly fatal mistake to have sent that protest, and so publically! Franz Joseph may harbor affection for his younger brother or, at least for their mother's sake, pretend that he does. But as Kaiser he turns first to the men around him, and those hardheads already considered Maximilian a near traitor for having dared criticize Vienna's barbaric measures against dissidents, and then, for having treated with Louis Napoleon.

To protest the Family Pact in this way—it was Charlotte who insisted they send the telegram to all the courts of Europe, and that moron, Schertzenlechner, and Monsieur Eloin and—oh, it was to have goaded the beasts with a red-hot poker. He should have waited. He should have been played the game with more subtlety, using back channels, letting those who needed to, save face. Now, with the Family Pact in force, should Maximilian return to Europe, his pensions, his position, his ability to choose where to reside, where to travel, in short, his entire future would be at their mercy. He would be as a turtle without a carapace.

One never should have listened to Charlotte. One never should have allowed her, so young a woman, to exert such influence. Charlotte is forever meddling! She meddled in matters with the church; it would not be fair to blame the break with the pope on her, but perhaps her overly frank manner with the papal emissary—? It did not serve. (Well, Father Fischer remains in Rome; he has not yet picked apart that Gordian knot.) Charlotte, with her habitual rigidity, takes everything in a manner deadly serious. She suffers paralyzing headaches. She has been so emotional about her father's death. This is why one must protect her from unpleasantness. One has given her the general tint of things, but specifics are best left unmentioned (for example, that the Iturbides, those ingrates, have gone to the U.S. minister in Paris to stir up an intrigue). One cannot discuss with Charlotte the possibility of abdication. If it happens—it might not—it is Bazaine's fault! For letting the guerrillas walk all over him. The armies are bleeding more deserters every day, Bazaine admits it! More money, General Almonte says, more, more— while the French go on robbing the customhouses.

Monsieur Langlais may be a wizard with numbers, but no mere man can bring forth loaves and fishes.

Impunitatis cupido . . . magnis semper conatibus adversa—The desire of escape . . . that foe to all great enterprises, as Tacitus said.

But one is weary to the bones. Oh, to be a child again! To run free in the world! One could retire, this very summer, to the Adriatic, visit the island of Lacroma . . . one might make experiments with aeronautics . . . Reread Goethe and Seneca . . . pen one's memoirs . . .

But would the Kaiser permit even that? From Vienna, Charlie reports that one's popularity remains very strong, especially among the Hungarians. So the Hofburg could consider one's mere presence within the confines of the empire a threat. Monsieur Eloin agrees. Perhaps the superior strategy would be to first, for some two or perhaps three years, establish residence in a neutral country—but which one?

A cigar smoldering between his lips, Maximilian leafs through his atlas, a prodigious tome bound in navy blue morocco leather, its pages gilded: The Sandwich Islands . . . Tahiti . . . he wets a finger and turns another rustling page . . . Australia's Botany Bay . . .

Rajasthan? Say, a yearlong expedition to ride elephants and shoot tigers?

But one's happy fantasies are cut short. The Austrian ambassador is ushered in.

His Excellency stands taller than Maximilian by a full three inches. Dressed in white linen trousers, a white blouse, and incongruously black boots, Count Guido von Thun has muttonchop sidewhiskers, low-set dark eyebrows, and the focused gaze of a stork about to pincer a fish. Having returned Maximilian's greeting, stooping slightly, Count von Thun tries out his heavily accented Spanish on the prince, who is sprawled on the carpet, stacking his blocks.

"*Mucho gusto en conocerle* . . . Pleased to meet you . . ."

"*Hola!*" says the child, but without looking up.

His frock, Count von Thun cannot help noticing, is covered with grass stains. There is a frightful bruise on his left arm, just above the elbow.

"A right nice tower you have built there with your blocks."

Agustín kicks it over with his sandal.

"Was that a castle?"

Agustín runs to Maximilian and clings to his leg.

Count von Thun persists. "How old are you?"

Shyly, Agustín holds up four fingers.

Maximilian, tousling the child's hair, says, "You little liar! I know how old you are."

Count von Thun had assumed the child was at least four. Agustín, biting his lip, holds up two fingers.

"That's right, little cousin," Maximilian says, "but you are almost three, aren't you?"

Agustín nods.

"And you know when your birthday is, don't you?"

Agustín swings his head, "No."

"I know you know when it is," Maximilian says. "Ho!" Agustín has crawled under the desk. Maximilian bends down, both hands on his thighs: "What are you doing under there?"

The ambassador, beetling his brow, rubs his chin, and then he scratches behind his ear. *What is this about?* There is a reason that, for his—that is, Vienna's—benefit, Maximilian makes a fuss over this infant, but what is it? That one is supposed to see this so-called prince—this really is a stretch—as his Heir? That the idea is, one should run cable Count Rechberg, *Do convince the Kaiser to send over a nephew lest the House of Habsburg lose this golden opportunity?* War is coming with Prussia, perhaps as soon as May. The Kaiser needs Mexico like he needs a hole in the head. Austria cannot afford to make an enemy of the United States. (Already, Austria's ambassador to Washington is under orders to maintain strict neutrality with regard to Mexico.) To allow a few thousand volunteers to ship over was a concession made out of family loyalty, to give Maximilian *something*.

And the Austrian volunteers might have achieved *something*, had Bazaine not kept them scattered, sent off on operations both trivial and absurdly dangerous. Count von Thun's cousin, General von Thun, is the commanding officer of the Austrian volunteers. Last time they had spoken of Bazaine, he'd nearly choked with rage.

In any event, at the rate Mexico is falling into bankruptcy and lawlessness, Maximilian shall have to abdicate. The question is, when will he do it?

And this little boy? It was spectacularly stupid of Maximilian to have his mother arrested and deported. According to the police reports, she has taken her case to the U.S. minister in Paris. Typical of Maximilian! He coddles his enemies, and then when they go after him, he plays the ostrich. Faced with unpleasant decisions, he procrastinates—the most inane game. Which is how Maximilian got himself into such a tangle over that Family Pact. It was beyond ingenuous for Maximilian to claim he'd been surprised by it; Count Rechburg had presented the terms very clearly and early on. *Geltungsbedürfnis,* the need to show off—that has always been the weak chink in Maximilian's armor.

Count von Thun does not have any feeling of charity for Maximilian's byzantine fooleries. He never has. He takes out his handkerchief and mops his brow. Dressing all in white is not defense enough against this heat.

It offends him that capable officers are dying. He shall never forget his grief: Captain Karl Kurtzrock and sixty ulans slaughtered in Ahuacatlán. The Austrian volunteers, for the most part, roam around the sierra battling these monkeys, and stagecoach robbers and kidnappers with names like Loco de López, Hongos, and El Tuerto. Austrians should be serving the Kaiser, not this chimera of *l'empire du Mexique* dreamed up in the Tuileries. And to begin with, it was a scandal for an Austrian archduke to have condescended to accept a throne from a Bonaparte.

Further, this position has been no boon to Count von Thun's career. One of Austria's most highly regarded diplomats, he has been posted to Mexico not because Mexico matters but because its sovereign happens to be the Kaiser's brother. Count von Thun would prefer Muscovite snowstorms to this puny farce. Look at this office: the upholstery, the paintings, the elaborately carved credenza—and, according to intelligence, Maximilian has been regularly corresponding with his decorators in Trieste! It seems he is less interested in governing than in furnishing his Italian plaything. The latest letter intercepted was an order for a thousand nightingales to be placed in the open aviary behind the parterre overlooking the Bay of Grignano!

Out of the corner of his eye, Count von Thun spots the atlas open to . . . Rajasthan?

"*Dulce de cacahuate?*" Maximilian says, lifting an orange and black clay bowl from the edge of his desk. A pot like a pumpkin.

"A what, sir?"

"*Ca-ca-hua-te,* that is, 'peanut' in the language of our Aztecs." Maximilian waves his cigar over the neatly arranged rows of paper-wrapped candies the size of doubloons. "These come from Mexico City's finest *dulcería,* as we say, *Süßwarengeschäft.* El Paraíso Terrestre on the Calle de San Francisco."

"I do not know it."

"Shame. You must be sure to go there. "

"*Quiero un cacahuate,* I want a peanut," Agustín says from under the desk.

Maximilian says in Spanish, "I will give you one, little cousin, but not until you come out from under there."

"No!"

"Well then, little cousin, you may not have one."

Agustín says, tugging at Maximilian's trouser leg, "My rhino wants one."

"Your rhinoceros!" Maximilian says. "What color is your rhinoceros today?"

"Seven."

"No, that is a number. What color is your rhinocerous? Is he blue?"

"Tuesday."

"Your rhinoceros is Tuesday!" With a chuckle, Maximilian turns to the ambassador. In German, Maximilian says, "Your turn."

"Sir?"

"Ask him about his rhinoceros."

Noisily, the ambassador clears his throat. He bends down, one elbow on his knee, and peers under the desk. In his awkward Spanish, he says, "Where is the rhinoceros?"

"On your head!"

Count von Thun touches his head. "I do not feel it."

"He bite you!"

Having gone as far as his dignity permits, Count von Thun straightens. He still has the *dulce de cacahuate* in his hand.

In German, Maximilian says, "Try it. It is a marzipan of the peanut."

Count von Thun bites into his *dulce de cacahuate,* and nearly chokes. Truly, it is one of the most detestable things he can remember ever having tasted. Dry as chalk, it sticks to his teeth.

"Mmm," he says, making an effort to swallow. In the meantime the tyke has crawled over to the bookcase and begun pulling out books.

Maximilian says suddenly, "I have been thinking of India." He lifts his chin and, in the direction of the open door, exhales a pencil-stream of smoke.

"Ah?" Books go on thumping to the floor—and there is another noise. Just outside the door, the emperor's bodyguard has begun snoring.

"As I was telling your British counterpart, the other day, we Mexicans have much to learn from their example in India."

"Hmm." Count von Thun wishes he could have a glass of water and tries, discreetly, behind his handkerchief, to clean his teeth with his tongue.

"As their Hindus have demonstrated, elephants are most useful in logging hardwoods in mountainous terrain."

"Hmm."

"We have extensive hardwood forests all along our Gulf Coast and in Yucatan and Chiapas." (Another thump.) "As well as in the north as far as Chihuahua. Mahogany, oak, walnut, really, what we have is a cornucopia of hardwoods."

"You would import working elephants for logging?"

"Precisely."

"From India?"

"New York City. Our consul there has been in negotiations with a circus."

It takes all of Count von Thun's diplomatic nerve to maintain a straight face.

"But," Maximilian continues, "we are already benefitting from a number of extraordinary innovations. I am sure you know all about our *henequén,* or sisal hemp production in our very rich haciendas in Yucatan? Now, in Lower California, our northwestern peninsula, with the aid of the modern diving apparatus, we will be expanding the exploitation of our pearl beds along the Sea of Cortez."

"Ah."

"Near the islands off La Paz, in Lower California, one of our Yaqui divers has brought up a black pearl the size of a lemon."

"Hmm?"

"But the shape of a pear."

"Hmm."

"It weighed in at three hundred and fifty seven grains."

"Ah."

"There was an article about it in *Le Moniteur*."

"Hmm."

Maximilian goes on in this vein, Count von Thun carefully calibrating his reactions—or rather, noises—to fall within the range distant from disdain on the one hand and false enthusiasm on the other. To put it undiplomatically, Maximilian is full of beans. They are standing in the center of the room; behind Maximilian's shoulder, between the two oil paintings of Popocatépetl and Iztaccíhuatl, a prize-winning cockroach works its way down the wall. On the tiles, close enough that Count von Thun could put out his boot and crush them, a line of ants marches toward the door. The air stirs. Maximilian's expression suddenly fixes on something outside. Count von Thun turns his head.

"You missed it," Maximilian says.

"What?"

"A hummingbird. There is a nest under the eaves. The other day I found the gardener up on a ladder. He meant to remove it, but I forbade it." Maximilian goes over to his desk and comes back with a tin plate covered with a handkerchief. "Lift it up."

Upon the plate rests a thumb-sized lump of feathers: a hummingbird. "Professor Bilimek's treasure of the morning. A cat got it."

"Fast cat."

Maximilian squints through the smoke of his cigar. "Pick it up."

"Another Aztec delicacy?"

Maximilian laughs.

Count von Thun cups the cadaver in his palms. For the first time he is genuinely astonished. "It does not weigh anything."

"Our Aztecs call the hummingbird feather *huitzilihuitl*, or pure spirit. It is breath and sun."

Count von Thun rolls it from the one palm to the other. Its feathers are black, yet they shimmer with all the colors of the rainbow.

Maximilian says, "It is the only bird capable of flying backward."

Count von Thun replaces the cadaver on the plate. Pleasantries dispensed with, this is the moment for Maximilian to bring up business.

Instead, Maximilian puffs his cigar. He looks around himself and then, suddenly, says in English, "Hello?" He dips his head under the desk. "Little cousin?" He straightens. In German: "Where is he?"

Count von Thun shakes his head. He follows Maximilian outside.

"Sir!" The emperor's bodyguard has snapped to shocked attention. He squares his heels.

Maximilian says, "Where is the prince?"

"Sir! I have not seen him, sir!"

Maximilian yawns. To Count von Thun, he says, "Can't have gone far." He taps some ash onto the grass. "Shall we?"

Music floats over the lawn. Along the pathway by the fountain, in the cool beneath a coconut palm silvered with sun, a maid hurries past with a teetering basket of towels on her head. Maximilian and the ambassador continue down the veranda in the direction of their luncheon (the smell of baked fish becoming stronger), and just as they approach the flowered mass of the table, they hear, this time from the other side of the hedges, from the steps that lead down to the horse stables, the child's screams.

CHEZ ITURBIDE

*T*he instant the child's arm snapped, on the other side of the world, in her seat at the Paris Opéra, his mother began to fan herself desperately. Her lips parted, as if suddenly she beheld, not down upon the milling stage but hovering before her in midair, the gruesome vision.

Every cell in her body knew that her child had been hurt; he was crying for her. Flooded with helpless anguish, she began to weep. Angelo, exasperated, whispered into her ear: "Get a hold of yourself."

"Something has happened to the baby!"

"Darling, *please.*" Angelo put his hand over hers, less to comfort than to quiet her. He had so hoped the distraction of this evening at the opera would settle her nerves, and these were expensive box seats—front row, with a clear view across the orchestra pit, of the imperial box. Behind the tricolor bunting, Louis Napoleon sat watching the stage intently. Eugénie was regal as a marble Diana, supremely aware of the eyes upon her. At her throat (much remarked upon before the curtain came up) sparkled a ruby the size of a walnut, and in her hair an aigrette of ebony feathers and diamonds. The foreign minister, Drouyn de Lhuys and his wife were seated to the left of the imperial couple, Madame in precipitous décolletage and a necklace of sapphires. Even in the dim, as she turned her head: blue sparkles. Perhaps, Angelo considered, it was this mute proximity to the objects of their efforts—so cruelly tantalizing, why, he could have tossed a glove and it might have landed in the emperor's lap. Was that what had set Alicia off? But, as he'd always told himself, it's God's own mystery what fancies flit about in a woman's head.

A crash of cymbals. On the stage the crowd of garishly costumed peasants parted, and to a solitary violoncello's F sharp stretched taut, Adelina Patti glided toward the footlights, raised one luminous arm gloved to the elbow, splayed her fingers, and uplifted her rib cage into a glorious aria—ruined by his wife. Half the theater, it seemed, including Eugénie, glanced in their direction. The stern matron in the next box glared at Alicia.

"Shsh!" someone behind them hissed.

Angelo scraped back his chair and took his wife by the arm.

Outside, Alicia could not stop crying. Under the arcade they stood in the bone-chilling night, their breath a ghost between them. Angelo reminded her, Drouyn de Lhuys was not their only line of communication to the emperor. There was Dr.Evans, Bigelow's extra-official and direct conduit, it turned out, to the innermost salons of the Tuileries. (The week before Christmas, Dr. Evans had extracted Agustín Gerónimo's molar.) And as Alicia well knew, a friend of a friend of Agustín Gerónimo had agreed to write to Maximilian. It could be a month before Maximilian might read it, but, Angelo said, the letter was on its way. And Bigelow had cabled his counterpart in Vienna, who could be counted on to put a word in at the Hofburg, and that would be sure to embarrass Maximilian.

"Bigelow cabled Vienna! Why did you not tell me?"

Her face broke his heart. "Because, darling, I just found it out and we were rushing to make the curtain." He put his arm around her waist. "You see, things are moving. But we must have patience."

Alicia turned away from him. Her voice had become brittle. "Something has happened to the baby. I know it."

"You must stop exciting your mind." He gave her his handkerchief; she blew her nose. Once she'd finished, he pushed a hand at her back. "Shall we?" He meant to take her back to the hotel.

But Alicia stayed right where she was. She cast a glance about her and sniffed the air. She adjusted her fox-fur wrapper. "Do you know what?"

"What."

She twisted her mouth. "I *loathe* this city."

Angelo closed his eyes. The previous summer, when they were negotiating with the empress, Alicia had repeatedly declared that to live in Paris would be *le rêve de ma vie—la grande vie—le douceur de vivre*—she'd trotted out her schoolgirl French every chance she got. But now she turned her tear-stained face back to his. In the gaslights she looked gray and haggard. He did not want to look at her. He looked at his watch. He wondered, very angrily, what he might do with the rest of this wasted evening.

She said, "Don't you hate Paris, too?"

He examined his shoes.

"Don't you?" she insisted.

"In a way."

"It is *de trop*. Gigantically overrated!"

"Yes," he said, only because he did not want to be standing out in the night air.

"Adelina Patti is a mediocrity of a soprano. *De mal en pis.*"

He had decided to placate her. "Yes," he said, though, absolutely, he disagreed.

"We should be given a refund."

"Yes, darling, tomorrow."

Alicia turned on him fiercely, her little beaded bag swinging on her wrist. "The Opéra does *not* give refunds."

"Yes."

She stamped her shoe. "*Yes!* Is that all you can say, 'yes'? You are—" But then she saw the look in his eyes. They both knew what she had been about to blurt out. When she'd tried that on him the other day, he had answered her, with a coolness he had never shown her before, *If you think so little of your husband, I suggest you consider going back to live with your mother.* She now cried out, "Oh, oh!" covering her eyes; she swooned, but he caught her, pulling her back up as if she were a rag doll. He had lost his patience.

He said, gripping her arm, this time without compromise, "Come. You can cry oceans in the hotel."

• • •

The curious thing was, the moment her husband said that, Alicia's tears dried up and she has not shed one in the two weeks since. It is February 14, as it happens, Ash Wednesday, the first day of Lent. She is much grieved that, socially, the winter has been a complete *folie.* Not having been received at court, what then could Madame de Iturbide be expected to be invited to? All the savoir faire in the world would not gain her entrée through those elegant doors behind the high walls of the Faubourg.

Lent: one is supposed to give up something in penance, but why should she, when she has sacrificed her whole heart? Or rather, had it ripped out of her! What kind of a God can be so cruel as to allow her to suffer so? Could it all be a fraud? Does He even exist? A sin of a question, she thinks. Ought she to confess her spiritual decay? She intended to, back in December, however, the English-speaking priest was not there. Confessing in French? What a bother.

But maybe the problem is that she has been praying to the wrong saint. San Judas Tadeo, Saint Jude Thaddeus, patron saint of impossible causes— what was Doña Juliana thinking to suggest him? It would have been better to get started with the Santo Niño de Atocha, protector of children and prisoners. But nobody cares about that one here in France.

The past weekend, their nephew Salvador had been let out of his school, Sainte Barbe des Champs. "Can we ride horses in the Bois?" Salvador said. "I want a horse. I would be so happy to have a horse."

"Might find one on the menu," Agustín Gerónimo quipped. But not even Agustín Cosme laughed.

Salvador, with his angel-fish eyes, his unruly hair, has grown a full inch; he is nearly as tall as Angelo, though so skinny he might blow away in a stiff wind. To put some meat on his bones, they took him to la Maison Dorée. It was full of Yankees, nouveaux riche. The couple at the next table was shamelessly eavesdropping. Shyly, as the waiter was handing round the menus, Salvador asked, had there been any news of the baby?

"Not from Pepa directly," Angelo said. They had heard from their relative in Toluca, José Malo, and also secondhand—from Angelo's sister, Sabina, the nun in Philadelphia—that the baby was healthy.

Alicia, dry-eyed, said, "Your auntie Pepa has stolen him, you see."

Alicia has taken to casting down these truths, how they shatter like goblets. In the silence that follows—a silence like that of a farm in snowfall—she does not cry.

"Sister," Agustín Gerónimo gently chided Alicia. "Let us forgive Pepa. It is Maximilian who will decide matters."

Alicia keeps her hand locked around her other wrist. But sometimes, she cannot help it, she twists her hair. She's developed a bald spot she has to keep covered with a curl. She bites her fingernails. Fragments of songs, little earworms, tunnel into her brain, *Da de da de boom-bah* . . . They've rented a piano; after hearing Salvador play, for several days, over and over, she kept hearing the first three stanzas of *Hail Columbia*. Two days ago, she awoke with these words ringing in her head: *the stone was shattered by the silence.* Outside it is forever gray. If the feeling that envelops her had a color, it would be a sooty, pulsing red. She always feels cold, but her anger—fury of a Hecuba!—is a sun that has dried the sea to a vast gritty plain. And on that anger shines, on and on, ferocious, obscene. There is no shadow, no contrast. Only the rash at the back of her scalp. A stye. A sore throat for the first week of December, and a running fever at Christmas. Pounding headaches, and this never-ending sandpaper ache, the hollowness in her chest.

Cables, letters go out into a world so enormous, it seems beyond logic that the same sun and moon shine over Mexico City as over Paris. One night, she awoke and for some reason felt drawn to the window. She parted the drapes and there, balanced like a ball upon the mansard roof across the street, was the moon. Her dream, though fading, still held bright in her mind: she'd been in her bed in Rosedale in the room she shared with her sisters and, for some reason, gone to the window. She looked out and there, high above the Potomac, hung the moon. The orchards, the fields, the houses and buildings of Georgetown, all the way down to the warehouses and the bone factory and the wharves, the scene was blanketed in snow. Beneath the window, the hedges along the driveway were shining pillows. A doe leapt across the drive.

Then, wisp that it was, the dream vanished.

At the window, she whispered to the Paris moon, "Take my love to my little boy."

Her child! To think of him, she put her hands to her ribs.

"M is for moon, who sings a tune."

Moon: a big yellow cheese. Her baby was sitting on her lap while they looked at the book.

"N is for nut, rolling down the roof of a hut. O is for opossum, which, roasted is very toothsome."

And the Paris moon, pale and mottled, seemed to offer its smiling benevolence. Its glow iced the shingles of that roof, the outer fold of the drapes, and her left sleeve.

Yes, in the turn of the clock, it would shine upon Mexico.

Her fingertips warming the glass, she went on gazing at this strange pearl, eye of the sky. After a while, it moved up and shrank to half its size. A scarf of cloud drifted across it.

Three weeks ago Louis Napoleon announced to the Corps Législatif that he would be withdrawing his troops from Mexico in stages, beginning in October. Paris is still abuzz: is this an admission of defeat or a signal of success? Louis Napoleon claims that the Mexican imperial government is strong enough to stand unaided. Mr. Bigelow, however, claims that the "archduke's" government will collapse. It is too early for anyone in Paris to do other than guess at Maximilian's reaction; it may well be that the news of Louis Napoleon's decision has not yet even reached Veracruz.

What did this mean for getting the baby back?

"Prob'ly nothin'," Agustín Gerónimo said.

"Anything," Angelo countered.

Alicia: "If Maximilian abdicates—?"

Angelo: "I expect he will remove his court to Trieste."

Alicia's hands flew to her cheeks. "Trieste! We shall have to go *there*—"

"Darling," Angelo interrupted. "Let us take one day at a time."

Agustín Gerónimo kept his pipe in his teeth. "Eh, dottle. Maximilian's not—" But the rest of what he wanted to say was drowned in coughing.

• • •

Yes, time has crawled on bloody knees all the way to Ash Wednesday. At midday mass in La Madeleine, front row center, on one of the plain rush-bottomed chairs, Alicia sits, arms crossed, with a puckered expression. Behind the altar, a stone Mary Magdalene ascends to heaven in the arms of a pair of angels. When Alicia first set eyes on these sculptures nearly two months ago, she leaned over and whispered to Angelo, "Aren't they beautiful?" Washington had nothing of this caliber. (Georgetown's Holy Trinity was so Spartan, the reverend used to joke that it could pass for Presbyterian.) But now, halfway into February, the bitterest of her life, Alicia decides that the face of this sculpted saint and imaginary winged creatures are simply dégagé: blasé as three artist's models, which is exactly what they are. French tarts!

In gloria Dei Patris Amen . . . The priest, his back to the congregation, drones on. She is glad she does not have to look at him: he looks like a demented barber. Altar boys swing their censers, trailing poufs of smoke. The little bell rings. Because she has not confessed, Alicia does not join the queue to receive communion.

Last year on Ash Wednesday, they all went to mass at the Templo de la Profesa. On Tuesday, the Calle de San Francisco had been full of the din and clang of bands, and barefoot Indians stumbling around stupefied with pulque. By Wednesday, however, that street had been swept clean as a penny by the Zouave crew. As Alicia and her sister-in-law rounded the corner, they passed one last African in a fez and red pantaloons, raking down the gutter.

"I am beginning to have hope," Pepa said, pressing her hoopskirt so that it tipped up, not so much as to reveal an ankle but enough to get her safely over the high threshold.

"Me, too," Alice said.

In the dark of the vestibule, Pepa suddenly put her hand on Alicia's arm. "For Lent, let us give up *all* sweets."

"O Moses!" Alicia had laughed. "*All* sweets? I could not endure *that*."

"Nonsense. We'll do it together."

That afternoon, however, after forgoing not only the pie but her customary two lumps of sugar in her coffee, Alicia had come upon Pepa in the pantry, with her fingers in a box of bonbons! The memory of that now sends Alicia into a silent rage. She exhales through her nose.

Domine Deus, Agnus Dei, Filius Patris . . . the priest intones.

Angelo shuffles back to his chair. He kneels and rests his forehead on clasped hands. She wants to shove him in the back. *Can you not see, no one is listening? How can you tell me I am the one with the over-excited imagination? Why, that "host" on your tongue, it's a scrap of flour! Get yourself examined by the nerve-doctor!*

Arch-backed in her chair, Alicia sits as still as the silhouette on a coin. Suddenly, out of nowhere, something so funny pops into her head she can't help laughing out loud: it was the way her brother Oseola, after he came out of the swimming pond, would put his cupped hand in his armpit and flap his elbow to make fart noises.

Angelo lifts his head. This time he doesn't shush her; he only touches her wrist.

They come out of La Madeleine into a shadowless, hammer-dull day. A crowd of beggars, legless veterans, and pigeons. Angelo turns his collar up; Alicia pulls her fox-fur wrapper close. Her quilted and seal-fur-trimmed bonnet and muff are not enough to keep her from shivering. Angelo, wincing as he hobbles, has fallen victim to the gout. Again.

Ash Wednesday, as all the days, plods on in boots of lead, remorse and anger dragging behind each moment like Frankenstein's creature. So many useless days of needlework, reading novels, newspapers, magazines; learning to play a mandolin (but then one of its strings broke), games of whist and jackstraws, driving, singing, letter writing, trudging the echoing galleries of the Louvre, buying heaps of things—a paperweight shaped like a chimpanzee, monogrammed stationery, sugar plums at Boissier.

The Grand-Hôtel's hydraulic lift: how delighted Salvador was at first to ride it up and down. So noisy, so confining. It made her feel like a pea in aspic.

Back in her room, she changes clothes for the third time. Then she goes out for gloves to match the dress with bachlik fichu she's having made by Worth. "*Bonjour,* Madame de Iturbide." The clerk slides out trays of merchandise, one after the other, and another, and Alicia yearns to ask, not *Would you have this in a darker hue?* but *Can you not see the axe in my chest? Where is God's mercy, that no one will pull it out by the handle?*

On the most simple of errands, Alicia must confront children on every boulevard: bundled into prams, holding their nursemaid's hand, carried on their father's shoulders, riding by, wee rosy faces, in whatever fiacre. On along and up the Champs-Elysées, she strolls, stopping here and there to peer in at amber bracelets, pictures of Tahiti, Turkish carpets, chinoiseries, but it does not matter where she is, what she is doing, in her mind, over and over, there comes the image, bright as life, of Pepa in the carriage, clutching the baby.

Alicia remembers the last kiss she pressed into her baby's cheek—so vividly, it seems she can close her eyes, put out her hand, and caress that warm downy skin. Most of all she remembers her baby's curls; her fingers tousling his curls, and his sweet talcum scent with a soupçon of raisin and roses—her baby's smell. She would know it with her eyes closed.

It has been for five soul-deadening months that Alicia asks, *How could Pepa, who claimed she loved her, have done this to her?* Filled her head with princess dreams and lies, conniving lies, obvious now as the stink of a polecat! Alicia hates Maximilian and Carlota, but the one who brings the bile to her throat is Pepa.

Pepa promised: "I shall write to you every single day."

But in Veracruz there was nothing, in La Havana there was nothing, nothing in New York, nothing in Washington, or London, in Saint Nazaire, or now in Paris—in Paris since late November—not one blessed word.

All Alicia has of her baby is a lock of his hair and his photograph, taken the day of his christening: he was then a bald-headed little man, just able to sit up. Much as she cherishes this picture and has, a hundred times, wept over it, this is not who he is now. April 2, the day after Easter, will be his third birthday. What does he look like now? Fruitlessly, she has searched the shops of Paris for his carte de visite—she has found one of Crown Prince Rudolph, the Prince of Wales, Prince Chulalongkorn of Siam, General Bazaine,

John Wilkes Booth, that of every silly little actress and opera singer and poodle-trainer.

Oh, what have they done with his curls? What words, what songs has he learned to sing? Does he have his toy bunny, his blocks, his blue ball? She trembles for his safety. The Child of France has had measles. To stanch the rumors that he was on his deathbed, they sent him out for a drive before he was fully recovered, he relapsed—and nearly died, so the more scandalous newspapers say. And that eight-year-old dauphin whose parents were beheaded in the Place de la Révolution? Agustín Gerónimo said, "No worries, sister, the dauphin escaped." Out of the many stories, the one he judged most likely was that the dauphin was residing incognito in a London suburb. If alive today, the dauphin would be an old man some eighty years old. But their Paris guidebook says that no, the fairy stories are not true; the pretenders are every one of them shysters. What really happened was, after his mother, Marie-Antoinette, was taken to the guillotine, the little prince was not locked but bricked into a windowless cell in the Temple Tower. Alone in the dark, in his own filth, he was slowly starved to death. As a souvenir, someone took a knife and cut out his heart. Dr. Evans has told them that last July, Mr. Bigelow's four-year-old son died of a fever in the brain. Willie Lincoln died in the White House. Heaven is filled with the souls of children. *Dust thou art, and unto dust shalt thou return.* Before she realizes what she is doing—at the corner of the rue du Faubourg Saint Honoré—Alicia has tucked her furled umbrella under her other arm, and crossed herself, and kissed the knuckle of her thumb.

Later, after buying five hair ornaments, three lengths of satin ribbon in magenta, mauve, and violet, and more silk hose than three women could wear out in a year, as she sits by herself eating a pistachio ice cream in the dining room of the Grand-Hôtel (a hall so out of scale—the adverts claim it can seat eight hundred—that it always, even with as many as two hundred people, feels empty), Alicia remembers that she has not yet decided what to give up for Lent. It goes without saying, meat is off the menu. Angelo is giving up his evening glass of Madeira. Agustín Gerónimo had first thought of giving up his pipe but then decided that, instead, he would sacrifice butter on his rolls.

"And croissants?" Angelo had asked.

"What?"

"Brother, they've a lot of butter."

Agustín Gerónimo had coughed. "Can't see it, doesn't count."

They argue about the daftest things. For his gout Angelo soaks his feet in a bath of salt, ammonia, and camphor.

"That's not enough camphor," Agustín Gerónimo said.

"There's plenty."

"Ya hafta be able to smell it a mile away."

"You can smell it in the hallway."

"Well, *you* can."

"That's right, I can."

They had spent last evening in Agustín Cosme's tavern; both had sick headaches this morning. Angelo has this boy's book of nautical yarns he sometimes takes out, a smelly old leather-bound thing their father gave him; it's falling to pieces. Every once in a while, Agustín Gerónimo lets him read it aloud, but that usually ends badly, because at the worst possible moment, Agustín Gerónimo makes a loud guffaw.

Alicia scrapes the spoon along the bottom of the dish and she remembers: she used to give her baby tastes of fruit ices. The *nieve de limón* was his favorite. The ice was carted down from Iztaccíhuatl. At the piano, she would hold him on her lap and let him bang at the keys. They sang the alphabet song and "Mary Had a Little Lamb." When they went for a ride, in the coziness of their buggy, she would throw her shawl over his curls and bump noses and sing-song, *We're snug as two bugs in a rug!*

When Angelo came home at midday, he would grab the baby, toss him up in the air, saying in English, "Hi baby, high to the sky!"

"High!" Agustín would say.

"You want to go high again?"

"No." He would shake his curls.

"You want Papa to set you down?"

"No!"

"Well, little man, I shall have to swing you in the Big Clock!" The baby's shoe clipped the vase, which broke, splashing over the carpet.

"How you spoil him," Alicia said, and Angelo laughed at her. He said, "Who talks?"

Soon Atín, as he called himself, was learning to walk. Mother and baby had a game: he would crawl under her hoop skirt and then cling to her leg as she walked. *¿Dónde está mi Agustinito?* Where is my Agustinito? Lupe would play along, scurrying up and down, knocking on cupboards and doors, crying out in her tiny tremulous voice, "Agustín, *chiquitín*, is he hiding here? Bless me, where could he be, my little heart?"

There was Lupe bringing him to her after his bath, his hair wild from the towel, his skin satiny with talcum . . . The angel's breath weight of his arms around her neck . . . In his bedroom there was a drum-shaped table, and on the little featherbed in his crib, a calico quilt his grandmother had made for him. The way slats of sunlight came in through the shutters, filling the ceiling with a melon-like glow. The plank floors of heart-of-pine. On that drum-table, there was a silver rattle that had been a gift from Doña Juliana, and a silver cup, just big enough to hold a quail's egg, from General and Madame Almonte.

It is safer to think about ice cream. This pistachio ice cream is delicious: she licks the little spoon clean.

As penance, she could give up ice cream, she thinks. But she won't. She waves for the waiter, the handsome one, his apron fresh from the laundry and tied tightly around his hips. Carrying a tray of *beignets aux pommes*, he glides right by. How provoking! She is provoked by many things, among them, that she has been dining here nearly every day for more than two months and the staff have yet to address her by her title.

To another waiter, she calls out, "Garçon!" And when that achieves no effect (the waiter continues to the back counter, where he begins filling a salt cellar), she waves her hand above her head at yet another, as if, so it seems to the matron at the next table, to a chum at a country fair.

"*Dieser Amerikaner!* These Americans!" the matron mutters to her husband, who goes on with his *soupe à l'oignon*. After two more spoonfuls of the over-salted broth (markedly inferior to the *Zwiebelsuppe* he had at home last week), the Prussian count dabs at his mustache. With the ease of the most magnificent stag in the forest, he lifts his gray head. His baleful gaze roves over the mostly empty dining room until it settles upon the extraordinary but morose-looking creature at the next table. He remembers her; he had seen her dining with, presumably, her husband, last night. They were speaking English but he did not take them for English. In fact, he wondered whether this pair might not be the worshipers of the molten calf that his acquaintance, Dr. Evans, had spoken of at the dinner at the Prussian embassy. It appeared that this couple—the prince a Mexican, the princess a highborn American (if such a thing be conceivable)—had, in exchange for pensions and honors, handed over their son to Maximilian von Habsburg. The mother regretted it at once; their object in coming to Paris was to secure the return of their infant. Dr. Evans, as he has the ear of Louis Napoleon, was brought onboard this scheme by the American minister. Being a Prussian, this count has a low estimation of Maximilian von Habsburg. As a matter of principle, he has a low estimation of all things Austrian. Vienna, to this Berliner, is the epitome of laxity, immorality, and decadence. He also has a low estimation of anything connected with the primitive. Mexico, in a word, is primitive; he has zero interest in learning anything about it. Furthermore, he has a low estimation of Dr. Evans, a man of obscure birth, elevated to distinction by his friendship with a personage far above his station who, as a consequence, has a cloying sense of his own importance. A tooth-puller in the court of France! Dr. Evans is a messenger at best; a useful gossip, and one would do best to steer well clear of such company on a brief sojourn. He has come to Paris to put a stop to his wife's nagging. She insists on seeing the sights now, in this ridiculous season, because the situation between France and Prussia is a tinderbox awaiting a spark. It is not Berlin that will go down in flames.

"*Garçon!*" Madame de Iturbide has flagged her man. Petulantly, she pushes her empty dish to the corner of the tablecloth. "I want another."

"*Oui, madam.*"

She fixes the imperturbable waiter with a pout: "Tell the chef, I won't have a doll's portion."

"With or without whipped cream?"

Alicia answers in a voice that contains the Apocalypse: "*With.*"

❦

BASKET OF CRABS

A leader must see things not as he would wish them to be, but as they are. General François-Achille Bazaine, supreme commander of the French Imperial Forces in Mexico, is no novel reader. He remembers once, years ago, being told about a novel that was fashionable with intellectuals and other pointlessly affected people, which described, over the course of hundreds of pages, a whore's fall from one of the towers of Notre Dame. How the pins in her hair came loose one by one, her gown went thus-way, and on and on in the most convoluted and microscopic detail. He had permitted his first wife, Marie, to read him a few pages of the opening chapter. He would have traded those ten minutes for an hour of torture. *"Basta!"* he said, and he stood up, took the book from her hands, and threw it in the fire. "You are going to foul your mind with this trash." She slapped him. He was young then and arrogant. Had he known better, a lot of things might have been different with Marie. Perhaps she would be alive today. He is alive because of her, that is the irony. Fifteen years in the sands of Algeria, in France, the battlefields of Solferino, the Crimea, over the ocean to Mexico, and all through the long lonely year of the siege for the city of Puebla, it was her love that had been his talisman—and then, when he called for her, to learn she had died in Paris, in the arms of her lover, an actor! The shock of it, a bayonet to the solar plexus.

Bazaine had survived it, but with a new understanding of how, when one surrenders one's heart, grievously one can be wounded. And how much more vulnerable one is when one has a child. His Mexican wife, Pepita, is expecting his first child. His love for his little family frightens him as nothing has frightened him before. Not that Pepita would love another, he has too much dogged courage for that class of fear. It's this: he must protect his family, but the Mexican Empire is that whore, falling. Because of Maximilian's airy-fairy extravagances, the experiment has failed. Should Maximilian hesitate much more before he abdicates, short of a miracle, there is only one way this will end: in a blood-soaked heap.

The army maxim: never reinforce failure.

The last contingent of the French troops is scheduled to evacuate from Veracruz, in a mere year and six months, in October 1867—and possibly, as it would be, in Bazaine's view, advisable, the schedule may be accelerated. Once the French are gone, there will be reprisals. Pepita's family's property may be confiscated, her aunt Doña Juliana—God knows. Until then, it will be a grinding, heavy-hearted wait. As supreme commander, Bazaine as a point of honor will be Last Man Out, that is, the last French soldier to lift his boot from Mexican soil.

Would Pepita's family have permitted the marriage had they known it would turn into this? A question, to Bazaine, as useless as dropping a bucket down a dry well.

Yes, some had thought him ridiculous for courting a sixteen-year-old. In Algeria some had thought him ridiculous for courting Marie—then known as the Señorita María Soledad Tormo, barely out of childhood and the most alluring flamenco artist in the colony. A rose tucked behind one ear, she would tip her head back to blow smoke rings, a series of them, *ha, ha, ha.* When she was not dancing with her castanets, her beautifully shaped arms jangled with bangles; when she slipped out of a room, her orange-blossom perfume—concocted by witches in the souk—lingered, intoxicating. His commanding officer had warned him, "With marriage to such a person, you are throwing away your future." But Bazaine was then in his thirties. His father had abandoned his mother. His social connections were few, and he lacked the polish, and, as he imagined, the proclivity to the ass-kissing necessary to secure the ones that could yield results.

Out in western Algeria, who else would have this battle-scarred legionnaire? He didn't give a rat's pecker what some stuffed shirt had to say about his personal decisions. Bazaine trusted his gut—in this matter of love, as on the battlefield. And consider his brother officers' wives: thick-waisted, doughy-faced prudes and gossips. Naturally, they were envious of the youthful and vivacious Señorita Tormo; naturally the men were jealous. Time and again, Bazaine had proved himself—but for having come out of an elite school, they imagined themselves superior. As he used to say to his Marie, *They know how to use an oyster fork, so they think that gives them the right to stab us in the back with it.*

Pepita could be Marie's twin—the dimple on her chin, her graceful arms; above all, her fearless, head-high personality. It was at a Mexico City ball that he first saw her, whirling past in the embrace of some Mexican lieutenant, and for a gut-wrenching moment, there at the edge of the parquet, a glass of champagne gone warm in his hand, he thought his Marie had come back to life. He had to have this woman—he did not care who she was! But it turned out, wasn't he the lucky bastard? Pepita is a de la Peña, not the richest but one of the most prominent and respected families of Mexico. General and Madame Almonte went into raptures over the idea of a match. The shrimp that sleeps gets carried off by the current, that is Madame Almonte's personal motto—he liked her for that. Not two days passed, but she had done her round of visits, and voilà! Pepita's aunt, the widow of a president, was commissioned to play chaperone. Maximilian and Charlotte warmly encouraged it. Louis Napoleon and Eugénie gave enthusiastic approval. And Pepita had, she truly had, fallen in love with him. Bazaine may have conquered Mexico, but the conquest of this señorita's heart was his proudest accomplishment.

Yesterday afternoon, he came up behind his little wife, massaging her shoulders. His voice was gruff from years of barking orders, but to Pepita he spoke softly.

"What are you reading, hmm? A little book?"

"Poetry," she said.

"*A ver* . . . Let me see." He lifted the book from her hands. With his thumb, as on a pack of cards, he rifled the gilt-edged pages. Latin on the left, Spanish on the facing pages. He recognized a few names: Virgil, Ovid, Dante. On the flyleaf, an inscription had been was made in Spanish.

To Madame Bazaine,
dear tocaya,

Your affectionate friend,
Pepa

Bazaine's Spanish was fluent but it was not his native tongue. "What is a *tocaya?*"

"We share the same Christian name."

"Who is Pepa?"

"Princess Iturbide."

He raised one bushy eyebrow. "I did not imagine Princess Iturbide to be your friend."

Pepita turned around in her chair as far as she could, given her girth; she rested her pretty chin on the back of her hand. "Why not?"

He did not answer with what came directly to mind, that, to begin with, there was a gulf of difference in their ages (in fact, Princess Iturbide was the same age as himself). A pretentious flatterer and self-important schemer, that was his opinion of that old prune. But he left this all unsaid. "It was my impression you had taken Doña Alicia's side in the family quarrel over the little boy."

"I did. And I do, but Mexico is a—"

"*Pañuelo* . . . a handkerchief."

"*Mon amour,*" Pepita said with a little laugh, pinching her fingers together. "I tell you, it is a *pañuelitito.*" Deftly, she took the book back. "Shall I read some to you?"

"This old man would like nothing better. But there is not enough light here for your delicate eyes."

Pepita opened her mouth to disagree, for her eyes were not in the least delicate—but, looking around, she realized that the dusk had come upon them quite suddenly.

She took his hand and led him into the drawing room. The use of this palace, one of the most beautiful in all of Mexico, had been granted to them by Maximilian upon their marriage, last June. Though they came into their drawing room for one reason or another almost every day, these nine months later, it had not ceased to amaze them: its cavernous size, the masses of flowers, heaps of fruit, gilt furnishings for an entertainment of two hundred people, and screens, and two lustrous pianos, and landscape paintings with herds of sheep in them, and all multiplied in the gilt-framed mirrors. Outside the western window, the sun's rim had nearly slipped behind the mountains; chandeliers threw diamonds of rainbow light on rosy walls. In the stretches between the many carpets, parquet floors gleamed slicks of gold. Like two children, they sat down on their sofa—not close enough that, were a servant to happen by, Madame Bazaine would have been in any way embarrassed, but his knee pressed into her hoopskirt. He could smell the sweetness of her breath.

She said, opening the book, "I am no good at Latin."

He patted her belly. "Spanish," he commanded.

Pepita read a few poems, but not well; she stumbled over the longer words. But what did this matter to a devoted husband? Soothed by the ministrations of his own angel, the weary warrior's chin fell to his chest. He squeezed her hand and closed his eyes.

Since his marriage General Bazaine has become obtuse, so the young officers who work most closely with him remark with bewilderment and concern. The situation is deteriorating by the day. One says to the other, and the other to the next one, *The only thing organized in this country seems to be thievery.* In their stunning incompetence, those Austrian volunteers allowed General Porfirio Díaz to escape—now the insurgents are on the verge of free reign, bombing, shooting, kidnapping, terrorizing innocent citizens. And the Yankees, still parked at the Rio Grande, have been egging the Juaristas on, with more money, more weapons. Maximilian, off in his Petit Trianon in Cuernavaca, has the temerity to blame France for the consequences of his own blunders. France is extricating herself from this imbroglio but with what shreds of honor left to her? Does General Bazaine not see the damage being done to morale?

Captain Charles Blanchot, his aide-de-camp, is so consternated that often, sighing deeply, he stops in midsentence and presses his fingertips to his forehead.

Twenty years the general's junior, Captain Blanchot has an imperious nose, ill-disguised by an impeccably groomed rectangle of a mustache, and a small mouth set in a permanent expression Mexicans recognize as contempt. His brass buttons polished to candle-shine, whip-sharp and ambitious Captain Blanchot is proud to serve the supreme commander, this legend of the French Foreign Legion, the lowly sergeant who evidenced such courage under fire, such coup d'oeil, he had moved up through the ranks like a rocket. But Captain Blanchot was proud to begin with, proud above all to have been born French, which is, *bien sûr*, to be superior to the entire world.

Captain Blanchot's wife, an American from Louisiana, though still in the bloom of youth, is a few years older than Madame Bazaine—which is to say, more alert to the hazards of the present moment. It was she who had brought to her husband's attention the rumors that are spreading, very dangerous ones, for they are being repeated by none other than Princess Iturbide, whom his mother-in-law, Mrs. Yorke, had happened to find herself seated next to at the widow de Gómez Pedraza's.

The walls have ears.

Ever since his days running the Bureau Arabe, it has been General Bazaine's custom to invite his aide for a morning ride (he escort being ordered to maintain a distance of no more than fifty and no less than thirty meters, that is, just out of earshot). To his credit, the general has cultivated the habit of listening; he keeps his cigar clamped in his teeth. This morning, as they came upon the first field, Captain Blanchot brought his mount alongside and opened with this salvo:

"Sir, there has been a serious attack on your personal dignity. They say you are importing French dressmaking supplies through the army's supply lines."

Bazaine pulled the cigar from his mouth. "What?"

"Dressmaking supplies. They say you are selling them through a dressmaker here."

Captain Blanchot could not discern the general's reaction; the visor of his kepi threw the grizzled profile into shadow. Bazaine shifted slightly in his saddle and slowed, but merely to steer his mount around a pothole. Beyond Chapultepec Castle, the twin snowcaps of Popocatépetl and Iztaccíhuatl floated in the hazy distance. The haze was from the sweet-smelling fires to the south; the season for burning cane has begun. The sky directly above, however, was a dome of the profoundest blue.

With the sangfroid that had made him famous, the general put his cigar back in his mouth. "What's her name?"

"Mademoiselle Louise."

"Never heard of her."

"All the officers know her."

Bazaine laughed heartily. "One of those, eh?"

"Sir, it is being generally repeated."

"*Oof!* Ridiculous."

Blanchot, brittle with indignation: "Infamous, sir."

They rode on, pulling to the side to allow a donkey cart to squeeze past.

The general had many matters on his mind this morning, among them, the military situation in Tlaxcala and the financing for the payrolls, which had become a white-knuckled trapeze act. As per the Treaty of Miramar, the costs of the occupation were to be borne by the Mexican treasury; however, that treasury has been bled dry by interest payments to the House of Jecker, the English debts, and Maximilian's unmitigated profligacy. The silver mines have not been bringing in anywhere near the projected revenues, and with the loss of cities and ports to the insurgents, and no small dose of corruption, the customhouses' receipts have plummeted. Late last month, while Maximilian was enjoying the fauna and flora of Cuernavaca, Monsieur Langlais, having sifted through the ledgers in preparation of a long overdue budget, was found dead in his bed. A heart attack? Or had he been deliberately poisoned? Bazaine suspects the latter, because, when moving at speed, he sent Captain Blanchot to retrieve Langlais's papers, lest they fall into improvident hands, an aide to the French ambassador barred the door. That quickly, all of Langlais's papers had disappeared into Ambassador Dano's custody!

Dano and his cronies: they may have been the source of this fresh slander against himself—a ruse to divert attention from their profiteering! Isn't this some basket of crabs, Bazaine thought, and he was about to change the subject, when, noticing his aide's wounded expression, he thought better of it.

"There is more you want to tell me?"

"Sir, you always told me that I should feel free to tell you anything."

"That's right."

"Princess Iturbide repeats this slander."

"*Ah, ça.*" Bazaine dipped his head to avoid a low-hanging branch. Straightening, he hacked up a gob of spit into a bank of nopal cactus.

"Sir, the princess claims that her information comes straight from the empress's wardrobe maid."

"Well now." He laughed again. "I cannot worry my old gray head with a wardrobe maid's tattle."

"But sir, if Princess Iturbide is repeating it, I believe it comes from the highest levels."

Bazaine swatted some flies. "Bah."

"That Austrian Machiavelli, he's capable—"

"Heard the latest?" Bazaine interrupted. "You've heard it from your wife already, I'll wager. In Cuernavaca, Maximilian's taken the Indian gardener's daughter for his lover."

"Oh, that."

"You believe it?"

"Most do."

"I'd sooner believe it, if it was the gardener." Bazaine laughed.

"But sir—"

Bazaine interrupted, "When things become difficult, rumors crop up. It is inevitable."

"But sir, they are saying you have taken one million dollars."

A jolt of electricity passed between them. They had come to the edge of a steep slope carpeted with jagged, soot-black lava rocks; here, the sun full on his face, General Bazaine halted.

Breeze disturbed the fur on their horses' necks. With a loud splattering, Captain Blanchot's horse urinated.

"They are saying, sir, that you have received one million dollars in exchange for rendering the Mexican Empire with the least possible resistance."

"Son, I swear to you, and I swear before my Maker, I do not have a sou to my name other than my salary."

"Yes, but—"

"And you know that my residence, and everything in it, the furniture, the paintings, it all belongs to the government."

"Yes, but you could defend yourself! You could open the books, gather the evidence, show—"

Bazaine put his hand up. He shook his head, *no, no.* "Son, you did right by telling me. Always, you should feel free to tell me. But understand, it is impossible to disprove what is not true."

The captain's mouth had become extremely small. "But sir—"

"*Alors,*" the General said gruffly. "A cock does not play hens' games."

A year ago, Bazaine told Almonte, "The Arabs have a saying. *He sleeps, but his feet are baking in the sun.*"

"I have told Maximilian as much."

But where, really, do Almonte's loyalties lie? How long until he jumps horse? In January, the U.S. secretary of state met with Santa Anna on the island of Saint Thomas. Seward on a pleasure cruise, bah! Almonte must have known about the meeting, or maybe not, but he knows it now.

A Mexican empire? Well, that's pasting some feathers together and calling it a duck!

So much money, so many opportunities squandered. How different things could have been.

"It breaks my heart," Doña Juliana de Gómez Pedraza said. The other morning, she'd come to pay an early morning visit to her niece; Bazaine, still in his babouches, found the women knitting. He had the Mexican *mozo* bring tea—as he liked it, steeped with a fistful of mint and plenty of sugar. (A Mexican *mozo:* another thing his men grumbled over.) He had told Pepita she could bring any and all of her family when they evacuated. He could protect them, he could get them out. Again, he extended the invitation to the widow de Gómez Pedraza. Doña Juliana thanked him profusely, but she was too old, she said. In France, what would she do? She'd have to improve her French. There wasn't much of it to improve. She tapped her temple. "It's full up with memories."

"Bah," Bazaine said, though in truth, Doña Juliana was old. Her moist, sagging eyes reminded him of his mother's.

"Besides," she said, "you won't allow me to take my harpsichord."

"You can play the accordion, why not?"

She laughed at him.

Affectionately, he teased Doña Juliana, whom he had grown to know so well when he had courted her niece. In a way, he'd had to court her also. He looked out for her as best he could. After that vicious robbery last December, when her old cook was murdered, he assigned a pair of Zouaves to guard her house. She'd insisted she was going to quit Mexico City for Querétaro, where she had some relations, but when she tried to sell her house, there were no buyers, and she gave up the idea.

"*Ay,* Doña Juliana, you think you won't have your hot chocolate in Paris?"

"Not the good chocolate."

He bowed his head, the way a waiter would. *"Un chocolat chaud, madame?"*

Doña Juliana clicked her tongue. In Spanish she said, "Impossible!"

"Madame. À coeur vaillant, rien d'impossible."

But she did not understand him. Pepita, meanwhile, went on knitting, the needles clacking softly over her belly. The ball of yarn trembled at her feet. Doña Juliana picked up her work again, a sweater for Pepita's baby. All that was left to be knitted was a cuff. She would have finished this one last week, she said, had her arthritis not been bothering her. Because of her cataracts, she often dropped a stitch, and then she had to unravel her work and begin anew. Nonetheless, the cedar trunk was nearly to its brim with sweaters, blankets, bibs, booties, a christening gown and bonnet, each item enfolded in muslin.

Lorgnette to her eye, Doña Juliana said, "Now tell me, General, in complete confidence . . . What will become of little Agustín?"

Bazaine pursed his lips and blew across the top of his tea. They all knew the boy's arm had been broken. The court had been a long time in Cuernavaca, and when in Mexico City, Princess Iturbide kept her nephew sequestered. Maximilian's personal physician, Dr. Semeleder, was attending the child. The arm would be, he assured the princess, "good as new." In the meantime, however, as the princess confided to Mrs. Yorke, she did not intend to demoralize Mexicans by letting the Heir Presumptive be seen in a plaster and sling.

There were other reasons, however, that the child had turned into an embarrassment for Maximilian. Last month, a *New York Times* dated January 9, arrived on the steamer—*La Sociedad* had not reported it, of course, but, within a matter of days anyone who was anyone in Mexico City knew that, in the U.S. House of Representatives, a Kentucky congressman had called for a presidential investigation of the "so-called" emperor of Mexico's "kidnapping an American child."

Doña Juliana said, "You seem to think we all need to leave with you or be slaughtered by the Juaristas. Well, what about this innocent?"

Bazaine turned up his palms. "Unless Maximilian decides—"

Doña Juliana interrupted. "I should think Carlota would have some influence."

"Charlotte?" Out of habit, Bazaine used her French name. He scratched at the back of his neck. His sentiments about the empress, whom he and his men had initially revered as their own countrywoman, had become less than respectful. Many things had brought down his estimation of Charlotte; in fact, the final straw had been her refusal, last September, to receive Doña Alicia de Iturbide. Charlotte may have been young, but not young enough to excuse this heartless and cowardly refusal to look at the consequences. Bazaine had gone to the palace to see her personally and he had beseeched her to reconsider. But the empress of Mexico, in her diamond earrings, had simply stared back at him with the eyes of an inanimate object.

This week a delegation from her brother, the king of the Belgians, is visiting Mexico City. Reports from the secret police are that Maximilian has not bothered to remove himself from Cuernavaca, and the things Charlotte has been telling these Belgians are so fantastic! It seems she is losing her grip on reality.

Finally, Bazaine spoke. "Have you asked Princess Iturbide what she plans to do?"

"She tells me she has no intention of leaving."

"What does she say about Maximilian? Does she think he'll abdicate?"

"She tells me that Maximilian is a man of the highest honor, a member of the House of Habsburg. He would sooner go back to Europe in his coffin."

Bazaine rubbed his jaw.

Doña Juliana still held the lorgnette to her eye. "Pepa says the Mexican Empire will last for a thousand years."

A thousand years? Bazaine leaned back and looked at the ceiling. There hung an elaborate gold-and-glass chandelier. He could not help but wonder what it had cost. In Acapulco, the garrison was running low on ammunition. In Veracruz, the supply of hardtack had been spoilt by mold.

Doña Juliana's voice went up half an octave. "A child should be with its parents."

Pepita shot a glance at her husband, who had once again gone as silent as the Sphinx. He had told her the details of his meeting, back in September, with Doña Alicia de Iturbide. He had also told her, and she was never to repeat it, that his police agents inspected Maximilian's correspondence, and on the subject of this child there had been some real head-shakers. Recently, Maximilian's ambassador to Queen Victoria had been questioned at length about the Iturbide family by Foreign Secretary Lord Clarendon. The ambassador's report to Maximilian reeked of embarrassment. *Good God*, Bazaine had said to his wife. *His own ambassador doesn't understand the damn thing.*

Doña Juliana said, "I have Don Angel's books in crates upstairs in my house. I don't know what to do with them." She massaged her knuckles and the joints of her fingers. "I don't know," she said, suddenly, "I don't know . . ." She burst into tears.

"Auntie . . ." Pepita came over and put her arms around Doña Juliana.

"I am sorry," Doña Juliana sobbed, "I am sorry." She knew she had embarrassed the general.

"Do not be," Pepita said. "But, Auntie, we will miss you so much. I'll wear out my soul with worry for you. Oh, won't you change your mind?"

In the office, after lunch, hours later in the day than was his custom before his marriage, General Bazaine has his boots shined. The shoeshine boy rubs the cloth, making a soft chuffing.

The window is ajar; the papers on the massive mahogany desk quiver from the breeze. On the opposite side of the desk, Captain Blanchot says, apropos of the angry protests by his officers in Chihuahua, "You are caught between the Mexican anvil and the French hammer."

"*Oof.*" Bazaine makes a grimace of indigestion. Fist to his mouth, he belches. (He'd promised Pepita he wouldn't, but he'd had seconds on the beef enchiladas.) It is out of character, but his mind is wandering, while his aide finishes up with the latest stupidity regarding those visiting Belgians (another police report, about Charlotte's tea party and their visit to the museum of antiquities). Then, the day's field reports. Bitterly, Bazaine thinks how, had he been given the men and materiel to do the job, he could have sunk the foundations to make this Mexican Empire stand, yes, as Princess Iturbide said, for a thousand years. Had he not taken Oaxaca?

Oaxaca: forgotten already, the months of backbreaking work, roads carved through the mountains, and then the siege of the city, buckets of blood sacrificed. Buckets of French blood, fine officers, good men, boys green with lives unlived, their bodies stacked up like cordwood and then rolled into ditches. Matamoros, Monterrey, Saltillo, Chihuahua, Zacatecas, Tampico, Guadalajara, all pissed away.

It is his signature on the letters that go to the mothers and fathers in Lyons, Marseille, Limoges, the little villages, little farms . . . "For the glory of France," their boys have been shot, stabbed, burned alive and castrated, disemboweled. For the glory of *nada* they die of typhoid, cholera, gangrene, syphilis, meningitis, yellow fever. And such stupid things: they shoot each other by accident; one lost a knife fight with an Austrian corporal, another had his kneecap shattered in a duel, and then after a week in the hospital the fever took him down. Another, in a drunken stupor, runover by a garbage wagon. Many times Bazaine has toured the military hospitals. The smells, the piteous cries, have begun to invade his dreams. The Mexicans, too, have been subjected to unspeakable suffering. Bazaine did not use to dwell on such matters. He'd had a steel trap of a mind: *It is not for a soldier to judge*, he'd liked to say. *My orders are, kill the enemy. When they're dead, Jesus Christ, he can judge them.*

To lead, one must first learn to follow. To follow, one must learn not to judge. One must, as a blinkered workhorse, plod forward. One does not see all that the leader sees—intelligence from London and Washington, Moscow and Berlin, the myriad political and financial considerations to be weighed one against the other, carefully calibrated, the decoded dispatches of the secret police. One sits at the desk of the supreme command here in Mexico, not upon the throne in the Tuileries.

Louis Napoleon has decided to withdraw from Mexico, and Bazaine's orders are to prepare for that—to break down the whole goddamned edifice. A mere two weeks ago, Louis Napoleon's letter found Maximilian in Cuernavaca. Shortly thereafter, Bazaine had the less than pleasant task of going to Mexico City's Imperial Palace. At the news of the impending withdrawal, Maximilian returned from Cuernavaca in a white-hot rage; Charlotte nearly had to be given smelling salts. After months of antagonism with those two, Bazaine had felt so sorry, so goddamned sorry, that, though they were raising their voices with him, though he had been angered so many times by their ineptitude and ingratitude, he himself nearly wept. They were all on this ship together, this ship that was going to be scuttled. He did not protest when Maximilian said, "This is a violation of the Treaty of Miramar." Charlotte plunged in, "The *grossest* violation!" She clenched and unclenched her fists, her eyes unnaturally large, all whites. "A treaty is *not* a rag to wipe the floor!" she cried. "It is a *solemn contract!*"

These two overlooked the obvious, which was that neither were they upholding that treaty. It was clear as sunshine, the Mexican treasury was to finance the costs of the occupation. But the money had never been sufficient, and credit was exhausted. Financial calculations, now more a question of splitting bristles on a gnat's butt, were, in all events, within the entirely opaque purview of Ambassador Dano.

"Madame," Bazaine said in as even a tone as he could manage, "I do not make treaties."

After Charlotte flounced out of the room, Bazaine said to Maximilian, "In the interest of securing the safety of Your Majesty's person and household, I respectfully request that you keep me fully apprised of the proceedings for abdication." That Austrian raised his nose and glared down with pure hate.

"Abdicate?" Maximilian nearly spit the word. "We will do no such thing." But Bazaine knew perfectly well that, since late autumn, Maximilian had been corresponding with his decorators in Trieste. They were working on Miramar Castle, adding furniture, planting hedges, painting—for what purpose other than to receive himself and his entourage? Furthermore, Maximilian had sent Count Bombelles to Vienna with instructions to renegotiate his Family Pact. Once Vienna conceded something palatable to his dignity, or his dignity could shrink to fit, Maximilian would leap off this cactus throne. So why, in the meantime, did he have to be such an obfuscating prick about it?

As the Arabs say, *water in a mirage is not water you can drink.* In his darker moments, Bazaine wishes he could grab Maximilian by the collar and shout in his face: *Face the facts!* Face the goddamn facts!

All men, all money, all energies must go to the coming conflict with Prussia—the future of France, the future of Louis Napoleon's throne, depend on it. There is no glory at the end of the road called Mexico. No victory parade for its veterans. Bazaine's only hope is for his sovereign's gratitude for his unbending loyalty and duty well done. Bazaine's duty now, pleasureless as a year's diet of hardtack, amounts to a massive logistical task: get the boys home, the horses, the artillery, what to do with the ammunition, the mules, the wagons, calculate the supplies, food, water, clothing, coal, animal feed. It is *cuentachiles,* counting chiles—and in the meantime, keeping tempers soothed, keeping morale from disintegrating, and avoiding unnecessary bloodshed—above all, hostilities with U.S. troops at the border. The Mexican Empire may be a house of cards, but until the day the French Imperial Forces evacuate, that house must remain standing.

This picture would have been a different one had Maximilian made use of the past year to build up his own army, put his treasury in order, state his policies clearly, and execute them with resolve. But Maximilian seems to think the sun shines out the crack of his ass. His Majesty the Magnanimous, granting amnesty to guerrillas and toadying to their sympathizers, throwing costly balls, granting pensions, commissioning his *viennoiseries,* gardens, statues, whole boulevards, and when the whim took him, off he went, dillydallying about Indian villages, Aztec ruins, collecting butterflies—setting up an Imperial Residence in Cuernavaca! He could play the despot, too—that dunderheaded October 3rd Black Decree, summary execution of anyone found with a weapon. There is not a French officer in Mexico who has not been galled by the puerile stupidity of this Austrian's decisions. For example, to kidnap Doña Alicia de Iturbide. It made the ugliest of impressions. When he told Pepita what Maximilian had said about them, her expression grew hot. "Bald lies!" she cried. Bazaine had also queried her aunt, Doña Juliana. She had answered him with strained dignity that perhaps Agustín Gerónimo was a bit eccentric, but Angelo was a highly respected diplomat. All of the Iturbides were great patriots. And no, Doña Juliana swore it, the sons of the Liberator had no ambition but to live quietly. In returning to Mexico City last September, Doña Alicia, God help her, was nothing more than a mother with a broken heart.

To arrest her was a ham-handed cruelty—but there too, Maximilian was inconstant. Flip-flop: His Majesty the Merciful permitted the Iturbides to leave Mexico unmolested. And where did they go? Washington where they met with Seward! And now the Iturbides are set up in Paris, where they have ample opportunity to intrigue with the U.S. minister there—who, at Seward's instigation, is putting the screws on Louis Napoleon to get out of Mexico! And Maximilian, deluded dreamer, seems to believe that republic can be induced to recognize his empire! It did not help that he had that beans-for-brains of a foreign minister, Ramírez. Well, that one's another rat off this sinking ship . . .

Bullet-fast, a green bird flies into the room.

"Blanchot," he interrupts.

His aide lowers the report he was reading.

The general, coolly extending his other boot to be polished, aims his gaze beyond his aide's left shoulder. Captain Blanchot turns around. A parrot flutters at the ceiling. Suddenly, it dives across the room, past the door to the map room, and over to the racks of muskets fixed with bayonets.

Blanchot takes in a sharp breath. "Jesus."

"He won't land there." As if in answer, the bird swoops over their heads, behind the general, to the flags, silks of the Cavalry, the Foreign Legion, the Navy, *Tirailleurs algériens,* Zouaves, Infantry . . . It finds no purchase on a flag's pike, nor on the frame of Louis Napoleon's portrait. Off the parrot flies to the other wall, an array from floor to ceiling of sabers and Arab daggers. It settles on a tasseled handle, ruffles its feathers, and lets out an ear-piercing shriek.

The shoeshine boy lifts his head. The rag still in his other hand, he crosses himself. Then he whistles. "Titis, Titis," he says. The parrot, bobbing its head, whistles back.

"Whose pet?" Bazaine says in Spanish.

"The apothecary's."

"At the bottom of the street?"

"*Sí, señor.*"

Bazaine tells Blanchot to shut the window. "Run get a basket, son," he commands the shoeshine boy, who stares at him with a wrinkled forehead. Bazaine sighs. He'd forgotten to switch back to Spanish. "*Una canasta, hijo.*"

"*Sí, señor.*" The boy flashes out the door.

Captain Blanchot, having fastened the window, felt something shift— not so much the air in the general's office but the fabric of time itself, for he felt as though he were watching the commotion not as it was happening but as if he had already seen it all in a dream—the general going after the parrot with his own jacket; the secretary, climbing on top of the general's desk in his stockinged feet and then slipping, sliding, as with a broom, he tries to shoo it off the cornice near the ceiling; the bird trapped at last between the bookcase and a potted palm; the shoeshine boy coming down upon it with the wastebasket, so that, to the poor squawking bird, it must seem some gigantic maw.

Captain Blanchot made a quick inspection of the carpet. (He detests parrots; they stink and they shit like sieves.) The carpet, on the east side, behind the potted palm, had faded to a color that reminded him of the stain on an amputee's bandage. Highly particular about decoration, Blanchot had requisitioned a new carpet six months ago. When the inventory of the latest shipment from France, to his disgust (is there no respect for the chain of command?) did not include the carpet, nor carpets of any sort, he had his wife look at the one the widow de Gómez Pedraza wanted to sell. A threadbare old thing, she'd said it was, and its smell suggested it had absorbed a bucketful of mop water. The carpet Doña Concha Aguayo was offering for sale was no better.

The sun had moved; the office was cast into gloom.

"Shall I light the lamp, sir?"

The general put on his spectacles, which made his eyes seem even smaller. "Save the kerosene, son."

Captain Blanchot sat down opposite the desk. He picked up the report he had been reading. But the general unhooked his spectacles, folded them, and lay them on the blotting paper. He offered Blanchot a cigar. The cigar box, one of innumerable gifts, was more a chest; it was inlaid with an intricate rectangular design of polished bone, turtle shell, and silver studs. The cigars, too, were a gift, and the onyx ashtray. Over on the table by the door sat a staggeringly large the basket of oranges and another of dates, from the head of customs in Veracruz. The silver coffee service, from Don Eusebio. The silver sugar tongs, from the owner of some stables the army rented in Tlalpan. Blanchot remembered, at the general's wedding in the Imperial Palace last June, in the hallway, passing by, he had glimpsed the gifts—a glittering mountain. Bazaine did not look for these things, but they came. There was no stopping them. Was it really a mere three years ago that Bazaine's headquarters were a mud-spattered field tent? That they were working at a rickety campaign desk, on folding stools, the crash and boom of the artillery all around them?

The general had lit his cigar. He stretched an arm over the back of his chair. A rope of smoke wound toward the ceiling.

"My first wife kept a parrot. Not one of these noisy *loros*. An African gray."

Captain Blanchot, stiff in his chair, the field report on his lap, puffed at his cigar. He knew that the first Madame Bazaine had not committed suicide, as wags claimed, but the rest of the gossip about her was, alas, based on fact.

Bazaine said, "Ever seen an African gray?"

"Yes, sir. Beautiful bird, sir."

The general gazed out the window. "Hers could imitate a human voice. It was like her child. It went everywhere with her." He stretched out his left leg. He turned his ankle to inspect the polish on his boot. A suggestion of a smile came to his lips. He said, looking out the window again, "It could ululate like a Berber woman."

"Ulu—?"

"Never heard that?"

"No, sir."

The look in the general's eye was very far away. "You haven't lived, son. You haven't lived."

It seemed to Captain Blanchot that the general was going to say something more, but he rubbed his hand over his face, then plugged his cigar back between his teeth.

"Proceed," he said.

RÍO FRÍO

*T*he Belgians had enjoyed their visit to Mexico City immensely. Although it had not gone unremarked (feathers were ruffled) that Maximilian remained in Cuernavaca, and that certain senior French officers did not attend the entertainments, in all, they judged their mission a success. They were proud of Charlotte—their own princess—"swan of our Old World gifted to the New," as one of their members toasted her, after having imbibed a few too many cups of champagne (and made some tasteless remarks about "our ginger-colored protegés.") Also, they had seen an exotic land; they'd had a true-blue adventure and their steamer trunks and valises were crammed with the souvenirs to prove it. Of the delegation, no single member was more satisfied, more inspired, more, well, overflowing with joie de vivre about the whole thing than Baron Charles d'Huart.

An intimate friend and *officier d'ordonnance* of Charlotte's brother Philippe, duke of Flanders, Baron d'Huart might have been described as dashing had he not developed a paunch and double chin. Since departing Ostend in late January, he had been unable to maintain his regime of fencing and hunting. The crossing had been brutal. For days, frigid gales had tossed the ship like a firkin in a tub; some feared they'd be shipwrecked off the Azores. Unlike the others, confined to their cabins with nausea, Baron d'Huart often joked he must have Viking blood and went on eating and drinking without pause.

By the time they docked in Veracruz, he had consumed prodigious quantities of foie gras, bonbons, and champagne. And in Mexico, well, was there anything more delicious than a humble taco of beans with this marvelous sprig of an herb called the *epazote*? And he indulged in the candies—*dulces de cacahuates*, the cigar-shaped *camotes*, lime-skins stuffed with sugared lard, and the almond nougat "buttons" soaked in honey—baskets of candies were left in his quarters and replenished each day. At the farewell dinner at Chapultepec Castle, under his cummerbund, he had to leave the waist of his trousers undone.

The round of balls and dinners had been intense. All of the Belgians, and especially Baron d'Huart, were limp with relief to finally get out of court dress: the coats bristling with decorations and epaulettes, the clanking swords, the hats with feathers. This morning, for this first leg of the journey home, he'd thrown on his roomiest breeches and favorite deerskin jacket.

He is riding up top with the driver, who wears a sombrero with the circumference of a buggy wheel. Baron d'Huart had started out wearing his sombrero—a loosely woven one, not so big as the driver's but the biggest they had in that labyrinth of an Aztec market—but once the coach climbed to altitude and the air turned chilly, he exchanged it for the poppy-red cap he wore for grouse hunting in the autumn.

It is late; their coach has just departed from the inn at Río Frío. The sun having fallen behind the trees, the road is bathed in the blue shadow of the brief, disconcertingly brief, Mexican twilight. Baron d'Huart throws his shoulders back and fills his lungs with the pine-scented air.

"*Que fresco!* How fresh!" he says, eager to practice his Spanish on his companion.

The driver, throwing his lash, makes no reply.

Had the driver been a Belgian, Baron d'Huart would have been infuriated by such insolence; he would have had him fired. But the driver is a Mexican; to Baron d'Huart, a creature who forms a part of a tableau that is, in the altogether, picturesque. Baron d'Huart simply shrugs. He thinks to himself, *vraiment*, these Mexicans are an inscrutable race. But Mexico itself, why, Charlotte had every right to be proud, it is a world richer than he'd imagined. A land of dessicated cacti, hardly. Such a wealth of haciendas—they'd seen many from the highway, and they'd been shown photographs—vast plantings of agave, corn, sugar, coffee, cotton, and hemp. And what breathtaking scenery! Why the devil is he the only one with the gumption to enjoy it? He could not bear to keep himself cramped inside the coach, everyone smoking, snoring, sweating, when up here one can partake of an ever-changing panorama: now an Alpine Eden of rocky cliffs, sparkling rivulets, this forest for the Knights of the Grail. In the slice of Memling blue above, an eagle soars.

He does not know the word for "eagle" in Spanish. He points at the sky. "*Pajaro grande . . .* big bird."

Again, the driver makes no reply.

Again, Baron d'Huart shrugs, though this time with a sad little sigh. He gives his cap a tug, and he muses:

Mexico City—Mexicans aside—well, it is a wonder. Its cavernous cathedral makes Saints Michel et Gudule in Brussels a mere chapel. Though Mexico's Imperial Palace could in no way be compared to the gothic splendors of the Maison du Roi, it is nothing for Charlotte to be ashamed of. As for Chapultepec Castle, though excessively gusty out on the terrace, it offers far superior vistas than the Château Royale at Laeken. It is more on the order of Sorrento's. One had to agree with Princess Iturbide, the sunsets over the Valley of Anahuac are incomparable. *Mais oui,* and ever so much more with an orchestra playing Chopin.

Yes, they were shown the New World's Land of Canaan, its oceans teaming with pearls; yet-to-be-worked seams of gold, silver, copper, gypsum; fertile lands for tobacco, sugar, coffee, sisal hemp, cotton, and—all one would need is a proper lash—troops of natives to work them. Mexicans, being an inherently indolent people, cannot be expected to progress on their own. The mining engineers come from Belgium, Germany, Italy, and France; the telegraph and railway men are preponderantly Englishmen, Yankees, and American Southerners. Commodore Maury, the world's great oceanographer, has offered his services to the Mexican Empire. Yes, what excellent fortune that the Confederacy has fallen, for so many of its good men have come to Mexico: Baron d'Huart had had pleasant conversations with a Dr. Gwin and a Colonel Talcott and a Judge Perkins. There were Confederate generals by the bagful: Shelby, Harris, and one by the most amusing name, Slaughter, who has set up a sawmill in Orizaba.

Orizaba: on the way inland from the coast, when the Belgian party had stopped there, General Slaughter had given them a present of his oranges. Oranges! After those solid weeks at sea—after the heat and stench of Veracruz, that vulture-infested port where one hardly dared touch anything to one's lips—to have arrived in Orizaba, sweet-smelling Orizaba, to gardens of bougainvillea and gardenias, to cut-open oranges, cut-open oranges squeezed over cups of shaved ice—ice from the volcano, the Pico de Orizaba—it was as a gift from Olympus itself.

Phagomen kai piomen, aurion gar thanoumeta. He couldn't resist quoting Epicurus.

Then he drank a whole glass of juice, straight.

From Río Frío, it is another two days' journey to Orizaba. (Apparently, one must be grateful that this is the dry season.) From Orizaba to Veracruz, one can expect another long day, and from Veracruz to Ostend, by sea, a grueling three weeks. Then, Brussels at the end of March: the trees bare, the fields mud.

Baron d'Huart considers another attempt at conversation with the driver, but, *"Ya!"* the driver bellows, lashing his team with new violence.

What is the hurry, for the love of Christ.

This stick-in-the-mud did not want to proceed from Río Frío without an escort. This morning, from Mexico City, they had an escort, a gang of Zouaves, bronzed tattooed louts. There was supposed to have been a relief escort waiting for them in Río Frío. Where was it? The answer was the universal chorus in this country: *Quién sabe.*

Those Zouaves, following their orders, turned around.

An escort. Oh, the driver had to have an escort.

The fort at Río Frío was unmanned. Why that was, no one could say. Clearly it wasn't needed. So, why an escort?

Es la costumbre, the driver said. It's the custom. He insisted they wait in Río Frío until the escort showed up. There was an inn that must have seen better days when a couple from Bordeaux was running it; in all events, said couple from Bordeaux was nowhere in evidence. The stairs up to the porch were falling apart; the only decoration, nailed to the outside wall and left to molder, were the brittle-looking pelts of an ocelot and a wolf. It was the sort of porch that might have offered a row of rocking chairs, but there were no chairs. Inside, the party sat on benches. The food smelled of rancid grease and the cutlery, dumped without ceremony in the middle of the table, had been rinsed but not washed. The little raisin of a granny who served them said there was (curiously, she used the English) apple pie, but after such an execrable repast, no one, not even the adventurous Baron d'Huart, had the stomach to attempt it.

They went outside. Up against a crumbling stone wall, an emaciated bitch nursed two puppies. Chewed-up corncobs strewn about, cruddy with dust. Flies everywhere.

Still no escort. The driver proposed that they overnight in this hole. The Mexican Imperial Army officer accompanying the party also thought this advisable. General Foury, head of the Belgian delegation, refused. He said he would not touch a mattress in this inn, not by the tip of a barge pole. Overnighting in such a place was a sure recipe for sickness and diarrhea.

A dozen Zouaves, what for? To be sure, Mexico still has isolated pockets with remnant bands of Apaches, Yaquis, and suchlike savages who have yet to taste the fruits of civilization, but these are in the far north. Charlotte assured General Foury that, except for the few areas (mostly near the Texas border), where insurgents have recently been active, the country has been pacified. General Foury and the others had heard about holdups in the neighborhood of Río Frío. He asked Charlotte straight: "What about security on the corridor between Mexico City and Veracruz?"

Charlotte smiled at the question. "You must have seen yourself, large convoys make their way along it every day."

That was true. On their way in from Veracruz, they had seen innumerable coaches, troop wagons, wagons of merchandise, droves of cattle. "But what about the bandits," General Foury insisted. "Have they been cleared out?"

"Newspapers profit on sensationalism."

"Don't I know," General Foury laughed gently.

"I can assure you," Charlotte said. "You are perfectly safe."

Subsequently, at a dinner party, Baron van der Smissen, commander of the Belgian volunteers, confided that the French troops in Mexico are so poorly disciplined, they have committed so many atrocities, they have become genuinely hated. There is less concern here than many presume in Europe about the coming French evacuation; actually, it would be a good thing to see the French go. At that dinner party, there was a Mexican general, a gnome by the name of Almonte. He did not disagree when Colonel Talcott said, angrily, that the French troops are sucking more out of the Mexican treasury than they are worth. The Mexicans, Talcott said, can stand up on their own. The Mexican Imperial Army was being trained and equipped— many Belgian and Austrian officers, Confederates, too, many experts in all matters from artillery to cavalry to logistics, are aiding in this enterprise. And by the way, a contingent of several thousand Austrian volunteers is scheduled to arrive in Mexico this May.

"Viva Maximilian! Viva Carlota!" Glasses clinked all around.

In Río Frío, at half past five, General Foury decided that they had waited long enough for this phantasmagorical escort of French Zouaves. *Allons donc!* They would drive on through the night to the city of Puebla, where they could be assured of hygienic lodgings and good food. Baron d'Huart was not the only one who agreed wholeheartedly, and besides, he was plum out of patience with the fuss that had been made over them over the past two weeks. As they were the delegation from the new king of the Belgians, protocol dictated certain things—but so much formality had become chafing. From the moment they disembarked at Veracruz, they had been escorted absolutely everywhere, morning to night their activities preordained to the minute. At first, one passively devoured the scenery, as one might whilst leaning back upon the cushions of a Venetian gondola. But soon one began to feel like a valise hauled about from place to place, or rather a schoolboy, for at every moment, it seemed, there was some professor prattling on. The cathedral: and in this chapel, the story of Our Lady of Guadalupe, and in that chapel, the story of Our Lady of Loreto, and in the next chapel, the story of San Felipe de Jesús, martyred in Nagasaki, and the remains of the Emperor Iturbide, oh, every blessed one of that cathedral's chapels. The Basilica of Guadalupe. Chapultepec Castle and Chapultepec Park and Chapultepec Zoo. The baths of Montezuma. The Pyramid of the Sun and the Pyramid of the Moon. The Museum of Natural History. The Museum of Antiquities, and a viewing of the Aztec Sun Stone. A canoe ride among Xochimilco's *chinampas*. A bull-fight, a fandango, an exposition upon the meaning of this dance, and the meaning of that dance. In the market they were surrounded by a phalanx of escorts and guided to first, the sombreros; second, the masks of Moors and Christians; third, clay whatnots and jewelry and all about the tribes who made them, their language, their costumes. Bloody hell! San Angel, Coyoacán, the snake-infested lava beds of El Pedregal? No, no going in there, that is not on the schedule, no, that would not be of interest to you, sir, no, believe me, there is nothing to see in that street, no sir, very sorry sir, no time for an excursion to Popocatépetl—

When an excursion to Popocatépetl was the single thing Baron d'Huart had been most keen to do! He has never forgotten, as a boy, reading in Bernal Diaz's *The True History of the Conquest of Mexico*, how Hernán Cortez, requiring sulphur for his guns, sent two men down into that smoking crater by ropes.

And to hunt the rare breed of antelope found only on the flanks of the Pico de Orizaba: that was his other ambition. He coveted a trophy for the main hall in his chateau.

Charlotte said, "Our Indians call the Pico de Orizaba 'Citlaltépetl,' which means Star Mountain."

Miss Know-It-All, her brothers called her. Baron d'Huart had last seen her three years ago in Brussels, when she had been her usual frosty self. But now, even in mourning for her father, she was so friendly, infinitely solicitous. "You must come back, and when you do, I shall personally arrange for an expert guide to take you to the summit."

Was any sovereign more regal? The Belgians all agreed. Mexico agreed with her like nothing else.

Did she not miss the Old World?

"Never," Charlotte said. "I am *completely* happy here."

The highway has leveled out; the coach picked up speed. Baron d'Huart's thoughts wander back to one of the dinner parties, when he happened to have been seated next to Princess Iturbide. This august lady had been granted her title by virtue of being a daughter of Mexico's Liberator, the Emperor Iturbide. Her French was not so good as she seemed to think it was. To almost every other thing, she'd said, *"Pardonnez-moi?"* After the first course, he'd turned to the lady on his other side, Madame Almonte, wife of that gnome-like general. She smelled overwhelmingly of attar of roses—verily, enough to leave one destitute of appetite. Her French was too rickety a construction to attempt to stand on; fortunately, they could converse in English.

"What do you think of Mexico?"

Madame Almonte began with this tritest of questions, but only as an opening to press upon him certain points. She seemed to have the notion that he, the *officier d'ordonnance* of the duke of Flanders, was destined to be Europe's own oracle on the question of Mexico. Peculiar and very disagreeable was her habit of gripping one's arm for emphasis.

Wasn't this just the luck, caught between two crones, whilst directly across the table, half-obscured by the heaps of flowers and candles, just a whisper too far to be able to exchange a word, was a creature worthy of the brush of Botticelli. A Fragonard's goddess of Love! What was her name? How she had brought the spoon of sorbet to her laughing lips, an image that, once it appeared in mind, made his brain feel—a loud crack—it had exploded.

The sound reverberated through the trees.

Baron d'Huart, a ghost of a smile still on his face, fell backward. The mules bolted, the coach shook violently, and in a moment—in the midst of a hail of gunfire—his body bounced off, onto the road.

❦

ONE STAYS THE COURSE

ears ago, in the Latomia of Syracuse, Maximilian was shown the grave of an American cadet who had been shot in a duel. Syracuse: its landscape denuded, its harbor silted up, the town, shining beacon of the Ancient World, dirty, ragged. The Sicilian sun was ever-fierce, but this did not prevent the denizens from dressing head-to-toe in black, their faces weathered, dark, hard. The Latomia lay a short hike beyond a dusty olive grove and a stream where old women were beating laundry with stones. Goat bells clanked in the distance. In this quarry where, according to Thucydides, thousands of Athenian sailors had been imprisoned after their defeat in 413 B.C., the wall of rock, ablaze with sun, carved the sky like a scimitar. The cadet's grave was but a narrow space in the wall. To die and be buried in a place so strange, so far from one's fatherland (Maximilian pictured the boy's home as a clapboard house on the salt-lashed coast of Connecticut), it was so sad, so indescribably sad. He had never forgotten it.

In March, at the news that Baron d'Huart had been murdered, Maximilian and Dr. Semeleder abandoned Cuernavaca, riding straight through the night to Río Frío. There, while Semeleder attended the wounded, Maximilian was shown the body and given the particulars. The French military escort from Río Frío had never appeared—the Belgians, official emissaries of the empress's brother, King Leopold II, had been left unprotected. Maximilian kept shaking his head in grief, in rage, it was unbelievable.

What would they say now in the courts of Europe about his government?

It was Bazaine's fault: this absurd, this inexcusable dereliction of duty.

A casket suitable for conveying the body back to Mexico City did not arrive until afternoon. They loaded it onto the back of a wagon. Then, after sprinkling in a liberal quantity of borax, they nailed the lid shut.

Blow after devastating blow. Since that day, Maximilian cannot conceive of worse, but it comes, and another, knocking him down, down this hellish stairway of humiliation. March, April, May, June, and now, July, the worst yet, this gob-sock: his angel, his empress—the empress of Mexico—has left for Paris.

For some time, Maximilian had been flirting with the idea of abdication—in truth, though he'd said nothing to anyone until this week, since last summer when the military situation first began deteriorating. Over the past months, his thoughts had been turning more and more frequently to his castle by the sea in Trieste—its landscaping, the decor for the Throne Room, the aviary— perhaps an aquarium? These projects, and his botanizing, have been his escape, his amusement, and—well—altogether necessary, for, as he tells himself when he glances at the ballooning expenses, Miramar is the face of Mexico in Europe. What impression would it give in Vienna if Miramar were left unfinished, its park untended? It goes without saying, for a sovereign, the scrupulous maintenance of prestige is paramount.

To Charlotte, however, he did not have the heart to confess that he longed to return to private life, or at least a position with smaller, more manageable concerns. In his mind's eye, he could see himself at his desk there, the Bay of Grignano outside the window behind him, and before him his library, with its marble busts of Homer, Shakespeare, Dante, Goethe aglow with the light from that sea.

He missed his mother, too.

But he'd had such a horror of the afterlife—stripped of his throne, who would he be? Charlie, whom he'd despatched to Vienna to renegotiate the Family Pact, had, in essence, thrown himself at a brick wall. The bitterest betrayal, however, was not the Family Pact, but the Kaiser's order—one's own brother's order!—to hold back the desperately needed contingent of Austrian volunteers at the docks at Trieste. That treachery, which had humiliated him before the army, the French, and his own court, happened three months ago. The Americans had been threatening Franz Joseph that, if those Austrian volunteers departed for Mexico, the U.S. minister in Vienna would demand his passport. Franz Joseph's excuse for capitulating? That he needed the men for the conflict with Prussia. Bah!

If Maximilian were to abdicate, those Americans would be puffed up, and he, mere worm, would have to grovel before Franz Joseph and his camarilla. What insultingly paltry pensions might Vienna begrudge an inconvenient younger brother? No longer an archduke of the House of Habsburg, Maximilian would be ex-emperor of a memory, a mirage. By what protocol would he be treated? Could he even show his person in the Hofburg? What would his status be in Paris, in Brussels, in Lisbon, in London? The Vatican? Caricatures in the French newspapers ridicule him as a Don Quixote spurring a Mexican burro—how much worse would it be without his having even windmills to tilt at! The lord chamberlains, the masters of ceremony, he knew how they worked, how they would find the most pettifogging ways to humiliate him.

Bonaparte on Saint Helena. Louis-Philippe wasting away in Claremont. Portugal's Dom Pedro. Uncle Ferdinand I, a simpleton respected by no one. Murat. Iturbide. None of these was a pretty story.

But the Mexican Empire had sunk feet, torso, and shoulders into a quagmire. Chihuahua definitively lost, as were Matamoros, Mazatlán, Tampico—all the revenues from those customhouses either cut off or captured by the enemy, and the whole state of Guerrero in an uproar of banditry. The insurgents have been steadily gaining ground from the north, from the west, from the south. U.S. troops still poised at the border, Seward intrigues with Santa Anna, and meanwhile Señora Juárez has been fêted with a state dinner at the White House!

And now, in an ultimatum that arrived in Mexico City on June 28, Louis Napoleon is not only withdrawing his troops, in reply to Maximilian's protest and counterproposal, he heaps all blame upon Mexico! No new troops, no new money, and if French troops are to remain for any time at all, France must have complete control of the customhouses and one-half of all government revenues. Should this be refused, all French troops will immediately be embarked, the Treaty of Miramar null and void.

These terms are not only an insult, they are impossible. A quarter of all revenues were already going to the English debt. And without French troops to contend with, how much longer can it be before the Yankees run their "stars and stripes" over the Imperial Palace? As for the Family Pact—well, Maximilian would take his chances that something could be arranged ex post facto. When the ship catches fire, you jump into the sea, or what?

Two of Bazaine's men helped him draw up a proclamation of abdication. But as Maximilian sat down at his desk to sign it, his soul tore in two. Abdication: the freedom his soul had yearned for and, in the same package, monstrous, galling failure. His stomach in his heart and his heart in his throat, he had, hesitatingly, picked up the quill. He was about to dip it into the ink, when he thought: No! No, it would not be right to do this without Charlotte as his witness. And he needed her now, more than he had ever needed anyone.

Charlotte, summoned, did not even read the document. She grabbed the pen from his hand. "Abdication is excusable only in old men and idiots!" Hadn't her father told them, what a grievous mistake for her grandfather Louis-Philippe to have abdicated? It was the ruin of his honor, the ruin of the dynasty, and a tragedy not only for France but for all of Europe! If *cher* Papa were alive, what would he say to this? He had died of something else, but if he hadn't, *this* indeed would have killed him! What would her brother, Leopold, say to this, and Franz Joseph? And Queen Victoria? "Sovereignty is the most precious of all possessions. Emperors do *not* give themselves up! So long as there is an emperor, there is an empire, though he have but six feet of ground, for the empire is *nothing* without the emperor."

"But there is nothing left I can do."

She stared at him with such ferocity, he feared she was about to raise her voice, but instead, with a voice full of love, she said: "But there is something I can do."

She made her case with the passion of a Joan of Arc: Louis Napoleon was the victim of a massive conspiracy. Confronted by the true facts, presented by herself, in person, Louis Napoleon will recall Bazaine, he will maintain troops in Mexico, he will send more money—in sum, he will renew, with vigor, his devotion to the just and vital cause.

Stunned, Maximilian said nothing.

Charlotte shook a finger. "Louis Napoleon's honor and the interests of France will demand it!"

In the gale force of his wife's will, Maximilian felt something in himself unmoor and begin to drift . . .

"But," he stammered, "it is dangerous in the extreme to travel this time of year." There was yellow fever, and Campeche and Tabasco were beset with cholera.

Charlotte answered stoutly, *Had she not represented him in Yucatan?*

Maximilian twisted his hands. Nervously, he turned his rings around. The Totonac bowl of bonbons, the door, the inkpot, the clock, the drapes—his gaze found no place to rest. Suddenly he wanted Father Fischer, for his feelings had fallen into chaos. Honor: yes! He was not sure, however, should he trust himself to decide, should he allow his wife to undertake such a desperate mission? Was it valiant—or insane, trying to sail into a countervailing wind without a mast, without a rudder, a venture out over the Atlantic without coal? Father Fischer, however, had not yet returned from Rome. Ramírez, his foreign minister, would have offered a carefully considered opinion, honestly given—but on Bazaine's insistence, he had been fired. There was their Belgian advisor, but whatever the circumstance, Monsieur Eloin took Charlotte's views as his lodestar. Whom else?

Maximilian realized, with a lurch in his stomach, that not one of his cabinet ministers, not one of the high-ranking clergy, and certainly not Princess Iturbide would approve of his even considering abdication. If he signed this proclamation of abdication, a document concocted in the office of General Bazaine, their respect would transmute, instantly, to contempt.

Charlotte's parting words still ring in his ears: "Faith, Max! Hold tight to your faith in God's will!"

Her entourage comprised Charlie Bombelles, Foreign Minister Castillo, General Uraga, young Dr. Bohuslavek, the chamberlain Don Felipe del Barrio and his wife, Herr and Frau von Kuhacsevich, and an army of maids and lackeys. It has been little more than twenty-four hours since their middle-of-the-night departure from Mexico City. Maximilian accompanied Charlotte twenty miles out, to the village of Ajotla. There, by the still dark highway, in the dull shadow of an agave, the air rent by the screams of roosters, he kissed her hands. He kissed her hair. For the first time in a very long time he held her in his arms. He could feel her bosom rising, falling with her breath. She lay her cheek on his shoulder. He loved her; he did. His arms emptied, limp by his sides, he sobbed like a little child. He could not look: he only heard the sounds of her shoes on the gravel, and then up the steps to her carriage. The door clicked shut. Dr. Semeleder and Grill, his valet, had to support him; they lifted him back into his carriage.

Back in Chapultepec Castle, his feelings gone numb, her absence felt, at first, like a reprieve. Now it feels like what it is: an amputation.

He has a terrible foreboding that he will never see Charlotte again. Nor Charlie, his companion from childhood. Nor the von Kuhacseviches. None of them. They will have sailed off the edge of the earth.

"Good morning, Your Majesty." Grill peels open the drapes.

Maximilian can barely bring himself to open his eyes. The very air here is leeched. It is all so ugly. The water stains on the wall behind the crucifix. The smears on the windowpane. The bedraggled, over-soaked plants cluttering the terrace. No snowcapped volcanoes, no glittering vistas: dawn over the Valley of Anahuac is a horse blanket. One is sick of it, sick of it all, sick of being sick. Cramps, sweats, shivering, the most god-awful nightmares—one wakes into bone-deep fatigue.

"Your robe, sir."

One inserts an arm. One inserts the other arm.

Perhaps one should have signed that proclamation. No, Charlotte was right. As Tacitus said, *For he who would have an empire, there is no middle ground: it is the heights or the precipice.* So, it was no miscalculation to send her to Paris, it was genius!

However, what if . . . ?

General Almonte, now one's ambassador to France: what Faustian bargains has he made? On his way to Paris in May, Almonte sojourned on the island of Saint Thomas. One had instructed Charlotte, first thing on arrival in Paris, after securing an emergency loan, to put it to Almonte directly: Did he meet with General Santa Anna?

Oh, what a labyrinth one has sent her into.

The robe's belt is drawn tight and knotted around one's waist.

She cannot have gone far beyond the city of Puebla. Another chamberlain, Count del Valle, shall be sent racing after her this morning, with the last letters—one shall write to her with the most cheering words, first thing.

Or, ought one to wire ahead, to Orizaba? Wait!

They could go home together. They should: the Mexican Empire, eaten out from its core, cannot stand. Blood has been spilled for it, a tragedy, why compound it? One mustn't spill more!

To go or not to go? To abdicate or not to abdicate? And these are not the same question because one could go, as emperor, leaving a regency in place—

The seraphim lightness of freedom: to fly to one's own Miramar, spend the last, long, fig-and-honey days of August cruising the Adriatic . . . recuperating one's health on the island of Lacroma . . . feasting on the perfume of roses . . . lulled by Charlotte's mandolin, and the rush of the surf.

Bazaine, lying jackal, presses you to abdicate so that he, serving himself with the big spoon, can take it all! Do you really imagine Louis Napoleon would give up Mexico? Bazaine and his wife and her family are behind this, they want Mexico to be a French Protectorate, another Algeria. They push you into a corner where it appears you have no choice but to abdicate—the one who has no choice is Louis Napoleon. In accepting this throne, we have rendered him an unparalleled service. He owes us an enormous debt. I will lay it out plainly, the true situation. Have faith!

One is the emperor. And an emperor, captain of his country, does not abandon ship. Through the storm—cresting, plunging, washed with spray— one grips the wheel. One stays the course.

One . . . collapses into the chair.

The beard. After the tossing and turning in the night, it's a nest of tangles. Grill combs it out. Then, the mustache comb. Grill upturns the blue bottle of Zweigschein's, rubs his palms together vigorously, then swipes his hands over the beard. The trimming scissors: snip a bit here, snip, a bit there. Once finished Grill carries the heavy mirror around to the back of one's chair. With the hand mirror, one inspects the back of one's head. One dislikes that curl at the nape, but one has not the strength to quibble. Gone are the days when one had the strength to attack the dispatch box before breakfast. One cannot even stomach breakfast.

Grill brings the vest, shirt, and trousers, all folded over his arm.

Oh, the siren call of sleep . . . one is weary, weary as the last mammoth staggering over the Siberian tundra . . . But if Charlotte is soldier enough to make that hellish journey, by God, one can haul one's sack of bones to the office and write her a letter.

Grill knots the tie at one's neck.

One stands, chest out, before the mirror. The frock coat.

The boutonniere?

Grill fastens it in.

One does look all the part.

In the office in the Imperial Palace: a bonbon, in contradiction to Dr. Semeleder's orders, has gone down tolerably well. Out the open window, a hubbub of cries and whistles rises from the Plaza Mayor: mango-sellers, pulque-vendors, bank clerks, beggars . . . one's subjects. How many weeks have gone by and one has not thought of it? That one's palace stands upon the ruins of Montezuma's. Montezuma, whose feathered shield adorns one's office. Montezuma, who had welcomed Cortez as Quetzalcóatl, the feathered serpent-god returned, as was prophesied, from the east. Quetzalcóatl: giver of civilization, time, and the tracking of the stars. He came with magical animals—horses; he came with magical weapons—muskets and cannon. Montezuma's shield was Cortez's gift to his Caesar, Carlos I, king of Aragon, Castile, Naples, and Sicily, ruler of the Burgundian territories, and Holy Roman Emperor—from whom one is directly descended.

Charlie, returning from his mission to Vienna, brought back Montezuma's shield. For this one could almost forgive Franz Joseph. But why could Franz Joseph not also give up Montezuma's headdress of jewels and quetzal feathers? One had specifically requested the headdress, together with the shield, at the outset. For Franz Joseph, it would have been a small concession—of the mountain of treasures he has in Vienna, that and a pfennig would not be missed. Wasn't it obvious? It would have meant a great deal to bring Montezuma's "crown" and shield back to Mexico—the symbolism of that, right at the beginning, would have been powerful. But no. The All-Highest would not grudge them. Everything for himself. Nothing for oneself. It is ever thus.

The dispatch box. That bottomless trough of donkeywork.

"Not now."

"Sorry, sorry, sir . . ." Blasio shuffles out, walking backward.

Blasio, that stupid boy. How he had pleaded to go with the empress to Europe—as if it were a holiday. To play the flaneur on the boulevards of Paris! His chance to see the Louvre! He'll be sent along soon enough.

One clenches one's fists. Cresting, plunging—grip that wheel. *Get a grip.* One takes it coolly. One takes up the quill. One sets it down again. One mops one's brow. Mops one's tears.

Dearly beloved angel:

I have not the words to tell you, my angel, my star, how I have felt since you left, how my wounded heart suffers. All the joy of life has died in me; only duty keeps me on my feet. Nevertheless, our sacrifice is good, everyone sees it now, and they show me twice as much love and loyalty. All true friends have rushed to my side with great heart. Given that now I must not only perform the duties of father of the country, but also mother, yesterday I went to the evening promenade. Never have they greeted me so cordially and with such kindness. Throughout the city it is the same. From their carriages and balconies, they salute me. I have been deeply moved. They truly comprehend my immense sacrifice. Yesterday the excellent General Mejía was with me. He is more determined, loyal, and wise than ever. He has never lost his valor; to the contrary, he is a tower of strength.

My sole diversion now is work. Yesterday I renewed the conferences on the legal code. The second volume should appear on the 16th of September. Yesterday we received Santa Anna's famous proclamation, which is so foolish and so entertaining that I ordered it published today in its entirety and without commentary. You will receive a few copies.

Del Valle can tell you many more details. I saw him yesterday and I told him how much I am counting on him to take care of you, my love. For the love of God, do not eat fruit, do not walk from one side to the other in the sun, and do not set foot on land in Havana nor in Saint Thomas. I could die of worry when you are ill! I press you to my wounded and suffering heart.

Your forever loyal
Max
My cordial respects to your retinue.

One calls for the dispatch box. The first thing, slap in the face, a letter from Angel de Iturbide. Blasio begins reading.

"Once again I appeal to your venerable and noble sentiments, because my wife and I have suffered horribly from the moment we could no longer see our unfortunate child. We are—"

"No, just the gist of it."

"Same as the last letter."

Those Iturbides, whining about everything. No one has been paid in Paris since the end of February. The Palatine Guard, including Charlie, and the Austrian and Belgian volunteers—none has been paid since May. These are men who would give their lives! And this ingrate expects special treatment? After sneaking into Washington, contriving to meet with Seward, and in Paris intriguing with the U.S. minister, he and his brothers ought to be shot for treason. "Unfortunate child"—ha! Unbelievable.

One waves one's hand. "File it with the others." One presses one's hand to one's ribs, a spear of agony.

• • •

Prior to the luncheon, one rendezvouses with Princess Iturbide. In accord with protocol, the princess, a person of the second rank, has been waiting for the sovereign in the Throne Room for a half hour prior to the appointed time—but she is as alert as a sentry.

"Your Majesty." Pressing a hand to her hip, she sinks into the deepest curtsey yet.

One extends one's hand for the kiss.

One has been made aware that she has arranged, an expense out of her own pocket, to have masses said for the empress's safe and successful journey. It is a lesson one learned, painfully, in the last days of one's governorship of Lombardy-Venetia: when things become agitated, the wheat separates from the chaff, that is, the true friends, which are few, and the bonny weather friends, which are legion, reveal themselves by their deeds. La Prima, the cousin, as one calls Princess Iturbide, is a true friend. Father Fischer spoke of her with alpine esteem: that had been her entrée. After the deaths of Char-lotte's father and then, in March, of her Grand-maman, La Prima's compan-ionship was a great comfort to her. Whilst one was in Cuernavaca and touring the provinces, La Prima and Charlotte spent many an afternoon tête-à-tête. One would not have believed it if one had not witnessed it with one's own blue eyes: when she said goodbye, Charlotte, in violation of all protocol, threw her arms around La Prima's neck. She cried, *Could I but save this poor unfortunate nation, I should then feel I have done a great work.* La Prima an-swered, *You already have and you are, God bless you.* It pleases one to have La Prima and the little cousin back in their apartments. Alas, the reason for their return, the lack of guards to spare, was an unfortunate one.

"You may rise."

They proceed to the Painting Gallery where, here and there, buckets have been positioned to catch the leaks. The rainy season began back in May; it pours nearly every afternoon at four and whenever else the Maker pleases.

"Though not so heavily as last year."

"What troubles me is this air."

"Very miasmatic."

"It is colder than yesterday."

"If it weren't so humid."

The carpets having been removed for cleaning and repair, their footsteps echo. Pale light from the inner patio splashes the tiles. They walk into the shadow of a massive Venetian chandelier; past the portrait of the Liberator (that ageless Mars, doppelgänger of Murat, a hand on the hilt of his sword, the other forever pointing to his Plan of Iguala), and then, La Prima falling just behind one, into the Iturbide Salon where the small crowd of guests, who are of the third, fourth, and other ranks, await, having been divided by the Master of Ceremonies: gentlemen along the windows; ladies along the opposite wall. There are but two ladies: a banker's wife and daughter, a creature out of a fairytale and with freckles on her nose. The archbishop. Ambassadors Campbell-Scarlett and von Thun. Ah, Baron Stefan Herzfeld.

"My good man."

"Your Majesty."

Herzfeld: one's long ago aide-de-camp, one of the finest men in the Austrian Navy. As the Mexican Empire's consul-general in Vienna, Herzfeld had achieved little, but then, with Franz Joseph, it might have been easier to squeeze blood out of a turnip. Brave, loyal, handsome Herzfeld: unlike so many others—Gallotti, one's consul in Rome; and in fact, so many Mexican expatriates who bethought an empire a fine idea unless they might actually have to set foot in it—Herzfeld was unafraid to come to Mexico.

The Master of Ceremonies advises that the table is ready; one strides into the dining room, and the orchestra strikes up the National Anthem. (Short a violinist, one observes.)

The footman who pulls out one's chair is in green velvet. Is this a third-class lunch? No, one specified second-class, in which case the footmen should be in black, with black stockings. In the centerpiece, the edge of one petal of a *Phalaenopsis* orchid has browned. And the water goblets: some appear to be as much as ten centimeters closer to the salt cellars from one place to the next. Well, Frau von Kuhacsevich has gone to Europe with the empress; things are bound to slip.

One turns to La Prima. "And how is the little cousin?"

"In the garden."

One clears one's throat. Louder: *"How* is he?"

"Dr. Semeleder has pronounced him good as new."

"No runny noses?"

"Oh, no."

"I shall be taking him with me to Cuernavaca tomorrow."

"Am I to go as well?"

"No." One turns to the banker's wife. Not the freshest peach on the tree. For the menu—consommé with quail egg, *huachinango* in garlic-butter sauce, duck à la Périgaux, salad with walnuts and truffles, Tüdos's pièce de résistence, fruit of Lake Texcoco, *cuisses de grenouille*—one has no appetite. One is served one's plate of unbuttered rice and boiled chicken, Dr. Semeleder's hair shirt for the palate. One pokes the fork tines at the meat. Cardboard would be more appetizing. (One did press Dr. Semeleder, might one have a bit of sauce? Verboten!) It is nearing three o'clock: the dining room, despite the lamps, has turned into a sea of gloom. Thunder cracks overhead. One allows the footman to remove one's plate. The meal, thank God, is finished, and in record time.

But no siesta for the weary—back to the office, where Herzfeld, expert navigator, has undertaken to chart a course through the finances. One leaves Herzfeld with his pencils and clacking abacus and escapes to the window. Below a blackened sky, the Plaza Mayor, emptied of people, is awash in rain. Mud bubbles up from the hole for the last of the four new fountains. *Ojalá,* as they say, God willing, the landscaping will be completed before month's end. This was one of the last projects for which there was funding. It cheers one to see it proceeding. When one first arrived, this plaza, heart of the nation, was a shadeless stretch of Sahara and this palace, so-called, a fetid hulk (its ground floor had been used as a jail and some of the walls were still covered in graffiti). General Almonte could not have moved heaven and earth in a day, but, man alive, how difficult could it have been to arrange a room or two with cots, clean linen, and washbasins? The emperor of Mexico had had to spend his first night in this palace stretched out on a billiard table! Its empress had had to sleep fully clothed in a chair. As one had remarked to Charlotte, there is a shamelessness in poverty—and poverty is not only material; it is also aesthetic.

As water makes a desert bloom, so it is with the Teutonic sensibility applied to Mexico.

It has been gratifying in the extreme to show Herzfeld the multitude of improvements, all fruits of less than two and a half years: this Plaza Mayor; this palace—every room luxuriously appointed; the Museum of Natural History and the National Museum and the National Theater; the Paseo de la Emperatriz; the refurbished zoo, the decor and landscaping in Chapultepec Castle . . . Truly, one has shaped Mexico City into a world-class capital.

Charlotte's eyes had a powerful shine. *To throw away your magnificent work would be an ungodly sin. Days of glory are to come! Great glory! Hold fast, Max. Have faith!*

Near sunset the sky begins to clear and with it Maximilian's melancholy. Feeling years younger, he invites Herzfeld up to the flat-roof, which extends the entire length of the palace. The air, moist and breezy, smells metallic. Behind the towers of the cathedral, the rain-washed sky is a parfait of raspberry and mango, to the north, fast-moving shreds of mist.

"Welcome aboard," Maximilian says.

Herzfeld squares his heels. "Thank you, sir!"

To the southwest, in the coppery distance, a flock of water birds hangs in the sky like a snake. To the east rise the darkening silhouettes of Popocatépetl and Iztaccíhuatl. As they stroll, Maximilian points out the more prominent domes: the Archbishop's Palace, the College of San Ildefonso, the Convent of Santa Inés, the Hospital de Jesús where, "Did you know? Cortez's bones are mortared into the side wall behind the altar."

Below, in the Plaza Mayor, a clattering as Sawerthal's orchestra sets up for the evening's concert: horns and flutes catch the light. The street that divides the plaza from the forecourt of the cathedral is a patchwork of shining puddles, one large enough to reflect the façade tinged with alpenglow, an image that—as an Indian *tameme,* carrying a gentleman on his back, sets out across its expanse—wavers and then dissipates.

Herzfeld has long ago learned to synchronize his pace to Maximilian's. (Onboard ship, the archduke's all-weather exercise was one dozen laps from stem to stern.) It might seem, at times, that Maximilian walks quickly, but his pace, in fact, is languid. What gains him ground is the length of his legs. Easily distracted, however, he slows, stops, and more often than not, loses count of the laps.

Pigeons, unsettled, fly above the Plaza Mayor like some vast unraveling scarf.

"Over there—" Maximilian points with his cigar out to the west. "That is the Palace of Buenavista, a gem of Neo-classical architecture by Manuel Tolsá. Look sharp, you might see one of its finials."

Herzfeld adjusts the focus on his spyglass. "Affirmative."

"To give you an idea of things, where we are standing now was the site of Montezuma's palace, the center of the island city of Tenochtitlán. And that, where you see that finial, was the shore, where one of the causeways went out over the lake."

"The Indian Venice."

"The Egypt of the Americas." The sky's colors have deepened into the fieriest reds: ox blood and pomegranate. "You know, Herzfeld, I sometimes think the Spaniards made a mistake to drain the lake."

"It must have been so beautiful, the water reflecting the sky."

"You understand me perfectly."

At the two men's approach, sparrows spray into the sky. Suddenly, Maximilian halts. He puts a fist on his hip. "Do you remember Naples? The sunset from the Capodimonte? Until I saw these Mexican sunsets, I would have said that sunset was the most ravishing on earth."

"Yes, this—"

"Or," Maximilian interrupts, "the sunset from the Kasbah of Algiers, do you think?"

"Do I think, sir?"

"Yes, what do you think, Herzfeld, after these Mexican sunsets, which was the most sublime on earth, the sunset from the Capodimonte or the sunset from the Kasbah of Algiers?"

"I would have to say, neither. For me, Funchal."

Maximilian looks at Herzfeld with utter incredulity. "Funchal?"

"Funchal, sir."

"Ha!" Maximilian shakes his head, laughing. "Have it your way."

The polka music has begun; they stroll on with a lighter step. What did Herzfeld think, would they manage to lay that transatlantic cable? What were the latest developments in Hungary? And Serbia? The situation in Lombardy? What was Herzfeld's opinion of the Prussians' so-called "needle-gun"?

Austria is at war with Prussia—but Austria has an ally in France. It will be a minor conflict, over by summer's end, certainly before the harvest, didn't Herzfeld think?

No, actually, Herzfeld feared it would turn into a widening conflagration. Austria would need him.

"You would not consider it inadvisable for me to abdicate?"

"Affirmative."

"Well, Herzfeld." Maximilian tried to make a little joke. "You also think my Totonac bowl is decorated with a—"

"Centipede."

"Caterpillar, Herzfeld. That *is* a *caterpillar*."

The concert concludes with a march by Donizetti: a Niagara of violins. With a spatter of applause, Maximilian and Herzfeld have arrived back at the stairwell. The cavity exudes a mildewy smell. The air has turned colder. In the breeze Maximilian holds onto the brim of his hat.

"Was that a dozen?"

"Nine laps, sir."

Maximilian drops his cigar and crushes it under his boot heel. "I have decided to take a vacation in Cuernavaca. We'll kedge over there, only a couple days' journey. It is the most enchanting village, you will fall in love with it. It is not so low as the hot-lands, nor high as this Altiplano; it sits, therefore, in a bowl of eternal springtime. My gardens are abloom with roses. What's more, this is the week, the single week of the entire year, when the *Diethria anna,* a butterfly of the *Nymphalidae* family, is most numerous. Crimson and black, and on the underside of the hind wings are the most distinctive markings: two eighty-eights."

"Extraordinary."

"Professor Bilimek prefers to call those markings, 'the twin infinities.' You know, Herzfeld, when you see a thing like that you know there is a God."

"Indeed there is, sir."

Maximilian takes a step down, and Herzfeld moves to follow, but suddenly Maximilian changes his mind. He comes back up onto the roof, and with a deep breath, swiveling his head all around, he takes in the sky. Then, he elbows Herzfeld.

"Funchal?"

"Funchal."

"My *good* man!"

August 20, 1866

※

IN THE GRAND-HÔTEL

*I*t reminds Alicia of Washington, the air so stagnant and dense in the Salon des Dames, this secluded corner of the lobby of the Grand-Hôtel, where, by means of one-way windows, ladies can, with complete privacy, observe the comings and goings—the sort of thing that makes hayseeds go all agog. Madame Almonte's insistence on this venue for a meeting in itself is peculiar.

Polish a penny 'til it shines like the sun—it remains a penny. This saying of Mrs. Green's comes, unkindly, into her daughter's mind, as still cackling with laughter, Madame Almonte brushes a tear from her cheek.

Madame Almonte may be wife of an ambassador, and chief lady-of-honor to an empress, but Alicia reflects, her deportment has all the polish of a Kentucky schoolteacher's. Recounting the perfect mess of the empress's arrival, Madame Almonte has to set down her glass of orangeade; yet again, she rocks back in her chair, helpless with laughter. Alicia, fanning herself against the heat, gives a tight-lipped smile. She has already heard about the fantastic string of humiliating mix-ups—hasn't all of Paris? The telegram announcing the empress's arrival landed at the Mexican legation only shortly before her ship docked at Saint Nazaire. Relations between Maximilian and General Bazaine had so deteriorated that Bazaine was not even informed of the empress's departure; he read about it in *La Sociedad*. From San Luis Potosí, where Bazaine was on a tour of inspection, he immediately sent Louis Napoleon a telegram, but as *Le Moniteur* called the story of the empress's departure a hoax, there had been no one from Paris, save the Almontes, to receive Her Majesty on the quayside. The mayor of Saint Nazaire could find no such thing as a Mexican tricolor, so—Almonte assured him it was better than a French flag—he ran a Peruvian flag up the pole! The French foreign minister, apprised of the horror show, was livid; Carlota, apoplectic. Madame Almonte's laughter is not malicious, no: Alicia recognizes a quintessentially Mexican sense of humor. It is, against naked humiliation, the only armor one owns.

Alicia, however, is not Mexican. Her sense of humor is a mild one. Perhaps this, after all, was the thing she'd given up for Lent. And Lent—over for everyone else ages ago—it just drags on. To hold her child in her arms: the longing inside her is a suspended screech—and a clanging of worries. Everything is turning to ashes! O Moses, won't Madame Almonte just shut up?

The ghoulish laughter grows louder: Then, after rushing ahead to Paris to prepare, Madame and General Almonte went to receive Carlota at the Montparnasse railway station, while the French—Drouyn de Lhuys, the whole party, all gussied up in their uniforms, the bouquets of flowers, red carpet, court carriages waiting to whisk the empress to the Tuileries—went (she throws out her hands), for reasons known only to themselves, to the Gare d'Orléans! Madame Almonte claps her hands and tosses her head to the side: torrents of laughter. This in the lobby, hushed as a church, of the most fashionable hotel in Paris! The clerk at the theater-booking desk has leaned out over his counter, to have a long-nosed look.

Alicia sips her orangeade and then flicks open her fan. If she were that clerk, or just another tourist happening through here, she'd take Madame Almonte for a Turkish lunatic. Why does Madame Almonte feel the need to make such a scandal? And wear such appalling shoes? Comfort for her bunions is all she cares about, it seems. And that mantilla, in Paris, what *mauvais goût*. Well, it's August; being here at all is mortifying in the extreme when *tout le monde* has gone to Biarritz, or to shoot in Scotland or Sweden. Mr. Bigelow and family, having more bourgeois tastes, are on an excursion in the Alps. Alicia is not glad about much of anything, but she is glad, grateful, now that she thinks about it, to be absconded behind this one-way mirror and phalanx of palm trees.

On the other side of the glass, the doorman helps another party in. Alicia had saluted him by name, but he did not recognize her. Has she changed so much since she was resident here? She feels no affection for this place: it is too big, too impersonal, and, moreover, the scene of some of the most cheerless days of her life. At the end of February, when they discovered their pensions were frozen, to economize, the Iturbides removed to an arrondissement so obscure she cannot bring herself to pronounce it. The boardinghouse (for that is, properly, what it is) has walls the color of tobacco spit and a proprietress who looks like the sort of person who would conduct séances. Alicia has been suffering from head-splitting migraines; Angelo, the gout; Agustín Gerónimo's cough thunders through the paper-thin walls. As for Agustín Cosme, he seems to have fused his shirtsleeves to the zinc of the counter in his tavern. Angelo, breaking protocol, has begun sending entreaties directly to Maximilian, who seems impervious to embarrassment, nor has the "archduke" a shred of compassion, so, why should she? In a curio shop on the Rue des Ecoles, one day, she found a voodoo puppet. She has been sticking hat pins in it.

It was not until late last spring, when General and Madame Almonte arrived from Mexico, that the Iturbides learned the true gravity of their situation. To Angelo, Almonte spoke plainly. The experiment was finished. He had known in February, with the news that Louis Napoleon had announced his schedule for the withdrawal of his troops. But what about the Mexican Imperial Army? Angelo asked. Almonte put on the face of a man discussing the death of his own child. Oh, there had been money for decorations and jewels, for balls and theaters, but not for officers' salaries. Not rifles, blankets, kettles, boots. The Mexican Imperial Army was broken. What little there was left of it would disperse—he snapped his fingers—like that. Almonte put out one fist. "The Army of the Mexican Republic, here." He put out the other fist, then opened it, wiggling his fingers. "Caciques here." Then, he clasped his hands together. "This is how it will be."

Being dispatched to France as Mexico's ambassador, Almonte had as much as won the lottery, for he would not be in Mexico in the end, when the Juaristas would want the satisfaction of having him shot. Of course, Maximilian wanted Almonte out of Mexico because he considered him a rival. That had been Maximilian's great mistake, Almonte told Angelo, to have kept him at arm's distance, bestowing upon him honors but not power, inviting him to dinners, to balls, every glittering reception, but listening more to the orchestra than to his advice. Maximilian should have trusted Almonte (here he thumped himself on the chest). Why, why did Maximilian put foreigners such as that Belgian Monsieur Eloin, Father Fischer, and the French, first? This was Mexico! Foreigners might be better educated, they might have the fancy manners, but did they understand Mexico? Not even Bazaine, sharp as a fox about guerrilla warfare, understood Mexico—no, not in the gut.

Yes, Almonte admitted to Angelo, on his way to Paris he had stopped on the island of Saint Thomas to meet with Santa Anna—a meal and a smoke with an old comrade-at-arms. Santa Anna had trouble walking; the stump of his leg had become excruciatingly tender. Yes, Santa Anna was trying to get up a coup, but more out of habit than in all seriousness. *The old warrior is bored, don't you see? He cannot raise the capital or the support—the only support that matters—of the United States.*

And Almonte himself?

The Iturbides had noticed, Almonte had developed a habit of licking the sides of his mouth. It was most unattractive and, behind his back, commented on.

Madame Almonte confided to Angelo that the general's abdomen was chronically swollen; his hip joints painfully tender. He was leaving blood in the chamber pot. They expected that Maximilian would set up his court-in-exile at his castle in Trieste. His courtiers' pensions would have to be paid, well, somebody had to pay them, by Vienna. Madame Almonte had begun studying her guidebook to Trieste.

As for the Iturbides, their plan was to remain in Paris for the duration. At some point, Angelo and Alicia hoped to be reunited with their son, in Paris or Havana or New York, and then they could go to Washington, to stay with Mrs. Green at Rosedale. From there, Angelo will petition President Juárez for permission to return to Mexico.

May, June, July: the days of summer had drooped by, each slower, hotter, emptier than the last. And then, in August: this bomb—a crater a hundred miles wide—Carlota was about to land in Paris!

But in those summer months, France, and, in fact, the entire face of the continent, had changed. Austria had been defeated at Sadowa—or, Königgrätz, as the Prussians called it. At the cost of thirty-five thousand casualties, Bismarck's war machine had delivered the German Federation to Prussia— Prussia, bristling with bellicosity—and where, the newspapers went wagging, were thirty thousand of France's soldiers? *Oof!* On the far side of an ocean! Louis Napoleon, backed into a corner, had been compelled to announce a withdrawal from Mexico, but the logistics of transporting so many men, horses, and matériel are complex. However urgent, it will take months, and however painful, it will take money to get them all home. A chorus of voices laments, so much treasure, so many lives lost, and all for what purpose? The Austrian archduke has proved himself inept and the Mexicans, unworthy people, unwilling to stand up for themselves. *La plus grande pensée du règne*— as Louis Napoleon called his Mexican expedition, an intervention energetically promoted by his Eugénie, his Spanish Catholic wife (beholden to Rome)—has degenerated into an unmitigated calamity: military, political, diplomatic, and financial. France has been dishonored, thoroughly undermined. The newspapers are baying: Which bankers, which war contractors, which cronies have fattened their pockets at the citizens' expense?

For Louis Napoleon, stricken with kidney stones, the subject of Mexico is the last one he can bear to hear about. The ghastly, unbelievable news that the empress of Mexico was on her way to Paris sharpened the agony of his suffering. By the time she had made her way out of the Montparnasse railway station, and in fulminating consternation, checked into the Grand-Hôtel (taking the entire first floor, paid for with the emergency funds for Mexico City's dike repairs), Louis Napoleon was writhing in his bedsheets, wishing, praying to sweet Jesus he were dead.

But for Alicia de Iturbide, had the miracle she has been begging God to send finally come? Because confronted with the true facts, by herself, in person, surely, Carlota, who will have no reason to keep the baby, will give him back!

Angelo dashed a letter to Maximilian: again, he begged for the return of their child, he reminded that they had not been paid since February, he said, *my wife's health has been failing and, I fear, with no end to her grief, the consequences could be fatal.*

General Almonte presented Angelo's letter to Carlota. She did not acknowledge it. That was two days ago.

"Do not lose heart," Madame Almonte had counseled Alicia, with a powerful squeeze to her arm.

Extricating herself from Madame Almonte's clutches, Alicia drew herself up and spoke as the daughter of the naval officer that she was: "I shall not lose heart until the day I die."

But Madame Almonte was genuinely trying to help. Fortunately, as Monsieur Eloin had been sent on a mission to Vienna, a Mexican in the empress's retinue, Count del Valle, had taken charge of Her Majesty's schedule. Madame Almonte had assured Alicia, with yet another vice-like squeeze to her arm, *We will get you in.* It seemed a solid assurance, for Madame Almonte, resuming her duties as chief lady-of-honor, was now close by Carlota's side, all day, every day—indeed, Madame Almonte, and the one other lady-in-waiting, Madame del Barrio, accompanied the empress on her visits with Eugénie and her ladies. Count del Valle, however, remained unshakable in his refusal to assign a slot to an Iturbide. The empress was besieged by bankers, merchants, diplomats, supplicants of a thousand stripes; such ungrateful subjects as those Iturbides, he said, were unworthy of their sovereign's time. General Almonte's personal intervention achieved nothing but a strange intelligence, that Carlota had a fixed idea that Bazaine instructed the Iturbides to appear in Paris precisely to humiliate her.

"No," General Almonte had protested to the empress. "The Iturbides are here because His Majesty sent them here. They have been resident in this city since late last year."

In the empress's salon, a mirror with a gilded frame stretched from the floor to the ceiling. Carlota, standing near the window, happened to turn and therein she saw that her crinolines—it was no help they were black—were a mess with wrinkles. Mathilde had ironed them, but the clothes had been in a trunk for weeks, and that trunk, stupidly, loaded upside down. Carlota met her own eyes with familiar loathing. *Your pissy little problems. Stinking sinner. You deserve to die.* She was hearing voices again, louder, sometimes roaring in the core of her brain, though now they subsided to a low hiss. For having just had two cups of coffee, she felt strangely sleepy.

Her Majesty turned back to General Almonte, addressing the space about a foot above his head.

"Conspiracy surrounds us. We are aware—" her eyes fluttered—"of their connivance with Bazaine."

"No, but—"

"When you visited St Saint Thomas . . ." Her tongue felt thick. "On Saint St Thomas. . . . What. . . . tell me . . . what did you talk over with Santa Anna?"

"Your Majesty, with all due respect, I have already answered that question."

"You . . . may. . . . leave us . . . now." With a swish, she turned her back on General Almonte. In the mirror she saw that General Almonte did not walk backward out of the room with the proper respect for his sovereign. He had, for the first time, turned his back on her.

General Almonte was so mortified by Her Majesty's ingratitude that he fell sick. Perhaps, his abdomen distended, he really was growing a tumor.

And now what? Angelo and Alicia turned to Madame Almonte.

Madame Almonte allowed that, no, Carlota would not be going to Belgium because she was protesting King Leopold II's halt to the recruiting of volunteers for Mexico. Her Majesty's relations with her brother, strained by the negotiations over their father's inheritance, were very bad. Neither was Carlota going to Vienna, because she was protesting Kaiser Franz Joseph's withholding the Austrian volunteers at the docks at Trieste. Her Majesty's relations with her brother-in-law were very bad also. Carlota had not shared her intentions, Madame Almonte said, but she guessed that, most likely, once business was concluded in Paris, Her Majesty would go to Rome. Mexico's consul in Rome, Galloti, had finally found the courage to comply with Maximilian's summons to Mexico; who knew?

"And Father Fischer?"

"Father Fischer has already departed for Mexico.

"When can I see the empress?"

"My dear," Madame Almonte soothed, patting Alicia's hand. "You must have patience."

Patience! For Alicia, the Almontes were a repository of the most unattractive presumption, grasping naïveté, self-serving meddling, and inflated amour propre; these were a pair of fish far out of water, and if they were now lying prone, exhausted, on the verge of extinction, she had no pity and no patience, for them, for anyone.

Alicia leveled her gaze at the wife of Mexico's ambassador, as she would at a servant she was about to dismiss. "Carlota can receive me tomorrow, or else."

"Or else what?"

"I shall confront her in public."

"Where do you pretend?"

"Where it suits me. What's more, I shall bring with me, as my witness, Mr. Buffum, the correspondent for the *New York Herald.*"

"You could be arrested."

"You forget, I have already been arrested."

Alice's tone won her no affection from Madame Almonte, however, the latter was eager to do a favor for her family. Don Angel, especially, could be claimed as an old friend from Washington—this when friends were growing scarcer by the day.

Madame Almonte therefore related Alicia's dangerous ultimatum not to that complacently arrogant Count del Valle, but to Count Bombelles; not only had he been the head of the Palatine Guard, but he was the most trusted of Maximilian's camarilla, and, here in Europe, responsible for Her Majesty's personal security. Consequently, after the empress retired for the evening, Bombelles slipped the appointment book under his jacket. Madame Almonte and Bombelles rendezvoused in the Salon des Dames, this quiet corner of the lobby, secluded from general view by the bank of palm trees and the one-way windows. Bombelles's breath smelled of beer.

"Let me see it," said Madame Almonte. Bombelles hesitated; Madame Almonte wrested the appointment book out of his hands. She quickly read through the schedule for Monday, August 20, and seeing a wide-open space at ten o'clock, wrote in, MADAME DE I.

"You are welcome," Bombelles said coldly as he pulled the book back.

"*You* should be thanking *me*."

They exchanged vulpine stares. Then, at the same time, they both huffed.

And so it is that Alicia's interview with Carlota is today at ten o'clock. With impatient flicks, Alicia goes on fanning herself. She stops, suddenly, and leans over the table for her orangeade. But the sticky-sweet liquid has turned disagreeably warm. On the other side of the one-way window, an extravagantly dressed young woman swans up the stairs.

"Isn't that Adelina Patti?" says Madame Almonte.

Alicia pushes at the scrap of mint floating upon the surface of her orangeade. "I wouldn't care if it was."

"Really? Adelina Patti?"

"She is completely overrated."

"I know people who would give their right arm to hear her sing."

"I heard her sing once. I walked out."

"Really!"

Alicia looks over Madame Almonte's shoulder, to the clock that stands sentry at the foot of the staircase. Four minutes to the appointed hour. Alicia last saw Carlota when she and Pepa came to retrieve the baby—eleven months ago.

Alicia, barely listening to Madame Almonte's prattle, jiggles her ankle: three and a half minutes more.

She smacks the fan closed. Two.

And one day, a black, black day, Alicia had driven the point of her manicure scissors through Carlota's carte de visite—it was the one of the empress in profile, with flowers in her coiffure. Then, because Alicia had ruined it, and she was ashamed, she tore it in two, and then she tore those two pieces into tiny pieces and she threw them all into the stove. *I hate you, I hate you,* she cried over and over, sobbing into her hands.

One . . .

Madame Almonte says, "I saw Alexandre Dumas the other day."

Alicia tucks a stray curl behind her ear. She smooths her skirt. "Do I look disarranged?"

Madame Almonte dips her head, the better to spy through the palm fronds (Bombelles has gained the stairs). Distractedly, she offers, "You look lovely as always, dear."

Alicia pats the side of her head. "My hair?"

"Your hair looks fine."

Alicia rises and throws back her shoulders. Deep inside, she feels a riptide of strength.

"Go," Madame Almonte says, giving Alicia an utterly unnecessary nudge.

Not five minutes before Alicia de Iturbide appears in the corridor outside the empress's reception salon, Frau von Kuhacsevich came upon the empress's wardrobe maid.

"*Ach*, Matty! Guess who I just saw down in the lobby having a tête-à-tête?"

"What do you mean?"

"La Almonte and La Iturbide. They were *conferring*."

From behind an armload of petticoats, Mathilde Doblinger, her forehead beaded with sweat, simply looked at her.

The Mistress of the Imperial Household lowered her voice. "Matty, they were having a *private conversation*. I overheard some of it."

At just this moment the empress's personal physician rounded the corner. "*Grüss Gott!*" Young Dr. Bohuslavek bowed deeply to the Mistress of the Imperial Household, kissing her hand before, stiffly, offering Mathilde, a mere maid, a nod—though the doctor's and the maid's relationship has developed into one of far greater respect and mutual confidence than Frau von Kuhacsevich has yet intuited. Over the weeks of a difficult journey made more dangerous by haste, Dr. Bohuslavek has been made acutely aware of the multitude of concerns for Charlotte. She is young—younger than himself—and, fragile female, burdened with responsibilities that would make a Bismarck stagger. Insomnia, nail-chewing, lace-tearing, crying jags, poor appetite, disjointed speech, and extended brooding silences: a diagnosis of hysteria is not contra-indicated. Upon his own counsel—as a medical doctor, he need consult no one—least of all the patient, as she is the most likely to resist it—Dr. Bohuslavek prescribed a sedative. Mathilde has been dosing the empress's coffee, two drops per cup.

Frau von Kuhacsevich whispered, "Doctor! Guess who I just now saw in the lobby, tête-à-tête?"

His hat was back on his head. "Dear lady, I beg your pardon, I cannot tarry."

"I have to go, also." Mathilde hurried away down the hall.

"Well!" Frau von Kuhacsevich pipped to herself as, with a subtle click, the door behind her unlatched. It was the door, an ornately carved and gilded confection of white and rose pink, to the antechamber of the empress's reception salon. The door swung in, revealing a patch of flowered carpet, a length of wainscoting, and then a lunette table crowned by an overflowing fruit basket—the morning's offering from the Tuileries. In a rustle of crinolines and a waft of the most expensive perfume, out came Madame del Barrio, the empress's other lady-in-waiting—the only one who had accompanied her from Mexico. A generation younger and of a markedly different social provenance than La Almonte, Madame del Barrio, who could pass for French, was dressed in a delphinium blue frock with the same style ruffled sleeves with lilac grosgrain trimmings as the ones Eugénie wore the other day. Neither was her coiffure what she wore in Mexico: *comme il faut,* combed back close to the ears, with two expertly shaped and shellacked "loaves" rising straight up from the forehead and back over, very like ram's horns; these tapered, just behind pearl-and-sapphire pendant earrings, not into points, but the flourish of a foursome of sausage-like ringlets.

"*Ah, bonjour!*" Madame del Barrio continued in French: "I thought I'd heard something."

Frau von Kuhacsevich, suddenly self-conscious, tugged at her lace cap. "Guess who I saw down in the lobby having a tête-à-tête?" She dropped her voice to scarcely a whisper: "La Almonte and La Iturbide."

"Ah!" Madame del Barrio covered her mouth with her fingers.

"I overhead some of it."

Madame del Barrio pulled the door shut behind her. "Pray tell."

"Come!" Frau von Kuhacsevich hurried Madame del Barrio down the corridor and around two corners and, pushing aside a trolley with the leavings of someone's breakfast, into the service stairwell. In less time than it would take to bring a cup of coffee to boil, the pair of them piece together a story too scrumptious to question, that La Almonte—in league with General Bazaine, who is, in turn, therefore, in league with Santa Anna, and in receipt of millions of dollars to render the Mexican Empire with the least possible resistance, and has been conspiring with the Iturbides who are conspiring with Bazaine, whose Mexican wife's family wants Louis Napoleon to abolish the throne and make Mexico a protectorate so that they can all go on enriching themselves by importing dressmaking supplies and whatnot without paying customs duties, has—Frau von Kuhacsevich interrupted—poisoned Count del Valle.

"What!" Madame del Barrio said.

"You did not know he has been indisposed?"

Madame del Barrio's earrings trembled.

Frau von Kuhacsevich whispered: "A laxative."

No need to speak a word: both ladies vividly recall Monsieur Langlais's mysterious demise. Monsieur Langlais, who had been preparing the budget and, in so doing, delving deep into the customhouses ledgers, had been seen all around Mexico City and in Cuernacava; then, suddenly, he was dead. It could have been a heart attack, but it could have been, well, it was rumored that a well-known apothecary shop, one very near General Bazaine's office by the way, had been broken into, and a quantity of strychnine stolen. Carlota herself claimed to have been poisoned in Yucatan. There had been, to date, three attempts on the emperor's life. Pistols, bombs, knives, snake venom, arsenic—around a throne, anything was possible.

"But," asked Madame del Barrio, "what has this to do with La Almonte and La Iturbide?"

"Guess who is the empress's ten o'clock?"

In her astonishment Madame del Barrio does not even cover her mouth. She concludes at once that, with Count del Valle indisposed, it is Bombelles who must be in charge of the empress's appointments. Bombelles, Madame del Barrio had learned from her first day onboard ship, is an aficionado of late-night drinking, billiards, and dice games, as is Frau von Kuhacsevich's husband, the Purser of the Imperial Household. These Austrians live in each others' pockets, as it were, for they have been together, attached to Maximilian's household, since before Maximilian's marriage. Madame del Barrio, alas, does not speak German. She switches to Spanish.

"*Válgame Dios.*"

Frau von Kuhacsevich answers in her unique amalgam of Spanish and Italian, "*Debemos de presar nuestras orejas a la parete.* We must press our ears to the wall."

"But it is ten, we must hurry!"

"No, we are exactly where we need to be." Frau von Kuhacsevich removes her earring, tucks it into her pocket, and places her cheek against the wall. This is somewhat more troublesome a maneuver for Madame del Barrio, however, because of her coiffure.

Bombelles knows a better place to eavesdrop than the service stairwell. Like a palace, a big city hotel is a Swiss cheese. As the *agents de sûreté publique,* the French police spies, would say, to listen in, *c'est simple comme bonjour.* Around the second corner from that antechamber, just before the service stairwell, is an innocent-looking little door: it appears to be the door to a broom closet. Bombelles was simply doing his duty on the first day to inspect the immediate surroundings when, with his penknife, he jimmied the lock. The setup was impressive. Coiled on the floor lay a tube that ran underneath the wall. On the other side of that wall, in the empress's reception salon, was a chest of drawers just tall enough that, to see the top of it, he had to, inconveniently, stand on tiptoe. This meant that a man of shorter stature such as Count del Valle, or a woman, would not notice that the tube connected—this was delightful—with a brass vase placed there. This vase had four rosettes of elaborate open grillwork. These were the receptacles for sound. The "vase," filled with silk violets, was an apparatus that must have been made by a doctor for the deaf: it worked brilliantly.

Bombelles has always resented Carlota. As the son of their tutor (who was himself the son of the third husband of the archduchess Marie-Louise), Bombelles grew up alongside the archdukes in the Hofburg: a boy's paradise. He can take his pleasure in women (he's happy to pay for it), but he dislikes women; he shares the conviction of many a Jesuit, that the so-called weaker sex cannot be trusted; they are mentally inferior and sow-like. The Belgian princess, in Bombelles's opinion, was the worst possible choice for a wife: always with her nose in a book, so pious, so pushy. Almost all his life, Max had been the Heir Presumptive to the throne of Austria! And, after the birth of Prince Rudolph, next in line! If not for her, Max never would have accepted a foreign throne, certainly he never would have signed that Family Pact. Her selfish ambition is disgusting. When Max was sick, sicker than he had ever been in his life, prostrate in his bed—she barged in, ignoring Dr. Jilek's anguished protests, and she forced Maximilian into it. Trying to fix that ungodly mistake has been the focus of the last several months of Bombelles's life. He's had to go all the way to Vienna, where he could do nothing, then back to Mexico, and now, again to Europe. Fool's missions. She will not have children, so what was she thinking to covet a crown? General Almonte had been furious, he had actually turned a shade of purple, when he found out that, after several childless years—they've been married since 1857—Their Majesties do not sleep together. Carlota, always scheming, comes up with these mad, crude solutions; then, having set the ship on fire, she becomes hysterical.

Bombelles has placed the tube in his ear. He knows that France's business with Mexico, *c'est fini*—for, were it otherwise, would he have this closet to himself? In the ten days Carlota has been in residence in the royal suite, the police spies have not used this closet once. She could meet with the queen of England and the powers that be could not care less. But what damage can this Jezebel still do to Max? In the dark Bombelles holds his breath: the first voice, somber in tone and without inflection, he recognizes as hers.

"*You are much changed* since I saw you last."

"I have suffered so terribly in these many months. You also are much changed."

"State your business."

(Rustling sounds. Then, much louder:) "I beg you, give me back my child!"

"I have done you great honor in granting you this interview. You should not make me regret it."

"How is he?" (Louder:) "Tell me how he is!"

"He is well."

"What else, what more! Oh, my child!"

"He improves every day in person and intelligence."

"Oh . . . oh . . ." (Rustling.) "If you only knew what worry, what grief has weighed upon my heart!"

"I am treating your child with the greatest kindness. I am supporting it with my own money."

"I ask nothing more than the privilege of supporting him myself!"

"Yourself?"

"Yes, myself!"

"If we give you back your child, you should refund the money the emperor has paid to your family."

"Those pensions were granted to the Emperor Iturbide's family, many years ago. The emperor did not give us that money; he reinstated a debt of the nation. Besides, since February we have not been paid."

"I bid you adieu."

"No! No, if this is your condition, we will pay it. I would pay anything rather than be deprived of my child!"

"You affixed your signature to a solemn contract, that your child is to be educated by the emperor."

"But I did not forfeit in any way my legal right to the possession of my child."

"You have this advice from foreign lawyers, I suppose."

"No! From Mexican lawyers of the highest character."

"Ah! Then you received this advice before giving up your child to us."

"No, Your Majesty, I received it when I returned from Mexico City to the city of Puebla, after I had been kidnapped."

"Kidnapped? That is ridiculous."

"I was arrested and taken out of Mexico City against my will."

"The emperor did right. You should not have come back to Mexico City. And you did wrong to address yourself to General Bazaine instead of the emperor."

"At that time I did not know of the misunderstanding between them."

"There is no misunderstanding. It was not, however, an affair for General Bazaine. You have always acted badly toward us. You stood aloof from us when we first came to Mexico. And now you show no gratitude to the emperor for having made your son and nephew princes."

"My husband and his siblings are the children of a legitimate emperor, and if they had not borne their titles, it was because they had not cared to."

"He was not of royal blood. Whether or not that was a legitimate throne is debatable."

"Many are saying the same about your throne, and that you keep my son to bolster your favor among the Mexican people."

"What advantage can your son be to me? The emperor and I are both young. We may have children of our own."

"I earnestly hope so, if that will restore me mine."

"You may have other children."

"I do not know. I am sure of this one and I want him."

"For how long are you willing to give him up to us?"

"Not an hour longer than I am compelled to!"

"I advise you to write to the emperor yourself."

"I have done so many times and received no reply."

"Write again. And write politely."

After this, the voices become muffled, indistinct. Then, like the descent of a curtain: definitive silence.

Bombelles, a little too quickly, closes the door behind him. On the other side of the wall, Charlotte, momentarily alone, startles. She'd heard something—inside the wall—that was not the hydraulic lift.

In the street below, a whip cracks. Voices.

"Bombelles?" she says. She has never taken the liberty of calling him Charlie. She does not trust him.

"Your Majesty." He smoothly bows.

"Have them send in a fresh pot of coffee."

September 30, 1866

NIGHT IN THE ETERNAL CITY

*R*ome's Piazza del Popolo: its marble lions and obelisk naked to the hot sky, morning shimmering up from the pavement. Before the doors to the church of Santa Maria del Popolo, Carlota furls her parasol—a black parasol, black to match her dress and mutilated bonnet. Madame del Barrio, close behind, furls her parasol also. They have already seen this church. Her Majesty and the remnants of her retinue have been in Rome now for five days. They seem to be going in circles. Madame del Barrio does not know what to do. Count Bombelles, the one person who would, was—by Her Majesty's order, given coldly—left behind in Trieste. Radonetz (one of Maximilian's most trusted men in charge of the administration of Miramar Castle), Her Majesty had, quite violently, accused of thievery. The Almontes—abandoned in Paris. Monsieur Eloin—dispatched to Brussels. It is all crashing down around them, and Carlota is obsessed with the notion that Louis Napoleon conspires to poison her. She is mad. *You can see it in her eyes,* said Frau von Kuhacsevich. *Deplorable,* Count del Valle said. *What will become of us all?* And Dr. Bohuslavek, he is so terribly young, he seems unsure of himself. He is afraid.

Madame del Barrio hands the two parasols, hers and the empress's, to José Luis Blasio. Blasio had arrived at Trieste two weeks ago, bearing Maximilian's instructions for Her Majesty's meeting with His Holiness here in Rome. And what happened in that meeting? In the three days that have gone by,

Her Majesty has not uttered one word about it, nonetheless, they all guessed the cruel thrust of it, for, on her return to the hotel from the Vatican, she instructed Count del Valle to dismiss—immediately—the pope's honor guard and the French military band.

In Santa Maria del Popolo's vestibule, after Her Majesty, Madame del Barrio and Blasio have knelt and crossed themselves, Blasio catches Madame del Barrio's eye. She can read his lips.

"Not again?"

What else can they do but obey their sovereign? Madame del Barrio can only hope that, perhaps, by midday Her Majesty will have exhausted herself. Her Majesty has not eaten since the day before yesterday, and then only nuts and oranges she insisted on peeling with her own hands. Mathilde, her maid, told Dr. Bohuslavek, who told Frau von Kuhacsevich, that Carlota sucked like a peasant at those oranges, for the water, she says, and the wine, *all* the liquids served to her are poisoned. Carlota cannot be reasoned with. This morning, a feverish flush in her cheeks, first thing, she flew to the Trevi Fountain, where she removed her gloves, bent over, and scooped the water with her hands! She then tore the veil from her bonnet, and wiped her face with that. *Here, at least, it will not be poisoned. I was so thirsty!*

Madame del Barrio and Blasio follow Her Majesty down the nave of Santa Maria del Popolo, pretending to listen to her rambling about its artistic treasures. Whenever the empress looks away, they dart glances at one another. She's speaking unnaturally fast, leaping from Bernini, to something Goethe wrote, to the Bible—

"Do you understand?" she asks Madame del Barrio.

"Yes, ma'am."

Carlota addresses the air to the left of her ear: "The time has come for silence."

Blasio drops one of the parasols.

"Silence!" Carlota cries.

Their footsteps echo, ten, eleven, twelve, and suddenly, she stops. Before the Caravaggio, she lights a taper. She falls upon the marble floor, and pressing her hands together in prayer, she seems to beseech the terrible scene itself:

Saint Peter crucified, upside down. The golden tones of the old man's flesh; the stake driven through the hand; the mouth agape in agony . . .

Not knowing what else to do, her lady and her secretary both kneel, the one a little way behind Her Majesty and to the left; the other to her right.

Madame del Barrio, her hand over her mouth, darts Blasio another look.

Carlota flings opens her arms, as if upon a crucifix. And then—they clearly hear it—her stomach growls.

There was, one long month and a half ago, a shard of a moment when it seemed to Charlotte that this nightmare was about to transmute into the Apotheosis of the True Destiny, when she drove up to Saint Cloud, and saw that, waiting there to receive her, stood Prince Louis.

She had come to Saint Cloud for her interview with Louis Napoleon: the aim of so many weeks, so much worry, letters and telegrams. She had been thinking of nothing else for weeks. So much depended this. She had become agitated, unable to eat. All the way in from the Grand-Hôtel, Charlotte was in such a state, she gripped Madame Almonte's hand. Madame Almonte gripped it back. The one Charlotte wanted, more than anyone, was her father. But her father was dead. Her brother, King Leopold II, cared not a fig, unless there was money in it for him. The Kaiser, in betraying her husband, had made himself her enemy. About Mexico Queen Victoria had shown only ignorance and priggish disdain. Grand-maman was also dead, she had not approved from the beginning. No one approved of Maximilan accepting this crown, except such as Louis Napoleon. And Madame Almonte. Together, in Charlotte's lap, their hands made one big fist. Charlotte could feel the little bones in her hand being crushed. "Thank you," she said to Madame Almonte, and at the look in her other lady, Madame del Barrio's eyes, they all three burst into tears. But then, as the terrible wheels rolled over the gravel of that drive and finally creaked to a halt, there—at the window: that shining boy in his uniform.

The Child of France. He calmed her so, like a puff of opium. His beautifully molded mouth was set in, not so much a smile but a unique expression at once elegant, martial, and kind. She knew this was a child who would be kind to his pets. He would speak to them; the pictures in their minds would float above his head like kites; he would know when they wanted water.

She accepted his small gloved hand. With what satisfaction she saw that, pinned to his chest, was the medal of the Order of the Mexican Eagle. It flashed in the sun.

Such sun. Madame del Barrio balanced the parasol over Charlotte's head.

Prince Louis led her up the path. He had celebrated his tenth birthday; and he was going to be devastatingly handsome.

"My, Louis, you have grown."

"Did you have a pleasant journey?"

"I had the journey God wished me to have."

Perfume of roses and gladiolas drifted in from the other side of the hedge. A dog barked in the distance. Their shoes made such noise upon the gravel. The sounds, the smells, they seemed to have blue shapes and conical colors.

"Did you call at Fort-de-France?" he asked.

"Not this time."

"Where did your ship take on coal?"

"Havana and Saint Thomas."

"Did you see any sperm whales?"

"No, but many dolphins."

They strode past the line of Praetorian guards. For some reason, they bothered her. She felt a noxious but scentless emanation from their gazes: disapproval. Pity. She, empress of Mexico, was not a human being to them. They, rigid as if cast in bronze, were not human beings to her. From beneath their visors, they were watching her with alien intelligence, as they would watch a prisoner being escorted to her execution.

As Prince Louis led her up the steps, she remembered to ask about his accident. In July he had fallen from his trapeze and suffered a concussion, from which, obviously, he was recovered.

"I am quite well now, thank you."

He did not ask her about Orizaba, as he did the last time. He asked nothing about Mexico. He recited no pretty list of native fruits and vegetables. At the top of the steps was Eugénie, and here Prince Louis, squaring his heels, took his leave. Eugenie brought Charlotte and her ladies inside: into the lair of Mephistopheles.

Todo es inútil, All is useless, she had telegrammed Max. If she never saw this Babylon again, she told Madame del Barrio, it would be too soon. She could not return to Mexico, not yet. Rome—she needed to go see His Holiness—but prudence made her go first to Trieste, and there await Maximilian's instructions.

Miramar, their ivory castle on the Bay of Grignano: its parterre, so lovingly designed and cared for, its pines and oaks and ilex trees receiving the sweet sea breezes. The gardener and his wife cried tears of happiness to see her. There were several cats she recognized, and three black kittens, darling fur balls. But how peculiar, like having become a ghost in her own life, to go into these rooms, Maximilian's library, his wood-paneled office. There was where he sat at his desk reading, writing letters. There was where he took his breakfast, there where he played billiards with Bombelles and Schertzenlechner. The music room with her pianoforte; she touched the keys but found no will to play. Her boudoir. For their wedding gift, the city of Milan had given them a bed. It was still there. She threw herself upon it—and cried.

Free of her, Max could have married a more suitable princess. Someone like Princess María Amelia de Braganza, his first love who died on Madeira. What a splendid empress she would have made, and her own half-brother, Dom Pedro II, Brazil's emperor of the Divine Holy Spirit. María Amelia, she was so sweet, so pure. Their children would have been beautiful.

And it occurred to Charlotte, and not for the first time, that it would have been better for Maximilian if she had died in Yucatan. She had begun to suspect this had been intended for her; two of the servants on that expedition contracted yellow fever. Scrupulously she had avoided fruit; nonetheless, attacked by headaches, dizziness—she was sure of it, she had been poisoned. Among the ruins of Uxmal, she had been overcome by a nameless dread that left her, for some minutes, unable to speak. The heat. The whirring hiss of insects. The sky: staccato of swallows. That nauseating smell of bat droppings. She did not know how it happened, perhaps she had floated to the top of that pyramid—there she was, empress of Mexico, surveying a realm of rubble, and encircling it all, trackless jungle.

Useless woman, she told herself. *Useless* to her husband, *useless* to her country—anchor on too short a chain, making the whole ship list. She should have produced an heir. It was so crucial for the stability of an empire—this empire of nine million; this empire larger than England, Scotland, Ireland, France, Spain, Sicily, Sardinia, and Prussia combined; this empire commanding two oceans—*of course* Louis Napoleon was jealous! And Almonte and Bazaine. With Carlota gotten rid of, it would be easier to replace Maximilian with General Bazaine—ah, wouldn't it. Franz Joseph was afraid of her also—for she alone had dared to stand up to the All-Highest—All-Highest of that cobbled-together empire. All of Austria, all of Hungary, the provinces—they loved Max.

These were the incontrovertible, shocking facts: nearly 550 million francs' worth of debt had been issued in Paris, of which 6 percent had been paid to the Mexican Imperial Treasury.

She knew she was being drugged. Her handwriting had become ragged. It was a titanic struggle to keep a leash on her thoughts, they raced and tumbled, faded into a kind of noisy fog. She was a doe, frozen in the middle of a clearing: enemies encircling her . . . creeping closer . . .

Woe to the vanquished, wrote Countess Hulst, in a letter of such venom and cowardice, it sickened her. Countess Hulst, her governess, had been opposed to the Mexican project from its inception, but now—in refusing the honor of the medal of the Order of San Carlos, now, in such insulting tones, now even she—even Countess Hulst had succumbed to the sirens of the Demon:

> *I told you so, I told you that you should not accept the crown of Mexico. You accepted it, and now look at the price you are so rightfully paying. Do not tempt Providence any further: get out of that deadly undertaking now, while you still have your honor and there is not too much danger.*

Fortified by indignation, Charlotte wrote to Max, *the republic is as poor a mother as Protestantism, and the monarchy is humanity's salvation.* This was no time to lay down arms! Sovereignty is a treasure more precious than life itself.

She had come to Rome two days before her appointment with the Holy Father. The first thing she learned upon arriving at the Albergo di Roma was that Mexico's consul, Galloti, whom she had been anxious to see had just left Mexico, returning to Rome, when he died onboard ship. His aide, a Mexican by the name of Velázquez de Leon, went on about how Galloti had so many times begged off Maximilian's summons, for he was so afraid of the yellow fever.

More probably, Charlotte suspected, Galloti had been poisoned.

Next, she learned that the German painter who had given the imperial party their tour of the sights back in 1864 had died. Roman fever, the concierge said. She brooded on that. He, too, must have been poisoned, for he was the picture of health, and with what strong thighs he climbed the steps of the Coliseum and, in the Forum, leapt like a gazelle over those fallen columns. Italians were wizards with poison. A jealous rival—a pinch of arsenic stirred in his beer!

When Henry IV visited the Louvre, he would touch only eggs he had boiled and peeled himself. The Jewish doctor Lopes tried to poison Queen Elizabeth by smearing poison on the pommel of her saddle; he was hanged, drawn, and quartered. Isn't it obvious, Prince Albert, Queen Victoria's consort, was poisoned? He was a Saxe-Coburg, the English conspired against him. Or—ah—the Fenians, they did it. Lead, antimony, mandrake—an overdose of tincture of laudanum, is that not what General Bazaine's first wife, supposedly, killed herself with? But perhaps she was not a suicide! *Strychnos Nux Vomica* works lightning-fast, but its bitter taste must be masked by honey; its victim dies with her hands in claws and spine so arched that only the head and the heels touch the bed. The Borgias had their formulae: crushed glass, belladonna, wolfsbane. Cleopatra: snake venom. Socrates: hemlock. Livia poisoned Augustus; Tiberius poisoned Germanicus. Agrippina fed Claudius a dish of poison mushrooms. Napoleon Bonaparte was given gargantuan doses of arsenic, that is why his body did not decompose. Neither did Marie-Louise of Bourbon's, and before she died, her fingernails fell off. Nero favored cherry laurel water, which contains cyanide. The signs of cyanide poisoning are anxiety, headache, drowsiness—check, check, check! (Her heart is pounding in her chest—)

Saint Peter was martyred in the Neronian gardens, at the foot of the Janiculum: Is not the Holy Father the successor of Saint Peter, first Apostle of the Son of God?

Her stomach makes another growl.

"*Pater noster* . . . Our father who art in Heaven . . . ," she begins, but then, as if possessed, she jerks her head back. Suddenly, she's on her feet again and swanning down the nave. It happens so quickly that Blasio scarcely has the chance to run ahead and open the door for her.

Her Majesty orders the coachman, "*Il Vaticano. È urgente!*"

Caray, the Vatican? Madame del Barrio does not dare ask what Her Majesty wants to see there. The carriage hurtles into the traffic; soon it clatters onto the bridge over the Tiber. In the nearing distance, the dome of Saint Peter's gleams through molten sunlight. They have already—three days ago, when Her Majesty had her audience with the pope—been given an extensive tour of the Vatican's museums. They had not seen the half of the Vatican, and still, it was more than a body could digest in a lifetime: the stupendous basilica with Bernini's baldachino overlooking the crypt of Saint Peter, Michelangelo's *Pietà*, all the gold, all the marble of all colors, the Sistine Chapel, Raphael's frescos, gallery upon gallery of Egyptian gold, Greek amphorae, Etruscan and Roman mosaics, busts, statues, sarcophagi, untold chalices, urns, and silken robes embroidered in China, paintings by Titian, Da Vinci, more Raphaels, more Michelangelos, *Adoration of the Magi* by Pinturrichio, and in the library, maps, illuminated manuscripts, incunabula . . .

What more could Her Majesty possibly want to see?

And that had not been Carlota's first visit to the Vatican. Often she spoke of her confirmation, when the pope first gave her the benediction, as he did again, three years ago, on her departure for Mexico. As she had told Madame del Barrio, taking communion from the Holy Father's hand was one of the most moving experiences of her life. In Saint Peter's, what had impressed her (more than the great art) were the confessionals, their little signs—"Italiano"; "Français"; "English"; "Español." That Christians of all the world could come here, to the True Home of the True Church, it was sublime consolation. To speak of it, her eyes had filled with tears.

Perhaps Her Majesty wants to confess?

Her Majesty puts her head out the window. She cries to the driver, "Not that entrance! I am going to see the pope!"

Horrified, Madame del Barrio says, "But Your Majesty is not dressed for an audience with the pope!"

"You forget, Manuelita, it is the emperors who make the rules of etiquette. They themselves are above them."

After this smoldering rebuke, Madame del Barrio falls silent.

In her impeccable Italian, Carlota instructs the driver, "Take my secretary back to the hotel. You need not return for me."

Madame del Barrio follows Carlota past the Swiss Guards, into the residential compound, and up the steps. The pope's secretary emerges. Blinking with surprise, he bows to Her Majesty.

"I must see the Holy Father."

"That is impossible. His Holiness is having his breakfast."

"I do not care. Tell him I am here."

In a moment, the pope's secretary ushers Her Majesty in; Madame del Barrio, cringing with embarrassment, watches the door to the pope's private chamber click shut.

The pope extends his hand for the empress of Mexico to kiss his ring—but she's collapsed at his feet, sobbing, her lips upon his slipper!

"*Per piacere* . . . Please, please help me, Father, I beg you! Louis Napoleon is trying to assassinate me!"

"What—assassinate—you?"

"Louis Napoleon has sent his spies, vipers nest in my own household, the von Kuhacseviches, and the doctor, and Vázquez de Leon and Count del Valle!"

"Vázquez del Leon and Count del Valle? What are you saying?"

"They are in Satan's pay."

"No, these are good men, your loyal subjects—"

"*Tutti, tutti* . . . All, all of them have been bribed . . . I beg you, Father, give me asylum! Inside the Vatican, it is the only place I can be safe!"

"Inside—?"

Again she kisses his slipper. "Permit me to sleep at your feet."

"No, no—"

"Give me a bedroom then!"

Never has a woman, not even a nun, slept beneath the roof of the Vatican. "Impossible!"

"Then I shall sleep in the corridor! I would sleep on the floor, oh Father . . ." she heaves with sobs, "Oh, Father, I am so afraid . . . The poison . . ."

The pope looks up to see the undisguised disgust on his secretary's face, but being a man of gentle nature and genuine good heart, the pope wonders, could it be? In centuries past, a pope or two has been poisoned, is this not so? He has to shift his weight; Her Majesty is clinging to his ankles. "There, there." He pats the top of her head. But his nascent credulity, a fine, fattening montgolfier, all of a sudden deflates: she's jumped up and stuck her fingers into his cup of chocolate. She licks her fingers.

"I am starving! Everything they give me is poisoned!"

"Well, my goodness, well! I'll have them bring you a cup of chocolate."

"No! I will only drink out of Your Holiness's cup; if they know it is for me, it will be poisoned."

"In that case, by all means—"

She tips back his cup, gulping it to the dregs. She then licks the inner lip of it. Her pupils seem dilated; there is a strange light in her eyes. She rushes to his desk and snatches up the silver goblet.

"Father, give me this so that I may drink without being poisoned."

A souvenir of a visit to the shrine of Our Lady of Loreto, it is such a large and heavy goblet he has never used it for drinking. To his astonishment—and at this point, he hadn't thought he could be astonished any further—with her teeth, Her Majesty tears off one tie of her bonnet and, knotting the ribbon around the neck of the goblet, thus secures it to her belt.

"Now, Father, I want to discuss Mexico." She plants herself on a sofa.

This is the opportunity for his secretary to slip out and alert Cardinal Antonelli.

"Yes?" the pope says smoothly, easing back into his chair.

She begins a breathless ramble on the province of Yucatan, San Luis Potosí, the archbishop of Mexico—a farrago of nonsense, accusation, and natural history, but then she interrupts herself: "What is the most effective antidote to poison?"

"The rosary and prayer, my child."

She asks him again. His answer does not deviate.

The Demon has given this madwoman the tentacles of an octopus. Not until nearly midday, thanks to Cardinal Antonelli's behind-the-scenes orchestration, is the pope finally able to give her the slip. Her lady, being closely questioned, had informed Cardinal Antonelli that the empress is an aficionada of illuminated manuscripts. The pope, therefore, led Her Mexican Majesty into the library and, just as he slid open the drawer of a cabinet and took out one to show her, very quietly, in came the cardinal and Madame del Barrio.

"Father, this is as beautiful as anything by Memling."

"Bright colors, yes," agreed the pope.

"The script is Gothic."

"Yes, my child, it is . . ."

With chocolate-stained fingers, she turned another page of the thirteenth-century treasure. "Ah! The story of the good shepherd . . ."

"Look at the little sheep," the pope said, "how finely drawn they are."

"Their hooves, their tiny ears . . ."

"Very nice . . . a very nice story. . . . I should like to sit here and listen to you read it," he said. "Would you do that for me?"

"Sit here?"

"Yes. Sit here and read me the story."

When, after a little while, Her Majesty looked up and did not see the Holy Father, she became agitated, but Madame del Barrio, feigning an exaggerated interest in the manuscript, managed to calm her. This part of the library was the first of the Paoline rooms. They had been in here the other day, admiring the ceiling frescos and the many paintings commemorating the donations made by European sovereigns: *The Donation by Emperor Constantine I to Pope Sylvester I; The Emperor Ludwig I, the Pius, confirms to Pasquale I the Donations Made by His Ancestors;* and more: Otto I the Great; Otto IV of Wittelsbach; Frederick II; Rodolfo I; and last, *Henry VII, the legate of Albert I of Habsburg, King of the Romans confirms the rights of the Holy See to Pope Boniface VIII.*

She insisted on reciting the complete title of each painting. Only then could she be induced to proceed, very hesitantly, clutching tightly to Madame del Barrio's arm, into the second of the Paoline rooms. Here, again, the frescos of angels and commemorations of the ancient donations, and the elaborately inlaid poplar cabinets with the coat of arms of the Borghese: crowned eagle and winged dragon. This library, a wonder of this world, contained the proceedings of the trial of Galileo, the absolution of the Knights of Templar, the—

Her Majesty interrupted. Was that door there not to the stairway to the Tower of the Winds, the Vatican's astronomical observatory? Because the other day, they had not seen that.

It was closed, Cardinal Antonelli said.

Why was it closed?

It was being used as a bedroom.

"Ah, I could sleep there!"

Smoothly, Cardinal Antonelli suggested a tour of the Vatican gardens; Her Majesty accepted. And thus was she ushered out of the building.

For Mexico, alas, the pope could do nothing. The Vatican would not, nay, could not presume to pressure Louis Napoleon when it was his bayonets preventing the loss of Rome to the Italian patriots. Nor could the Vatican take any step whatsoever in regards to Mexico without the support of its clergy, which had not been forthcoming. While the Mexican Republic had confis-

cated church property, neither had Maximilian's imperial government reinstated it. Furthermore, neither had Maximilian respected the Catholic as the
One True Faith. He had been encouraging Protestants to immigrate from
Europe and the Confederacy. It was said that both his personal physician and
one of his closest advisors were Jews. It was also rumored—widely retailed in
Vienna—that, when he was viceroy, in Milan, secretly, Maximilian had been
inducted into the Freemasons.

There was not yet a concordat with Mexico. It had both surprised Cardinal Antonelli and embarrassed him before the pontiff that the empress of
Mexico had come to Rome at all. But the Vatican did care, and profoundly,
about the health of its relations with the ruling families of Austria, France,
and the many other Catholic principalities to which this disturbed young
woman was related by blood. Cardinal Antonelli had already sent word to the
Belgian ambassador; the king would need to have a family member take custody of his sister. Count Bombelles and a certain Dr. Jilek, the cardinal ascertained, had been summoned from Trieste yesterday, but it would be a few
days until these people could be expected in Rome. A madwoman in the Vatican! He would have a better idea what to do with a greased pig. For now,
Cardinal Antonelli would have to rely on two Roman alienists, a white-
bearded professor and his well-muscled colleague, to whom the cardinal lent
priests' garb and presented to Her Mexican Majesty as "Papal Chamberlains."
The alienists bowed deeply before her.

In the gardens, she dipped the pope's goblet into a fountain and drank
from it. They all—Cardinal Antonelli, Madame del Barrio, and the two "Papal Chamberlains"—behaved as if this were normal. Cardinal Antonelli's
purpose was to induce her to return to the Albergo di Roma, peaceably and
immediately. It was imperative that the Vatican wash its hands, as it were, of
responsibility for what was an appalling and unprecedented scandal. In the
garden Carlota went into ecstasies over the statue of a fawn; she had to discuss the manner of pruning a certain topiary—she would not budge from the
gardens. As it was well into the afternoon, Cardinal Antonelli, seeing no decent alternative, invited the women to lunch. Carlota ate heartily, but only
from the plate of her lady.

A hot meal of soup, pasta, and roast lamb seemed to have lulled her, and Cardinal Antonelli was now able to convince her, that, as he had, in accord with her wishes, arranged the arrest of her Viennese doctor, and others in her retinue, she should go back to the Albergo di Roma.

Outside, the same carriage and coachman that had brought her were waiting. In a thistley tone she said to the coachman, "I told you not to wait for me."

"I personally recalled him for you," Cardinal Antonelli said. "He is the best driver in Rome."

"Is he?"

"He is famous. No one drives a carriage more expertly, more safely." Antonelli bowed. "Madame, he is entirely at your disposal."

Carlota climbed inside with her lady. But before the guard could secure the latch, Carlota reemerged. The pope's goblet, still tied to her waist, banged against the edge of the door.

She addressed the cardinal. "I will not have to see the ones who want to kill me?"

"Your Highness is very safe."

"I will not see traitors nor thieves nor liars?"

"You will not."

"No poisoners?"

"None."

"You are sure, all the conspirators are gone?"

He cleared his throat. "Absolutely all."

She turned around. But after one hesitant step up, she stopped. "My chamberlain, Count del Valle, has been arrested also?"

"Yes, Your Highness."

"They are all gone?"

"All gone."

She climbed back inside. But then—the door popped open—she climbed back out.

"What about my servant, Mathilde Doblinger?"

"According to your wishes, Madame, she has also been arrested."

"And the von Kuhacseviches?"

"Yes."

The cardinal inclined his head with solemnity.

At the foot of the marble steps, the cardinal waited. His obsidian eyes narrowed. He wanted to be certain that that carriage would not be coming back. Only when the vehicle, gaining speed, had passed out of earshot did he turn, and quickly, so that his scarlet robes billowed out. With his characteristic energy, he took the stairs. His footsteps were perfectly regular, like the beating of a drum.

When Charlotte arrived at the Albergo di Roma, no hacks waited outside at the curb. The sidewalk had been cleared of its flower-sellers, touts, shoe-shine boys, and beggars.

"Where are the porters?" she asked her lady.

"I do not know, Your Majesty," Madame del Barrio replied.

"They had to arrest them also?"

Madame del Barrio stammered, "Yes—I suppose."

In the lobby, beneath the sign that said TUTTE LA COMODITÀ MODERNA, a hastily folded newspaper had been abandoned on a sofa; a tea service and half-eaten plates of cake covered a table.

"And the concierge?"

"I do not know."

"You know very little, Manuelita."

Madame del Barrio blushed and stared at her gloves.

Upstairs, in the hallway, they encountered no one. At the door to her suite, Charlotte waited for Madame del Barrio to open it with the key. As if pulled by some unseen hand on the other side, the door creaked in. The room, hot, gloom-soaked, was agitated by the sounds of traffic. One of the windows overlooking the Corso had been left ajar.

After the sumptuousness of the Vatican, this "royal suite" looked so mean. The upholstery should have been replaced; the arms on some of the chairs had been rubbed bald. The furnishings seemed sparse and overwrought. In what was left of the sunlight, every stain and scuff stood out. Beneath a bulls-eye mirror, a torn thumb of wallpaper shivered.

Madame del Barrio lit the lamp on the mantel.

From the threshold Charlotte said, "Shut the window."

Madame del Barrio pulled the window in.

"I won't come in."

"Why not?"

"Someone is hiding behind the drapes!"

"No, ma'am." Madame del Barrio gathered the drapes in her arms, and turned them inside out. "You see?"

"Look behind the sofa."

"No one is there, Your Majesty."

"The divan!"

"No, ma'am. It is safe."

Carlota put a foot inside, but at once she withdrew it. From the hallway, she said: "Check the bedrooms."

In a moment, Madame del Barrio came back to the door. "Your Majesty . . ." There was no need to whisper, but she whispered: *"It is quite safe."*

Charlotte stepped over the threshold and immediately, she knew—her arms turned to gooseflesh—something was wrong.

"Where is Mathilde?"

"Your Majesty wanted her arrested."

"Oh, that's right. You take my hat, then."

"Perhaps Your Majesty might lie down and rest?"

"Yes, Manuelita, I would like to rest."

"Take my arm."

"Thank you . . ." Before the door to her bedroom, Charlotte shrank back and screamed, "The key!"

"The key?" There was no key in the door to the bedroom.

"They have taken it! They plan to lock me inside! Then they can murder me!" She tore the hat out of her lady's hands and flung it back on her head.

"Where is Your Majesty going?" Madame del Barrio cried, running after her. The answer came when they were both, breathless, on the sidewalk once again. Carlota flagged a passing hack.

"Il Vaticano. È urgente!"

• • •

In a matter of minutes the empress's retinue emerged from their rooms—new rooms on higher floors—and swarmed down into her salon, where the same lamp Madame del Barrio had just lit, flickered weakly on the mantel.

Frau von Kuhacsevich, first to arrive, lit another lamp; out of sheer nerves she went about plumping the sofa cushions. Then, as she feared she would faint, she sank, despondent, into the sofa. José Louis Blasio took the edge of that sofa and sat hunched with his hands between his knees. Count del Valle commandeered the mantel, but the chamberlain, del Barrio, Madame del Barrio's husband, ousted him, and he in turn was interrupted by the Mexico's acting consul in Rome, Velázquez de Leon, and he by Herr Jakob von Kuhacsevich who allowed, he may have only been the Purser of the Imperial Household, but he'd known Maximilian and Charlotte since before their marriage, and—

Someone said they'd heard her screaming about a key.

Ein Schlüssel!

Una llave.

Where is it?

Who took it?

What key?

Dr. Bohuslavek moved into the circle. He dangled the key from his fingers. "The one to her bedroom."

By Jove.

Caray!

What possessed you?

Upon whose authority?

"Upon my honor," Dr. Bohuslavek said stiffly, but he was so very young and he looked as if he were about to cry. "I took the key in case, in the night, she should go into a rage."

Now you've done it!

Wooden-headed!

Said nothing to me—a mi no me dijo—

Die Dringlichkeit der Situation steht außer Frage—

Fresh out of medical school, thinks he knows everything.

From the sofa Frau von Kuhasevich wailed, "Now she'll never trust any of us!"

Frightened her out of her wits—

Already out of her wits—

Hysterischer Anfall—

The bromide in her coffee, someone gave her cannabis, all the symptoms—

Blunder after blunder—

The voices barraged him; the men crowded into him. The doctor, so as not to fall into the chair, had to take a step back. The chair's leg made a squeak on the floor. Dr. Bohuslavek took out his handkerchief and disguised his emotion with noisy coughing.

But these were delicate people with delicate manners; soon, like a summer shower, their angry words had passed.

"Dr. Bohuslavek," Frau von Kuhacsevich began in her most generous and careful Spanish, "I know that you were only doing what you thought best."

Yes, perhaps the only thing that could be done.

Count Bombelles and Dr. Jilek—

Be here soon enough.

And her brother, the Count of Flanders.

"*Ach,* Matty," Frau von Kuhacsevich said, turning to the maid who had been hovering in the doorway. "What is to become of us?" She said this in German, but it needed no translation.

Mathilde Doblinger knit her hands together. She looked at Count del Valle. They all, the whole circle of them, looked at Count del Valle.

Count del Valle held his hand to his cheek as if, in this way, he could keep his teeth inside his head. He was a shining specimen of New World aristocrat from his shoes to his cravat, from his manicured nails to his waxed mustache. Slowly, the be-ringed fingers came down to his chin. He gave his chin a scratch.

Pigeons had gathered on the ledge.

Frau von Kuhacsevich thought, if only Father Fischer were here. He could dispense that healing balm of spiritual solace. Poor Charlotte; she has no family, no friend of her own rank to confide in. Perhaps Princess Iturbide—perhaps. Pointless conjecture.

It was all pointless.

Frau von Kuhacsevich began to weep.

THE ROAD TO ORIZABA

*I*n Mexico City's axe-bright morning, Mrs. Yorke's parlor has all the ambiance of a cave of gloom. Princess Iturbide, the visitor around whom Mrs. Yorke and the others form a rapt circle, lowers her teacup to her lap and her voice to the gruffness, if not the chocolately smoothness, of Father Fischer's:

"Do not doubt it! The Mexican Empire will endure for a thousand years!"

"Father Fischer said that?" Astounded, Doña Juliana de Gómez Pedraza fastens her lorgnette to her eye. Has Princess Iturbide lost her senses? For the word, directly from her niece, Madame Bazaine, is that Maximilian has received a stern letter from Louis Napoleon ("not an ecu or one man more") and has been convinced, finally, to abdicate. Carlota is said to be too ill, no one knows of what, to return to Mexico. What to believe? What does it matter? Maximilian's goose is cooked, and only by a miracle of Lazarus will it rise from its pan and waddle out of the oven! As all of Mexico City knows, three days ago, at three in the morning, from Chapultepec Castle, Maximilian, a wagon-train of luggage and an escort of three hundred Austrian Hussars up and fled—what other word is there? By now, the highway may have brought Maximilian past Río Frío and perhaps as far as Puebla.

"Yes," Princess Iturbide says, "Father Fischer said exactly that, and I will tell you what's more." She fixes Madame Bazaine, who perches on the divan to her left, with an "I-dare-you" but not altogether unfriendly look. Princess

Iturbide—abandoned without income, without a bodyguard (Weissbrunn took off, whether with his regiment or what, she knows not), and with an innocent child in her care, and fewer "friends" by the day—walks a tightrope, and she knows it. She needs General Bazaine's protection, if all fails, and she and Prince Agustín are to escape with their lives. She has been mortified—to her core—by Maximilian's abrupt departure—"*me voy a mi pueblo,*" like a servant!—but! Princess Iturbide is not one to set aside so hastily her sacred duty to serve her country. Is she not her father's daughter? She has had to sell her diamond bracelet (and at a price that constituted robbery!) that she might stock her pantry, feed her horses, and continue to have her coiffure arranged by a professional, rather than be seen in an anonymous old-lady's lace cap, as Doña Juliana has been reduced to doing. On the lapel of her jacket she wears a brooch rimmed in pearls, with a miniature portrait of Prince Agustín, her message to all: Make no mistake where my loyalties lie.

Thank Heaven for Father Fischer!

It was Father Fischer who convinced the cabinet not to resign en bloc should Maximilian abandon the capital, and he who engineered the synod. Prelates from every corner of the empire are arriving. The Holy Church, reaffirmed, will help Maximilian raise a new army and vanquish the Juaristas.

Princess Iturbide continues, "It is a grave miscalculation to imagine that, being a gentleman and a Habsburg, Maximilian would ever entertain the idea of 'abdication.' He will only go so far as Orizaba, for purely practical motives of being closer to whatever news may come from the empress, and, on the advice of his doctor."

Doña Juliana exchanges a grim glance with her niece. Mrs. Yorke, wedged into a corner of her sofa, horrified, covers her mouth.

Princess Iturbide, an ironclad of calm, surges on: "Dr. Basch has diagnosed His Majesty with a mild case of malaria. Father Fischer suggested Orizaba as having the most salubrious climate for His Majesty to rest and recuperate."

"Orizaba, *salubrious?*" Madame Blanchot scoffs. "All I remember is its ghastly nonstop drizzle, the—what do they call it?"

Mrs. Yorke answers, in the tone of an undertaker: "The *chipichipi.*"

From the opposite end of Princess Iturbide's sofa, in a curiously accented Spanish, half-Baltimore-half-Cuban, comes the remark: "Ah, but Orizaba's luscious oranges, kisses from the sun itself!"

All eyes turn to the newcomer who has interjected this vivacious impertinence. A consensus about this person has not quite gelled. Princess Iturbide's attitude toward her is one of open-armed indulgence, for Father Fischer befriended this lady and her husband on the ship from New York to Veracruz and has warmly recommended her. A darling out of Washington—acquainted, so she claims, with President Johnson, many senators, and members of Congress, and what's more—she is a real princess, married (in a Catholic mass, Saint Patrick's on F Street) to Prince Felix Salm-Salm, then serving in the U.S. Army. She and her prince have come to Mexico that he might see action in the civilizing cause of his fellow German, for whom, he says, he has always felt a deep sympathy. Princess Salm-Salm has no child, but a black-and-tan terrier named Jimmy, who sits by her skirts on the sofa, alert as a little sphinx, with her dainty hand resting upon his velvet head. (Jimmy's favorite foods, she has confided to all, are veal, oysters, and the yolks of hard-boiled eggs.)

What none but Princess Iturbide knows is that, thanks to Father Fischer, overriding the bitter and absurd jealousies of senior Austrian offers who refused to accept a Prussian, and some of whom have gone so far as to assert that "Prince Salm-Salm" is an imposter, the Salm-Salms had been invited to dine in Chapultepec *en petit comité* with Maximilian. They were to be given a mission more vital, more brilliant, than any military action: to take two million dollars in gold to Washington and there secure U.S. recognition for the Mexican Empire. Thus, the "open sesame" for trade—the trade Mexico so desperately thirsts for! And colonists, crowds of them, the best people! Mexico may have been abandoned by the Old World with its musty prejudices and fossilized rivalries, but it could be embraced by the new, the brash powerhouse of its neighbor to the north—with this, yes, miracles can happen!

Why, in circumstances far more dire, had not Frederick the Great of Prussia had his last-minute reprieve?

The Salm-Salms' dinner was canceled, however, when the news from

Rome and Miramar left Maximilian unable to speak. And this was when Princess Iturbide nearly came to blows with Dr. Semeleder's replacement, another Johnny-come-lately, that presumptuous Viennese Hebrew. Dr. Basch barred Maximilian's bedroom door and refused to let Princess Iturbide—La Prima!—in to talk sense to Maximilian—it was outrageous!! But Father Fischer is wise to all of these things . . .

Do not doubt it! For Princess Iturbide, and all those of the conservative party, Father Fischer's words have been a comfort beyond price.

As soon as the two princesses have left, Mrs. Yorke, whisking the dog hairs off her sofa, says, "I hardly know what to think."

She means, about Maximilian, but Madame Blanchot misunderstands. "They say she performed in a circus."

The Viscountess de Noue has arrived, shaking loose her mantilla, and with a toss of her head so that her earrings bobble, and with venomous delight: "In Baltimore."

"Baltimore!"

The Viscountess de Noue slides onto the sofa next to Madame Blanchot. "When she married Salm-Salm in Washington, she told me, she did not speak German and he did not speak English."

"Ah ça!"

Laughter all around. Soon Madame Bazaine and her aunt, Doña Juliana, take their leave, and the coterie switches to French, and a freer dissection of Princess Salm-Salm's hapless groom, *très ridicule,* wrinkly codger, can't go back to Europe because he owes money from Paris to Vienna, and so on. To listen to unkind gossip is not really Mrs. Yorke's style, however. Much as it perturbs her to find herself and her daughters mixed into such uncertain society as with these queer adventurers—who knows, the "Salm-Salms" could be imposters, after all—she is anxious to glean what information she can, for they are all, all of them together, as she likes to say, in the same "tussie-mussie," the same clutch of herbs and flowers and perhaps, well, some weeds, too. A terrible storm is descending upon them. Her plan: to leave Mexico under the protection of her son-in-law, Captain Blanchot, that is, with General Bazaine's caravan, the last contingent of the French troops to evacuate, early in the new year.

By the time her youngest, Sara, has returned from her morning's excursion to Chapultepec, the small raisin cake, to its last crumb, has been eaten. The tea, though piping hot and served with limes, is so weak it tastes insipid. These days, tea is almost as costly as silver!

Mrs. Yorke pours her visitors fresh cups.

Sara, who went up to the castle with a party of French officers and curious friends, recounts what they saw: shirts left hanging in a closet; cupboard doors wide open, a plate of toast on a bedside table. The fine things, the carpets and paintings, tapestries, silver, most of the light fixtures and statuary, have all been removed. Birds were flying about the stairwell.

They picture this in silence. They had all been invited, at one time or another, to a ball or one of the empress's Monday *tertulias* in the palace downtown, but the castle, being the Imperial Residence, was unknown to these ladies, except from a distance. All of Mexico City, all of the entire Valley of Anahuac, in fact, had vantage points from which to see it there, emerging like a ship from its foamy sea of ahuehuete trees in the surrounding park below. Proud Chapultepec Castle, its windows sparkling in the sun, tufa pink at sunset, had always stood like a vault for a sovereign's secret and beautiful dreams.

"The thieves worked so fast?" Mrs. Yorke says.

"Captain Blanchot said it was deliberate, everything had been carefully packed to be sent to Europe."

The viscountess says, "Yesterday, my coachman heard it from Princess Iturbide's, that with his own eyes, he saw crates marked 'To the Super-Intendant, Miramar Castle.'"

Outside Mrs. Yorke's window, a sudden rattle of wheels over the cobblestones. Then, the knife-sharpener's shrill whistle and the fading cries of a vegetable-seller. Yet no one speaks, each communing with her own private reflections, fears, judgments, sympathies, disdains, which is to say, knitting into some semblance of logic a why, a how, and especially, whose fault it is that it has come to this *sauve qui peut*. The spell is broken, at last, by the hostess, who says something that surprises everyone, most of all herself:

"Poor Princess Iturbide."

No one answers. No one likes Princess Iturbide.

Mrs. Yorke trembles. An emotion she has not before acknowledged, in regards to the princess, wells up from her heart into her throat, which feels very tight. Four years ago, Mrs. Yorke's own son, carrying a message for Mr. Thomas Corwin, was waylaid by bandits and murdered on the highway near Perote.

"You—you have children, or you will, with God's blessing. You have your whole lives in front of you."

The viscountess blinks. Little Sara takes in a sharp breath.

Mrs. Yorke, embarrassed, looks away. Her eyes, moistly, rest on the piano. It is a handsome piece of furniture and though its innards would not impress a concert-hall maestro, one of the French officers billeted in her spare room keeps it in fine tune. Soon, she will be obliged to sell it, or give it away, and in the days to come, some desperate Mexican may hack it to bits for firewood . . . but for now . . . She pats her youngest's hand, and, switching to English:

"Sara, darling—" she gives her a gentle nudge. "Play us some Schubert."

In an hacienda outside Puebla, from an unseen corner of the back patio come the labored strains of a march by Chopin. In its dining room, a rustic hall, Maximilian, vaguely, in German:

"It is the music, more than anything, that I miss."

Professor Bilimek, with sympathy, but unusual liberty: "The band, they do their best."

Maximilian gazes out the window, where Popocatépetl, but an hour ago, magnificently glistening, had disappeared behind mist. The view has been degraded to a muddy field and a herd of appallingly filthy sheep. He pokes a fork at Tüdos's *amuse-gueule* of overripe melon and pickled nopal. Professor Bilimek and Dr. Basch try to buoy his spirits, which have never sunk so low . . . to the very waterline . . . no. . . .

They *have* sunk this low once before: when he learned that his betrothed, his beloved angel, Princess María Amelia de Braganza, had died in her mother's arms on the island of Madeira. That solid-granite grief, pressing so heavily on one's chest, one feels one cannot breathe!

Poor Charlotte!

A king who is about to forfeit his kingdom, is his sorrow but a pinch of salt compared to that of a bereaved husband?

After Louis Napoleon's brutal betrayal, Charlotte fell ill, of what, no one could say. One had assumed it was the Roman fever. The blow of blows came last week with Charlie's telegram from Miramar. Herzfeld had some trouble deciphering it, or pretended to. He read it aloud, haltingly. *Her Majesty's . . . safe . . . arrival. Dr. Reidel called in, and . . . Dr. Reidel not having given up hope . . .*

"Dr. Reidel, do you know him?" Maximilian asked Dr. Basch.

"He is the director of the Vienna Lunatic Asylum."

A block of ice in his stomach. It was as if he had been told she was dead—but she was not—and—ah!—still—he could go to her! A magnetic force seemed to pull him—*to Charlotte! To Miramar!* How he had neglected her, why had he not seen, of course, oh God, of course, intelligent as she was, a female brain was incapable of sustaining the strain of so much responsibility, and over the years she had weakened it with excessive reading, he should have recognized that, what had he been thinking to send her to Yucatan, then to Paris—Rome—oh! And her father had died and her beloved Grand-maman, and she was so heartbroken—she must have, oh, oh . . . *What had he done?* He *had* to go to her. At once! To their ivory castle by the sea, where he would take her in his arms, and away—away from cold, dark Europe, to the healing sun of Corfu.

Or Patmos.

Rajasthan. Tahiti. The Great Wall of China!

Were she not well enough, they could stay close to home and, come spring, cruise up the Adriatic to Lacroma, their private island of pines and myrtle and, in the ruin of Richard the Lionhearted's refuge, its peace broken only by the murmur of the sea and birdsong, cascades of the most fragrant roses . . .

He longed with all his soul to go out upon the sea again, to cross that Lake of Oblivion.

Maximilian ordered Dr. Basch to keep Princess Iturbide away. He decided he was going to go to Charlotte, damn the consequences, damn that woman's shouting at poor Dr. Basch.

After a sleepless night, however, a certain worry began to unravel his idea: But if he went to the empress, would his subjects believe this was his sole motive for the journey? Would they think their sovereign was abandoning them?

Herzfeld, who had advocated abdication, allowed that, well, it could appear that way.

"It *certainly* would appear that way," Father Fischer said.

Father Fischer: six solid feet of soutane, below which were Roman-made shoes with buckles and soles thick enough to withstand a walk the length of Mexico, up and down, forty times.

His Majesty was not tempted by the devil of abdication?

"No, no. Oh, no. That I would never do."

Maximilian had given Charlotte his word. But . . . if . . . she were no longer in her right mind?

Or . . . perhaps he could leave Mexico, for a little while without signing any piece of paper . . . Was it not so that, before God, and before her father, and all their family, he had made a vow to honor and protect her?

Maximilian asked Dr. Basch, "Will *anyone* believe that my going to Europe is only because of the empress's illness?"

Dr. Basch, apparently, did not yet feel confident enough in his place nor his experience to commit to an unequivocal answer. Maximilian talked and talked, in circles and then into knots.

His health had broken down, he suffered night sweats, fevers, stabbing stomach pains, and those pains in the liver, too, and when Dr. Basch diagnosed him with malaria, Maximilian confided to Herzfeld, "I have decided to abdicate."

Herzfeld's response was swift. "Very good, sir."

"You think it wise?"

"Affirmative."

Herzfeld's counsel was a lifesaver on these drowning seas. "My good man," Maximilian said. "Your unbiased opinion. You *really* consider it wise?"

"Louis Napoleon has not upheld his part of the bargain. He has broken the Treaty of Miramar. The military situation and the finances—"

"But I have no future in Austria . . . Father Fischer maintains that—"

"Get out now, sir, when you have the chance."

And so, from Chapultepec Castle, the orders went to Veracruz, where the imperial luggage was already being loaded on the ship, to prepare for Maximilian's arrival—but then, like a bull that has been whistled at, Father Fischer came in with thunder:

"If Herzfeld were not such a good friend of Your Majesty's, I would suspect him of being in the pay of France." How much blood had been shed for this holy enterprise, what catastrophic consequences would be unleashed, more blood on his hands, and the stain of dishonor!

Maximilian, weakly: "But what honor is there in abandoning my helpless wife?"

Father Fischer did not answer that. Smoothly switching gears: "Your Majesty's grief over the empress's illness is entirely understandable." With priestly gentleness, he brought his hands together, fingertips to his lips. His eyes slid over to Dr. Basch. Dr. Basch looked at Professor Bilimek, the gentle botanist and Capuchin friar with whom, on many a butterfly-catching expedition, Maximilian had probed his spiritual concerns. Professor Bilimek had, more than once, when pressed, offered his opinion that the October 3rd Decree was unchristian, and that, in the current circumstance, Maximilian should abdicate. But now, under the wilting gaze of present company, the botanist, stroking a beard that had grown very white, stared at the mute oracle of his shoes.

Maximilian twisted his ring. Everything had already been planned, the October 3rd Decree repealed, furnishings and papers put into crates. He felt like a prisoner who had been pardoned—and then at the gates, vistas before him, grabbed back by the collar.

"I cannot remain here—I *must*—"

Father Fischer interrupted, holding up both palms. "Orizaba." He quoted Goethe, *Über allen Gipfeln ist Ruh* . . . Over all the mountaintops is peace. "Your Majesty is not well. Leave this climate. In Orizaba, Your Majesty can rest, and then—" Father Fischer rubbed his hands together—"with more information from Europe and the United States, Your Majesty can better see to the bottom of things."

No, Father Fischer went on, by no means should Herzfeld come along. Herzfeld must remain in Mexico City, for who better to take charge of critical tasks such as assuring the Austrian and Belgian volunteers that it is true that the empress is ill, and that these brave men have certainly not been abandoned?

Father Fischer would hasten to Orizaba, to arrange for His Majesty's reception there.

Mexicalcingo. Ajotla. (For security reasons, initially, Maximilian was taking a very round-about and back route toward Orizaba.) Then Hacienda Socyapán, where, during a lengthy walk, Professor Bilimeck convinced Maximilian to stand firm in his decision—that is, to rescind the October 3rd Decree and, then, abdicate. But then Maximilian decided not to abdicate, at least not yet, for Hacienda Socyapán was, by no means, a sufficiently dignified venue for such an important act. And so, in limbo, back on the road to Orizaba, and on to another, tired, nondescript, hacienda.

Broth, fragrant with sherry, arrives in a clay pot. Outside the dining-room window, the mist begins to lift. Already a slice of Wedgwood blue hangs above the hump of Popocatépetl.

Long ago, with Charlie and Professor Bilimek, he had climbed it partway. He had wanted to see into the famous crater into which Cortez's men had been lowered by means of ropes, that they might replenish their supply of sulphur. But Maximilian and his men did not have the heavy clothes and crampons. Nor time. There has never been enough time.

Maximilian cocks his ear toward the music. "Donazetti?"

Dr. Basch, just as the set ends: "Verdi, sir."

Professor Bilimek slurps his soup.

Etiquette dictates that no one speak in the presence of the sovereign until spoken to; therefore, in tautest silence, the three men butter their bread.

On leaving Chapultepec, Maximilian's mind had rocked like the carriage itself. Hoist sails, weigh anchor? Furl sails, drop anchor? To leave Mexico or not to leave Mexico—forever—or, temporarily, for Charlotte's sake? That one was here in Mexico at all was for her sake. But her admonition rang in his ears: *Emperors do not give themselves up! So long as there is an emperor, there is an empire, though he have but six feet of ground, for the empire is nothing without the emperor.*

Was he Sisyphus or Hercules, Tantalus or Icarus, or all of them, all at the same time? He felt himself living in a nightmare painted by Hieronymus Bosch.

What if he were to arrive in Miramar to find that Dr. Reidel has already cured her? His journey would be for naught, and Mexico, in its sovereign's absence, could be lost forever. Ludicrous he would be then—no longer a member of the House of Habsburg, he would have nothing, be nothing—a laughingstock, the Rigoletto of Europe!

On the other hand, without the French, the treasury run dry, the Juaristas gaining strength by the day, Almonte conniving with Santa Anna, the empire is doomed.

This swindle foisted upon him by Louis Napoleon, heir of Krampus!

Bitter is the memory of that letter Louis Napoleon sent when Maximilian, not yet having affixed his signature to that accursed Family Pact, had decided to refuse the crown, and Louis Napoleon answered thus:

What would you really think of me if, when Your Imperial Highness had already reached Mexico, I were suddenly to say that I can no longer fulfill the conditions to which I have set my signature?

As a matter of principle, Maximilian refused to receive General Bazaine— but Bazaine's man, Pierron, urged him to abdicate. Pierron said the same Bazaine had said, *The Juaristas will not show you the mercy you have shown them.*

And how to forget that scene in Claremont with Charlotte's Grand-maman when, as they were leaving, she gripped Charlotte's hands, crying, *"They will assassinate you!"*

In his childhood, the older ones often spoke of their aunt and cousin, Marie-Antoinette.

The guillotine.

A noose.

An axe, a sword, a dagger, a barber's razor.

Poison.

He'd had a presentiment, from the time he was a small boy, that his would not be a natural death.

A firing squad: that was Iturbide's fate.

As for the Iturbides . . . What to do, what to do—each avenue of this maze sticky as a piece of *tzictli*. For to return the prince to his parents would annul the contract, and signal that the empire has no future, while to keep him . . . By what right take an innocent child to the possible abyss? How to steer between the Scylla of La Prima and the Charybdis of Doña Alicia and the other Iturbides? To satisfy the former would cause the latter to persist in their scandal, a scandal perhaps fatal to conservative support in Mexico, fatal to all hope for U.S. recognition. The parents have departed Paris for Washington. They continue to send letters, always the same drumbeat of a request: their child.

One is not an ogre. But neither is one a doormat!

What in the dither to do, with dignity, about the boy?

It was beneath one's dignity to consult a subordinate about a family matter. But, before leaving Chapultepec, one had spoken with Father Fischer about the question of U.S. recognition. It would be imperiled, would it not, by keeping the child of a U.S. citizen against that citizen's will?

"Your Majesty," Father Fischer said, bringing out the rosary beads, "I resolutely advise deferring *any* decisions until reaching Orizaba."

Now, a waltz by Strauss. Dr. Basch tucks into the salad of citrus, cilantro, and sheep cheese.

Professor Bilimek, discreetly, behind his fist, burps.

Outside, in the gray, the filthy dog barks after its filthy sheep.

And in that other morning on the highway nearing Río Frío, Maximilian awoke to the sharp air as in a trance. Wrapped in his cloak, his limbs feeling stiff as a mummy's, his forehead damp with fever, he looked out at a forest clotted with such bluish light it seemed to him filled with spirits of the dead. He had just been dreaming of a butterfly frozen in the snow. He recognized the clearing by the road, where, only six months before, Baron d'Huart's body had been laid out and covered with a blanket. A small cross marked it. And behind it, a shadow—of a rock?—seemed the very blood that had oozed, attracting flies, from the head wound.

From a cliff, an eagle had winged low over the road and then the treetops.

And as the imperial carriage clattered on toward Puebla, he felt he were traveling back in time, to the beginning, each turn in the road reminding him that what had appeared a harbinger of glory was, in reality, a milestone on the road to calamity. He had been failed by the French, in every way. At the inn in Ajotla, he crossed paths with Louis Napoleon's emissary, General Castelnau, who was on his way to Mexico City to urge him to abdicate. Because this was what Louis Napoleon, that back-stabber, wanted him to do, Maximilian refused to receive Castelnau.

This morning, in this hacienda outside Puebla, at the break of dawn, Maximilian had summoned Dr. Basch. On the edge of his camp bed, weakly, for he had hardly slept, Maximilian put his elbows on his knees and his head in his hands.

In Veracruz, the *Novara*, its hold packed with his archive, his furnishings, his treasures, was waiting for him to board. But in Orizaba, Father Fischer . . . Oh, God.

Dr. Basch took his wrist, to check his pulse.

Maximilian's voice dwindled to a whisper. "Should the empress die, I would have no heart to fight."

Dr. Basch said only, "Elevate your feet, sir."

His head on the pillow again, Maximilian let out a ragged breath. "Whatever happens, I want no more blood shed on my account."

Dr. Basch merely nodded.

"But . . . a captain does not abandon ship."

"There are many metaphors, sir."

When he woke, with a surge of energy, Maximilian wrote two letters: the first, to Doña Alicia de Iturbide; the second, to Princess Iturbide.

Madam:

The repeated instances in which you and your husband have addressed to me, directly and indirectly, requesting that I return your son Agustín, and thereby annul the contract that you and other members of your family, of your own free will, signed with me last year, have obliged me, finally, to instruct Princess Iturbide to deliver him to his closest relative, Don José Malo, that you may give him your final instructions.

In fulfilling the repeated requests by yourself, your husband, and others of your family members, I hereby cede all responsibility for having violated the contract, which was made for the exclusive benefit of your son and your family, to you, who have broken it.

With my best wishes for your happiness, Yours Truly,

Maximilian

My dear cousin,

The repeated instances in which our dear Agustín's parents and elder uncle have unceasingly requested that I return their child and, in consequence, annul the contract which they entered into of their own free and spontaneous will, have obliged me, finally, after a long struggle in my own mind, to send a letter today to Señora Doña Alicia de Iturbide, advising her that her son shall be in the custody of his uncle, Don José Malo, so that the parents can make arrangements to claim him to their own perfect satisfaction.

I beg you, therefore, to deliver him and all of his belongings, to Se-
ñor Malo.

I know the profound sentiments this directive will cause you and that
this sacrifice is no less for you than it has been for me. However, both conve-
nience and the fear that the parents and uncles may cause yet greater scan-
dals, has made this sacrifice imperative.

I very sincerely share your understandable sorrow and I assure you
that the conduct of other members of your family in no way changes the very
affectionate feelings of friendship on both my part and that of the Empress.

Receive the assurances of esteem and benevolence of yours truly, your
cousin,

Maximilian

Sealed with the imperial stamps, the two envelopes were turned over to
the courier—the first, for Veracruz and ultimately Washington, D.C.; the
second, for Mexico City.

A weight, not all of it, but a terrible piece of it, had lifted from his heart.

He had no idea where he might find himself a month from now—in Miramar, with Charlotte; in the Hofburg with his family; in Mexico City, or
some other Mexican town, in a general's uniform with saber, and a pistol in
his hands.

The late morning sun was smiling and so, with Professor Bilimek, he
went off for three blessed hours of botanizing. They visited a waterfall. The
botanist filled every one of his little jars. They spoke of nothing but birds and
beetles, butterflies and ferns.

Strauss. On the other side of the dining room's barred window, crows con-
gregate along the fence. Then, again, from the patio, Chopin. A Kasbah-like
sunset burnishes the back wall, behind Dr. Basch.

Broiled tongue, and potatoes sauteed with chopped maguey flowers.

The sheep bleat. The dog barks. Clacking sounds, as the three men, heads bowed, cut their meat.

In that patio, Sawerthal brought down his baton. The Hussars folded their music stands and their instruments into their cases; in another moment, the patio was empty but for a few scattered blossoms of bougainvillea. The last to cross it were the cornetist and a violinist. The cornetist, buttoning his jacket, for the air had turned cool, accidentally bumped the violinist with his case.

"Beg your pardon," he said.

"Don't mention it," said the other.

They both owed fantastic sums to a certain Weissbrunn, one of those who had been left behind to defend the capital. Perhaps they would never see him again. Or perhaps they would.

"Are you game for cards?" said the one.

"Dice," said the other. He turned back his cuffs, as he did so, passing his violin case from one hand, and then to the other. The lining under the cuffs was hardly regulation: purple silk with a stamped pattern of Chinese dragons.

Where had he had that done? The admiring cornetist wanted to know.

"Mademoiselle Louise."

As they came around the corner, chickens scattered. A rooster came flying at their boots; the violinist gave that impudent bird a kick—which probably killed it; but neither of the men bothered to look back. They started up the path to their barracks, a crude setup in the barn. Beyond the roof of the hacienda's chapel shone the persimmon pink hump of the great snowcapped volcano.

"The Mexican Matterhorn," said the cornetist.

"I've never seen the Matterhorn," said the violinist.

There was a dissatisfaction in their tone. They had not been paid. They had not—yet—seen action. True, for the rest of their lives, they could boast of their exploits in "Amerika," serving the younger brother of the Kaiser. Still,

Mexico had not—yet—matched their expectations, so searingly romantic, nourished on stories of the Conquistadors, and boys' adventure books, including such exotica as scrappy translations of X. Salvatierra and Fenimore Cooper.

"You've seen Stromboli."

"*Ja.*"

"And Vesuvius?" (They had come to Mexico on different boats.)

"Fogged in that day."

They did not know if they were going on to Veracruz, and from there, who knew by what route, to Christmas at home or back to Mexico City. Or what. Not knowing, forever waiting, that was the Purgatory of being a soldier.

When it's all said and done, said the one—this was years later, the First World War breaking out over their old white heads—*you're a raisin baked in a cake.* After Mexico, they would meet again, by pure happenstance, in Weissbrunn's daughter's tavern in Ölmutz. Maximilian's portrait hung over the mirror that spanned the bar. They raised their steins, "To Max!" They carved their initials and "MEXIKO 1864-1867" into the ancient, almost black wood of their table. They talked of their children. They both had grandchildren who loved to go into the attic and try on their old uniforms, the boots, play with the saber and rust-locked pistols. The one had a granddaughter who'd taken his silver medal for "Merito Militar"—*and you know what the naughty monkey did with it? Hung it as a picture in her doll-house!* Roars of laughter. And then, after more beers, remembering all the ones who were gone, tears.

But now, in an hacienda outside of Puebla in the sunset of October 25, 1866, with a brisk and swinging stride, the two young Hussars come through the gate and out onto the road. A church bell clangs. From so far away that the sound is almost like birdcalls, a pack of dogs howl. A star has come out; then two. Now the volcano, soot gray with dusk, is full before them, making any other comment impossible.

"I want to get up there."

"All the way?"

"The flank." A soft clicking as the violinist turns the dice in his pocket. "There's a rare breed of antelope."

They could be bivouacked here for a day, for a week, or a month. Everyone has a conjecture, but no one knows. If, on a Sunday, a man went up onto the flank of that heap of rock to bag an antelope, well, it might be his one and only chance!

A tiny granny, hunched under a load of firewood, scuttles past.

The cornetist kicks at a loose cobblestone and it rolls, wobblingly, into a thicket of cactus. It is almost too dark to see. Here, by a crumbling adobe wall, they stop and light their cigars.

BOOK THREE

*pero es cierto que el dolor nos avisa con tiempo su
llegada*

*but it is true that sorrow announces its arrival
beforehand*

—CONCEPCIÓN LOMBARDO DE MIRAMÓN,

MEMORIAS

AN UNEXPECTED VISITOR

*Y*ears blurred by. Fourteen of them having passed, in March 1882, Mr. John Bigelow, retired from diplomatic service and now a gentleman farmer, journalist, and lawyer active in New York civic enterprises, determined to visit the sister republic. He had always been an eclectic traveler, ever-ready to inspect the home of some obscure French philosopher, Alpine hamlets, undertake the rigors of Sicily, even (as part of his research for the cause of abolition) Jamaica and Haiti. Having played a modest role in, as he always claimed, the nonetheless *inevitable* demise of the Archduke Maximilian's soi-disant "imperial" government, he was curious to see Veracruz, the pyramids of Cholula, Chapultepec Castle—in short, the sights. Above all, however, his purpose had been to inform the readers of *Harper's New Monthly Magazine,* and therefore himself, about the Mexican railroads, a question of special interest on Wall Street.

A three-week itinerary having both sated his curiosity and definitively depleted his patience, in Orizaba, Bigelow and his eldest daughter, Grace, boarded the train for the last leg of their journey back to Veracruz. Grace had filled her steamer-trunk with exotic horse-gear (saddle, bridle, stirrups, and a smart, snug-fitting little jacket and matching sombrero). She had found much to amuse her, though she disliked the food, and the pesky beggars, and she thought bullfights, for the way they exposed the horses to being gored, an abomination. Her father, however, had, on the whole formed a less than stellar opinion of Mexico and its prospects. Certain regions had potential, one could not deny it, but the conjectures of such as Baron von Humboldt—whose now decades-old researches had so enthralled Louis Napoleon, poor Maximilian, and now, so many of these latter-day promoters—amounted to nothing but fairy tales. Mexico remained sunk in a mire of banditry and poverty, both the result of pervasive and systematic financial, political, and spiritual corruption. Why, it turned out that even Mexico City's Protestant bishop was involved in financial shenanigans! As Bigelow confided to his diary: *The horse he showed us was not such as Jesus rode into Jerusalem on.*

Forever after, forever after, the clack of the wheels on the track seemed to chant, as the blue-tiled domes of Orizaba and the station's squad of cavalry grew smaller. A sweet smell was fierce in their nostrils: Bigelow and Grace looked out their windows, through smears of grime: from the foothills of the snowcapped Pico de Orizaba to the meadows yonder, plumes of smoke billowed. This was the season for burning cane. Ahead, where the track curved, hovering above it was a cloud of buzzards and other birds of prey.

Madame de Iturbide had said, in ten years time, her son would be president.

In Mexico City, Bigelow and his daughter had met young Don Agustín. A well-mannered cadet in the Colegio Militar, he was tall—remarkably so for a Mexican—and altogether Anglo-Saxon in his complexion. In a portrait, if not for a franker gaze than any Habsburg's, he might have passed for a younger sibling of Crown Prince Rudolph.

After her husband's death, Madame de Iturbide had educated her son in Washington and, for a spell, a Jesuit boys' college in Belgium. That college, his mother said with quite the sparkle, was not far from the castle where Carlota had been, these many years, locked away. And Carlota, Madame de Iturbide claimed, was not so *folle* as they made out. On her father's death she inherited six million dollars; her brother, King Leopold II wanted to prevent her from remarrying, to keep that money for himself.

So, Grace asked Agustín, had he seen Carlota?

"No," Agustín said.

Bigelow had liked the boy's frankness. Grace, at twenty-nine, was closer in age than his grandfatherly self. What was her opinion of him?

Oh, he seemed nice enough.

Bigelow was very much enjoying his daughter's company, but there were times, and this had been one of them, when he especially missed his wife's conversation. Mrs. Bigelow was the wisest, most perceptive little person, articulate and, in private, forthcoming with her unvarnished opinions. But Mrs. Bigelow also had a spiritual side, a deep well of compassion that, he knew, helped temper his sometimes excessive severity. *Judge not, that ye be not judged*—unlike himself, Mrs. Bigelow did not have to chastise herself in this regard. As she often said, *no matter how you pour it, there are always two sides to a pancake.* It had been a sore disappointment for him that, instead of coming with him to Mexico, she had elected to visit some of her connections in England.

Would Mrs. Bigelow have agreed with him? He had the sense the young Iturbide was doomed. (Are we not all doomed?) An overreaching mother, an improvident country—miscreants, marauders, and kidnappers abounded on every street corner and turn of the highway, if one were to believe the stories—but more than this lay behind his intuition. How not to dwell on days gone by? Louis Napoleon and his only son—that poor child, so tender an age when his father surrendered to the Prussians, the glittering capital sandbagged, starved. In exile, still suffering from stones, the French Caesar ascended to his Maker's Kingdom from a bed of agony, and infinitely more would his agonies have been had he known what cruel trap Destiny laid for his boy. Three years ago, on a reconnoiter with the British Army in the South African bush, Prince Louis, aged twenty-three, was killed by Zulu spears.

Methodic in his travels, Bigelow was always avid to make the acquaintance of key players, but it was late in the game when he bethought himself to look up the Iturbides. He'd had some justification, however, not to think of it sooner. The Juárez government, having tried and then condemned Maximilian to death before a firing squad, was hardly likely to have issued passports to the Iturbides. True, a parade of years had gone by. Juárez himself was dead and buried. The "Republic" was now in the firm grip of one of his generals, Don Porfirio Díaz, a Mexican species of Augustus, who, whether in the office of the presidency or behind it, controlled the army and the revenues—and would, in the manner of Machiavelli it appeared, open the gates of Mexico's Holy of Holies to any class of foreigners so long as they offered gold enough to grease his palm. But Bigelow assumed that, having recovered their boy, the Iturbides would have stayed on in Europe where, as for so many Americans, their dollars stretched to lengths unimaginable at home. He himself had kept his family for several years in Berlin for the benefit of the children's education.

In Mexico City, Bigelow's first foray was to the U.S. legation where he and Grace made the acquaintance of the ambassador, who turned out to be a judge from Louisiana. In his ignorance of the country, its geography, history, politics, and cultural personalities, this individual revealed all the enterprise of a man who, having consumed a mint julep or three, was content to siesta in his hammock.

Grace had asked the judge about the Mexican ambassador in Washington (she meant Don Matías Romero, a distinguished and very patriotic gentleman mentioned at length in Lester's *Mexican Republic* for his exploits on behalf of the republic during the French Intervention). "Is Romero a Spaniard?"

"No," the judge said darkly. "He is an Indian."

"An Indian? How is that?"

The judge answered, "His father was a priest and his mother a nigger. If that doesn't make an Indian, what does?"

From his recent reading, on the train in, Bigelow realized the judge had confounded Romero with General Almonte.

On leaving, Bigelow muttered, "Tom Corwin, where are you?"

"Who is Tom Corwin?" asked Grace, taking her father's arm.

"He was our minister to Mexico—and a better man than myself."

"Oh, Pa, you're too modest."

Bigelow, feeling the altitude, wanted to rest; Grace wanted to go as far afield as the floating gardens of Xochimilco. They compromised and went to view the Aztec Sun Stone. In a bookstall Grace found a colored map of Mexico prior to the U.S. invasion of 1847. Bigelow was very pleased to spend only four reales for an unblemished copy of the trial of Maximilian. (He was also offered a document from the archives of the Inquisition, but as it appeared to be authentic, he did not trust it had come into this dealer's hands by blameless methods. Accordingly, he refused it.)

After his interview with the head of the Casa de Moneda and a director of the Mexican Central Railway, next on the touristic itinerary was the cathedral—a prospect that, though he felt duty bound to see it, in truth held little interest for Bigelow, for it would be, the guidebook assured, entirely Spanish in its aspect, and he had toured so many cathedrals in Europe (most recently, last summer, those of Monreale, Palermo, and Naples). They all piled together in his mind, these excesses of masonry and stained glass, gold enough for herds of Golden Calves, the vividly gruesome images of martyrdom, relics of hair, teeth, finger bones enshrined in silver—so many priest-ridden medievalities—the bells, the smells, the drone of tour guides, and the murmur of their sheep-like charges, all muddled together like voices in dreams. His soul found no repose in such places.

He would have no priest of Rome come between himself and his Savior!

To get into the vestibule, they had to run a gamut of whining and importuning beggars, the blind, the crippled, the aged, the leprous, and filthy Indian women suckling infants. Once inside, their guide fell to one knee and made the sign of the cross, a gesture finished with a kiss on the thumb.

His name was Ignacio Pérez. He wore expensive-looking brogues, but his shirtsleeves were rolled up to the elbows. He had a thick shock of shiny hair and strong-looking teeth, which made him appear young; his long, beak-like nose and dark, sunken cheeks made him appear old. He might have been twenty-five or fifty-five; it was impossible for Bigelow to tell which.

"It looks like a jail," Grace whispered. All along the western wall, one after the other, stretched a chain of cell-like chapels, their treasures, ivory-faced saints, crucifixes, age-dark paintings, reliquaries, secured behind locked iron bars.

"Look at this, Pa."

"This," Ignacio Pérez began, "is the chapel of San José de—"

"No," Grace interrupted. "I mean these." She indicated a heap of ribbons and rags and shoestrings, each knotted to a pad-lock—brass locks, iron locks, square, round, big, minuscule. Bigelow counted thirty, forty—

"By Jove, what a lot of locks," he exclaimed.

"These," Ignacio Pérez said, "are offerings to a very important saint, San Ramón Nonato."

Neither Bigelow nor his daughter could recall having heard of said saint. Bigelow took a step backward, to clear the path for a blind couple, the man probing, *tap, tap,* with what appeared to be a broken-off broom handle, the woman shuffling behind, her hands clamped to his shoulders and her face, wanderingly alive, to the ceiling.

"You see," Ignacio Pérez said, "we are near the confessionals? San Ramón Nonato protects us against gossip, rumor, and false testimony."

"Interesting," Bigelow allowed. He strolled on, his hands joined behind his back. Daniel Webster had a theory that, in the long run, the people who fed on milk would dominate the people who fed on oil. Exchange "milk" and "oil" for "Protestantism" and "Catholicism," Bigelow thought, and there you have it. He believed in tolerance and the separation of church and state, but how far could a country get when its people had all their thinking done for them and they were all taught to obey the dictates of Rome?

Before the chapel of (so the placard said) San Judas Tadeo, an ancient granny, barefooted and with dirty ankles, was praying, eyes closed, into her clenched hands.

Grace, having given this individual a wide berth, whispered loudly to their guide, "Is that woman worshiping Judas!"

Ignacio Pérez smiled wanly. Apparently, he was used to this question. "No, not Judas Iscariot. This is, as you say in English, Saint Jude Thaddeus."

"Who?"

"Grace!" her father said, raising an eyebrow. "You haven't been reading your Bible."

"San Judas Tadeo," their guide went on, "is the patron of impossible causes. After Our Lady of Guadalupe, some say that San Judas Tadeo is the most beloved by us Mexicans." He crossed himself for a second time. "I myself was saved from the yellow fever. He has granted many millions of miracles."

Bunkum, Bigelow thought. But, it was eerie enough to startle him, the moment the word "miracles" left their guide's lips, from somewhere beyond the choir stalls on the other side of the nave, a falsetto, sweet and clear as a crystal bell, began to intone a prayer. *Santa Maria, ora pro nobis . . .*

With this beautiful music in their ears, they came to one of the last chapels, that of San Felipe de Jesús, the first Mexican saint, a missionary martyred in Nagasaki, which explained the enormous cage-like pagoda of gold-leafed bamboo set out front of the chapel's bars. This chapel received little sunlight; had their guide not explained each of the several paintings set into the altar—the mutilation of San Felipe's ear, San Felipe's premonition, San Felipe's crucifixion, the intercession of the Holy Child, and so on—Bigelow would have been able to make neither head nor tail out of them.

"San Felipe was martyred on February 5, 1597. And you know what, in his family home in Mexico City, on that very day . . ."

Bigelow and Grace said nothing but waited politely.

"There was an old dried up fig tree on the patio, and it came back to life and gave fruit."

"Hmm," Bigelow said. He coughed.

Having finished his story, their guide stepped down, but he did not move on. He was waiting for them to notice something.

Grace said, "What is that fancy chair in there?"

Bigelow had not noticed any such thing. He came close, stepped up, grasped the bars, and peered into the gloom. In the far right-hand corner, beneath a red, white, and green flag, there was indeed a golden armchair—a throne—its legs and arms carved to resemble sheaves of wheat.

"That," said Ignacio Pérez, "was the throne of the Liberator, Emperor Don Agustín de Iturbide."

Bigelow noticed now the plinth, a marble the gray of foie-gras, set into that right-hand wall, and above it, an urn. Above that—one really had to look to see it—was a portrait of the man in profile.

Mexico's George Washington, as it were. Iturbide, Bigelow thought, looked rather like Murat, king of Naples.

Was there any way to unlock this chapel and go inside?

No. The chapels would not be opened to the public until All Souls, the Day of the Dead.

The lettering of the inscription in the plinth was too small to read from this vantage point. From memory, Ignacio Pérez recited his own translation, and with such feeling that it was no puzzle to guess his sympathies.

Agustín de Iturbide, author of national independence. Fellow patriots, cry for him. Passersby, admire him. Here lie the remains of a hero. His soul rests in the bosom of God.

The singing on the other side of the church had ceased. The priest spoke, the voices chanted; they went on, back and forth, like surf.

Did their guide know anything about the Liberator's descendants?

There was one, a lady.

Doña Alicia de Iturbide?

He was unable to say if that was her Christian name or not. She lived in the Hotel Comonfort, he knew that. And she was stone-deaf and in a wheelchair.

At the Hotel Comonfort, the concierge made Bigelow understand that the lady in residence was not the one he had in mind. But he was in luck, for Doña Alicia had just returned from the United States and she was staying in the hotel across the street. At that hotel, Bigelow ascertained that she was no longer in residence; however, he might find her at home. Her house, a short drive yonder to the head of the Alameda, was the one directly facing *El Caballito,* the equestrian statue by Tolsá of King Carlos III.

At said destination, he found such a fine-looking house as would not be out of place in the most elegantly modern of Paris's arrondissements. But Doña Alicia was not to be found here, either. The porter, by means of gesture, brought Bigelow around the corner. Here was a well-weathered door, by its side a small hole from which hung an unremarkable cord made of hemp, knotted at the end. Bigelow pulled it. An eye appeared in the grate above the handle. Scraping sounds (in a moment, he would realize this was of a stool being removed) and then, the door opened to reveal two children, one dark, the other Spanish-looking, both very untidy and neither in the least intelligible. Presently, a servant appeared, as untidy as those children, her braids as greasy-looking as her apron, but she had a smiling face and patient manner, as well as—this was a boon—knowledge of a few words of English.

"Tomorrow," she said. "*Doña Alicia estará aquí, si dios quiere,* tomorrow."

"At what time?"

She shook her head in incomprehension. "*Sorry I no understand.*"

Bigelow scribbled a quick note, that he and his daughter were at the Hotel San Carlos, and he handed over his card. This disappeared into the apron's pocket and, with what he took to be polite wishes for a pleasant day, the door closed.

The following morning being a Sunday, Bigelow attended the service at the Protestant church. On his return to the hotel, in the lobby, he found Grace with Madame de Iturbide.

From the sofa by the window, she floated up to greet him—breathlessly— "Mr. Bigelow!"

The years telescoped to an instant. He would have recognized her any-where: her crown of fine, fair hair, apple chin (perhaps a little bit plumper). He took her hand in both of his. For a long moment—so long that Grace be-gan to shift in her seat—neither let go.

"What a pleasure, what a pleasure," he said, at last taking his chair.

They took a little tea, and then a long lunch. She would have insisted on having them to her house to dine, Madame de Iturbide said, but the main rooms were undergoing renovations. As a widow (alas, Don Angel had died several years ago), she had been inclined to remain in Washington near her family. It was Mexico's minister of war who had convinced her to bring her son back to Mexico. Her son was a Mexican, the last of his family, and his country needed him. After a year or so at the Colegio Militar, he would be made a captain and an aide-de-camp. Then, they would see.

It took little prompting on Bigelow's part for the floodgates to open: Don Porfirio Díaz?

"A journeyman tailor from Oaxaca, Díaz joined the revolt against Maxi-milian, and he made himself indispensable to President Juárez in such wise that, after Juárez's death, well . . ." She took a sip of wine. "Díaz came in with nothing and left the office worth more than a million dollars."

"A million dollars!"

"More than a million dollars."

And what of the current president, González?

"His wife left him. She owns a millinery shop, the one around the corner from this hotel." Madame de Iturbide turned to Grace. "Quite nice hats. Though I am sure you can find better in New York."

She had unending information and opinions about various personages' marriages. Don Porfirio Díaz had recently married the teenaged daughter of a lawyer by the name of Romero Rubio. *"Un mariage de l'ambition,"* Madame de Iturbide summed that up, using the French—which reminded Bigelow of General Bazaine.

Hadn't Bazaine married a very young Mexican señorita?

"Pepita de la Peña." Madame de Iturbide knew her well. "But that was nothing compared to his first marriage. *Oof!*" According to Madame de Iturbide, while serving in North Africa, Bazaine purchased a little Spanish girl and her mother from Mogador slave traders. He had the child educated in a French convent and then, when he judged her ready, obliged her to marry him. But she never loved him. While in the Crimea, she took up with some of his brother officers, and when he was sent to Mexico, used that opportunity to carry on with an actor. Bazaine sent for her; but she refused to come. He insisted. She acquiesced, apparently. The night before she was to depart Paris, she gave a really recherché dinner for thirty persons. "The Count of Montholon, France's minister to Washington, was one of the guests; he told me these facts. After the guests retired, Madame Bazaine took poison."

Bigelow looked at his daughter; his daughter looked at the clock. Madame de Iturbide, however, blissfully unaware of her effect on her audience, nodded slowly. "Yes, poison."

"Bazaine," interjected Bigelow, "was nonetheless highly respected by several of our senior generals." He was thinking, in particular, of some things General Sheridan had said.

"Grant was here."

"Ah?"

"He is very unpopular."

Bigelow would have liked to steer the conversation back to General Bazaine, for he wanted to know more about the second Madame Bazaine, who a few years ago—after Bazaine's surrender to the Prussians at Metz and subsequent trial and imprisonment for treason—had orchestrated her husband's escape from the Île Sainte Marguerite, an exploit so audacious, so cunning, so thoroughly romantic, it was as a chapter out of a novel by Dumas, *père* or *fils*. Madame de Iturbide, however, was compelled to make him understand that when ex-President U.S. Grant visited recently, the Mexican government put him up at a house and paid all expenses to the fabulous sum of one hundred thousand dollars. A Mexican gentleman gave an entertainment costing some other fabulous sum, and Grant had not troubled to thank anyone.

"Grant's ingratitude was shocking," she concluded.

"Hmmm," said Bigelow. He had his own grudge against Grant, who in 1870 refused an appointment for his son to West Point as these were reserved for sons of "those who had served the Union during the war"—one of the most galling insults he had received in his life, for what, then, had been his years of service in Paris? But this he did not share.

The next afternoon, Bigelow and his daughter called again on Madame de Iturbide. Her house was as she said, in a state of some chaos. The windows had all been thrown open, to air out the smell of glue and turpentine. The drawing room featured new sofas and an expensive-looking piano, and many bookshelves, their moldings painted a slick-looking asparagus green, but all stood empty—a disappointment, as there were few things he relished more than perusing the libraries of others. In the dining room, the furniture covered by bedsheets, the walls had been only partially papered. The paper appeared to be Oriental in theme. Great curls of it lay on the floor in a corner.

The servant who had answered the door the other day (wearing a cleaner apron but not cleaner hair) brought in a tray of coffee and strawberry pie with whipped cream.

A round of pleasantries. He told Madame de Iturbide about their visit to the Palace of the Inquisition and the Jesuit colleges. Grace went into raptures about a certain horse she had seen in Chapultepec Park. Bigelow and Grace both accepted another slice of pie.

These many years, Bigelow had been harboring a question. He feared it was impertinent, but the opportunity being a singular one, he went ahead and asked it.

"Why, really, did Maximilian want to adopt your child?"

Madame de Iturbide set down her cup of coffee.

"Carlota had no children. The Austrian doctor in their retinue diagnosed a malformation. There was a doctor in New York, Dr. Sims?"

Bigelow shook his head.

"Well, Dr. Sims was summoned to Mexico. But he said he would undertake the journey only for all expenses and thirty thousand dollars."

"Thirty thousand dollars!"

"In cash, to be paid prior to his departure from New York." Madame de Iturbide picked up her cup of coffee. She stirred it, twice, and then set it back down.

"Thirty thousand," Bigelow said encouragingly. "That was a lot more money than it is today."

"Maximilian did not want to spend it. General Almonte got up an intrigue, that he should apply to the pope for an annulment."

"An annulment!"

"Oh, yes, and Maximilian would have done it, too."

She then told Bigelow about the negotiations Carlota initiated with her and her family, the visits, the bouquets, all the pretty promises. For Grace's benefit Madame de Iturbide recounted the story of her change of heart in the city of Puebla, her frantic return to Mexico City, her appeal to General Bazaine, and her arrest by Maximilian's Palatine Guards.

The scene of her long-ago interview with him in Paris burned bright in Bigelow's mind: the oak desk, the overstuffed file boxes, the persistent smell of wet umbrellas. Only a month afterward, in December 1866, he had resigned, at last, and the American community in Paris gave him a dinner, such a dinner—he remembers good friends, Dr. Evans and Buffum, the *New York Herald* correspondent, raising their glasses of champagne . . .

Having given up his post and returned to New York (it turned out, only temporarily), Bigelow followed the news from Mexico—that poor deluded archduke's decision to fight on with the last shred of his support, the clerical faction. (Had Maximilian lost his gimbals?) Then the siege at Querétaro, Maximilian's capture, trial and, no one with a Christian sensibility welcomed this, his execution by firing squad. But Bigelow did not know the details of the Iturbides' story.

Had Madame de Iturbide been in Paris when Carlota came to see Louis Napoleon that summer?

"It was August 1866." And she told him, word for word, how she had confronted Carlota in the Grand-Hôtel.

"What an extraordinary narrative! Have you written it out?"

"In part."

"I would very much like to read it."

She turned away and lifted the coffee pot.

Bigelow pressed, "I do hope you would consider allowing me to read it." He was an experienced newspaper editor, and, he mentioned, he was writing his own memoirs.

She said, coyly, pouring, "All my papers are packed away in boxes right now."

She then resumed her story, how she and her husband and elder brother-in-law returned that autumn to New York, where, in the Metropolitan Hotel, her brother-in-law died. He was buried, next to his mother, the empress, in the family vault in Philadelphia's church of Saint John the Evangelist. Doña Alicia and her husband took refuge in her family's country estate in Washington, in the heights above Georgetown. Nearing Christmas, word came to them that Maximilian had relinquished custody of their boy, and the archbishop of Mexico named a steamer that, in the spring of 1867, en route to Europe, would be stopping at Havana. They raced to Cuba, boarded that steamer, and over the vociferous protests of that scheming sister-in-law, took back their son.

Her son was a topic of endless fascination for Madame de Iturbide. She told many stories about his childhood in Georgetown. Bigelow, bemused, indulged his hostess. He, himself, was blessed with a tribe of offspring. He was inordinately proud of each and every one and could imagine the pride a parent must feel for an only child. And, too, her voice had that cooing quality, that accent unique to the old Maryland families, which she shared with Mrs. Bigelow. That said, Mrs. Bigelow and Madame de Iturbides' characters, it seemed to him, could not have been more different.

Not until two days later, at a dinner dance at the Mexican foreign minister's, did Bigelow and Grace first meet the young Iturbide. He wore a beautiful uniform, and all eyes upon him, his adoring mother's most of all, he danced, youth in the prize of life, with flawless élan.

THE END

THE STORY OF THE STORY
OR,
AN EPILOGUE BY WAY OF ACKNOWLEDGMENTS

Once upon a time, or, I should say, more years ago than I would like to count, I was invited to a lunch in Mexico City. There in the dining room was an unusually handsome antique portrait of a youth—perhaps English?—cradling a rifle. The scenery included a nopal cactus and, upon a hill in the background, as in a Renaissance portrait . . .

Was that Chapultepec Castle?

Yes, my hostess told me, as our bowl of salad came out in the arms of the muchacha.

And who was the boy?

Agustín de Iturbide y Green, the prince of Mexico.

I had never heard of him. This astonished me. I was recently married to a Mexican, and I considered myself well educated. I realize now that we supposedly well-educated Americans rarely open our minds to the rich complexities of our southern neighbor. In part this is because we are lulled into an illusion that we already "know" Mexico. Our media drench us with ready-made images: the wetback; the bandido and the bullfighter and the mariachi; the narco-trafficker; the corrupt official with his Rolex, his yacht, his weekends in Vegas; the *pobres* in their sombreros and huaraches; the ubiquitous unibrowed Frida, and those sugar-sand beaches bereft of people other than, perhaps, long-limbed blondes in bikinis.

A prince! This meant an aristocracy, a theater for power: social, political, financial, economic, military. Certainly, revolutions have erupted in opposition to the idea, but it can be said that for many people a monarch and, by extension, the royal family serve as a focal point for the identity and unity of a nation. To most Americans and Mexicans today, this idea is absurd. But as I write these lines, the Belgians still have their king and the United Kingdom its queen.

These days, usually, one can satisfy one's idle curiosity with an Internet search. Back then, my search yielded nothing.

A few months later, halfway through reading Jasper Ridley's *Maximilian and Juárez,* I came upon the chapter "Alice Iturbide." My surprise at finding my own countrywoman, long ago, at the apex of this Mexican aristocracy—both antagonist and victim, motivated and blinded by who knew what medley of ambition, avarice, love, borrowed patriotism or naïveté—so intrigued me I knew at once I wanted to explore and expand the story into a novel.

Writing a book is like climbing a mountain: one step at a time eventually gets you to the summit, though perhaps, once, twice, or a hundred times, you might have to overnight in heavy weather, or retrace a deadend route and begin anew. In my case, before reaching much of any altitude at all, I fell, to use a Mexican expression, into an eggplant patch.

The eggplant patch was my initial reading of the main works on the period. In these the story of the little prince is either erroneously or so faintly told as to be—well, it wasn't anything to hang a novel on.

This is surprising, given the impressive quantity of research into the Second Empire, well documented in historiographies, most recently, Mexican historian Erika Pani's *El Segundo Imperio:Pasados de usos múltiples* (2004). In addition, the rise and fall of the Second Empire, Carlota's descent into madness and Maximilian's last days and execution, have been told and retold in movies, TV series, documentaries, as well as plays, operas, musicals, epic poems, and novels—but never, apart from a couple of problematic articles, has the story of the little prince been told on its own.

Back to that eggplant patch. Ridley claims that Alice first married Agustín Gerónimo, eldest son of the Emperor Iturbide, and then after his death married the second son, Angel. In the Washington, D.C. Marriage

Records I found the marriage of Alice and Angel of June 9, 1855, but never anywhere any evidence for her supposed first marriage to Agustín Gerónimo and in fact, as ample documentation in the Iturbide Family Archives in the Library of Congress shows, the elder bachelor brother traveled with Angel and Alice from Paris to New York, where after many years of ill-health he died in December 1866. (There, for anyone who wants to see them, are the microfiches of bills from New York's Clarendon Hotel, one Dr. John Metcalfe, and for the conveyance of Agustín Gerónimo's remains to Philadelphia, where they were interred in the family crypt in Saint John the Evangelist.) As for Angel, according to a privately printed Iturbide family genealogy, he died in Mexico City in 1872.

The best-known work on the Second Empire—and the first based on research into Maximilian's archive in Austria's Haus-, Hof-, und Staatsarchiv, Egon Caesar Conte Corti's *Maximilian und Charlotte*—offers what I now believe is an accurate account of the Iturbides' tangle with Maximilian, but in the sum of a single page.

Maximiliano íntimo: El Emperor Maximiliano y su corte, one of the indispensable eyewitness memoirs, by Maximilian's secretary, José Luis Blasio, similarly relegates the Iturbides to the briefest of mentions and, further, claims that "the little Agustín, then five years old, was the son of Angel de Iturbide, who had passed away, and an American woman." Three strikes there: the child was only two and a half years old, Angel was quite alive enough to have affixed his signature to Maximilian's contract, and—poor Alice! She did not even rate the mention of her name.

There are so many, but one more example: Sara Yorke Stevenson's *Maximilian in Mexico: A Woman's Reminiscences of the French Intervention 1862–1867,* a magnificent tome in all other respects, relegates the Iturbide affair to—I found this astonishing—a snippet of a footnote, apropos of Maximilian's flight from Chapultepec to Orizaba in late 1866.

I read and I read, but in these works about Maximilian, the Second Empire, and the French Intervention, whether a memoir or based on original research, when it came to the Iturbides the story was always the same: mystifying errors and vagueness.

Why, precisely, Maximilian would want to take custody of the Iturbide grandsons, and why Alice, her husband, and his siblings would agree to this, at least initially, were questions I could not begin to address when the Iturbides themselves remained obscure.

I knew there were archives on the Emperor Agustín de Iturbide in both Georgetown University and the Library of Congress, but I was still in Mexico City. So my first path out of the bramble was an unlikely one, and I found it thanks to Mexican economist and historian Eduardo Turrent, who granted me access to the Banco de México's Matías Romero archive. During the French Intervention, Romero, one of Mexico's great statesmen, served as the Mexican Republic's minister to Washington where he lobbied, gathering money and arms, against Maximilian. In Romero's archive, among countless treasures, I found several letters from Angel de Iturbide, anxiously requesting that he and his family be permitted to return to Mexico. These are dated August 1867, some two months after Maximilian's execution. They were sent from "Rosedale, near Georgetown, D.C."

Rosedale, Georgetown, D.C.: that was my lead. When I went to Washington, in addition to delving into those archives at Georgetown University and the Library of Congress, I went to the Washington Historical Society Library, the Peabody Room at Georgetown Public Library, and the Washingtoniana Division of the Martin Luther King Library. Alice's family turned out to be an old and prominent family, on both sides. It gave me a start to realize, after several visits to the Washington Historical Society Library, then housed in the Heurich mansion on New Hampshire Ave, that it was Alice's lace-capped grandmother, Rebecca Plater Forrest, whose portrait graced the vestibule. Over on Massachusetts Avenue, in stately Anderson House, the Society of the Cincinnati had the records of Agustín de Iturbide y Green's membership, descended as he was from the Revolutionary War hero General Uriah Forrest. And in the library of the Daughters of the American Revolution headquarters, I found a copy of the 1861 diary of his grandmother Ann Forrest Green. And about Rosedale, which crowns the knoll just behind the National Cathedral, several archives had newspaper clippings, some dating back to the 1930s and including interviews with Alice's family members. Also of enormous help were Washington, D.C., historian Louise Mann-Kenney's

Rosedale: The Eighteenth-Century Country Estate of General Uriah Forrest and a personal visit to Rosedale, one snow-dusted day in February.

The biggest trove of information about Alice and her son, however, I found in an unlikely place, for as far as I can determine, they had no association with it during their lifetimes: the archives of the Catholic University, in Washington, D.C. The rest of Agustín de Iturbide y Green's life is the subject of my next book, so here, suffice it to say, his career in the Mexican cavalry ended abruptly in 1890 when he was court-martialed and imprisoned for 340 days for having written a letter to a newspaper criticizing President Porfirio Díaz. On his release, he and his mother returned to Washington. In 1892 when she went alone to Mexico City to conclude some business, she died suddenly of blood poisoning from an infection to the foot. Soon another bout of inopportune truth-telling resulted in Agustín's expulsion from Washington's exclusive Metropolitan Club, though many of the members considered this so grossly unfair that years later there was an attempt, without his cooperation, to reinstate him as a member.

And so the onetime prince of Mexico, orphaned, ostracized, and plagued by chronic tuberculosis of the bone, made his living as a translator for the Franciscan Brothers and, later, as professor of French and Spanish at Georgetown. He nonetheless made a happy marriage, which lasted a decade until his death in 1925. The Catholic University archive, donated by his widow, Louise Kearney de Iturbide, contains his personal papers, scrapbooks, photographs, and her handwritten memoir, as well as many Washington area newspaper clippings, among them one dated 1939, "Memory of Imperial Fame: Princeling's Widow Refreshes Lost History," that shows the same portrait I had seen in Mexico City.

Why, having done so much original research, did I write the story as fiction? I wanted to tell it true, which means, of course, getting the facts as straight as possible but also, and this was the most interesting to me, telling an emotional truth. Why did Alice, Angel, Pepa, Maximilian, and Charlotte do what they did? Who encouraged and supported them, and who criticized, intimidated, and frustrated them—and for what motives? The answer is not only in historical and political analysis, but in their hearts, and the hearts of others can only be experienced with the imagination, that is, through fiction.

How much of this is fiction and how much is fact? We will never really know. Whether in a novel or a textbook, a character is not a real person, merely a metaphor. How good is the metaphor? All I can say is that, with some minor exceptions necessary to create what I hope is a harmonious narrative structure, I have done my utmost to render the facts and the contexts as accurately as possible. All the characters are based on real people, with the exceptions of Lupe, Chole, the bandits, the palace nannies Olivia and Tere, the murdered Count Villavaso, and the prince's bodyguard—though, in all these instances, real people did fulfill these or very similar roles, and I undertook extensive research into the sociology of the time and place to portray them, if imaginatively, as accurately as I could.

Several scenes incorporate lines of dialogue based, though loosely, with the tweaks and embellishments of fiction, on previously published works. These include: John Bigelow's interviews with Alice de Iturbide in "The Charm of Her Existence" and with French foreign minister Drouyn de Lhuys in *"Pas possible"* which rely on Bigelow's memoir, *Retrospections of an Active Life;* Alice de Iturbide's interview with Carlota in "In the Grand-Hôtel," which relies on Bigelow's article, "The Heir-Presumptive to the Imperial Crown of Mexico: Don Agustín de Iturbide" (*Harper's New Monthly Magazine,* April 1883); Captain Blanchot's exchange with General Bazaine about the rumors of the latter's supposed corruption in "Basket of Crabs," which relies on the former's *Mémoires: L'Intervention Française au Mexique;* and, finally, Bigelow's visit to Mexico and his meetings with Alice de Iturbide in the chapter "An Unexpected Visitor," which rely on his 1882 diary in the Manuscript Division of the New York Public Library.

Letters quoted in part and in whole (with some modifications for literary purposes) include: from Pedro Montezuma XV to Maximilian, (my translation, Kaiser Maximilian von Mexiko Archive, Library of Congress) and from Louis Napoleon to Maximilian (my translation, Egon Caesar Conte Corti, *Maximiliano y Carlota*), both in the chapter "The Archduke Maximilian or AEIOU"; from Madame de Iturbide to her son, Angel de Iturbide (my translation, Agustín de Iturbide Papers, Library of Congress), in "Past Midnight"; from A. [Agustín Gerónimo] de Iturbide to Maximilian, from Maximilian to Alice de Iturbide and from Alice Iturbide to Carlota (my translations, Kaiser Maximilian von Mexiko Archive, Haus-, Hof-, und Staatsarchiv) in "One Takes It Coolly"; from Alice de Iturbide to Maximilian (Bigelow, *Retrospections of an Active Life*) in "The Charm of Her Existence"; from Angel de Iturbide to Maximilian (my translation, Kaiser Maximilian von Mexiko Archive, Haus-, Hof-, und Staatsarchiv) and from Maximilian to Carlota (my translation from the Spanish translation, Konrad Ratz, ed., *Correspondencia inédita entre Maximiliano y Carlota*) in "One Stays the Course"; from Angel de Iturbide to Maximilian (my translation, Agustín de Iturbide Papers, Library of Congress) in "In the Grand-Hôtel"; from Countess Hulst to Carlota (Prince Michael of Greece, *The Empress of Farewells*) in "Night in the Eternal City"; and from Maximilian to Alice de Iturbide and Maximilian to Josefa de Iturbide (my translation, Kaiser Maximilian von Mexiko Archive, Haus-, Hof-, und Staatsarchiv) in "The Road to Orizaba."

A last word about research. There is no end to it. This may be true of any period, but it is especially true of Mexico in the 1860s, for Maximilian's presence there makes no sense without an understanding of both the Mexican and the international context—the American, Austrian, Belgian, French, Prussian, Russian, Italian, English, and so on. The histories, memoirs, and documents themselves reveal only scraps and, at best, patched-together swaths of the wider story; and many as these may be, precious few have been translated. To give one of many examples, *L'Intervention Française au Mexique*, the monumental three-volume memoir by Colonel Charles Blanchot, General Bazaine's aide-de-camp, has not yet been translated into Spanish, German, or English. In 2008 (more than 130 years after the fall of the Second Mexican Empire), Austrian historian Konrad Ratz, working from previously untranslated German documents, published *Tras las huellas de un desconocido* (In the footsteps of an unknown), with important new information about Maximilian's early education; his governorship of Lombardy-Venetia; his last doctor, Samuel Basch; Prince and Princess Salm-Salm; and the shadowy Father Fischer. I had already finished and placed my manuscript; Ratz's was the latest research I could utilize for this novel. No doubt more wonders are forthcoming. There are more archives I might have looked into. I could also try digging a hole to China. After these several years' work, with a great sigh, I simply declared, "pencils down."

As I said, writing a book is like climbing a mountain, and this climb was made possible by the aid of many sherpas. First, always, and most important, I thank my husband, Agustín Carstens, whose support in every way has been unstintingly generous. Together we visited many of the scenes in the novel, including Cuernavaca, Mexico City, Río Frío, Orizaba, Veracruz and, though no scenes set there appear in this novel, the theater for Second Empire's bloody end, the city of Querétaro. It was my husband's suggestion that we make a journey to Vienna, Venice, and Miramar Castle in Trieste, which proved to be an indispensible step in my attempt to understand Maximilian. I also found that I had much to learn from our visits to Brussels and Paris.

I also thank my parents, Roger and Carolyn Mansell, and sister, Alice Jean Mansell, for their support in so many ways. Another family member who cannot go without a mention is my pug dog, Picadou. From the beginning of this project, she has stayed close by my desk, ever-patient, content to nap for hours, but with the wherewithal to insist, when need be, that we both go outside for a breath of air and a long walk.

Many librarians have my thanks, among them those of the Banco de México (Matías Romero Archive); Biblioteca Lerdo de Tejada (*Sociedad* newspaper archive); Catholic University of America (Iturbide-Kearney Family Papers); Georgetown University's Lauinger Library (Agustín de Iturbide Collection); Daughters of the American Revolution Library; Haus-, Hof-, und Staatsarchiv, Vienna, Austria (Kaiser Maximilian von Mexiko Archive); Library of Congress, Washington, D.C., Manuscript Division (Agustín de Iturbide Papers, and Kaiser Maximilian von Mexiko Archive); District of Columbia Public Library, Peabody Room, Georgetown Regional Branch; Washingtoniana Division, Martin Luther King Library, Washington, D.C.; New York City Public Library, Manuscript Division (John Bigelow and Bigelow Family Papers); Rice University Fondren Library (Maximilian and Charlotte Collection); Washington Historical Society, Washington, D.C.;

University of California at Berkeley, Bancroft Library; University of Texas at Austin, Benson Latin American Collection.

My deep appreciation to the Ragdale Foundation, the Virginia Center for the Creative Arts, and Yaddo, which provided residencies—the time and peace for creative writing.

Thanks to *Potomac Review* for publishing the first excerpt from "The Darling of Rosedale."

To the Foundation for Youth for Understanding, then owner of Rosedale, for the tour.

So many have helped me by the gift of a book, an article, a document, a key suggestion, and more. In alphabetical order: Lupe Arrigunaga de Mancera, Kate Blackwell, Carmen Boone de Aguilar, José G. Aguilera Medrano, Margarita Carstens Lavista, Helen de Carstens, Francisco José Joel Castro y Ortiz, Mr. and Mrs. Edgar Chain, Teresa Franco, Amparo Gómez, José Antonio González Anaya, Miguel Hakim Simón, Carlos de Icaza, Samuel Maldonado, Dawn Marano, Ileana Ramírez Williams de del Cueto, Robert Ryal Miller, Emilio Quesada, Salvador Rueda, Oriana Tickell de Castelló, Eduardo Turrent, María Josefa Valerio, Eduardo Wallentin, Roberto Wallentin, and Nancy Zafris.

I have been truly fortunate in having thoughtful readers of the various chapters or versions of the manuscript, again in alphabetical order: Kate Blackwell, Ellen Prentiss Campbell, Sofía Carstens, Luis Cerda, Maxine Claire, Kathleen Currie, Katherine Davis, Nancy Eaton, Timothy Heyman, Javier Mancera Arrigunaga, Ann McLaughlin, Mary O'Keefe de O'Dogherty, Carolyn Parkhurst, Leslie Pietrzyk, Deborah Riner, Sara Mansfield Taber, Amy Stolls, and Mary Kay Zuravleff.

Thanks to Washington, D.C.'s Politics & Prose Bookstore and Taylor Real Estate, where my writers group, bless you all, met many a Thursday.

Thanks to Douglas Glover for the long ago but not forgotten, and truly inspiring lesson on the novel, and to Robert McKee for his magnificent workshop on story.

Warmest thanks to the "invisible cheerleaders," above all, Louise Kearney de Iturbide and the many people, now "on the other side of the veil," who appear as characters in the novel. I do not know whether I have done you justice, but oftentimes I have felt your friendly presence. In this regard, I am deeply grateful to Lyn Buchanan, for the tools to help me stretch my concepts of the mind and space-time. I have also had the invaluable aid of two gifted mediums, Diane Forestell May and Deborah Harrigan.

Any mistakes or shortcomings in this book are my own, of course.

Finally, heartfelt thanks to my editor, Greg Michalson, who recognized what I aimed to achieve with this book and patiently helped me, as far as I am able, to realize it. Thanks also to my agent, Christina Ward, who has been a bright and timely light for me. Thanks to Pippa Letsky for such superb copyediting. At this point the book leaves my hands, but to everyone at Unbridled Books, and all the people who bring the book to your hands, and you, dear reader, know that you have my gratitude.

Washington, D.C., and Mexico City, 2008

SELECTED BOOKS CONSULTED

Aguilar Ochoa, Arturo, ed. *La fotografía durante el Imperio de Maximiliano.*

Almonte, Juan Nepomuceno. *Guía de forasteros y repertorio de conocimientos útiles.*

Arróniz, Marcos. *Manual del viajero en México.* Paris, 1858.

Ávila, Lorenzo, ed. *Testimonios artísticos de un episodio fugáz 1864–1867.*

Basch, Dr. S. *Memories of Mexico: A History of the Last Ten Months of the Empire.* Translated by Hugh McAden Oechler.

Bigelow, John. *Retrospections of an Active Life.* 3 volumes.

Blanchot, Col. Charles. *Mémoires: L'Intervention Française au Mexique.* 3 volumes.

Blasio, José Luis. *Maximiliano íntimo: El Emperador Maximiliano y su corte.*

Buffum, E. Gould. *Sights and Sensations in France, Germany, and Switzerland; or, Experiences of an American Journalist in Europe.*

Clay, Mrs. *A Belle of the Fifties: Memoirs of Mrs. Clay, of Alabama, Covering Social and Political Life in Washington and the South, 1853–66.*

Conte Corti, Egon Caesar. *Maximiliano y Carlota.*

Cortina del Valle, Elena, ed. *De Miramar a México.*

Cossío, José L. *Guía retrospective de la ciudad de México.*

Fabiani, Rossella. *Miramare Castle: The Historic Museum.*

Evans, Henry Ridgely. *Old Georgetown on the Potomac.*

Evans, Dr. Thomas W. *The Second French Empire: Napoleon the Third; The Empress Eugénie; The Prince Imperial.*

Genealogía de la Familia Iturbide. Privately printed.

Gooch, Fanny Chambers. *Face to Face with the Mexicans.* Original, unedited edition.

Hamann, Brigitte. *Con Maximiliano en México: Del diario del príncipe Carl Khevenhüller, 1864–1867.*

Haslip, Joan. *The Crown of Mexico.*

Iturriaga de la Fuente, José N., ed. *Escritos mexicanos de Carlota de Bélgica.*

Kearney de Iturbide, Louise. *My Story.* Manuscript, Catholic University Archives.

Kolonitz, Paula. *Un viaje a México en 1864.* Translated by Neftali Beltrán.

Leech, Margaret. *Reveille in Washington, 1860–1865.*

Lombardo de Miramón, Concepción, *Memorias.*

Luca de Tena. *Ciudad de México en tiempos de Maximiliano.*

Magruder, Henry R. *Sketches of the Last Year of the Mexican Empire.*

Mann-Kenney, Louise. *Rosedale: The Eighteenth-Century Country Estate of General Uriah Forrest, Cleveland Park, Washington, D.C.*

Maximilian, Emperor of Mexico. *Recollections of My Life.* 3 volumes.

Meyer, Jean, ed. *Yo, el francés: Biografías y crónicas.*

Michael, Prince of Greece. *The Empress of Farewells: The Story of Charlotte, Empress of Mexico.*

Mikos, Charles, *et al. The Imperial House of Iturbide.*

Museo Nacional de Arte. *Testimonios artísticos de un episodio fugaz (1864-1867).*

Ortiz, Orlando. *Diré adiós a los señores: Vida cotidiana en la época de Maximiliano y Carlota.*

Pani, Erika. *El Segundo Imperio.*

Payno, Manuel. *The Bandits from Río Frío.* Translated by Alan Fluckey.

Quirarte, Martín. *Historiografía sobre el Imperio de Maximiliano.*

Ratz, Konrad, ed. *Correspondencia inédita entre Maximiliano y Carlota.*

Ratz, Konrad. *Tras las huellas de un desconocido.*

Reglamento para el servicio y ceremonial de la corte, 1865 and second edition, 1866.

Ridley, Jasper. *Maximilian and Juárez.*

Robertson, William Spence. *Iturbide de México.*

Romero de Terreros, Manuel. *La corte de Maximiliano: Cartas de don Ignacio Algara.*

Ruiz, Ramón Eduardo, ed., *An American in Maximilian's Mexico, 1865–1866: The Diaries of William Marshall Anderson.*

Salm-Salm, Felix. *The Diary of Prince Salm-Salm.*

Salm-Salm, Princess (Agnes). *Ten Years of My Life.*

Solares Robles, Laura. *La obra política de Manuel Gómez Pedraza.*

Stevenson, Sara Yorke. *Maximilian in Mexico: A Woman's Reminiscences of the French Intervention 1862–1867.*

Villalpando, José Manuel. *Maximiliano.*

Warner, William W. *At Peace with All Their Neighbors: Catholics and Catholicism in the National Capital, 1787–1860.*

Windle, Mary J. *Life in Washington.*

For more detailed notes on sources, as well as geneologies, photographs and more, please visit www.cmmayo.com